RECIPE FOR TROUBLE

DYLAN MORRISON

Storm
PUBLISHING

Ebook ISBN: 978-1-83700-154-5
Paperback ISBN: 978-1-83700-157-6

Cover design: My Lan Khuc
Cover images: My Lan Khuc

Published by Storm Publishing.
For further information, visit:
www.stormpublishing.co

ALSO BY DYLAN MORRISON

Fall Into You
Second Helpings
Comfort Read

For the people who taught me to cook, the people who taught me to eat, and the people who kept me fed. May your toast always land buttered side up.

PROLOGUE

Benjamin Blumenthal's life isn't empty. He tells himself so every morning.

Sure, he lives alone, with no one to keep him company but an ill-tempered cat; sure, most of his friends live out of town. Sure, his family's back in Michigan and don't exactly lower Ben's stress levels when they call—sure, he lives in one of the world's most vibrant cities, but he doesn't get out much. Sure, he works a soulless job that doesn't challenge him, that doesn't even value him enough to make him an official part of the team. So what? As far as Ben can tell, an empty life is a matter of perspective, and he's determined not to fall victim to self-pity or despair. He has his health. He has his apartment, his steady paycheck, his beloved if somewhat vicious cat, and great people in his life, however far away they might be. Maybe it's not much, but it's his, and it's enough.

It has to be enough, because it's everything he's got.

My life isn't empty, Ben thinks each morning as he gets ready for work; as he walks the six blocks to the subway; as he waits an interminable age for the subway to (hopefully) arrive. It runs through his mind on the bumpy ride to Formica Media's midtown offices, as he rides the elevator twenty-seven floors up and settles in at his cubicle. He clings to it as he sits through endless, mind-numbing meetings with coworkers he hardly knows and doesn't like, and through endless, mind-numbing projects on topics he's never cared about. As he rides the subway home, makes a needlessly elaborate dinner and gets ready for bed—as he lives through day after unchanging day, each one slipping by the same as the last —he reminds himself over and over so he doesn't forget it: *My life's not empty at all.*

ONE

There are some jobs so boring that those unlucky enough to work them spend each moment thinking longingly of the end of their day, when they can cast aside their email inboxes and sensible blazers and ride off into the sunset. Ben's job is so boring it makes those jobs look like lion taming.

The *idea* of the job isn't bad, which is to say that video editing itself isn't bad. Ben almost enjoys video editing. It's not like it's his passion or anything, but he studied it in school, and he knows he's good at it. It's even satisfying sometimes, to cut things together in a way that watches smoothly, to make each piece of a narrative slide into the next one, seamless to the naked eye.

That's not what Ben does for Formica, though. For Formica, Ben edits technical and instructional videos, and edits more technical and instructional videos, and sits through long strategy meetings about the technical and instructional videos he's going to be editing, in which no one ever says anything interesting or useful. Occasionally, he gets pulled away from this thrilling nightmare to edit advertisements, which is an equally boring, but usually morally worse, nightmare. His coworkers, many of whom have been present and unpleasant during some of Ben's less poised moments, have the emotional depth of a puddle between them, and roughly the same intelligence; his bosses, to the extent he can call them that, offer no guidance or encouragement, just deadlines to meet. Yet he puts up with it all, and in exchange enjoys the dubious pleasure of a permanent contractor role, a paycheck that would be higher if his role was *not* a contract position, benefits that cost him more than those of his less capable coworkers, and a small cube on the twenty-seventh floor where his spirit goes to die every morning.

So he spends most afternoons with a laptop set up in a variety of positions in one of the restaurants on the ground floor of the building. Sometimes he's perched on the edge of an armchair, absently running a hand through his dark hair; sometimes he's resting his chin on his hand, comforted by the familiar, bristly texture of his carefully maintained, closely cropped beard; sometimes he's hunched like a gargoyle over one of the mirror-finished, metallic tables, scowling balefully down at his own face, which would be pleasingly square if it weren't for his sharply pointed chin. However he's positioned, though, he's always doing the same thing: looking for interesting people to talk to while he works. It's that or lose his mind.

"Hey, kid," Rick says one such Thursday afternoon, as Ben walks through the door of Brew, the coffee shop on the west side of the building. They're in the last dregs of September, October only a day or two away and eager to bring its traditional weather, and it shows through the coffee shop's large glass windows; something that looks to be a combination of rain and sleet is whipping into them. Ben shudders very slightly, his mind skipping forward unpleasantly to his journey home tonight, and then wants to keep shuddering when Rick uses a foot to push a chair out from his table and says, "Pop a squat."

Ben looks at him balefully, hiking his computer bag up a little higher on his shoulder. Rick is... Rick. He's a perfectly nice guy, Ben supposes, but that's about all. The whole point of lurking in these terrible corporate restaurants during the afternoon is to be *free*, in case an actually fascinating person comes down from one of the many publishing outlets Formica counts under its vast corporate umbrella. They usually don't, but now and then he has a conversation that makes working in this building worthwhile.

Rick, a thickly mustachioed, salt-and-pepper-haired white guy on the far side of middle age, once spent a whole conversation describing to Ben a fish he caught; he'd used the word "slippery" eighteen times. Scintillating, he is not. But the conversational pickings are slim today, just Rick and weird sexist Kenny from the sports website on twenty-three, and Ben has vowed never to talk to *him* again. Rick, at least, works for *Gastronome*—and while Ben wouldn't necessarily call it the *best* cooking magazine on the market, it's one of his personal favorites, and he's been reading it since he was a child.

"Don't call me 'kid,'" Ben says, "and please never say 'pop a squat' ever again," but he sits down in the offered chair anyway.

Rick laughs. Rick, Ben notes a little wearily, is often laughing at things Ben says that he doesn't mean to be jokes. It's part of what makes him such a frustrating conversationalist—Ben's genuine attempts at humor fly right over his head, but Rick finds his actual personality hilarious.

"Look, kid," Rick says, in flagrant violation of the request made only moments before, "I think I might have something for you."

"Well, that's ominous," Ben says. "What kind of something? Animal, vegetable, or mineral?"

Again, Rick laughs. It really is very annoying. "A job, actually. Or—a project, I guess. You do video editing, right?"

"I... do," Ben says, surprised and, weirdly, a little touched. He's always assumed that his side of their conversations drifted out of Rick's head like so much smoke the minute Ben walked away, but apparently, Rick's been paying attention, at least occasionally. "Why?"

"Oh," Rick says, and waves a hand. "Upstairs wants us to do more—what'd they say—'accessible Gen Z content.' Some nonsense about how the modern consumer doesn't have the attention span to read a recipe or something. It all sounds pretty stupid to me, but." He shrugs, affecting a commiserating expression. "You know how it is, when upstairs comes calling."

The only person in Ben's life who he even remotely thinks of as "upstairs" is Mrs. C, the octogenarian who lives in the apartment above his, and Ben doesn't know how it is when she comes calling, because as far as he can tell she never steps past her front door. He does, pretty regularly, bring her some dinner when he's made too much for himself, but he doubts that's what Rick's talking about.

"Sure I do," Ben says. It's just easier. "What'd you have in mind?"

"Well," Rick says, and grits his teeth. "I've got this guy, one of my test cooks. He should've been perfect for it—real big personality, y'know? Teaches people in the kitchen all the time. Teaches classes, even! And one of the photographers who shoots for the magazine used to do video, so we figured, whatever, right? We'd shoot Pete making some dish and throw it online. Should've been no problem."

"But...?" Ben prompts, when Rick pauses to build the suspense. This, too, is a common feature of conversations with Rick, and one Ben finds particularly irksome.

"My guy's a disaster," Rick admits. "The minute the camera turned on, he totally lost it. Rambling, spilling things, burning stuff. It took him two and a half hours to demonstrate making the chicken and kale salad we put out in our last issue—"

"But that's a *twenty-minute recipe*," Ben says, aghast. "I made it myself last month! Even if you roast the chicken yourself instead of using a rotisserie—God, even if you go *insane* and decide to break down fresh artichokes—it shouldn't take more than an hour and a half!"

Rick blinks a few times, then beams at him. "Wow, kid, I'm flattered. You never told me you were a *reader*."

"Don't let it go to your head," Ben says, irritably. "And I told you, don't call me 'kid.' I'm like ten thousand years old inside."

"That's what they all say, at your age."

"*Do* they?" says Ben, who has yet to find another twenty-eight-year-old as ready as he is to be a crotchety old man. "Are you sure?"

"Eh," Rick says, and shrugs. "I haven't known what the kids are saying for years; I took a shot in the dark. Look, my point is: Would you mind taking a look at the footage? It's beyond help from the likes of us, and maybe from anyone, but I figure it can't hurt to bring in a professional." He lowers his voice, and, conspiratorially, adds, "You'd be doing me a big favor. I'd owe you one."

Ben, who has freelanced for too long to do any editing work simply for being owed one, narrows his eyes. "Is this favor a paying gig?"

"Oh, sure, sure," Rick says. He waves a hand, effectively (if probably unintentionally) establishing himself as someone with enough money to find discussing it at all a little gauche. Ben grimaces internally but knows it's the better part of politeness to keep the expression off his face. "Our standard contractor fee. I'll send over the paperwork with the footage. The powers that be will probably find a way to roll it into your next paycheck."

Ben bristles a little at the words "contractor fee," since the reminder that at Formica contractors are basically second-class citizens, less valued than their full-staff counterparts no matter what hours they keep, always rankles. Still, he's curious and bored enough that he agrees anyway, scrawls his email address down on a piece of paper Rick offers him and says he'll turn it around as quick as he can. After all, Ben does love food, and it'll be something new to do.

Also, the eight-year-old version of him would have lost his mind at the opportunity to do anything at all for *Gastronome*. For God's sake, he'd dressed up as a chef for three Halloweens in a row, with the toque and the white coat and everything, always carrying a copy of the magazine under his arm. A little part of Ben can't help but want to honor that, for all adulthood has taught him that reality rarely plays out the way you dream it will.

Rick heads off, and Ben spends a lazy hour cleaning out his inbox, trying to decide how long he can linger down here before someone notices he's gone. All his important work for the next two weeks is already finished, but Ben's learned the hard way that he's a lot faster than bosses tend to expect, and also that if he lets on, they'll start expecting the impossible. Still, there are appearances to maintain, and usually, at least one of the higher ups gets a little squirrely if he's away from his desk for too long.

He's started bracing himself to ascend back into the nightmare realm when the email comes in from Rick. Its subject line is *Don't say I didn't warn you, kid :)*, and Ben snarls an incoherent little noise under his breath at the indignity of the diminutive in writing. Then, to get a sense of what he's in for, he downloads and opens the attached file, ominously titled, *Pete Bailey—Gastronome—YouTube pilot raw footage—OHGOD*.

In the first two minutes, Ben's eyebrows go up. By minute five, his mouth is hanging open. After ten minutes, Ben pops into Formica's terrible, buggy chat client, selects the thread for his office, types, *Feeling kinda gross, thinking maybe I should head home?* into the window, adds a barfing emoji, and hits send. It only takes forty-five seconds for Jessica, his germophobic boss, to reply with a link to an article about a recent norovirus outbreak and all-caps instructions not to return to the office until Monday. Even faking sick is too easy at this job. Ben knows he can't get away with watching this anywhere that people can see or hear him, and he's not going to be able to wait until his day's done.

Ben packs up his laptop. He grabs an extra coffee, digs out his collapsible umbrella from the bottom of his messenger bag, and thanks God for the thousandth time that said bag is waterproof. Thus prepared, he takes to the streets.

They are punishing streets. They throw rain and slush into Ben's face with all the gleeful abandon of a clown with a pile of banana cream pies. It murders first his coffee cup, which he abandons in a trash can, and then his umbrella, which wasn't doing him much good anyway, and finally his will to live, although Ben thinks that one's less a murder and more a maiming, and that probably, in time, it will recover.

Still, he decides that in the circumstances, it might balance things out to indulge in an alcoholic beverage. For fortitude. For strength. As this is the sort of decision Ben typically finds himself making once every business quarter at most, it necessitates a detour to the nearest bodega, where he spends several minutes dithering over canned mixed drink options before selecting one more or less at random. Thus armed, he heads down into the subway and settles in at his platform to wait the typical small eternity for his train to arrive. He finds the computer on his lap again almost without realizing he's pulled it out and, wondering if maybe he's remembering it as worse than it is, starts watching the footage again from the top.

The guy in the video—Pete—is handsome in that relaxed, unintentional way Ben associates with people who had a great time in high school. There's something about him that's almost familiar, and he looks older than Ben, in probably his early thirties. His dark wavy hair, faded tight on the sides and left longer on top, clearly just lies that way, in the sort of easy dishevelment no one can pull off when they're trying. As if all that wasn't enough, he's broad shouldered and well muscled—not a full gym rat like Ben sometimes pulls on Grindr, but definitely visibly toned. It's a look Ben associates with rock climbers, although admittedly that may be situational bias, because he is also wearing the type of T-shirt-with-sleeves-cut-off Ben associates with rock climbers. However, the idiot has distinguished himself from the pack by electing to do this to a shirt with ASK ME ABOUT CANNED BEANS scrawled across the front in a gigantic, hideous font.

And Pete is, above anything else, an idiot. Sure—he's a little bit hot. Ben can admit that to himself, here in the safe anonymity of the New York City subway system, where anything could happen and does, every day. Pete is a little bit hot. That doesn't make it okay that somehow, despite having presumably been a talented enough chef to land one of the coveted, cushy positions as a *Gastronome* test cook, he has produced what has to be the single worst collection of cooking footage ever created by man.

"Hi!" Pete says, waving at the camera, in the first take. But he's holding a spoon in his waving hand, and it goes flying and hits someone nearly out of frame in the back of the head, and they yelp, and someone else off camera yells "CUT." With no pause for recovery, it's the next take, and Pete says, "Hi! I'm Pat," and then, "Wait, no I'm not," and then, nervously, like he's not quite sure it's the right answer, "Pete? I'm... Pete." They cut again, and then it's the hideous take after that, in which Pete holds up a bunch of greens and says, "This is kelp—kelp—KALE. Good God. But could we make it with kelp, do you think? I never thought about kelp— aw, wait, these are collards, actually. Uh. Are we still rolling?"

Ben misses his train. It goes whooshing by as Pete very earnestly tells the viewers that he thinks everyone can learn to cook while, next to him, a piece of notebook paper that clearly reads, *DEAR PETE, REMEMBER: BUY TARRAGON, TOILET PAPER. NO MORE HOISIN! LOVE PETE* inches towards the stove. It catches fire at the same moment Ben realizes that it's a local 1 train pulling away, and he releases a little gasp of surprised annoyance in the exact moment that Pete does on-screen.

That disquieting moment of similarity is enough to get Ben to close the computer. He tells himself he's not going to open it again until he has his mysterious mixed drink in his hand to dull the pain but only lasts five minutes before he finds himself reaching for the laptop again. An express 2 train chooses that exact moment to turn up, running as always on a secret schedule known only to itself, which is all that saves Ben from spending the next several hours on the platform. Instead, he spends the standing-room-only ride back to his apartment stewing about the video, and how on earth Pete even got a job, and how on earth *he*, Ben, is supposed to do *his* job and edit this nightmare into watchable content.

He walks the six blocks back to his apartment quickly, eager now to see the rest and assess how bad the damage is, and whether he has anything at all to work with. He gets the file cued on his home computer—which is two computers and a server, but who's counting—and says hi to Roux, his cat, who is nowhere to be seen but surely lurking somewhere.

Then, knowing as he does it that he'll regret it afterwards, he hits play.

The two and a half hours of footage take an eternity to pass. Ben drinks his whole mixed drink as he watches, in a half-numb stupor at the horror of it, blindly groping for the can because he can't tear his eyes away, not tasting what he swallows. It's... so awful. In his time freelancing, Ben has edited footage of weddings, school plays, speeches, concerts, recitals, dance performances, sports events, terrible student movies, a few low-budget web series, and one really upsetting video essay for a kid in his film program he never spoke to again. He's seen drunk people on camera, and awkward people on camera, and high school students on camera— Pete is worse than all of them. Pete is worse on camera than a *drunk, awkward high school student.* It absolutely boggles the mind.

At 5:15 p.m., Ben, who doesn't typically drink, stands up in mild outrage, wobbles somewhat, realizes perhaps he should have taken a closer look at the ABV on that can, and then decides it hardly matters, in the circumstances. He yanks his phone from his pocket, pulls up Rick's email, clicks on the phone number that Rick included at the bottom, and puts the call through.

"Richard Raleigh's phone, Richard Raleigh speaking," says Rick, which is when—very belatedly—Ben realizes that Rick from Brew is *Richard Raleigh,* the famously private, famously photo-shy editor-in-chief of *Gastronome.* All those insipid conversations over lattes, and he was Richard Raleigh the *whole time.*

"Have you *always* been Richard Raleigh?" Ben thinks, and also says, because he's drunk.

There's a pause, and then Rick starts laughing. "Since the day I was born, kid. I take it this is Ben?"

Ben thinks, somewhat hysterically, *You were Richard Raleigh the whole time you were telling me about the slippery fish??* Through heroic effort, he does not say this. Instead, he says, "Uh, yeah," and then, remembering why he was calling, adds, "Hey! This footage is a car wreck!"

"I tried to tell you," Rick says, still laughing. "Look, don't sweat it. I've been thinking about it, and maybe it's for the best it's bad. Might buy us another year or two before we really have to start producing consistent video content. God knows the staff don't want to do it; Pete about pitched a fit when I told him he was the one on the chopping block—"

"Why *was* he the one on the chopping block?" Ben demands. "Surely, the best thing to do here is to get one of the other test cooks to do it? Or, I mean, grab a pigeon off the street and put it in a little apron. It's bound to do a better job!"

"I like you, kid," says Rick, chuckling. "You're a riot. But it's gotta be Pete; that one's out of my hands. The bosses like him for it."

Aren't you the boss? Ben thinks. He isn't naive enough to say it, though; at Formica Media, everyone's got a boss, and usually several. "Maybe," he says instead, "you should send them the footage."

"Or maybe," Rick says, in coaxing tones, "you should do the best you can with what you've got, and we should post it. And then, when my bosses want to know *why* it's terrible, I can say that I did what they asked, and even brought in one of their very own in-house video editors to help with it, and this is simply the best we can do. And then they'll spend six months developing a video presence concept for us, and another six months gathering capital and hiring writers, and another six months writing, casting, and filming it, and meanwhile my team will get to go on with the work they're actually good at. What do you say?"

Ben stares at the wall for a long moment. Then, wearily, he says, "God. This was your plan all along, wasn't it?"

"Gotta jump, kid," Rick says cheerfully, which almost certainly means *yes*. "Good luck, but not too much, ya know?" He hangs up.

"Sometimes I really *hate* people," Ben says to Roux, who he has spotted underneath the couch. "What do you think about that, huh? Do you hate people?" She cocks her head inquisitively, meows as if in agreement, and then reaches up a paw to scratch a new mark into the already much-maligned couch fabric, which seems about right.

Ben decides it's the better part of valor to step away from all this for a moment. He leaves Roux to her cavalier destruction of his property and walks, slightly unsteadily, the few blocks to the nearest specialty grocer. The weather continues, but as he is now somewhat drunk, he doesn't care as much that he's being simultaneously frozen and drowned. And, anyway, he'd walk through almost any weather to get where he's going.

It's not that Ben moved to the Upper West Side for the food. He moved here because he lucked into an apartment he could afford six years ago, and finding that apartment was such an ordeal that he's planning on staying in it until he dies... But he has to admit, the food is nice. Every few blocks there's another grocery store, each one stocked with a hundred products none of the others have, and scattered between them are delis and bakeries, little hole-in-the-wall restaurants, and bodegas somehow selling the freshest-tasting melons Ben's ever had in his life.

It's a cook's paradise, and Ben is, first and foremost, a cook, however long it's been since he wore the title professionally. He grew up in his parents' restaurant—bussing tables by ten, working the counter at twelve, waiting by thirteen, line cook from his sixteenth birthday—and he made it to sous chef at Fleur de Sel, the French joint he worked at in college to make ends meet. He may have abandoned it all for a career that seemed, at the time, like it would bring him fewer barely covered medical bills, unnecessary injuries, and hours spent feeling like he'd been hit by a series of trains, but he'll always be that kid on some level, begging his mother to let him put his latest fixation on the menu.

Food, now as then, brings Ben peace, and he wanders through the grocery store at a pace much slower than everyone else, taking his time, breathing it all in. He's learned, over the years, how to do this without inconveniencing the rushed New Yorkers around him.

Ben dances lightly around the other shoppers, spins away from an oncoming cart, catches a falling avocado in midair when another customer knocks it down. The employees greet him by name, and he greets them by theirs, pleased to be a regular, to be known. Out in the world Ben may be small and strange, never quite fitting in anywhere, but here amongst the chocolate babkas and smoked salmons, he belongs.

He has a basket half-filled with the ingredients to make sausage and mushroom risotto—sometimes, when he's feeling particularly stressed, he finds it restful to take his aggression out via twenty to forty minutes of stirring—when it occurs to him that maybe he should make the chicken and kale salad from the video. He did it without issue last month, after all, and maybe having it fresh in his mind will help him figure out how on *earth* he's going to make Pete's attempt watchable.

Balancing his basket on his hip, he fishes his phone out of his pocket and pulls up the recipe on the *Gastronome* website. He doesn't even get a chance to scroll through it, though, before he notices the byline.

"He *wrote* the stupid recipe?!" Ben yells this, a little, at his phone screen. It's a credit to his fellow shoppers that not one of them so much as turns around; Ben would still be a little embarrassed, but honestly, he's occupied. Pete *wrote* it? Pete wrote the *recipe?* Pete got a job in the *Gastronome* test kitchen, and was hand-picked to create video content for them, and wrote the stupid *recipe*—for a salad that, horribly, was delicious when Ben made it, the flavors of all the components exquisitely balanced—and he couldn't just *phone it in*, or something, in front of the camera? *What?* It was bad enough when Ben thought it was some randomly selected dish, but Pete must have made it dozens of times while he was developing it. He must be able to make it with his *eyes* closed!

Already hating himself for it, Ben clicks on Pete's byline. Sure enough, it pulls up dozens of recipes, some of which are personal favorites of Ben's. One of them is the very risotto he was planning to make tonight, and he lets out a soft shriek on realizing it, nearly dropping his basket; then, hastily, he puts all the ingredients back and gets a few potato knishes and a pint of pasta salad to go.

Forget risotto. Forget cooking anything, at least for tonight. Ben knows what must have happened here now; Ben understands. The Formica execs want Pete to do this, and Pete doesn't want to do it, and Rick, Pete's boss, doesn't want him to do it, either. They must have—Pete must have *tanked it on purpose*, maybe at Rick's instruction or maybe because it was the only thing he could think of to do, and now they've got Ben looking at it as... plausible deniability or something. Not quite a patsy; a patsy might be more dignified. No, Ben's a *stooge*, only here to help sell their little con.

Ben goes home. He cracks his knuckles, eats a knish directly out of the foil envelope it came in, and gets right into editing the stupid video, the aggression that he intended to take out on the risotto going into the work. After a bit of effort, he's able to hack together a version that vaguely resembles a normal man making a normal salad in a normal amount of time, so long as you don't turn the audio on. With sound, of course, it's still the cooking show equivalent of a train accident, but Ben's got a plan for that little problem.

It's kind of a mean plan, if he's honest, but. Well. Pete decided to play the fool, didn't he? Ben's got no choice but to work with what he's got.

He pauses the video on the opening shot, Pete's mouth split in a wide grin. Ben was annoyed at being tricked a few hours ago, but he doesn't care about that anymore. Now he's angry, *furious*, at this stupid handsome face to whom everything must come so easily. At this stranger who has things Ben's dreamed of since he was a child, things Ben will *never* have, and who doesn't seem to care at all. At this man who's got it so good that he can afford to throw away something like this, an opportunity like this, because he doesn't *feel* like taking it, and because his life will sail on just the same either way. If nothing else, he's too breathtakingly attractive for it not to.

Ben stays up until nearly five in the morning, cutting things together, recording voice-over, adding captions and graphics, using Photoshop to scrawl *WHY???* over several particularly grim moments. Then he sends it to Rick, along with the signed paperwork, before he can change his mind.

TWO

For the next week, Ben's life proceeds as usual.

He gets up as usual, rides the train as usual, sits at work in nightmarish boredom as usual. His cat scratches him four times, as usual, and he forgives her four times, as usual; he tells himself, each day, that his life isn't empty, as usual. He makes chicken cacciatore and shrimp scampi and five-bean chili, distracting himself from his problems by cooking through them and then taking the leftovers upstairs to Mrs. C, as usual. It's the same as it ever was.

Except that the following Friday, he's sitting in his cubicle in his typical position—chin tilted down, shoulders up around his neck in a protective curl, one headphone in—when someone says, "Yo."

Ben wishes he didn't recognize the voice instantly, but spending almost ten hours editing footage of someone will do that to you. He's still hoping he's wrong, or having an aneurism or something, as he turns his chair... But, no. Of course, there he is, in all his hideous glory.

Pete looks bigger in person. Or, that's not quite right—in fact, Pete looks *more capable of beating Ben to a pulp* in person, his broad shoulders and well-muscled arms a lot more threatening up close. A little frantically, Ben curses himself for not thinking this through; it's all well and good to verbally eviscerate someone on video, but it's probably a better idea to do it to a person who isn't actively working in the same building as you are.

Also—not that it even bears thinking about—Pete is hotter in person. A lot hotter. His arms are crossed over his chest and he's scowling, but that doesn't do anything to minimize the sharp cut of his cheekbones, his full lips, his tousled hair. The footage didn't do him justice. If he wasn't wearing the same ASK ME ABOUT CANNED BEANS shirt, Ben might be too overcome with the combination of his own panic and Pete's frankly devastatingly good looks to do anything but sit here, staring, mute and horrified.

As it is, he finds himself opening his mouth and, almost against his will, saying, "For heaven's sake, is that the only shirt you *own?*"

Pete stares at him for a moment, and then bursts out laughing. Ben, despite an admitted surge of relief that this dude isn't here to try and throw down, raises his eyebrows and silently wills his rude, nosy coworkers to ignore the hysterical beefcake at his cubicle. He doubts they will, but a guy's gotta hope.

"Oh my God," Pete gasps, when he gets his laughter under control. "I had this whole plan, you know—I was gonna play like I was *mad* about it—but you're just *like* this, aren't you?"

"Like what?" Ben asks, not sure he wants to know.

"Oh, you know," Pete says, waving an expansive hand. His grin goes all the way to his eyes, crinkling them up at the corners, and Ben tries frantically to remember that he's angry at this guy, however attractive he might be. "Mean."

"Mean?" Ben repeats, suddenly finding it less difficult to hold onto his annoyance. "I'm not *mean*, I'm—"

"Exacting?" Pete suggests, eyes dancing. "Particular? Mean people usually have another word for it."

"Look," Ben says, nettled, "I'm sorry if I upset you or whatever, but that doesn't mean you get to come down to my office and—"

"Oh, no, let's be clear," Pete says, holding up a hand to shut Ben up. "I loved it. You're hilarious, man—and you saved my bacon on that video. I know it must have been straight-up garbage before you cut it up like that."

"I—what?" Ben stares at Pete, wondering if maybe he's having a stress-induced hallucination. "You—what?"

"I'm not very good on camera," Pete says, in the tones of an admission. He ducks his head and rubs the back of his neck, obviously uncomfortable. "When Rick told me I was going to have to do this, I seriously thought about quitting my job, which, believe me, would be a nightmare. But I watched the video last night, and honestly? It's pretty funny. And I know that was you, so I thought I'd come down here to... I mean, okay, to rib you a little, for making me look like such a jerk, but really to thank you. For fixing it, or whatever. Making it look like it could have been on purpose."

Oh my God, Ben thinks, *it wasn't on purpose?*

"Wait," Ben says, before he can stop himself, "you're just *like* this?"

Pete smiles, but it's very nearly a smirk. It takes Ben a second, and then he realizes he's more or less parroted back at Pete the exact question Pete asked him not five minutes ago. He scowls, and Pete's smile widens into a lazy, self-satisfied grin.

"Like what?" Pete says, all innocence.

"Possessed of the intelligence of your average housefly," Ben snaps, before he can temper his tongue. "A fool with a cast-iron pan! God, I thought maybe you were faking it or whatever on camera, trying to get out of it, but clearly, you couldn't fake your way out of a paper bag!"

This doesn't have the intended effect. Usually, when Ben snaps at someone, shows them the jagged edges of his personality, they make an annoyed face and immediately get away from him, which is the desired outcome. Ben's long since known that most people don't like him, the *real* him, with his complicated angles and his sharp tongue, and it hurts less to figure that out up front. It backfires on him occasionally, sure; sometimes they burst into tears, which is the living worst and always makes Ben feel like a terrible person, and sometimes they snap back, which inevitably ends badly for everyone. Every now and again someone laughs awkwardly and rolls their eyes, but that's about the best it ever gets.

Pete... Pete laughs again, a real laugh, his shoulders shaking. It's not like when Rick laughs at Ben's personality, either; there's always an edge of condescension to that, as though Ben is a particularly entertaining dog, which, admittedly, has made a little more sense since discovering he's *Richard Raleigh*. Pete's laughter is—more genuine. Kinder. It seems designed by nature to invite others to laugh along.

It's just a laugh, Benjamin! Ben thinks, semi-hysterical. *You're losing it! His hotness has hypnotized you! You can't snap at him until he goes away; he clearly enjoys it! Run for the hills!*

"I've known a lot of brilliant houseflies," Pete says, grin still wide. "They're basically geniuses, at least when it comes to avoiding me murdering them, so I think that's an unfair comparison. But I'm making 'A fool with a cast-iron pan' my new bio, like, everywhere."

Ben stares at him, trying to think of something to say that won't a) make him, Ben, look like a fool himself or b) make Pete do anything else inexplicable and unprecedented, to which Ben will have to respond. Eventually, because he's been sitting silently blinking for too long, he says, "Uh. Okay?"

Pete claps a hand on Ben's shoulder; Ben doesn't flinch, but only just. It's been a while since he's been touched by... well, by anyone, save the occasional app-sourced hookup, and the apps are enough of a nightmare to keep Ben from bothering most of the time. Pete's hand is warm through the thin cotton of Ben's T-shirt and Ben tries his best not to think about it, wills his face not to turn the color of a ripe tomato.

"It was nice to meet you, Ben," Pete says, and flashes that grin again, all easy amusement. "I gotta get back to work now, but seriously, thanks again. The video's going up tomorrow, and I don't feel like running away to the woods, where I'd probably die, so. I appreciate it."

"I'm not sure I feel good about that," Ben admits, a little faintly.

"I think it might be better for cooking—and humanity—if you went ahead and pulled a Henry David Thoreau." Feeling like a bit of a schmuck, he adds, "Assuming you'd, like, survive it, I suppose. I'm not wishing you death here."

"Very generous," Pete says, still smiling, shaking his head. He sounds... weirdly happy about it when, waving and turning to go, he adds, "I'm sure I'll see you around."

Ben doesn't watch him walk away. He doesn't. He *doesn't*.

That's Friday.

The video goes up Saturday; Rick sends him a link. Ben watches it again, feels vaguely proud of his work, and forwards it to a few friends. It's not *Citizen Kane* or anything, but it's amazingly decent given what Ben started with. He takes a moment to admire his own name in the credits, and maybe one more to marvel at Pete's utter buffoonery, then closes the window, closes his computer, and stops thinking about it. It's over and done with; no point dwelling on it, or on its star, or on that star's visit to Ben's cubicle.

He spends a quiet day bouncing around the city, grateful that the unholy union of rain and sleet has decided to take its talents to some other metropolitan area. Still, it's chilly out for all it's bright, motivating Ben to dig out his favorite scarf—thick and dark blue and knitted by his sister, though Ben has never told her how often he wears it—and loop it under his canvas jacket as he runs out the door. As always, he regrets it bitterly within three minutes of every subway ride he takes, and then is incredibly grateful for it within five minutes of being back aboveground; this, more than anything else, is what marks for Ben the beginning of the end of the year. Sure, it *starts* with going back and forth about whether he should have bothered with a scarf, but somehow, before he knows it, Ben will find himself surrounded by twinkling fairy lights and snow-covered bus benches and a really unnerving number of drunk guys in Santa costumes.

Trying to put this out of his mind—the holiday season, for Ben, has never been a particularly happy one, and he'd just as soon live in denial about the approach of another bone-chilling New York City winter—he occupies himself running errands for a while before swinging down to Union Square for the farmers market, peeking eagerly into the various booths and stalls. He's able to get a ham and cheese croissant for lunch, and eats it as he selects some gorgeous eggplants, a few bunches of scallions so bright and green that they could have been plucked from the earth that morning, and a variety of root vegetables, jams, and pastries. He stops at his favorite butcher for a chicken and then rides the subway home laden down with bags, wishing as he does whenever this happens that he was smart enough to buy one of those personal pushcarts, even though he knows, to his bones, that he never will.

Roux is full of furious energy when Ben arrives back at his apartment, and he spends half an hour or so being batted at and gently scratched for her entertainment. Then he roasts the chicken and eggplant, chars the scallions whole, and cuts them up. It's the work of a few minutes to use them to make a ginger-scallion slaw, and he slices the chicken, arranges it with the eggplant on two plates, heaps the slaw over it all, and takes both dishes up to the eleventh floor.

Mrs. C's apartment door is always decorated for the season; she takes pride in it, insists that it brings the building together. Ben's not sure anything could bring the collection of New Yorkers under this roof together, far removed as they are from the forced friendliness he grew up with in the Midwest, but it's nice that she cares about things like that. She's not totally wrong in any case—she and Ben only met because when he moved into this apartment six years ago, it was June, and she had a gigantic rainbow flag tacked to the door. He'd been locked out of his apartment during his first week, and walked around the building looking for kindly souls who might give him the super's number. He knocked; she answered. They've been friends ever since.

There are things Ben doesn't share with his parents when they call. The fact that his closest friend in New York—really, his only friend in New York—is a sassy housebound octogenarian who would probably starve without him is close to the top of this list. He has a rotating cast of made-up people, largely based on characters from television shows he knows they'll never see, that he talks about instead, because it's easier. Lord forbid he tell them he's lonely and leave them to set him up on some kind of *friend date* with someone who knows someone who met one of their friends a few summers ago in Hilton Head. The last time he'd let tried that, he'd ended up spending two hours at a bar in Midtown with a woman who explained to him, in great detail and with several enthusiastic, room-stopping demonstrations, her passionate love for ventriloquism. Never again.

Today, Mrs. C's door has a banner hanging across it that says, Welcome, Autumn! It looks like she ordered it, and probably the little dancing leaves and mushrooms tacked up beneath it, from a store for kindergarten teachers. Ben shakes his head, grinning. Her doors always entertain him; they're so bright and cheerful, at odds with her actual personality, and it tickles him that she insists on them anyway, even though she seems to loathe most of their shared neighbors.

He knocks; she answers. This is how the vast majority of Ben's evenings go.

"Benjamin, *darling*," she trills, beaming at him. Everything Mrs. C does is reminiscent of a Broadway actress aged out of the stage, and her greetings are no exception. "I see you've brought two plates up tonight—does that mean I am to be graced with your presence for the entirety of a meal?"

"Hi, Mrs. C," Ben says, and leans forward for the requisite air kiss on both cheeks. "Yeah, I thought I'd join you for dinner, if that's okay?"

"I would be only *too* delighted! Do come in." She sweeps away from the door, throwing the mink stole she wears anytime it's less than eighty degrees out over her shoulder, and Ben steps into the apartment.

The space is a little bit like a museum—as the old woman's home for the last twenty-five years, it's packed full of little pieces of New Yorks gone by. Ben's only lived in the city six years; it's been enough time to absorb, if not fully understand, that the place he knows and loves will somehow be the same and utterly different six years from now. There's a comfort in that, the relentless entropy of so many souls crammed into such a small space, but there's comfort too in Mrs. C's apartment, proof that what was still is, somewhere. Her walls are lined with old posters, local art from the sixties and seventies, one illegally obtained street sign. On the shelves are beautifully maintained little collections of miscellany, things like sea glass and old subway tokens displayed next to tiny works of silver sculpture or obviously expensive jewelry intended to be admired.

That, of course, is the other thing about Mrs. C—though she's never come out and said it, Ben knows she's rich, and not low-key rich, either. Mrs. C is rich enough that she once gave Ben an envelope with a cool two grand in it as a holiday present. Mrs. C is rich enough that she *owns* her apartment, which is... not small.

Ben asked her, once, why she picked this building. He didn't say, "You could obviously afford somewhere bigger and nicer," but he didn't have to; she gave him a shrewd look, then shrugged.

"I had three husbands in my time, darling," she said that night, over a meal Ben's forgotten now. Something with mushrooms, maybe; it's lost to the recollection of the ache in her voice. "The first was a cad; the second, a brute; the third was married to someone else when I met him, so I suppose he was a cheat. Regardless, he was my favorite. This was our place, before I stole him from her, and when death stole him from me, I came home to it. I don't suppose I'll ever find anywhere else." She sighed, and dabbed at her eyes, and then, with false brightness, said, "Well! That's enough of all that. Haven't you brought any dessert for me, dear child?"

Ben took the hint, has been taking it ever since. Every time he visits, he wonders if the agoraphobia is a recent development, or if, as he suspects, she walked back in here the day the third husband died and simply never found anything worth stepping outside for again. He doesn't mention it—she wouldn't want him to—but it clings to him, the suspicion, a sharp-edged little burr of human tragedy.

"What sort of supper have you brought for me tonight?" she demands, wheeling on him in the living room. She's pretty spry for a lady of her years, but Ben still holds his breath for a second as he watches her sit down in her favorite chair, dangerously low to the ground and—like all of her other furniture—chintz. "I do hope it's not that terrible fish again."

"I served you tilapia one time," Ben says, feigning outrage. They've had this conversation so many times that he almost finds it comforting. "Most people like my tilapia."

"I'm sure I don't have to tell you that most people have terrible taste," Mrs. C says primly. She sits, waiting, as Ben sets up a little folding tray table for her, then one for himself on the couch opposite. "That's one of the reasons I like you, darling; you know what's good when you see it. The fish, regrettably, is a blind spot."

Ben laughs, shaking his head. "That's a real backhanded compliment, but I'll take it."

"They're my specialty, as you well know," Mrs. C says.

Ben rolls his eyes, but not unhappily, and they eat in silence for a few minutes. They do, sometimes; they're both fairly solitary people by nature, and he thinks that's why silence tends to fall so easily between them. There's also the fact that Ben didn't grow up thinking of dinner as a time to sit and chat—the meal where that sort of thing occurred might have been *called* "family meal," but it took place primarily between the restaurant staff, and it happened around 4 p.m., in the Trattoria Luciana kitchens, before dinner service started up. Ben mostly missed it on school nights, often walking in as things were drawing to a close. He typically ate his own dinner one of two places: either fighting with his sister for his share, generally in front of the television, in the upstairs apartment where they lived, or downstairs over the sink in the restaurant's back of house, hunching and shoveling in a stolen manicotti or sausage as someone shouted, "Kid! Look alive! Behind!"

Regardless, Mrs. C doesn't ever seem to mind keeping a companionable silence. It's part of why Ben likes spending time with her. Around other people he does his best to listen more than he talks, but the nervous energy seems to bubble up out of his mouth if a moment of quiet stretches on for too long. But not here, in this little pocket of the past, with this strange, persnickety old woman. Mrs. C's apartment is always emanating soft jazz music, muted but still audible, from some other room, and sometimes Ben comes up here just to sit, to be quiet with someone else. He thinks it's a big part of why Mrs. C puts up with him, even though Ben's heard her tell a number of their other neighbors to, to put it somewhat more mildly than she ever did, go take a hike. She doesn't like most people, and some days Ben's pretty certain she doesn't like him very much, either, but she must be lonely. Ben's considered suggesting that she hire someone off the internet to sit in her apartment and breathe all day, but he does think there's a good chance she'd get murdered, so he's never brought it up.

Also, horribly, Ben's pretty sure he would miss her dreadfully if she threw him over for some Craigslist probable serial killer. This is what his life has come down to, and it's very sad for him, but it's true all the same.

"It's a good chicken," she admits, after a while. "Well seasoned. Not like that dreadful fish. *This time*, anyway."

Ben smiles down at the floor. "Thanks, Mrs. C. It means a lot."

She doesn't eat all of it, but then, she never does—she's frail, and old, and has a nurse come by several times a day to make sure she's eaten enough, and help her with something she tells Ben to "never mind his young little head about" whenever he asks. He takes it as a compliment that she eats any of what he brings over, honestly; she could afford to have something professional brought in, or eat one of the various, easily microwaved options stocked in the freezer, some of which were clearly prepared specially for her at various NYC landmark restaurants. In some ways, her continued acceptance of his extra dinner is the best endorsement for his cooking Ben's ever received. He knows that over the years she dined at some of the most exclusive tables in the city and ate meals Ben would give up a kidney for a single bite of. She'd told him, once, that she'd eaten a few times at *James Beard's* table, which had put Ben into such a state that he had to go pace around the hallway like an overexcited Pomeranian for a few minutes to cool down.

He's scraping her leftovers into Tupperware for her when he feels his phone buzz in his pocket. And then buzz again. And then buzz *again*. Assuming perhaps it's one of his more loquacious friends—a number of his old college pals have the tendency to pop up and send him multi-text screeds every now and again, especially if they've been drinking—Ben ignores it, and gathers up both plates to take back downstairs. As he wishes Mrs. C good night, he feels the phone buzz again, and then *again*, and then again and again and again and again, far too many times for it to be from one person. He hurries downstairs, not wanting to pull out his phone with plates in his hands and risk pitching to his death over the side of the emergency stairwell he always uses to get between his apartment and Mrs. C's, finding it faster and less frightening than the building's creaky old elevator.

He drops the plates hastily into the sink when he gets back into the apartment and pulls his phone, which has not stopped buzzing, from his pocket. It's warm to the touch, and he takes a second to try to brace himself—*maybe someone is dead; maybe a lot of people are dead; maybe it's the end of the world; maybe aliens have made first contact; maybe that guy who dumped me in high school won the Nobel Peace Prize*—before he lets himself look at the screen. He has seventeen missed calls, twenty-nine unread messages, and a number of notifications on his social media apps.

He clicks into the first message, which appears to be from his sister, Renata. It is, in fact, several messages in a row. Quite... quite a lot of messages. He scrolls up to the first one, where he's surprised and slightly horrified to find a link to Pete's cooking video, and his eyebrows climb nearly to his hairline as he reads her words below:

RENATA:

BEN OH MY GOD IS THIS YOU????? DOING THE VOICE-OVER???

RENATA:

oh my god you don't even have to answer me i KNOW it's you that's YOUR voice

RENATA:

isn't it? i'm going to feel stupid if you have a voice doppelganger i guess

RENATA:

or (please imagine i'm doing my aunt muriel impression rn) mAyBe i'Ve fOrGoTtEn yOuR vOiCe bEcAuSe YoU nEvEr CaLl mE, BeNjAmIn

RENATA:

oh my GOD wait it IS you, you're in the CREDITS THAT'S YOUR NAME THIS IS SO FLIPPING COOL!!!!

RENATA:

BENJAMIN CHICKENFACE BLUMENTHAL I CANNOT!!!!! BELIEVE!!!!!!! YOU DIDN'T TELL ME YOU WERE WORKING FOR GASTRONOME I AM GOING TO KILL YOU

RENATA:

YOU'VE ONLY BEEN TALKING ABOUT IT SINCE THE DAY YOU WERE BORN

RENATA:

do mom and dad know????? god mom's going to FLIP lolololol

RENATA:

ben?? you know this has gone SUPER viral right? like i just saw about six different people posting it on my feeds, it has like a couple million views i think

RENATA:

ben????????? are you dead??????

RENATA:

don't make me call you for real

"Oh my God," Ben says, staring down at his phone. His brain, short circuiting a little, naturally focuses on the important things first:

BEN:

My middle name is not "Chickenface." That was the FIRST name of your childhood stuffed pig, which made us all worry that you couldn't identify basic barnyard animals. Do NOT call me, it might make my phone explode

RENATA:

"chickenface" is a better middle name than "rochester"

BEN:

Be that as it may.

RENATA:

seriously: do mom and dad know??

BEN:

It's not a thing, Ren. It was a one-off job. Leave it.

RENATA:

they're GOING to find out u know

BEN:

I said leave it, okay?

RENATA:

ugh, you're so annoying. congratulations u big stupid celebrity

RENATA:

haha celeBRATy

RENATA:

because you're a brat

BEN:

I'm not a celebrity. And if either of us is the brat here...

RENATA:

wow great insult bro

RENATA:

so witty and original

RENATA:

however will i recover

RENATA:

maybe go deal with your exploding phone or something

BEN:

Yeah, will do. Thanks for the heads-up.

RENATA:

lollllll for sure. good luck with internet fame haha

Ben ignores this last as not worthy of reply, and then immediately regrets it when he... reads the rest of his messages. He'd assumed that Ren was exaggerating, since she tends to, but a number of other very online people in his life have reached out, too, expressing similar sentiments. He opens the link to the video, sure it's going to show him the same two thousand hits or so it did when he looked at it before lunch, and lets out a little shriek when the number is 2.2 *million*. 2.2 million?! It's only been *up* since this morning! It must be—a glitch, or something. An error, that's all. It couldn't possibly be real.

But... but could a glitch have generated all these comments? Ben scrolls through them, a little dizzily. Some of them say things about the recipe, but those are in the significant minority. Most of them are saying that Pete is hilarious, or that the video is hilarious, or that the editing is hilarious, or that he, Ben—the Voice-over Guy, as most of them are calling him—is hilarious.

And a glitch couldn't generate this email in his inbox, either, Rick's address, no subject, ten words: *Did too good a job, kid. My office. Monday. Early.*

Ben stares at it hard, and swallows.

THREE

The next thirty-six hours pass in a blur.

No; that's a lie. Ben *wishes* they would pass in a blur, because he thinks that might be less nauseating. The hours wash over him, somehow both agonizingly slow and much too fast, as though every second is one of those slow-motion explosions in an action film. So much is *happening* that it's hard to keep track of, but at the same time, those events are all taking place only on the small, glowing rectangle of his phone. His physical body mostly paces around inside his apartment like a caged animal, eyes glued to the screen, occasionally shoving a handful of cheese crackers into his mouth.

Ben talks to a lot of people on Saturday night—good friends, old friends, bad friends who have chosen this moment to slither back out of the woodwork—and doesn't sleep much, although he tries to. Mostly, he stares at the ceiling and thinks, *What have I done? And What's going to happen? And What's Rick going to say? And What am I supposed to do now?*

The ceiling does not offer him any advice, but at some point he must doze off a little, because when he blinks awake it's morning and he's got emails and messages from people who say they're with news channels and media companies, and can he confirm that he is the Ben Blumenthal from the viral *Gastronome* video, and would he care to comment on the video's success? Some of those messages are private, but a number of them are public, and on the social channels where they're public, Ben's follower count has... climbed. Not exactly dramatically, but enough to be noticeable, especially for someone like him, whose typical follower count anywhere tends to hover around twenty-five.

Even as he reads them, *new messages are still coming in*.

Ben, having begun, without noticing, the slow process of inching down off his pillow in anxious horror upon opening the first message, realizes abruptly that he is lying flat on his back, every part of his face below his eyes hidden under the covers, holding his phone in the air as far away as possible, as though hoping a bird will steal it. Having now been made aware of this, he should really move, but he finds himself all but frozen. For a single searing second, it's as though Ben's whole life has skipped its track, and he is poised, breathless, waiting to see where it will fall, and whether or not he'll survive.

Then he notices he also has a message from an unfamiliar number; when he clicks into that one, he scrambles bolt upright in bed, the stomach-flipping sensation of hurtling through the air... well. Not leaving him, exactly. Just... altering, somewhat.

PETE:

hey, it's pete.

PETE:

or should i say pat? lol.

PETE:

got your number from rick. sorry to message so early—don't feel like you have to respond or anything. i just wanted to touch base. this is a little crazy, right?

PETE:

> also if you are not ben and rick's given me the
> wrong number again: i'm very sorry to whoever
> you are, my boss is unbelievably bad at using his
> phone. please tell me if you are anyone other than
> ben blumenthal and i'll leave you to your morning.
> thanks.

Ben stares at his phone for a moment, his half-awake but already fully panicked brain not entirely sure what to do with this. His thumbs seem to move of their own accord.

BEN:

> "A little crazy?" Are you kidding me? It's
> completely insane! How did all these people find
> me?! Have you ever dealt with anything like this
> before? Because I have to tell you, my life is NOT
> usually this interesting.

BEN:

> Also, yes, this is Ben.

BEN:

> Also: What do you mean Rick sends out the wrong
> phone numbers? Do I need to start bracing for
> phone calls meant for... uh, whoever else Rick
> talks to?

Ben sits and stares at his phone after sending this for longer than is acceptable. An amount of time that some might call foolish. Ridiculous. Pathetic. When he catches himself at it, he scowls and puts the phone down; it's not like he cares that Pete texted him, anyway. It's not like it matters if Pete replies.

He gets up, mostly out of spite, and tries to ignore the various frantic dings from his phone. When that doesn't work, he silences it, quickly feeds Roux before she can start yowling at him, and then makes himself some breakfast. What breakfast that is he couldn't quite say—it seems, as he eats it, to be cereal with fruit, but he doesn't exactly remember putting it together, as though it happened entirely on muscle memory. Maybe he's still asleep? And this is all a dream? But Ben doesn't think his dreams would have a message from a lady looking to hire him to revitalize her channel about *cockatoo taxidermy*; his subconscious is simply not that creative. He can't remember the last time he even thought about a cockatoo.

Towards the end of the cereal, his control breaks, and he looks at his phone again. He flips past notifications as quickly as he can, trying not to read them, until he sees:

PETE:

probably no need to worry about rick; half the time i think he does it just to screw with me. but maybe look up any number he gives you before dialing, lol. one time i called what i thought was a source at betty crocker and instead was the state game and wildlife commissioner? asked her about cake mix, it didn't go great

PETE:

and yeah, i've dealt with something like this before. or sorta like it, anyway. plus, i've talked to rick, which i bet you haven't, because he's on a fishing trip this weekend and he's seriously peeved that he has to think about anything but walleye.

PETE:

here are the three rules of going viral: don't talk to anyone you don't know, don't post anything publicly, and don't look at your phone unless you absolutely have to, until we've had a chance to circle up with rick. turn it off, ideally, and def turn off all your notifications. nothing good comes of a panicked reply while something's still popping off. gotta get our ducks in a row before we shoot them.

PETE:

that's what rick said before he hung up on me, anyway. always possible he meant literally, though, since i'm only eighty percent sure it's a fishing trip.

PETE:

maybe he just really hates mallards

Ben laughs, a little surprised by being entertained enough to do so, at this last. Then he fiddles with his spoon for a minute, rattling it back and forth against the side of the cereal dish, thinking. Unfortunately, in his haze of bewilderment, he neglected to make himself any *coffee*, so the results of that thinking are... a mixed bag.

BEN:

That seems like solid advice; thanks.

BEN:

But what happens if the walleye decide to seek revenge on Rick? Drag him to the depths for his crimes against fishkind? I've got the impression it's maybe a lot of crimes. Am I supposed to live as a digital hermit forevermore, in that event?

Ben cringes the minute he sends the message, horror offering the clarity that coffee might have provided if only he'd been wise enough to make some. What a perfectly deranged thing for him to say to this virtual stranger—Rick's *crimes* against *fishkind*? A *digital hermit forevermore*? What was Ben *thinking*? He wishes fervently that he could unsend it, but as he's trying to figure out if that's possible, a reply pops up from Pete. And somehow, upon reading it, Ben finds himself helplessly drawn into an absurd conversation, not entirely sure how it's happening even as he's typing his replies.

PETE:

LOLLLLLLLLLL

PETE:

he IS lake placid's most wanted

PETE:

but the fish can't draw a very good likeness, so we might be safe here. they'll never ID him from the poster

BEN:

You're very quick to assume you know what the world looks like to a fish.

BEN:

Maybe the posters are capturing the fish-eye view. There's a lens named after them and everything, you know. The artwork could be incredibly representational, to a fish.

PETE:

how are you suggesting they capture him? capsize the boat? rain of walleye?

BEN:

Maybe they could enlist the help of the other local fishes. Surely they all must bear some sort of grudge by now. I don't know the man that well, but he's still managed to tell me countless stories of fish murder. They probably all want a piece.

PETE:

LOL. this has escalated rapidly to all-out fish war

BEN:

I mean, he does by all accounts seem to be a fish war criminal.

PETE:

am i a fish war criminal? for cooking so many of them?

BEN:

If you are, then I am, too. Maybe we all have something to fear from aquatic wildlife

PETE:

probably best to avoid the sea entirely, just to be safe

BEN:

Lake Placid is famously a lake.

PETE:

LOL. so true

PETE:

okay i gotta go. seriously tho: turn off your phone, go do something in real life. it'll help. you going to be at this rick meeting tomorrow AM?

Assuming my actual bosses let me off the hook,
then yeah, I'm planning on it.

cool. see you there

Ben types, *See you!* and deletes it, and then *Looking forward!* and then deletes it, and then, feeling disgusted with himself, slaps a thumbs-up emoji on the message before taking Pete's advice and turning his whole phone off. If it's mostly in horror at his own sudden and inexplicable inability to behave like a *normal human being*, then nobody but Ben needs to know about it.

He spends the rest of Sunday mostly trying and failing to clean his apartment. It's not that the apartment is even particularly dirty; Ben just needs to be *doing* something. Unfortunately, every third or fourth minute, he finds his thoughts drawn away again, cycling into some rumination or another. By the time he calls it quits for the day, orders some takeout, watches half a movie that slides out of his head instantaneously, and goes to bed, his apartment doesn't look any different than it did when he started.

He has considered roughly twenty-six different ways Rick might verbally eviscerate him, and another ten or eleven scenarios in which some Formica executive saunters into tomorrow's meeting and fires him, and has also spun out rather more possibilities than he cares to dwell upon about what Pete might say tomorrow when they're face-to-face. He didn't *seem* angry over those messages. He seemed the opposite of angry: helpful and surprisingly funny for a guy who, in the footage Ben watched, spent about ten minutes trying to pull up the word "spatula." But a lot can be lost through text. Maybe Pete's trying to lure him into a false sense of security, to better pummel him with rage tomorrow morning.

It occurs to Ben, at this point, to wonder why exactly he's so afraid that *anyone* will be angry at him. Surely, the video going viral is a good thing, right? It will make Formica money—it will make

Gastronome money—it will boost Pete's career. It might even boost *Ben's* career, if one can call it a career; Ben himself has never quite been able to. And yeah, okay, Rick had wanted Ben to tank it, so *he* might be a little annoyed, but... why would any of these people be angry, otherwise? What issue could they possibly have with Ben?

Well, Ben's brain, never quite able to decide if it's with him or against him when the chips are down, points out, *Pete might not be thrilled that three million people and counting heard you suggest he was less intelligent than a dog.* It's a compelling argument.

But then again... surely, Pete would have said something earlier, if he was upset. He's had plenty of opportunities! And Rick's *Richard Raleigh*, so he's had plenty of opportunities, too, ample time to pick up the phone and put in a call to get Ben fired, if that's what he wanted to do.

Things never seem to go as badly as Ben expects them to, and he tries to let that thought comfort him to sleep. Unfortunately, the inescapable other half of that idea—that sometimes the reason things don't go as badly as Ben expects them to is because they go *much* worse—renders his attempt at sleep less than successful. He tosses and turns and groans at the ceiling and plays with Roux for a while and then tosses and turns some more and finally, around 5 a.m., gives up and heads out to get a latte and whatever pastry he can force himself to choke down.

By the time he makes it to the small but high-gloss waiting area outside Rick's office, Monday morning at 9:15, Ben is jittery from too much coffee, slightly sick to his stomach with nerves, and can feel the beginnings of a tension headache pounding behind his eyes. He perches on one of the waiting area's chrome and white leather chairs, one leg bouncing up and down so quickly it might as well be vibrating, and waits.

It's only a minute before Pete slouches around the corner. He is not, for once, wearing his ASK ME ABOUT CANNED BEANS shirt; he's wearing black jeans, and a black T-shirt, and black canvas shoes that Ben recognizes immediately as kitchen-safe non-skid. This, of course, is a perfectly normal thing for him to be wearing: It's the unofficial uniform of kitchen staff everywhere, and far more ubiquitous than the white chef's coat, at least outside of a certain sort of establishment. At Fleur de Sel they'd made him wear whites after he made it to sous chef, but until then he was in black like everyone else. And at Trattoria Luciana there were no real rules on staff dress, beyond the highly necessary and insurance-mandated non-slip shoe requirement. But still, most people gravitated towards black, which didn't show stains, and tended to hold up in the wash, and was easy to keep identifiable and separated as work clothes.

This, Ben thinks, looking Pete over more appreciatively than he would dare allow himself on more sleep, is what Pete should have been wearing in that video. This is how Pete should dress *all the time*. In his canned beans T-shirt and standard blue jeans, Pete had been hot in a distracting but incidental way; he'd looked like someone you might do a quick double take at during a beach day, or aim to make a series of enjoyable mistakes with on a vacation. But in kitchen blacks, Pete looks... serious. Professional. *Competent*.

"Hello?" Pete says, waving a hand in front of Ben's face, which is when Ben snaps back into reality and realizes he has been *staring*. Horrified, he tries to think of some explanation for himself as Pete continues, "You good in there, man? You kinda look like you saw a ghost."

"I just didn't recognize you without your stupid bean shirt," Ben snaps, retreating in panic. "I was starting to think maybe you had a closet full of them. You know, like a cartoon character?"

As it did the other day, this flash of Ben's verbal claws makes Pete laugh. "Yeah, Rick said I had to dress like a real cook today. It looks like he trusted *you* to dress yourself, which you should take as a compliment."

Ben grimaces slightly down at his own outfit, which is a pair of skinny maroon chinos underneath a navy-blue quarter-zip striped sweater that his mother had given him for some holiday or birthday —Ben can't remember quite when, just that he'd thought, *When am I ever going to wear this? When has any outfit I've ever worn suggested a tendency to shop the Middle-Aged Straight Man Whose Wife Buys His Clothing Collection? Did you mean to get this for Dad?* But Ben is, nevertheless, wearing it today, largely because he'd realized, sometime around 7:30 in the morning, and after an almost entirely sleepless night that he *could* have spent handling it, that he was basically out of clean laundry. His is an outfit of necessity, one he has been bricking it over a little since he stepped out his front door, and he had to fight the urge to duck into a thrift store or something on the way here, to pick up something a little more... him.

Thankfully, instead of revealing any of this, Ben is able to contain himself to muttering, "He might live to regret it."

"Nah," Pete says, his brow crinkling for a second before the expression smooths away. He sits down in the chair next to Ben, relaxing into the cupped backrest instead of hovering at the very edge of the seat as though ready to spring into the air, the way Ben is. "You look great—that's what these execs like to see in the behind-the-scenes people, I think. Professional, a little creative, but not *too* creative. Too creative is expensive."

"So there are going to be execs in this meeting?" Ben asks. It's a Pyrrhic victory; on the one hand, he does manage not to say, *You got that from this outfit? This outfit that says, "The man who stands before you is wearing the very last pair of clean underpants he owns?" Are you kidding me right now?* This, truly, is an important and critical success. On the *other* hand, his voice audibly cracks with nervousness on the word "execs," so. All in all, a bit of a humiliating turnout.

But Pete doesn't jump on, or even seem to notice, this moment of visible weakness from Ben; he just waves a hand, and says, "Oh, yeah. Anywhere there's money, there's executives. That's how it works around here."

"Have you worked here a long time, then?" Ben asks. He sort of knows the answer—Pete's been working here long enough to have bylines going back at least six years—but that doesn't necessarily mean he's *only* been here for six years. He could have started some-where else at *Gastronome*, or at Formica, worked his way up to article writing and recipe development a dozen ways.

Pete shrugs, and a shadow seems to cross his expression for a moment. "Long enough to know how things... generally work around here, yeah. I wouldn't worry too much; they're going to be happy. It's a lot of traffic, and that's all they care about." He drops his voice low and adds, "Well, the execs will be happy. Rick... might be a little annoyed, honestly, but don't let him get to you. He's all bark, really."

"Unless you're a fish," Ben says, before he can think better of it, also keeping his voice pitched low.

Pete grins at him, shaking his head. "Right, yeah. Naturally. It's different for them."

Ben finds that, in spite of his nerves, a small smile is starting to play at the edges of his own mouth. "I guess if he *really* goes off on me, I could always let his location slip to the nearest school of walleye."

"Which would be where, exactly?" Pete's eyes are almost dancing now, and Ben finds himself settling back into his chair a little, his muscles releasing their rigid control of him by a fraction. "I have to imagine they'd have some trouble roaming the halls."

Ben opens his mouth to say—well, something, anyway, he would have figured it out—when the frosted-glass door that reads RICHARD RALEIGH swings open. From inside, Rick growls, "Tweedle Dumb! Tweedle Dumber! Inside, now!"

Ben grimaces as he jumps jerkily to his feet, but Pete rolls his eyes and, after standing and stretching lazily, bumps his shoulder lightly against Ben's and gives him a reassuring little smile. Then he takes a step ahead, draws in a deep breath, and enters the office first.

It doesn't help, Ben tells himself. It does not help; of course it doesn't help. Why would it help? What good is the brief pressure of Pete's shoulder against his, in the scheme of things?

Ridiculously, *stupidly*, he feels the ghostly sensation linger anyway, seeming to nudge him into the room a step or two behind Pete, as though Pete himself is chivvying him gently along. God, Ben needs to *sleep*; his brain is playing nasty little tricks on him, that's all it is. Nothing worth dwelling on—nothing he needs to worry about.

Rick is, at least, alone in the office. He's seated behind his desk by the time Ben shuts the door; his elbows are resting on the frosted-glass surface, hands folded, chin sitting on top of them. He is, in a word, glowering.

"What did I say to you?" Rick says, glaring first at Pete. "Even you can't have forgotten—it was only a week ago!"

"You said that the worst thing that could happen was for this to go well," Pete admits, rubbing the back of his neck with his hand. "Because if it went well, I'd have to do a bunch more of them, and since I'm such a disaster the minute we start rolling, I'd probably end up accidentally killing us all?"

Sharply, Rick says, "That's *not* what I—"

Pete waves off the rest of his sentence with an easy hand. "Oh, don't, I know. *You* said it would be bad because it would give the Formica executives an excuse to swoop in and change how everything works, but I have to say, I think my thing hits closer to the reality." He looks—a little sheepish, maybe, but that's all. None of the gut-churning anxiety that Ben himself is feeling appears to be manifesting for Pete in any way, in spite of the fact that working here is his full-time job, and so, of the two of them, he is at more risk of being in serious trouble. But he seems cheerful enough as he adds, "But, in my defense, you *told* me to lean into my natural tendencies, which I did, and I'm *really* sure I did a bad job, so. *Can* you blame me for this one? I don't know."

"Which brings me to *you*," Rick says, turning his glare on Ben. He turns his laptop around to face them without breaking gaze; it appears to have their video open, full screen, and Rick reaches over the top to hit play.

"Hi, I'm Pat!" the smaller, on-screen version of Pete says; the image freezes, and then, as a ghostly hand draws a little jester hat on Pete's head, Ben's voice-over comes in: "This is Pete."

On-screen, the video cuts to Pete waving his knife in one gesturing hand and saying, "Uh—hey—has anyone seen my knife? Chef's, six inches, wood handle—oh, I'm holding it." Then it cuts again, to Pete standing over a sizzling cast-iron pan full of chicken thighs and saying, "So for this recipe you want to burn the chicken —brown. Brown the chicken! You don't wanna burn it, I said that because I think this batch is—yeah, yep. Super burnt. Torched, actually. [BLEEP]!" The image cuts again, this time to Pete singing softly to himself as he washes the kale. "First, you put kale in! Then you give it a spin! Then you throw your croutons on—no, wait, what am I *doing*?"

There's another cut, to the clip of Pete accidentally tossing his spoon in the air, and the video freezes with it poised mid-flight. Ben's voice-over returns, wry this time: "If Pete can make this, anyone can. Even you. Maybe even your dog."

Rick pauses the video again and resumes glaring at Ben, although Ben supposes it's not as though he ever technically stopped. "This is *funny*, Ben. It's *entertaining*. I told you, didn't I? I was as clear as I could be without saying anything that could get me in hot water—don't do too good a job, I said! For the best if it's a little unwatchable, I said! But do you know what the internet loves, Ben? It loves to be *entertained*."

Ben's not usually great in a situation where someone is angry with him. His move is generally to apologize, and then apologize some more, and then sullenly feel resentful about apologizing later when he's had a chance to think it over and realizes he's not sure he did anything particularly wrong. So he doesn't know where within himself he finds the gumption to jerk a thumb at Pete and say, "I think that's his fault, really. If he'd been able to do even an *impression* of a remotely normal human being, *at all*, it wouldn't have come to this."

Pete snorts and then affects an expression of perfect, angelic innocence when Rick's glare whips towards him. "What? It was a cough."

"God help me," Rick mutters, and closes his laptop screen. "Look—I don't have much time before the boss gets here, but I need the two of you to understand something, okay? I think this is a doomed venture that we're all going to regret embarking upon, but it's too late for all that now. Sometimes, even if you know it's going to be a low-bite day, there's nothing for it but to go out on the lake and give your worms a good soaking anyway." When Rick receives, in response to this, the blank stares of two people who are not committed to the art of fishing, he sighs, clearly disappointed, and carries on. "People are going to get *involved* in this now. Powerful people, in this building. There's only so much I can do, at this point, to keep an eye out for either one of you. Pete, we've already talked about your... situation... and I'll do what I can, but—"

"I know," Pete says, and shrugs, and looks away. Ben wishes he'd say more, offer up a scrap of additional info to go off, but all Pete adds is, "It is what it is."

Rick frowns, looking for a second as though *he's* going to say more, and then dashes Ben's hopes by turning to face him. "*You*— look, this is not normally the advice I'd give, kid, but you're in a tricky spot here. This isn't the kind of work you usually do, and with this traffic, they want someone more tested. I lobbied for you, and I think it worked—the voice argument was pretty strong—but don't try to push back here, okay? Not yet. Just... agree, for now, until we can prove it wasn't a one-off, and I can work the rest of it out. Assuming you want to keep doing it, of course—editing for the show, that is."

"The... show," Ben repeats, slowly.

"Yes," Rick repeats, even slower, as though he's talking to a child. "This video has more than five million views now—they want a whole web show, Ben. Nine episodes to start, but probably more once they've worked out sponsorships—they want to cash in on the golden cow. If you don't want to do it, that's one thing, but I figured..." He sighs, and shakes his head, as though wrestling with some internal question, before he finishes, "Well, I think they're going to go ahead with it either way, so. I figured you'd probably want the option."

"They... want *me*," Ben says, hardly daring to believe it, "to edit a *show*? Like, officially?"

"'Want' is a strong word," Rick says with a grimace. "I'd say it's more of a—they've *agreed* to let you edit the show. On a temporary basis. To see how it goes. In case—and you understand that this is coming from them, not me—that video was a total fluke, and all you had in you creatively. No offense or anything, but your resume doesn't exactly... line up with this type of work."

"I still think it's ridiculous that they're not offering a full-time role immediately," Pete mutters, mulishly. "The whole *thing* is because of him! Without him it's two hours of footage of me basically—"

"Your objections have been noted for the record," Rick says sharply, with a quick glance towards his office door and a significant look at Pete, who clams his mouth shut tightly but manages to look a little mutinous about it. Lowering his voice to a hiss, Rick adds, "And I don't even disagree! But we both know how it *goes*, okay, and there's only so much I can do, so—can you trust me? That I'm trying?"

Pete folds his arms, and says, "Hmph," which normally Ben would be interested to note is not exactly a yes.

He's not interested to note it now, though. He's not interested in Rick's obvious concerns, or the various signs that this whole situation is steeped in a layer of something he, Ben, does not yet understand. He's not concerned about the red flags, or what he's going to do about his regular job, or the pay, or the fact that the executives didn't want him on board. He's not concerned about making a decision like this on so little sleep, or while his whole body is trembling slightly from caffeine and shock. He's not concerned about anything at all.

He, Ben, is going to edit a show for *Gastronome*. A real show! Sure, okay, a web show, and a weird show, and a show that's going to involve quite a lot of difficult work that will make Ben want to throw his computer out a window, but Ben wants to throw his computer out a window several times a day already, so that's a wash. And, most importantly, it's *for Gastronome*. It was one thing, less real, when it was Rick's weird attempted flop—a one-off, nothing job that didn't count. But this... Even if it doesn't work out long term, Ben's going to be able to put this on his *resume*. It's not just going to be technical editing and cutting together videos of weddings, or bar mitzvahs, or corporate conferences—it's going to be a *real creative job*, for a *real* publication, with recognition and actual status and its name scrawled on several of Ben's childhood Halloween costumes.

"Sure," Ben says, even though his moment to say this in the conversation passed some time ago. "I'll—I'll do it. Whatever you want, or the execs want, or whatever." Turning to Pete, abruptly realizing he doesn't know the answer, he asks, "*You're* doing it, right?" before he can think better of it. Before he can remind himself that really, he shouldn't care at all—if anything, he should want someone else, someone better and less all over the place on camera and *not* so distractingly good-looking that Ben *ever* finds himself staring at him like a dope.

And Pete... Pete gives Ben this look that Ben doesn't quite understand, sad and surprised and pleased and sorry, all at once. When he speaks, his voice is quiet. "Yeah, I'm doing it. One way or another, I'm doing whatever Formica Media asks me to do."

"Well," says a voice from the waiting area, "isn't that what we like to hear," and Ben turns in time to see a tall, sharply dressed, auburn-haired woman walk through the door.

FOUR

"Miranda," Rick says. He sounds very calm and entirely unsurprised when he adds, "I wasn't expecting you until ten."

"Richard," Miranda says coolly, inclining her head. "My last meeting wrapped early, so I thought I'd pop down and see if you were free to move this up." She turns to Ben and Pete, and smiles. "Which it would appear that you are; wonderful."

That's a lot of teeth you've got in your mouth, lady, Ben thinks, which is both entirely unhelpful in this moment and, honestly, not the heart and soul of kindness. She's a perfectly nice-looking woman, to the extent Ben is qualified to judge such things; a little fox-faced, maybe, but it works for her. It's not her fault there's something a bit uncanny about her smile, the faint suggestion that perhaps, somehow, she stole it off a shark.

"And *you* must Ben," she says, her tone taking on the slightest whiff of a condescending coo as she passes over her business card. She doesn't, Ben notes, greet Pete; she just nods to him tightly. "I'm Miranda Culter, Formica's Executive Director of Creative Strategy. That was quite the video the two of you made —the traffic bump we saw was *enormous*. Of course, we won't have a full picture of the year-over-year data until the end of the month, but—you know the traffic to that kale salad recipe broke the site for about twenty minutes on Saturday, right? A night-mare for our support staff, of course, and obviously, we hate to see the site have any downtime, but if it *has* to go down, you know?"

She pauses here, seeming to expect some sort of response from them, but Ben does *not* know; he has no idea what to say to this. Should he confirm that he is, in fact, Ben? That's the only part of her statement that he feels capable of replying to with any level of coherence, understanding, or accuracy. Is he supposed to care about the site going down for twenty minutes? Is he supposed to know what the "year-over-year numbers" are? Surely not; he doesn't even work here, at least not yet. Ben's almost positive that the technical videos he usually edits don't have those, and abso-lutely certain that, if they do, it's beyond his remit to know about them.

Luckily, Pete says, "Wow, that's wild; gotta be a first for kale traffic to break anything. A great day for brassica enthusiasts everywhere."

Ben bites the inside of his lip to keep from smiling; Rick shoots a quick but unmissable glare at Pete, there and gone again. But Miranda doesn't seem to notice that Pete's being sarcastic; she just offers another one of those unsettling, toothy smiles, this one slightly more brittle than before, and says, "I think you mean a great day for Formica Media. Listen—did Rick fill you in on the plan?"

"I'm not entirely sure I've been filled in on the plan myself," Rick says, leaning back in his chair and fixing her with a somewhat unpleasant smile of his own. Ben notices, a little belatedly, that he has not invited her to sit, and that there is no available chair. "So I thought I'd better leave that to you. Wouldn't want to put the cart before the horse, you know, or step on any toes."

"Kind of you," Miranda says, her smile seeming to brighten a watt or two. Not appearing bothered by the lack of chair, she leans over to the laptop on Rick's desk and says, "May I? I didn't want to lug my laptop all the way down here for this."

"I see you already are," Rick says. Ben notes one of his eyelids is twitching slightly. "So... be my guest."

"Great," Miranda says. She types for a moment, and then, much as Rick had, rotates the computer so only Pete and Ben can see the screen. Turning to face the two of them, and with her back to Rick, she stands next to the desk with one long finger resting lightly against the computer's arrow key, as though she'd never thought of wanting a chair, and says, "All right, gentlemen. This is the presentation I gave to the folks upstairs, but I'll try to dumb it down a little for you. Let's go through this point by point."

The slideshow that follows is... dizzying. So many numbers; so many charts; so much unacceptably hideous graphic design. Miranda flips through it so quickly Ben can hardly take in one slide before she's moving to the next, babbling in jargon that doesn't ever seem to relate to anything that's on the screen. Ben's absorbing roughly every third word, so his experience isn't a presentation so much as one of those weird, half-awake dreams he used to have as a teenager when he'd fall asleep with the television on. Miranda might as well be speaking another language, or be, if Ben's teenage dreams are going to serve as a reference point, a large and vaguely alarming pineapple singing odd snippets of the *Fresh Prince of Bel-Air* theme song.

But there is, at least, a production calendar; Ben can read one of those. And Miranda, thankfully, is kind enough to leave it on the screen for a whole forty-five seconds, so Ben has time to process... well, most of it, anyway. It looks like, as Rick said, they'll be doing nine videos, on some sort of staggered schedule that involves a step ominously labeled s&p. Pete appears to have two days to shoot most of the videos, and Ben three to edit them; S&P, on the other hand, is slotted to take a wildly vacillating amount of time, sometimes as little as a few days, sometimes as long as a week or two. It's honestly an incomprehensible timeline, and certainly doesn't give much insight into what the process is meant to be; Ben is reasonably sure Formica doesn't intend to salt and pepper the edited file before posting it, which is honestly his best guess.

Whatever it means, it looks like the videos will go live following the mysterious S&P. A handful of the prospective episodes are marked with intended themes—Halloween, Thanksgiving, Christmas—but others are blocked out with a list of SEO keywords, like "best ravioli sauce" or "fall recipes." That's clear enough, and Ben can certainly make three days work, even for Pete's... less than clean footage. After all, he'd done the last one in a single, unhinged night.

The only other slide he understands in the whole presentation is the last one, labeled, IN SUMMARY. This slide contains a single short paragraph, which Miranda recites verbatim without looking at the screen: "This engaging, non-traditional web show, to be shared for free on our website as well as across several widely accessible social channels, has the potential to direct significant traffic to the *Gastronome* brand, as well as to other Formica Media properties. Additionally, it offers us the ability to bring in supplementary revenue streams, such as episode sponsorships and brand engagement deals."

Still smiling that unsettling smile, Miranda pushes Rick's laptop closed with one hand, ignoring his annoyed little huff. "Of course," she says to Pete and Ben, her voice honey smooth, "we'll be using those additional revenue streams to offset production costs. This is still very much a pilot run—if it goes well, it has the potential to open up a whole new world of options for this... Well, let's say we've all commented on what an *adorably* old-fashioned food brand you are."

"How flattering," Rick mutters, through what sounds like gritted teeth.

"But if it goes *poorly*," Miranda continues, her back still to Rick, "well. Obviously, we'll all be very sorry about the missed opportunity, but we're hardly in the business of *losing* money, are we? Anyway, we'll cross that bridge when we come to it. Pete, of course, you and I have already touched base on your situation, and I can't imagine you need a refresher—"

"Nope," Pete says dryly. His face is very calm, but Ben notices his fingers flexing and releasing against the black denim of his jeans. "We remain crystal clear."

"Fantastic," Miranda says; the way she says it suggests, to Ben, that in fact it isn't fantastic at all. It certainly isn't fantastic when she turns to Ben and says, "You're an interesting case. Usually, we'd be bringing in someone a little more... experienced for something like this."

"Why didn't you, then?" Again, Pete sounds cool and calm, but his body language tells a different story—or Ben thinks it does, anyway. It occurs to him that he doesn't know, that this man is still more or less a stranger to him. Still, in spite of that or maybe because of it, it warms Ben a little when he adds, "I doubt *they* would have netted us five million views, or whatever it's at now."

"Five point seven-five," Miranda says crisply, and turns the smile on Ben again. "Perhaps Pete's right, and no one else *could* have done it. Certainly, the argument was put forward that it was your unique voice that led to the video's success; some found that argument convincing. I suppose we'll find out, won't we? For now, we've talked to your team on twenty-seven, and they've agreed to allow you a semi-remote model. So long as you make all your meetings and turn all your projects in on time, you're welcome to work wherever you like, whether that's out of their offices or the *Gastronome* suites. The time you bill to *Gastronome* will be at a slightly higher rate, since the work expected is of a different caliber. It's all in the contract." She pulls a thin stack of stapled paper out of her attaché and proffers it. "If you wouldn't mind taking a quick look and giving it a sign; it *is* a tight schedule for you, after all. You've got deliverables due to Standards and Practices quite soon, and they *will* need the full allotted time to review. Dave's a real stickler for that sort of thing."

"I *knew* it wasn't salt and pepper," Ben mutters, very much *not* intentionally, reaching out and grabbing the contract. Pete makes a sound that seems almost like a laugh for a second but turns out to be a cough; odd. Everyone else, thankfully, ignores it entirely.

It occurs to Ben, as he looks down at the contract in his hand, that it's quite a bit harder to read than he was expecting. He realizes after a mystified second that it's because his hand is shaking so badly that the paper is actively vibrating; whoops. Too much coffee and too little sleep, not enough to eat—Ben *purchased* a bear claw at his favorite coffee shop on the way into work, yes, but he'd been so nervous that it tasted sickeningly sweet. In the end, he'd put it back in its bag for later and, he realizes only now, left it behind on the subway.

Ben's always *doing* this in critical moments. Other people learned how, probably, to say rational, reasonable things to themselves, and then follow through with them, somewhere in their orderly, well-managed childhoods. Things like: "Hey, self, you have a big meeting tomorrow, why don't you make sure your laundry is done, and then go to bed at a reasonable hour, and get some sleep instead of lying awake in a torment of nerves! And then, in the morning, you can have a nice normal breakfast and only one coffee. Certainly, you would never go to a career-altering meeting on no breakfast and a coffee at five a.m., and then another at seven a.m., and then another at eight forty-five a.m.! Only a madman would do something like that." It must be nice, Ben thinks, to be that sort of person. Calming. Restful.

But Ben is the sort of person who grew up in chaos, always one more thing to do, one more problem to solve, one more crazy thing about to happen just when he thought the restaurant was finally closed for the night. So now, as an adult, he seeks chaos like a homing pigeon, flapping past cleaner and safer roosts to the one his heart knows as his own. If he cannot find chaos—if chaos is not, by fate or fortune, thrust upon him—then by God, Ben will create it for himself.

The paper shakes in his hand, reminding him that he is not, actually, free to sit and consider this any further. Quickly, Ben rests it on his lap, smooths it over, tries to read it. He realizes he has no chance of doing this almost immediately; he *can* read, of course, but his eyes are skipping over the words, aware that the other three are looking at him. God, had they noticed the paper shaking?

Miranda in particular would probably see it as a sign of weakness, and *Pete*—no, Ben doesn't have time to think about this right now. He's not going to be able to focus, not like this; anyway, hadn't Rick said that Ben should go along, for now? Not push back?

Ben makes a decision. It's not a great decision, certainly, but it's the only one available to him in the circumstances, and in a real way, he made it last week, when he realized who Rick was. He said it already: He's going to sign the contract. So, really, what does it matter what it says?

For another moment or two, Ben makes a show of reading it over anyway, not wanting to look like the rube that he is. He flips through the pages, scanning them without absorbing anything. Then he takes the pen Miranda offers him, rests the contract against the edge of Rick's desk, and scrawls *Benjamin Blumenthal* in his crabbed, spiky cursive.

"Good," Miranda says, all but snatching her pen and the contract out of Ben's hands. "That's settled. I have a ten ten meeting, so I have to dash, but I'll email you a copy of all this later, of course." Without turning to look at him, as she stalks towards the door, she adds, "Richard."

"Miranda," Rick returns, rolling his eyes at her retreating back. When the door has snicked shut behind her, he mutters, "Who *alive* schedules a meeting at ten ten? I swear she makes this stuff up." Then, to Ben and Pete, he snaps, "You two, clear out. I need to talk to some lures about all this."

Ben thinks that's a joke, but Pete very decidedly does not laugh and makes a wide-eyed face of warning at Ben when the corners of his mouth begin to twitch. Sure enough, a second later Rick pulls an enormous tackle box out from under his desk with an air of finality, opening it with a loud, foreboding click.

"Yeah, we'll... go," Pete says quickly. He stands and puts a brief, urging hand under Ben's elbow; Ben rises almost unthinkingly at his touch, light though it is, as if he's a marionette Pete's controlling. Distantly, he wonders if maybe he doesn't need something to eat quite *badly*, but that's a problem for later Ben to solve.

Still, he's not so far gone that he can't identify and walk out the door, so he does, waving awkwardly at a glaring Rick and then turning away with a grimace. Pete's close on his heels, and when the door closes behind them, Ben lets out a huge breath, feeling as though he's been holding it for the last forty-five minutes. "God. Did I black out in there? I feel like maybe I blacked out in there. Something about all that business talk always makes my brain... oozy."

Pete laughs, shaking his head. "Oozy, huh? I think that's the Miranda effect; she's not exactly well-liked around here, if it's any comfort. It's not just you. My friend Adina—she's one of the test cooks, you'll meet her—anyway, she says that every minute you spend with Miranda costs you two minutes of energy. Even being around her charges interest."

In spite of himself, Ben can't help but laugh. "Sorry to say it, but that *does* make me feel a little better. Really, they should let me skip the rest of the morning at my other job as compensation."

"I mean," Pete says, and shrugs, giving him a little grin. "The way I heard it, you don't have to go down there, so long as all your work is done and you don't have any meetings. Right? That's what she said? So... *do* you have any meetings?"

"I... guess not," Ben says, blinking slowly. "No. Mondays are a no-meeting day on twenty-seven. One of my bosses has a thing about it. And I don't have anything due until Thursday, and I did it last week, anyway."

"Well," Pete says, and shrugs. "There you go. How about a new employee orientation? You are technically working here now. You should come see where the magic happens." Pete pauses ruefully, and then, as he starts walking, says, "Well, I *say* magic, but I mean more horror show."

"It's not *that* bad," Ben protests, keeping pace with Pete and trying not to gape as they walk through the halls of *Gastronome's actual offices*. He knows the magazine wasn't always based in this building—they were moved in from their original location in Chelsea when Formica bought the magazine out—but it's still surreal, and fairly cool, to be here. Framed covers of various iconic issues line the walls, along with a few bronzed newspaper articles about important moments in the magazine's history. Ben notices, to his irritation, that somewhere in the middle of the wall there is a beautifully staged headshot of Rick, one that must be twenty years old but would still look great *anywhere in the actual magazine,* where people who might *encounter him later in their lives* might have a chance to view it. There is, below it, a little plaque below it that reads, RICHARD RALEIGH: NOT PICTURED, which makes Ben want to scream a little, for all he can tell it must be an inside joke.

"Really?" Pete says doubtfully, pulling Ben back to the moment.

Then, because he's not a very good liar, Ben can't help but add, "I mean, okay, it's not—it's not that good, either. But you *can* actually cook, right? When... whatever's happening in that footage isn't happening? It seems like you can." It does not seem like this, at least based on what Ben's seen of Pete's cooking so far; it simply *looks* like it based on his current outfit. This isn't a fair tool to use to assess such things, of course, but in Ben's defense he keeps accidentally ending up a step or two behind Pete, distracted by the densely packed wall of preserved moments from *Gastronome*'s past. This leaves him with a rather unfortunately thorough view of how well Pete is wearing his black jeans, which is doing a lot of heavy lifting for Ben's opinion of him, at this moment.

"Cross my heart and hope to die," Pete says, with an accompanying gesture across his chest, and then steps into a large, high-ceilinged, open room. "In fact, how about this? I'll prove it."

Ben steps into the room after him and has a disquieting sense of déjà vu. He's been in this room before—no. Of course not. This is the test kitchen, he realizes after a beat; he's never been here, but he spent ten hours watching footage of *Pete* being in here, standing... yes, just over there. Ben blinks as Pete crosses the room to the same butcher block-topped island he stood at to cook the kale salad. It's interesting to see it from a wider framing. There's a stand-alone range set into the counter, though no accompanying oven, and a number of pots and pans hanging from a rail on the wooden front panel of the island, which is itself painted a deep royal purple, the *Gastronome* brand's anchoring color since it was founded in—God, was it a hundred years ago this year? Ben finds he can't quite remember, even though he knew that date by heart when he was a kid. Then again, Ben's childhood was itself a hundred years ago, or it feels that way most days, so. Maybe it's not such a surprise he's lost track of some of the fine detail.

Regardless, Pete's isn't the only counter; there's five more, two behind him and then three more next to them, so that all six are lined up in two neat rows. Though no one else is in here at the moment, each counter is slightly personalized. His has what looks to be a ceramic hanging sculpture of a braided bunch of garlic dangling from one of the low overhead lights, and a large knife block in one corner that had only been half in frame during the video. Ben had spent maybe forty-five minutes of his ten total hours of editing puzzling over what on earth the thing *was*, and now that he's looking at it, he's annoyed it wasn't adjusted into the camera's sightline by whoever did the filming. It's an odd, gnarled piece of tree branch, bark removed and wood polished to a high shine, with thin, barely visible slots out of which a variety of colorful knife handles are jutting straight up. It alone speaks to Pete as a competent if unusual cook; a collection of knives like that takes time and money to assemble, and such a well-crafted home and display for them... He must care about them enormously.

"I know it's a lot to take in," Pete says, half-joking, "but you can join me, you know."

God, Ben must be staring. But the truth is, Pete's right—there *is* a lot to take in. He walks over to Pete's counter as if in a dream, craning his neck to look around him as he goes. God, there are ovens set into the walls—home *and* commercial—oh, and that's a door to a walk-in fridge, next to one which must be the walk-in freezer. But there are two home fridges in here, too, each with a masking tape label too far away for Ben to read, and what looks like a grill-top, and—

"Oh, wait, you need somewhere to sit," Pete says, shaking his head, and runs off for a moment. He returns with a little metal stool, which he sets down in front of his counter before, humming to himself, he opens the walk-in and disappears inside.

Ben, a little overwhelmed, sits down on the stool. But when Pete returns, laden with a carton of eggs and a jumble of produce he's barely containing in his arms, Ben realizes he has been silent much too long and says, "Uh, do you need like—help? With that?"

"Thanks, but nah," Pete says easily, and it seems that he doesn't. The Pete that Ben spent ten hours staring at on a screen in increasing certainty that he was minutes from death every second of his life—well, that Pete would have managed to find a banana peel, and slip on it, and throw everything in the air, and then have every egg somehow land directly on his face. But this Pete simply leans across his counter and sets everything down in one smooth movement, then slides the walk-in door shut on his way to a large basket that turns out to contain bread. Once he's bent and plucked a round blonde loaf out, he stops by a cabinet from which he selects several spices, drops it all off on the counter, and, still humming, opens one of the two fridges with a masking tape label. Closer now, Ben can squint and see that the fridge Pete reaches into is labeled GRABS, and the other one is labeled KEEPS.

"This is the freebie fridge," Pete explains, as he rummages around in it. "Anything in here is up for grabs, and—ha, yeah, I thought so." He emerges with a large plastic container atop which he has perched two glass pints of orange juice. "Rick has this buddy who's a juice wholesaler, and every once in a while, he brings in a case for us. It's honestly insane how good it is; you have to try it."

"I mean," Ben says, making a face. "If it's like a—a special thing for the staff, I wouldn't want to—"

"Oh, shut up," Pete says, grinning and waving a hand. "We've all tried it before; besides, I'm having one, too. The code of the fridges is very sacred here—if it's in Grabs, it's for grabs."

"And I assume if it's in Keeps, it's for keeps?" Ben asks, as Pete sets the bottle down in front of him.

"Oh, yeah," Pete says, shaking his head ruefully. "God help you if you take something somebody else put in Keeps; that's a serious offense. But the orange juice is yours—seriously. Nobody will mind."

Ben hesitates for a second, but then shrugs and says, "Thanks." As Pete begins to open containers and pull out pots and pans and cutting boards, Ben twists off the bottle cap and takes a sip of the juice; his eyes go wide. "Oh my *God*."

"See?"

"How is that so..." Ben pauses, not sure how to describe what it is, and takes another sip. "God, like—crisp and sweet and sour and so *orangey*, somehow, even though it's not quite like any orange juice I've ever tasted, and—*floral*, too, I think." He pauses, and then, realizing he has perhaps let himself get a bit carried away, corrects, "I mean, uh. It's... really good."

"Adina always pulls the floral note, too," Pete says, shaking his head. "My palate isn't that good—to me, it just tastes like incredible orange juice."

Ben ignores this implied compliment to his palate as so much nonsense; however incompetent he may be, Pete is still a professional, and Ben's ... well, whatever Ben is. But he feels the faint flush creeping up his neck anyway, betraying his pleasure even as he tells himself it's nothing at all.

He sips the orange juice instead, trying to enjoy every nuance of the flavor, and something about the sugar and the brightness must enliven a few of his critical thinking brain cells from the stupor in which they've spent most of the morning. Rather belatedly, it occurs to him to ask, "Uh, what are you doing, exactly?"

Pete grins at him as he pulls out an enormous hunk of what looks like—oh, God, is that *pastrami*? Homemade pastrami? With a thick smokey bark on the outside and beautiful marbling on the inside? Even cold, Ben can *smell* it, and he's suddenly ravenous, hungry like he hasn't eaten in a hundred years.

"I'm proving to you that I can cook," Pete says, settling the pastrami on a cutting board and pulling a wide-bladed butcher's knife from the block. "What's your bodega order, by the way?"

"Bacon, egg, and cheese, American, ketchup if it's the right brand and hot sauce otherwise, hard roll," Ben rattles off immediately, as if he's at the bodega counter with a line of impatient New Yorkers behind him.

"Ah, good," Pete says, peeling the onion and setting it down on another cutting board next to a small container of mushrooms and two red peppers. "You'll like this, then, I think."

"I'll—wait, are you making something for *me*?" Ben demands, abruptly horrified. "That's—oh my God, you don't have to do that! I don't—you don't have to—I mean, who says I'm even hungry?"

"Hmm. Hold this?" Pete says, plucking a piece of paper out of an open metal inbox screwed onto the side of his station. He offers it out to Ben; it looks to be a recipe for an enormous quantity of shakshuka.

Mystified, Ben takes it. And then, a second later, the flush that was starting to fade back down his neck flares all the way up to his cheeks when Pete gives the trembling paper a significant look.

"*That* says you're hungry," Pete says, plucking the paper back out of Ben's hands. "At least, in my significant experience of working with people who'll cook for everyone but themselves. Come on—it won't kill you to have a breakfast sandwich. Anyway, I made this pastrami myself, and it took me three days, and if *someone* doesn't eat the rest of it, it'll be depressing."

"Oh, I..." Ben says, badly wrong-footed. Pete must have—he must have noticed the paper shaking in Ben's hand back in the *office*. And instead of saying anything about it, he... led Ben down here and started *cooking for him*, and only bothered calling Ben out on it when Ben more or less forced his hand. That's—it's—atypical, that's what it is. Ben can't find a place to slot it in against the rest of his mental landscape.

Well. There's one place he could put it, actually. Oddly, horribly, it's somehow one of the hottest things that's ever happened to Ben, for reasons he can't entirely explain even to himself. Surely, some of it is just a function of the sheer, unbelievable hotness of Pete, which burns so intensely that Ben keeps finding himself having a hard time looking directly at him, as if those stupid cheekbones are the surface of the sun. But for someone *that hot* to be paying so much *attention* to Ben as to notice a little thing like a trembling paper in his hand—for someone that hot to follow up on that observation by addressing and solving the source of the problem—it isn't fair play, that's all. It suggests Pete as someone who might pay Ben the same curious, investigative attention in bed, take the time to think about what he'd like, what he'd find hot, what'd feel good. This is not a quality Ben has found in previous men this attractive, who have mostly paid him absolutely no attention at all.

He's not entirely mannerless, though, so instead of standing there openly staring at Pete like a fool, Ben thanks him, or tries to. What actually comes out of his mouth is, "I mean—thank you, I guess. Assuming you don't, like, cut your finger off in the process or anything. I have an intense allergy, you understand. To fingers. The hospital would need to be involved."

"Well, that does sound very serious, but I think we're probably good," Pete says, a chuckle running through his voice. Then, his smile going smaller and a little sheepish, he knocks lightly against the wooden butcher block and adds, "But maybe don't turn your phone camera on, yeah? In case. Wouldn't want you to go into anaphylactic shock or anything."

"Very considerate," Ben says faintly, at a bit of a loss, and takes a sip of orange juice to buy himself a moment to think of something else to say.

Nothing comes, but it seems nothing needs to; even as Ben's swallowing, Pete resumes humming. The tune is vaguely familiar to Ben, but he can't quite place it; it's cheerful, though, and in spite of not being particularly loud, it has the odd effect of lulling Ben into an easy silence. Somehow it suggests that there is no need to fill the space between them with words.

Instead, he watches with curiosity, and then surprise, and then steadily increasing astonishment, as Pete cooks. Without a camera on him, Pete is not just a competent cook; Pete is maybe the *most* competent cook Ben has *ever seen*. He grew up watching a long series of line cooks fall in, and often dramatically back out, of Trattoria Luciana over the years; some of his earliest memories are of standing at one of the prep stations, so young that his eyes barely crested the top of the cutting board, watching Luis or Samara or Wendy or Hiram or whoever was on the bottom of Daniel's list that week, cutting huge piles of onions and peppers and tomatoes into a fine dice.

Pete is faster than Luis or Samara or Wendy or Hiram, faster even than Ben's own mother, a terrifying woman who stubbornly wields a four-inch paring knife she's sharpened down to nearly nothing as though it's both a chef's knife and an extension of her hand. He slices a potato into neat, perfect chunks so quickly and so precisely that for a second Ben thinks that maybe he accidentally fell asleep, took one of those micro-naps Salvador Dalí was famous for, and missed part of the process. But then he watches Pete do it *again* with six more potatoes, easy as anything, and dump them all into the stock pot he placed on the stove earlier. He takes the pot to the sink, still whistling, and as he fills it, waves hello at someone who steps into the kitchen from the entrance on the other side of the room. The mysterious visitor drops a pile of bags on one of the far stations, disappearing again after a returning wave.

When Pete returns to the counter and sets the pot to boil, Ben wants to ask him exactly how much he's expected to *eat* here, but he's distracted again watching Pete chop peppers and onions and mushrooms and pile them up on the cutting board, then slice some of the pastrami into paper-thin strips and set it aside, before he chunks up the rest so quickly Ben barely sees the knife move. Pete's starting the onions, mushrooms, and peppers in a huge, well-oiled cast-iron on a back burner—he's seasoning them with salt and pepper—he's cracking four eggs into a bowl and whisking them, and seasoning those, too—he's turning the heat on under a stainless-steel skillet—he's cutting off four slices of the loaf of bread, which smells like sourdough, and absently offering Ben the heel. Ben takes it, and has a bite; it's good, hearty, a whole grain of some sort clearly running through it. The water hasn't even come to a *boil* yet; Pete hasn't stopped humming.

It's this, more than anything, that ends up breaking Ben's silence. "Is that... oh my God, man, is that 'Mah Nà Mah Nà'? From the *Muppets*?"

Pete shrugs as he stirs the sizzling skillet, nodding at the potato water as though in approval when it starts to bubble and throwing in some salt with his non-stirring hand. "Hey, don't knock the Muppets. Maybe the Swedish Chef is my personal hero. You don't know."

Ben snorts out half a laugh without entirely meaning to; he and Renata had grown up watching reruns of the original *Muppet Show*, and *Fraggle Rock*, and whatever else they could find, but it's been a long time since Ben thought about it. "My sincerest apologies to Jim Henson; I would never knock the Muppets." Then he watches in growing hunger as, into the now-hot stainless-steel skillet, Pete lays down several of the thin slices of pastrami. Ribboned with bright white fat, each slice immediately begins to sizzle and shrivel, and the smell they release makes Ben salivate in anticipation.

Luckily, it's quick after that. The pastrami doesn't take long at all to sear up into crisp little sheets of meat, and Pete piles them onto a small metal sheet tray and sets them aside. Into the same pan, he introduces the slices of bread, letting them toast up in the rendered pastrami fat. When they're golden on the bottom with specks of black pastrami spice, Pete evacuates the slices from the skillet, tosses in a little pat of butter, dumps in the eggs he seasoned and whisked earlier, and cooks them up into a soft, fluffy scramble in a minute flat. Finally, he spreads some sort of red paste from a jar—not a branded jar, clearly a homemade condiment of some kind—onto the top slices of bread, settles a handful of pre-washed arugula on the bottoms, and piles on pastrami and egg until he has two beautiful sandwiches. He puts each one onto another tiny sheet tray and places one in front of Ben with a small, slightly nervous smile.

"The moment of truth," Pete says, and his tone makes Ben a little unsure whether or not he's joking. Which—well, surely that's insane. After the skills Pete showed him, he couldn't possibly care about *Ben's* opinion of his work.

It is at this moment that Ben's stomach releases a grumble so audible that Ben imagines *Rick* can hear it, back in his office. Pete's smile spreads into something smugger. "Go on; eat it. The anticipation is killing me."

"Are you planning to stare at me the whole time?" Ben demands, a little horrified.

Pete holds up his hands and looks politely away, and thank God; the minute his eyeline is elsewhere, Ben snatches up the sandwich and takes an enormous bite.

The groan that he releases is loud, involuntary, and incredibly embarrassing. Still: "Holy crap, are you *kidding* me?" Ben demands, staring at the sandwich. "*Why* is that so *good*? It's just—eggs and pastrami and—what is this condiment?"

"Oh, it's, uh, sauce," Pete says, and shrugs. "Every week I throw some stuff together... into a sauce. Sometimes it's an herb sauce; this week it's roasted bell peppers and Calabrian chiles and some other stuff. Malt vinegar, maybe? Anyway, I thought it would go nice here."

"It does," Ben says, between mouthfuls. "*God*, sorry to like, inhale this—I was hungrier than I thought—"

"Nah, go ahead, eat," Pete says. He sounds pleased. In this, he's the same as every chef Ben's ever known, even his mother, even himself, to the extent that he is one: To the true cook, the cook who feels the call somewhere deep in their heart, there is no better feeling than seeing a satisfied eater at your table.

Ben does as he's told, and, as he finishes the sandwich, watches with interest as Pete, *while eating his own sandwich*, tests the potatoes for doneness, drains them into a colander using only one hand, and then transfers them all into the skillet with the onions and peppers. He seasons again, with a variety of spices as well as salt and pepper this time, and after a few minutes of sizzling, he throws the pastrami chunks in there, too.

"I hope that's not for me," Ben says, after he's polished off about half of the sandwich. "Not that it doesn't look good, but this is definitely a solid breakfast."

"Nah," Pete says again, easily. He's relaxed now, in his element; it's hard to reconcile with the Pete from the video, who stood in this very same space looking as out of his element as Ben might at, say, any professional sporting event. "Mondays are usually a late day for the test cooks; some of them party pretty hard on Sunday nights. They'll start rolling in soon, and it'll be a better day for everyone if they all eat something."

"Oh," Ben says, blinking. "That's... nice of you."

"Maybe I'm a nice person," Pete says. His eyes are dancing again. "Or maybe I work with a bunch of lunatics, and this is self-interest, because I don't want to get stabbed with a meat thermometer. Who can say?"

This wrings a genuine laugh from Ben. Then, as he watches Pete flip beautifully browned potatoes in three perfect, even sheets, he says, "Wow. So it really is the cameras, huh?"

"Yep," Pete says, and though his voice sounds cheerful, as it should with a stomach full of good, hearty food, the light falls away from his eyes. "The minute I can feel one on me, it all goes haywire, even though—listen, you spent much time in restaurants?"

"Some," Ben says, and shrugs. "I worked at one in college, and I grew up in my parents'."

"No kidding?" Pete looks startled. "What kind of place?"

"Oh, old-school Italian," Ben says, waving a hand. "My dad met my mom on a backpacking trip through Italy and brought her back to the States with him, so. In theory Mom handles the cooking and Dad handles the books—it's her name on the door and everything—but the reality is Dad's a more consistent cook than she is and she's better at math, so really she's the boss and he's the sous." Pete is staring at him now like perhaps he's abruptly grown the world's largest and most obtrusive pimple; it's all Ben can do not to pat at his own face as he snaps, "What? Do I have chile paste on my chin or something?"

"Nnno," Pete says slowly, and then seems to shake himself, and says, "Sorry, sorry. I grew up in a restaurant, too. My mom met my dad on a mission trip to Guatemala in the eighties, not that she stayed religious, in the end. She brought my dad back to Jersey with her, and *they* started a restaurant, where *I* grew up."

"You're kidding," Ben says; it's his turn to stare like a gobs-macked fish.

Pete shakes his head. "I'm really not. That's where I learned to cook; I just kept doing it the older I got. It sounds like your parents stayed together, though?"

"Yeah," Ben says, with a little shrug. "They're all in on the 'for better or worse,' I think."

"Mine split," Pete says, and sighs. "When I was eleven. Mom went back to school; she's an art therapist in Queens now. Dad still runs the restaurant in Jersey—they're pretty famous these days, which is cool for him, but when I was a kid—oh, never mind." He pauses, and then, stirring the hash although as far as Ben can tell it doesn't need it, adds, "Anyway, so long as I'm not in front of a camera, even if I'm talking to a big crowd, I'm totally chill. But the minute you hit record..." He shudders.

Ben has... more questions. But before he can ask them, the person who made a brief, slouching appearance before walks through the door again, followed by several others. Suddenly, Ben is surrounded by a group of people complaining about their hang-overs, and passing each other utensils, and sticking their forks right into Pete's skillet while he laughs, "Hold it, hold it, you animals! There's enough for all of you—plates, for the love of God, let's try to maintain standards. Get that fork away from my cast-iron, Jaelyn!"

It's a lot to take in, and though somewhere in the middle of it there is a rattled-off series of introductions, it happens simultaneously with so much cross-chatter that Ben doesn't catch any of it. He begins to feel rather acutely that he is out of place in this bright, beautiful office, with these people who have worn into each other's ways so thoroughly that even an outsider like him can see how well they move together. It reminds Ben, oddly, of walking in night after night a few minutes too late for Trattoria Luciana's family meal, everyone smiling and laughing at some joke that, somehow, they could never quite explain to him.

But after all of the test cooks, if they are all test cooks, have had some breakfast, Jaelyn says, "Hey, Pete! You talked to Rick and upstairs and everything, right? You know we're shooting today? I've got my stuff; I'll get set up."

Pete blanches, mutters, "Great," and immediately turns away and starts a loud conversation with the person nearest to him, whose name Ben did not manage to catch.

To Ben, Jaelyn says, "You're the edit guy, right? Cool work. Anything you want me to change?"

Ben's mouth says, "I want his knife block in the shot. The whole thing, please, not just half," before his brain can advise temperance and diplomacy in his response to this new work colleague.

"Oh," Jaelyn says, blinking. "That's—yeah, all right. I can move it over."

"And," Ben says, because he's on a roll now, and perhaps because this has already been such a surreal morning that he's not entirely convinced it all really happened, "I don't want any cuts. Just—roll. Whatever happens, 'til you're done."

Jaelyn's mouth drops open a little. After a second, she says, "Dude, are you *sure*? It'll be like, so many hours of footage. It took us *five* to get the two and a half I sent you last time."

Ben swallows hard, but: "I don't care. And don't tell him you're doing this, either; just stop cutting, and especially stop *saying* cut. He's worse after every cut, did you notice that? At the beginning of that footage, there were moments where he almost seemed human; by the end... not so much."

"Huh," Jaelyn says. She gives Ben a long look, and then shrugs and says, "You know what? I'll try it. Thanks." To Pete, she calls, "No escaping me, Peter! I'm setting up! T-minus five minutes!"

Pete turns away from his conversation and, to Ben's surprise, meets his eyes. There's a pleading expression in them, one that looks caught, trapped; that's a clear enough message, isn't it? Having Ben here for what's about to come must be the last thing Pete would want—Ben misjudged him, that angry night with the edit footage. He's not a lazy, uncommonly lucky person to whom everything is handed; it turns out he's generous, and perceptive, and unexpectedly kind, and looks out for his people. And Ben is a stranger to him, basically, and one who has insulted him roundly and profoundly to a seemingly ever-growing audience of millions of people.

Pete wants Ben to go, and it's the least Ben can do. He makes his excuses, gathers his things, and is out the door in the next five minutes, telling himself as he recycles his own orange juice bottle on the way out that it's the right choice.

But the look in Pete's eyes as Ben walked out, the way his face briefly fell into something that looked like genuine panic before it smoothed away again... Well, Ben would be lying if he said it didn't follow him all the way down to the twenty-seventh floor.

FIVE

Ben ends up spending most of the rest of his workday waiting around on twenty-seven for Jaelyn to upload the footage of Pete's attempt at performing for the camera. It is not a pleasant wait. Word of the video, and that Ben has been picked up for an additional contract with *Gastronome*, has clearly spread around the office. He's not sure which is worse: the obsequious, congratulatory messages from colleagues who have never bothered to be nice to him before, or the people who keep sarcastically saying things like, "Hey, big shot, you mind taking a crack at this video for us? I know it's a little beneath you."

At three thirty, unable to take it anymore, Ben retreats to Brew, where he impatiently refreshes his email inbox and jiggles his leg for a while before he remembers that he could just... go home. After all, Miranda said that he could work from wherever he liked, so long as all his deliverables were turned in on time; in fact, the words "semi-remote" had been bandied around. And certainly, his regular bosses hadn't seemed bothered about the whole thing—Jessica the germophobe had come by his desk and talked for twenty minutes about how she wishes they could all go remote, and then said she was glad he'd secured this new contract, as she'd be grateful to have one less vector of disease around. It was quite clear, as it always was with Jessica, that she meant this as a compliment, but Ben, as usual, found he had rather a hard time taking it as one.

Anyway, it's not likely anyone will miss him, so he throws his laptop in his bag, rides the subway home, stops in at his favorite coffee shop and decides, in a moment of self-care and personal growth and feeling, for once, pretty all right with the world, to order a nice soothing herbal tea instead of yet another cup of coffee. After all, Ben is becoming a bigger and better person. He's got a new job at the place he's always dreamed of working, and yeah, okay, Pete's still a disaster on camera, but he'd turned out to be... different in person. A much better cook than Ben thought, for one thing, which can only help them in the long run. And, he reflects as he walks towards his apartment with his still-steaming to-go cup, a lot *nicer*. It might be fun working with him, although "fun" is not a word Ben has ever particularly associated with the word "work," nor indeed "job" or "paycheck." But this was creative, and Pete was pretty funny, and the first video got *millions* of views, and now Ben just has to... do it again.

In a cruel and unhappy twist of fate, as Ben takes the first sip of what was billed to him as a calming ginger-chamomile blend, the icy hand of devastating stress closes around his midsection and twists. He *just* has to do it *again*? He doesn't even entirely know how he did it the first time! He was accidentally drunk and somewhat unfairly pissed off and drawing *devil horns* on Pete's *head*—how in God's name is Ben supposed to do it *again*?

Abruptly but entirely in a frenzy, Ben's casual, slightly self-satisfied stroll morphs into a hunched, unhappy scuttle. He hurries the rest of the way home, lets himself into his apartment, and presses his back against the door when he shuts it behind him, letting out a long breath and standing there for a moment. Once his nervous system gets the memo that he is not, in actual fact, in any kind of danger, he's able to push himself off the door and gather... Well. It's not *quite* all of himself that he manages to gather, if he's honest—there are some bits and pieces off screaming in various corners—but enough of himself, anyway, to be getting on with.

Naturally, his mother chooses this exact moment to call him; she has, in this specific and unfortunate sense, always had incredible timing.

Heart pounding in his chest—a ridiculous state of affairs, Ben knows, for speaking with one's own mother—he picks up the phone. "Hey, Ma."

"Oh, 'hey, Ma,' he says," Lucia says; Ben can hear her eyes rolling. Her voice still bears the faintest hint of her Italian accent most of the time, the bulk of it burned out of her vowels and cadences bit by bit as Ben grew up, but when she's annoyed at him —which is usually—it's always thicker. "'Hey, Ma!' Were you going to tell me you were working for *Gastronome* now, or was I supposed to find out in the papers with everyone else?"

"Ma, my contract video editing gig is not in the papers," Ben tries, knowing even as he does it that there isn't any point.

"Maybe not *today*," Lucia counters, drawing in a huge breath, "but—" and then the barrage begins. She's so proud of him; she's so embarrassed she had to hear about it from Bethany in her jazz tap class; does Ben know Bethany? Of course he knows Bethany, she's little Jeffrey's mother—Ben's little friend Jeffrey from when he was nine—no, surely not the Jeffrey who ended up in prison for that horrible business with—but wait, why is Ben trying to change the subject? It's such incredible news; it's such terrifying news; does Ben know how many creeps and weirdos are on the internet? Lucia felt like the belle of the ball out on her errands this morning— *everyone* wanted to know about her son the viral star—and how did Ben think it felt, for her to not even have talked to him yet? Has Ben thought about how hurt his father must be, not to have heard it from him? What was the pay like—oh, not enough, of course not. Are there going to be more videos—oh, yes? Well, at least she knew *that* first. Is Ben worried about that? Does he think he can handle that, all that pressure? Oh, she's so *proud* of him!

By the time, forty-five minutes later, she says, "All right, Benny, they're wrapping up family meal out there, I should go get ready to work the early crowd—Danny, do you want to say hello to your— ah, no, he's gone out the back. Ciao!" Ben is back against the door. He's also sitting on the floor, having slumped down against the slick wood surface as she went on and on and on. Roux, at least, is having a good time, and is sitting in his lap purring, but Ben... Well. It's not that he doesn't love his mother, it's just—

It's just that *sometimes*, what Ben would *really* like to do after one of her phone calls is give it the exact same treatment he gave Pete's first run of disastrous footage. He wants to record it and pop it into his editing software and pick it apart, pulling out each contradiction and logical fallacy and thing that really, really isn't helpful. He wants to scrawl things like *Why?* And *Who says that?* And *Do you honestly not find this exhausting?* over particularly choice moments, although that's not even possible in audio, and he's clearly losing his mind.

His fingers do twitch, though, with the pent-up frustration of years of one-sided conversations, all the things he's wanted to say that he's choked down because it wouldn't go well. Renata, of the two of them, was the one who would pipe up, push back, engage in the ongoing argument that was their family conversation. Ben has always been the type to put his head down and get on with things —someone had to, after all. The things still needed to be done.

But when he'd made that first video of Pete—yeah, sure, Ben had been drunk and annoyed and feeling a little vindictive. That had been part of it, maybe even most of it. But underneath all that, it had felt *good*, weirdly, hideously good, to let a part of himself he usually tries to keep a leash on get out and *run*.

He checks his email inbox, and, of course, has the same little jump scare he's been having for the last few days every time he checks his email inbox. Ben scrolls hastily past a lot of unsettling media requests that he realizes only now he *never asked Rick how to handle*, but then brightens somewhat when he sees an email from Jaelyn, in spite of the subject line, *Bet you $20 you regret saying "No Cuts."* Even the emoji she's included as the sole copy of the body of the email, which resembles a face melting like an ice cream cone, doesn't dim Ben's resolve.

He gets up off the stupid floor, because it's high time he did, and cracks his knuckles. Setting his laptop up on the kitchen counter, he starts pulling ingredients out of the fridge to make himself dinner as he watches through the—dear God, *four and a half hours* of footage? Well, whatever, it doesn't matter. He'll watch through the first part while he makes dinner, and then the rest over the course of the evening, and as he gets more and more annoyed with Pete's total inability to function on camera, his frustration will happily seize upon the outlet. Maybe he *was* worried about his repeat performance, but that was before his mother called him up to, among other things, suggest he should be worried about it. He's not about to give her the satisfaction of being *right*.

He hits play on the footage as he's gathering prep bowls, but as he's reaching over to preheat the oven, he pauses, transfixed by what's on the screen. The video's scrub bar reads nearly five minutes by the time Ben realizes he's just been *standing* there, horror-struck, his finger hovering in mid-air like he's trying to make contact with E.T.

At minute six, he orders a pizza.

The next several hours are, honestly, a bit grueling. Ben was expecting his frustration to mount as he watches Pete, but instead Ben finds what swells within him is sympathy. The man has simply got *problems*; now that Ben knows how Pete usually cooks, and without any cuts for him to hide in, it's a lot harder to find it funny.

Or, well. Okay. It is still... pretty funny. Ben feels guilty about it, but—there are moments, in spite of the strange knot of fellow feeling that seems to have sprouted in his chest since he last did this a week and a half ago, where he can't help but let out a *little* laughter. Pete's stupidly handsome face is so unusually expressive, for one thing, seeming to go rubbery with comical shock or dismay as he drops, spills, trips, and otherwise clatters his way around the kitchen he'd moved so easily in this morning. He's making a Halloween cocktail and appetizer; the appetizer is a seven-layer dip with a spiderweb drawn on top in sour cream, although if one counted the layers Pete attempts to make, screws up, and grimly throws away, it would be more like a twenty-five-layer dip. But the drink—it's a blueberry spritzer, and there must be some note somewhere that Pete needs to refer to it as a "Boo-Berry" spritzer, because between every actual take, captured on the long reel of uncut footage, is Jaelyn gently saying, "Okay, Pete, that was good, but could you try actually saying 'Boo-Berry' this time?"

But it becomes apparent, as the footage rolls on, that Pete cannot say "Boo-Berry." Pete can say "blueberry," and "blowberry," and "blackberry," and "boysenberry," and "gooseberry," and "bloo-bluh," and several creative swear words, none of which sound like the word "Boo-Berry" at all. The frustration is obviously getting to him; on what has to be his thirtieth attempt to spit the pun out of his mouth, Pete's composure snaps, and waving his knife in the air like a madman, he all but shrieks, "Blueberry—whoberry—*why*berry! Why are we even *doing* a blueberry cocktail, blueberries aren't even in *season*, no one has ever! In history! Thought, 'Wow, it's Halloween, I better have some "Boo-Berry" juice'—oh my *God*, tell me I didn't finally get it right in that *totally unusable take*?" This, as it turns out, proves to be Ben's breaking point as well, and he throws his head back and loses it laughing in spite of himself.

He has to pause the footage for a second to calm down and wipe his eyes, only to crack up again when, a few minutes later, Jaelyn appears in frame, glares, and grimly mouths, "No cuts, huh?" into the camera.

But actually, when Ben gets to the end of the footage, he opens up the email she sent him and types a quick reply: *Haha. You owe me $20.* He doesn't regret the "no cuts" call at all. Pete's—*bad*, still, of course, abominably bad, and it's harder to watch than the last round because sometimes, between attempts at demonstrating very basic cooking skills that Ben is now sure he could typically do drunk and half-dead and with his eyes closed, he looks truly wretched. It must, Ben can't help but think, be incredibly frustrating for him, to so abruptly be unable to access this skill that seems to be woven into his bedrock most of the time.

But the lack of cuts helps. Pete is still comically awful, awkward and forgetting what he's doing and ruining so many different dip layers that even Ben loses track of them. Even something as simple as guacamole proves a challenge: Somehow he manages to drown the first batch in so much lime juice that it's inedibly sour, oversalt the second round beyond the point of saving, and, without realizing it, accidentally dump so much cayenne pepper into the third that it renders the next fifteen minutes of footage borderline unusable, since it's just Pete jumping around in anguish, drinking water, drinking milk, panting, drinking more milk, cursing the heavens, and glaring at the bottle of cayenne pepper as though he intends to remember its sins here today.

Still, though, he's not as bad as he was, by the end of that first round of footage. Even in his haze of semi-drunk self-righteousness, Ben had not used any of the last half hour of what was sent for the initial video. It had felt—wrong, too personal. Even if Pete *had* been affecting his camera-triggered incompetence, which Ben now knows he was not, those last thirty minutes would have been him reaching a place within himself that Ben can't imagine anyone wanting broadcast out to the internet. His nervousness, or stage fright, or whatever you wanted to call it, had become so bad after hours and hours of hearing "Cut! Reset to go again!" that he was truly barely coherent. On his first watch Ben had turned it off, wincing, when Pete said, "It—that's—kale! The salad!" and then blinked blankly into the camera as though trying to remember why, exactly, that wasn't an appropriate sentence.

That doesn't happen this time. By the end of the *four and a half hours* of footage, Pete looks exhausted and wan and like he'd be willing to fight his way out of the test kitchen if it meant an escape from Jaelyn and her treacherous equipment, but he is at least speaking in more or less complete sentences. In some ways he's *better* at the tail end of the video, after the cayenne pepper incident, and Ben wonders idly as he starts to mark off clips to pull for the final cut whether the pain and frustration was distracting enough that Pete could almost forget a camera was on him. It's a theory, anyway, if at some point they want to try to shift things towards demonstrating to the audience that Pete can, actually, prepare a meal like a normal person sometimes.

That's not going to be possible with this video, though, and as Ben sinks into the editing, he finds that the lingering traces of his nerves fall away. He'd thought, before, that he was able to do this because he was angry at Pete—this time, stone-cold sober and wholly invested, he realizes he was able to do it because it's *fun*. This has always been what he's liked about editing, even with simple stuff like wedding videos; he can see the shape even this strange mess of footage wants to take, the way to make it seem funny and entertaining and, above all else, a little bit intentional. It's satisfying, especially here, to have the control and creative freedom to do as he likes, and it's also nice that it's about a topic about which he, Ben, happens to know so much. He always knows what Pete's *trying* to do, so it's easy to work around it and fill in the gaps.

It is somewhat slower work than it was the first time, without the fuel of misplaced tipsy rage. It takes him the better part of the rest of his night and then about half of the next day, working on it in bits and pieces in between his meetings on twenty-seven, to get the final cut of the Halloween video into a place he's happy with. He doesn't dare go up to the *Gastronome* offices to work—even though he knows technically he can, he doesn't want to abuse his privileges—but he thinks, a couple times, about stopping by to... say hi, or whatever, to Pete. Check in.

Every time he has this thought, it is, of course, followed by another thought, such as, *Why on earth would you do that?* Or *Don't you think that would be incredibly weird?* Or *What exactly are you planning to say to him, then?* "Hello, *person I hardly know and just eviscerated on video for the second time in as many weeks, I'm here to touch base on your emotional well-being!*" No. Pete has been kind to Ben, and that's because Ben is a weird little gremlin person and Pete is an incredibly attractive and competent man with, admittedly, a fairly significant camera-related flaw, but who, after all, does not have flaws? Ben himself has dozens and dozens of them, carefully cataloged in a little recipe box in his mind that he can flip through whenever he likes; it's stopping that's the problem. It wouldn't be the same thing, for Ben to go hovering around in Pete's workplace, as it was for Pete to swing by Ben's desk—for one thing, Pete had been doing that mostly to size him up, which was only fair, in the circumstances.

And if on Tuesday night, getting ready to lock the video back at his own apartment, Ben lingers for a moment on the disquieting notion that he is awfully worried about what Pete thinks of him, it hardly matters. He drowns out the thought in the rush of satisfaction he gets from sending the file to Dave in S&P, and closes his laptop pleased with work well done.

It's Thursday before Ben notices his mistake.

Wednesday is a nice day, a boring day, in which nothing much exciting happens at all; Thursday makes Ben long for Wednesday, and also, quite possibly, for death. His day is back-to-back meetings he has no business being in, and the technical video he finished a week ago for today's deadline suddenly needs three additional minutes edited in, and Renata keeps texting him complaining about some fight she's having with their father, which, as far as Ben can tell, started with a disagreement about the best type of lasagna and spiraled out from there.

So when the email comes through from Miranda a few minutes after five, he's braced for the worst. This is, probably, what saves them in the end—Ben has found it often is—but it doesn't ever make the experience of actually *finding* the worst any more enjoyable.

The email is Ben's promised copy of his contract, paperwork, the slideshow she showed them, and best of all, the production schedule. Relieved to finally have that to study properly and add to his own universe of calendars, Ben opens it eagerly as he rides the subway home, waiting an age for it to load on the spotty signal. His eyes skim eagerly over the first week and—stop.

He stares at it. For a long, frozen moment, that's all he does, the subway car alive and vibrant around him as Ben hovers, stilled, just outside of time in clear, world-sharpening horror. Then the train judders on its tracks and Ben seems to judder, too, his eyes skittering across the calendar before they land, again, on the offending tile.

Maybe he's reading it wrong? He stares at it again, willing the words and dates to reconfigure themselves into a different order; they don't. He closes his eyes, opens them—the same. This can't be a stress dream, he remembers how he got here, he *knows* he's awake; God, God, *God*, could it possibly be *right*? Because if it's right... if it's right, then he and Pete owe S&P *two* videos this week, not one. The Halloween one Ben already sent in was delivered on deadline, but they have another one slated to be sent off no later than—oh, God, even thinking it makes Ben feel a little sick—end of day *tomorrow*. He scrolls up to the body of the email, which he'd skimmed without really reading it because the first three paragraphs were a glaze of Miranda's jargon-heavy corporate babble. But there is, at the end, a chilling postscript: *And don't forget, Ben: If you blow a deadline, you're in breach of contract!*

The train lurches to a stop in... well, some station, anyway. It's not Ben's station; he's only been on the subway for a few minutes, and it's eight or nine stops between work and his apartment, depending on which station he opts to start at and whether or not the line has gone express. It doesn't matter—he has to get in touch with Pete. This whole thing is going to be over before it's started, and Ben's mother will *never* let him hear the end of it. He pulls out his phone and starts typing and then realizes speed is of the essence here, and messages are not going to be his fastest path. Shoving his phone into his pocket until he has the cell service to put a call through, he hurries towards the nearest exit and up onto the street.

He realizes unhappily, once he's blinking in the thin, waning light of an early October evening, that he's in Columbus Circle. His current mood is not comforted by the slick, shiny nature of this particular corner of the city, though there are days when it is. One of Ben's favorite things about New York is that there is a little pocket of it for every mood, a place where you will fit seamlessly amongst the scenery no matter how buoyant or unhappy or anxious or fired up. But one of his *least* favorite things is moments like this, where you turn up in precisely the wrong corner. Ben, right now, is in a St. Mark's mood; he wants to sit without permission on someone's front steps eating incredibly delicious dumplings that are still far too hot for human consumption, and then nurse his lightly burnt mouth while he considers an ill-advised tattoo. That is about the only thing he could think of that would make him feel less like a panicked animal right now.

But instead, he has a choice between the shiny, shopping-heavy district before him, or turning on his heel and storming into Central Park. He opts for the latter and, as the sound of the city begins to dampen ever so slightly against birdcall and chittering squirrels, he puts a call through to Pete, who answers on the second ring.

"Ben, hey!" Pete sounds cheerful; grimly, Ben thinks this conversation will probably take care of that. "To what do I owe the pleasure?"

"Did *you* know about the second video?" Ben demands, which is hardly any way to start a phone call.

He explains, as quickly as he can, when it becomes apparent that Pete has no idea what he's talking about. When Ben has communicated the gist of the problem, Pete mutters, "Freaking Miranda—I can't *tell* you how sure I am she did this on purpose; this is just like her. But—Ben, I'm so sorry, but I don't know *what* we're going to do here. I could make it back to the offices tonight, not until seven thirty or eight, but I know for sure Jaelyn's not around—she left this morning for a wedding in Minnesota."

Ben chews on his lip for a second, but: "I mean... I could shoot it, probably. It won't be as professional as her work, not by a long shot, but maybe we can lean into that? A little more casual? *Gastronome* After Dark? It'll still be better than *nothing*."

Pete laughs, but not happily. "Do you think so? I'm not sure how much more casual I can get before it's a medical condition. We might be entering *Weekend at Bernie's* territory, which I think the health codes frown upon when it comes to cooking."

Privately Ben thinks Pete's issue is probably that he is the exactly the opposite of casual while the camera is rolling, but it doesn't seem like the moment. "Well, yeah, actually? I think almost anything is better than me being in breach and you, I assume— well... you probably wouldn't get fired or anything, right? But—"

"Yeah, no, it wouldn't be good," Pete says, and swears. "I really did not want to have to do one of these again this week—do we have a concept, at least?"

"The guidelines say, 'Something for fall,'" Ben says drily, and, as Pete groans, says, "Yeah, my thoughts exactly. Completely vague, no direction, *anything* could be for fall—"

"Yeah, it's always easier to come up with something with parameters," Pete agrees. A pause, in which Ben almost thinks he can hear the distant sounds of the ocean. "Listen, I have an idea. Why don't we meet at seven thirty—where do you live, exactly?"

"Uhh, Upper West Side," Ben says, wincing slightly, and then hastily adds: "But it was one of those crazy situations, you know, I'm not like, secretly wealthy or anything. I went a little feral with the old real estate listings for a few months, and may or may not have snuck into a few invite-only open houses."

"Oh, you're *way* closer to the office than me, yeah, this is gonna work," Pete says, seeming to blow right past Ben's guilt by neighborhood association. "Listen—go to the grocery store and get ingredients, okay? Whatever says 'fall' to you, I guess. I'll meet you at the office at seven thirty, and I'll use them to make, uh... something. Dinner? Something."

"Fine, fine," Ben says, distracted by a small mob of pigeons that seem to be bobbing concerningly in his direction. "Seven thirty, ingredients, got it, bye," and he hangs up, too frenzied to worry that he's being rude. Then he spends several upsetting minutes trying to sidestep the pigeons, who are equally determined not to let him pass, before it occurs to him that he still needs to go back to his apartment. Slightly ashamed, Ben turns around and stalks back to the subway, and rides the several remaining stops to his usual station.

He blows through his apartment like a tornado, digging through old boxes looking for cameras and lenses he hasn't used in years now. Roux comes over and yowls at him after a while, so Ben gives himself five minutes of operating at a reasonable, measured pace to scratch her behind the ears and feed her a can of wet food; then he's running around again, looking for connecting cables and memory cards and all the other little things it would be a real pain to forget.

Twenty minutes after arriving, Ben's got a camera bag as ready as he's going to be able to get it. He says, "Wish me luck!" to Roux as he opens the door to leave, but she just stares at him, her wide green eyes unblinking, and delicately licks one cream-colored paw. This doesn't seem like an entirely good omen, but to cover his bases, Ben says, "Thanks," anyway, before hurrying down to his favorite grocery store.

As he's walking across the threshold, it occurs to him that he didn't ask Pete enough questions, but when he pulls his phone out to ask them, he sees he already has a message waiting:

PETE:

just remembered you've never cooked in the TK before. don't worry about like, pantry staples— flour, sugar, pasta, spices, we've got all that. just like, whatever fresh stuff you want me to use

BEN:

Okay, great. also, I don't know if you're allergic to anything? Or on some kind of Whole Keto I Only Eat Carbs Under the Full Moon diet or whatever

PETE:

LOLLLLLL

PETE:

yeah not me haha, i will happily eat carbs under
any moon—waning gibbous, waning crescent,
whatever. bread's still bread

PETE:

i am allergic to strawberries tho

BEN:

Duly noted, but since they're months out of
season and not associated with fall we should
be good

PETE:

that's why i didn't mention it, lol. you?

BEN:

Do I eat bread under a waning gibbous? Not
usually, but I wouldn't say it's a hard and fast
rule. Why?

PETE:

lolol no, the allergy thing

PETE:

should've asked before i made you that sandwich
the other day tbh

PETE:

other than your finger allergy, lol, that one i've got

BEN:

Oh! No, not really

BEN:

Technically I'm supposed to avoid too much acid
but that's not an allergy, it just messes my
stomach up a little, no big deal

PETE:

gotcha. i solemnly swear to go light on vinegar.

PETE:

please don't test me by getting tomatoes tho

PETE:

october tomatoes need to be drowned in vinegar,
okay, i don't make the rules

Ben looks up from his phone, startled. He's been wandering around in a bit of a daze for the last few minutes, grabbing things and dropping them in his basket almost at random between messages; he should take stock, probably, since time is relatively short. Instead, he takes a breath, trying to work out why he feels abruptly but profoundly off-kilter. He doesn't even know why he mentioned the acid thing—it's not like Ben's stomach's tendency to turn his constant churn of stress into a series of inconvenient ulcers is relevant to Pete in any way—or why it should make him feel so odd, now, for Pete to respond like this. Ben's own parents can't seem to keep track of it, constantly plopping down plate after plate of things drizzled in thick balsamic or drenched in a tomato sauce so well-reduced that, digestion-wise, it might as well be lemon juice.

In the end, he leaves the texts unanswered, mostly because when he half glances over his basket, he realizes there is an eggplant inside of it. An eggplant, of course, is a wonderful choice for dinner tonight, in the first full week of October, when the very last in-season specimens are still waiting to be taken home. Still, something about it itches at the back of Ben's brain, sets off the shrill, insistent warning alarm he associates with a mistake in progress. The production calendar seems to swim before his eyes, superseding the lemons and limes he's standing in front of for a moment. It's not a good idea to shop for what's in season tonight, because the video goes to S&P tomorrow and posts a week from now, at the earliest. So Ben should be grabbing ingredients that will be in season for the *back* half of the month, when people will actually be watching the video.

Huffing in annoyance at himself, Ben returns eggplant and corn as well as a bag of what had to have been the last good plums of the year. Those he is particularly regretful to leave behind, but there's nothing for it—no one outside of California will be able to find good plums by the middle of the month, and there's no point setting the audience up for failure.

He selects brussels sprouts and several pomegranates instead, and then swings back to the meat and fish counters. The meat counter is mobbed with after-work traffic, but the fish line is lighter, so Ben does what he'd usually do and gets what looks best in the case, which is sea scallops. At Pete's advice he skips any staples, but he does, on the theory that he's already picked up brussels sprouts and pomegranate, grab a small package of chopped pancetta on his way to wait in the interminable checkout line, too. It's not that he doesn't trust that Pete can cook—Ben *knows* that Pete can cook. But he also knows that in front of the camera, all bets are off, so it's better if Ben stacks the odds with an option for something *he* knows how to cook, too. That way, if Pete burns the scallops, or forgets the entire English language, Ben can... well, he can do *something*, anyway. Hopefully by the time he has to cross that bridge, he'll have figured out what.

After a seemingly endless wait, during which Ben still cannot muster a normal human reply to Pete's texts, he gets through the line and heads back downtown, crowded like a sardine into the standing-room-only subway crowd he'd been thrilled to miss when he'd cut out of work hours early. Resigned to his inevitable fate, Ben dissociates with the smooth practice of all seasoned New Yorkers, forgetting the weight of the groceries in his hand and the straps of his camera bag digging into his neck. He rocks to and fro with the turns of the train, his shoulder occasionally brushing against someone else's, too tightly packed against his fellow travelers to be in danger of falling down.

In spite of his haste, between the waits and the train rides and the frankly upsetting amount of time Ben spent standing around in various corners of Zabar's, typing furiously on his phone, Ben dashes into the *Gastronome* offices at 7:32 p.m., kicking himself for being late. But he finds Pete taking off his coat in the lobby, having clearly only just arrived himself.

"Hi. What's the hurry?" Pete says, cracking a grin. "We're basically going to my funeral, you know—I don't think we need to rush it."

"Oh my God, we're not going to your *funeral*," Ben snaps, too on edge from the impending deadline and two hours of running around to temper himself. "Are you always this dramatic about it? Do you walk into every one of these shoots thinking to yourself, 'Pete, you're going to die today?' Because honestly, that *would* basically explain why you're always acting like you're in a hostage situation and trying to communicate it to the audience."

Pete blinks, clearly surprised, and then laughs. "I don't know. I guess I kind of *do*, now that you say that."

"Well," Ben says, shouldering past him and walking back towards the kitchen, "maybe that's the problem, right? What if you tried... *not* thinking that?" A little voice in the back of Ben's mind sends him a brief memo, letting him know that later he'll look back on this moment and be embarrassed for taking charge like this. He ignores it.

"Does that usually work for you?" Pete says, falling easily into step with Ben; it sounds like a genuine question. "Deciding not to think about something?"

"Me? Oh, no," Ben says, waving a hand with a little laugh. "I'm still thinking about things I should have forgotten twenty years ago, myself. But, you know. Maybe you're normal."

"A bold assessment from someone who has watched all my footage," Pete says solemnly. Then he sighs. "Well, listen, before we turn the camera on and ruin the evening for everyone—what did you get?"

"*Seriously* that is so defeatist, it's like you want it to be a disaster," Ben complains, but they've reached the kitchen, so he unpacks his grocery bag onto Pete's counter in answer to Pete's actual question. "The wrapped package is scallops—they're what looked best in the case—and you can feel free to skip using whatever. I sometimes do this thing with pomegranate and brussels—"

"Oh, and the pancetta, yeah, I can see that," Pete says, tilting his head. "You *would* need a little balsamic for that, though—I have this fig one, that would be nice—and then the scallops would be a quick sear, and it all plates up on... Hmm. Does it want to be one dish or two, do you think? I could stack it all up on like, a polenta or something, but it seems like it might be a little busy."

Ben stares for a second; is Pete asking for his *opinion*? On the *food*? When he's a *professional*? Sure, okay, a professional with some significant problems, but still. Even when Ben had made sous at Fleur de Sel, the French restaurant where he worked in college, his role had been to *execute* the chef's vision, not opine on it. And in his parents' kitchen, he'll always be an overly eager, somewhat obnoxious little child, whose opinions on the dishes won't matter until he's old enough to count, to them, as an adult. Based on progress, Ben expects that day to come sometime in his own late eighties, when his parents themselves have been dead several decades, and even then, he expects their ghosts to be a little grudging about it.

But Pete stares back at him with wide, clear eyes, nothing in the expression but interest and curiosity. It's weirdly intoxicating.

"Uh. Let me consider for a second, yeah?" Ben swallows, and forces himself to start setting up camera equipment so he'll have something to do with his hands. Unfortunately, this means that within seconds he finds himself needing to mic Pete up, which, okay, maybe was a bit of a mistake. Standing close enough to Pete to clip the mic to his shirt, smoothing the wire down before passing him the battery pack to slide into his pocket; it does something to Ben, for some reason. Maybe it's the smell of whatever cologne Pete is wearing, or the scent of the shampoo he uses or something— clean and crisp and vaguely sandalwoody, Ben thinks, though he's not normally one to think much about sandalwood at all. It's a good smell, whatever it is. Distractingly good.

All in all, Ben's proud that his voice comes out normal and even as he steps back and says, "Okay. Yeah, honestly, I don't know that brussels want pancetta and balsamic *and* scallops *and* polenta. The fig vinegar sounds good, though; it's only a little acid and I always do vinegar, too—so maybe it's two dishes? Do you have a scallop in your repertoire somewhere?"

"Sure, until you hit record," Pete says ruefully. "I can think of a dozen things to do with them. Ceviche—although, I guess, acid—"

"I mean, you don't have to worry about that," Ben mutters, feeling himself start to flush slightly and willing the blood back down away from his neck. He stares hard at the camera equipment he's popping and slotting into place as he says, "It's for the video really, it doesn't matter if—"

"Come on, I'm not going to make something you can't eat," Pete says, rolling his eyes. "If I have to endure the nightmare of filming, *someone* had better enjoy it. And, anyway, scallops are easy, I could do a beer batter and fry them off, or a quick seafood stew, normally. But the minute the camera starts rolling—"

"I know, I know, shut up and stop thinking about it," Ben says, flapping a hand at him in a way that he'll recognize, some hours from now, as upsettingly reminiscent of his mother. "Look, which one's the most hard coded? Like, if you were on a desert island, totally wasted, and had to cook one scallop dish to survive—"

"What desert island is this?" Pete asks, cocking his head. He sounds amused. "Sounds like somebody needs to get a UN representative out there to check things out, stat."

"Oh my *God*, would you just answer the question?" Ben snaps, finally turning away from the tripod and camera and laptop and hard drives and connecting cables to glare at him.

Pete just offers him a slow, lazy grin, seeming to relax slightly as he leans back against his counter. "What? Am I annoying you?"

"You're avoiding the topic is what you're doing," Ben grumbles, trying to ignore the mysterious spike of pleasure he feels every time he takes a swipe at Pete and, in spite of his generally excellent aim and a long track record of unfortunate success, seems to miss. "You think that you're going to draw me into some involved conversation about sending the United Nations to Scallop or Die Island, and whether or not their authority extends to fictional islands, and what the conditions are for scallop-based survival—"

"It already seems like a lot more fun to—"

"And I *refuse*," Ben cuts him off sharply, "to be part of it. You and I have to make this video tonight one way or another, and I, for one, don't want to be here at three in the morning watching you struggling to remember how to use a *knife*, okay, I have an appointment with my pillow! I cannot be late! And you could do this with your *eyes* closed, it's so clearly a mental block—for the love of God, what is your easiest scallop dish!"

"Seared on a pesto pasta," Pete says, blinking at him in what appears to be surprise. "Done it a thousand times."

"Fantastic," Ben says, shaking his head. "Do we have all the ingredients for that? I do *not* want to go back to the grocery store."

"Oh. Yes," Pete says, still blinking. He opens his mouth, as if to say something else, and then, after a moment of standing there like a fish who has had the misfortune of encountering Rick, closes it again.

"Then we are in business!" Ben says, clapping his hands together. "Okay, I'm set up, so here's my theory—I'm going to turn the camera on at some point, right, and not mention it, and we're going to stop talking about it. Camera? What camera? We're just two—" Ben hesitates for a bare second in panic; are they friends, at this point? Can he call them friends? Is that too familiar? Luckily, a useful word falls into his mind before he can spiral too far off course and he finishes, hastily, "—colleagues who are making some food together. Okay?"

"You don't have to do that, you know." It's the first time Ben's ever heard Pete sound genuinely unhappy, at least in person; it's weirdly heart-wrenching. "Coddle me, or whatever. I don't—I don't have any illusions about my performance, okay? You don't have to pretend like you can get something good out of me—"

"Dude, I'm getting millions of views off your *bad* footage," Ben says. He doesn't know why he said it—it's bolder, more arrogant, than he'd usually let himself be—but, riding the impulse, he subtly hits the record button on the camera while Pete's looking broodily out the window. "This is not about quality, it's about not having like, you know, a completely miserable time? I don't care if it's bad, and it's probably better, honestly, if it is. I just think the next few hours will pass a lot faster for everyone if you're not, like, wishing for death every minute of them."

"Oh," Pete says again. Then, a slightly confused smile tipping up one side of his mouth, he adds, "Uh. Okay, then. Where should I start?"

Jaelyn, Ben knows, had been largely silent during the takes; this, he knew, was entirely correct and professional of her. The phrase "Quiet on the set" became ubiquitous for a reason, after all. If this was a bigger budget show, there'd be a proper director, too, giving directions and guidance between takes. But Pete doesn't have that, and no one else is in here, and Ben has perfect confidence, in this specific case, that the editor who is going to receive this footage will be able to work around his voice.

"Why don't you start with the scallop dish? You could always try just telling me what's in it, you know? A little breakdown for the audience? Might be a good place to get into things."

Ben realizes immediately that saying the word "audience" was a mistake; what hint of cheer there was in Pete's expression drains away, and his gaze flicks down to the little red light on the front of the camera, betraying it as recording. His Adam's apple bobs as he swallows.

"You got this," Ben says, hoping he sounds more confident than he feels. "Just... start cooking, okay? You know what to do; you've made this a million times. What are the ingredients of the dish? Let's start there."

"Right," Pete says, as if to himself. "I can do this—right." He blinks, and turns to the camera, and smiles before he says, "Today we're making scallop pasta with scallops. The ingredients are scallops, and—uh—scallops, and... um... did I say scallops?"

Ben bites back a groan. It's going to be a long night.

It is a long night. By the time Pete has successfully produced both dishes, which should have, in totality, taken him roughly an hour, it's nearly 11 p.m., and things in the kitchen have become a little chaotic. They've gone through, in Ben's opinion, all the stages of creative grief—horror, anguish, denial, more aggressive denial, horror again, sullen acceptance, resurgence of anguish, and hey, might be worth trying that denial one more time—before landing in a final resting place of mild hysteria. Pete has burned scallops and sprouts and so much pancetta they had to switch to bacon they raided from the walk-in freezer; he has shattered a large bottle of fancy fig vinegar; he has said the word "shrimp" when he meant to say "scallop" twenty-six times; he has developed a slight twitch under his left eye.

But he has also, for the last hour or so, seemed a little better. A little more normal. Ben thinks the questions help a little—if Pete is answering a direct query, or trying to demonstrate something specific upon request, he's a little more likely to do a vague impression of normal human speech.

Mostly, though, if Ben's honest, he thinks it's the hysteria that is carrying the day. Pete is too lost in cackling over every little thing that goes wrong to worry about what *will* go wrong, and whenever something does, it makes it all that much more hilarious. Even some of what goes right ends up striking either him or Ben in a funny way, and the minute one of them even snickers, the other one totally loses it laughing, which ruins a lot of takes. It's nice, anyway, honestly, to see him do even a few simple cooking tasks correctly while the camera is on him, even if Ben is a little worried that, given all the laughing, the footage is going to make him look like he's on some sort of drug.

At the moment, the source of their laughter is the finished meal Pete has produced.

"Why did I think," Pete says, gasping in between peals of mirth, "that this was going to look good together? Oh my God, it's a pile of pasta... next to a pile of brussels sprouts..."

"It is a bit," Ben says, a helpless chuckle escaping him, too, "well, sort of... some heaps? Heaps for dinner."

"*Heaps* for *dinner*," Pete gasps, and then he's howling with laughter again, which, Ben thinks, is a sign of how far gone they both are. "Heaps for dinner" is not a funny joke—it's not even really a sentence. They've just been in here, locked together in this absurd situation, a few hours too long.

"Okay, you have to wrap this up so we can actually *eat* it," Ben says, trying to get his own laughter under control. "It might be heaps, but it is dinner and I'm *hungry*, just... say anything. Any wrap-it-up thing, I can make work."

And then it happens. Pete turns to face the camera, but he's looking at Ben, pushing his hair back out of his eyes with one hand; he's smiling, the last hint of amusement still evident in his crinkling eyes, in the tone of his voice, when he says, "Look, okay, the truth is, when it comes to cooking, sometimes it's all going to go the way you're hoping, and you're going to get beautiful dishes that make everyone ask for seconds. And sometimes, you know, you're going to get something that tastes like the dog made it. Or something like this, which tastes good—wait, I should make sure it *does* taste good before I say that, huh?"

Pete picks up a fork and tries the vegetable dish first. He makes quite a gratifying noise of pleasure upon tasting the sprouts, especially since he'd asked for Ben's guidance multiple times while preparing it, taking his cues for the quantities and ratios. Nodding firmly at it, Pete turns his attention to the scallop pasta, which earns another—although, Ben notes, a little pleased about it, less emphatic—noise of approval. "Yep, both good. Anyway, what I was saying is sometimes you end up in a situation like this, where the flavor is great but the overall presentation is a bit... kind of... uh. Bad? And in those moments, you have to remind yourself"—and here he pauses, and smiles, and spears a brussels sprout, and seems to lift a toast to the camera with his fork—"just keep cooking."

It's a golden moment, a perfect moment. It's so astonishingly cogent, reads so cleanly as Ben watches it record on the view screen, that Ben stands there for a second, his eyes bugging out of his head, before he finds the voice to say, "Uhh, right, cut! That's a wrap, I think. That was *good*, dude."

"Oh, hunger has made you delirious," Pete says, but Ben

notices he ducks his head to conceal what looks like a smile. "Eat something, please, it's basically the middle of the night and I've trapped you here watching me burn things—"

"Seriously, that last bit was *genuinely* well done," Ben argues, but then Pete pushes a plate over to him and hunger overrides altruism and honesty. He takes a bite of the scallop pasta first, and groans out loud without meaning to, the sharp, salty crust of the scallop fading to an almost creamy sweetness, set perfectly against the herbaceous zing of the pesto. "*God*, I hope people make this, it's *amazing*."

"Nah, the brussels are better," Pete says. "Even if I did ruin the fig vinegar—you were right, the red wine option is really nice."

"My mom always had it in the kitchen," Ben says, shrugging. "And the recipe's hardly original, just something I make sometimes when I need to trick myself into eating a vegetable. It's nothing special."

Pete frowns, but then he turns the conversation to the best places to get scallops in the city, and Ben allows himself to be towed away from the topic with relief. He tells himself it's relief, anyway. If it feels almost like regret—if it feels, a little, like he wishes Pete would have poked and prodded at that statement until a hot ball of words choked its way up out of Ben's mouth and submitted itself to Pete's cheerful assessment—well. It's nothing more than a consequence of the lateness of the hour, and the absurdness of the circumstances.

But Pete waits while Ben finishes eating, even though he's the slower of the two of them, and helps him pack up the camera equipment, and they wash the dishes together, rather than leave them for the morning crew to deal with. Pete cracks jokes, seeming relieved and relaxed and less drained by the whole experience than usual, or at least than he usually seems on film. Maybe this is normal, and the minute the camera shuts off, he is always hit with a shot of this cheerful, positive energy. It's possible, certainly. Likely, even.

Ben is not, in general, a particularly hopeful person. Hope is a fool's errand more than it's not—it leaves you open to disappoint-ment, and Ben so hates to be disappointed. But here, a few minutes from midnight, as Pete walks Ben to his train even as he explains that he still has to make it back to *Jersey*, Ben allows himself the indulgence of thinking maybe it *isn't* normal. Maybe Pete's buoyant energy under the halogen glow of the streetlamps is because something about Ben's presence eased something for him. It would be nice to think that, wouldn't it? If nothing else, it would make it easier for Ben to admit to himself that something about being around Pete seems to have a similar effect on him, unwinding some part of himself that is usually tangled up and pulled taut.

They say good night at the mouth of the subway, and Ben thinks, for a wild second, about that first impression he had of Pete, in his sleeveless ASK ME ABOUT CANNED BEANS shirt. Suddenly the thought of encountering Pete on a vacation, or in a bar, or in any context other than the most important professional opportu-nity Ben's ever had... Well. It makes Ben's mouth go a little dry.

"I should go," he says, his voice only creaking slightly with the effort. "Lots to, uh. Edit."

"Right, right," Pete says. "And I've got to fight my way back across the river, of course. Thanks for your help tonight, okay?"

And, for a second, he twitches forward, like—like he's going to hug Ben, maybe, or—or lean down and kiss him, carefully at first and then more deeply, drawing him close, and Ben could lose himself in it entirely. They'd be jostled, probably, by hurrying, irri-tated New Yorkers, and eventually Pete would break away and laugh and say, "Come on, come on, let's find somewhere better to be," and they'd duck into an alley and confirm they were alone, and Ben would make *absolutely sure* his Grindr location settings were off, and then Pete would smile and reach for his belt and—

—oh, but it doesn't matter. It's nothing, anyway, probably, a trick of the flickering lights; a second later, Pete's waving cheerfully over his shoulder, gone before Ben can so much as say good night.

SIX

The rest of October rips past Ben like an overdue bullet train, time streaking recklessly by, each day sliding between his hands like silk before he can totally get a grip on it.

It's not that it's a *bad* thing, exactly. Ben's lived months—years, even—wallowing in such depths where time seemed to become thin and hollow, the minutes stretched out meaningless before him and then flattening to nothing in his memory. This, thankfully, isn't like that. He's, for once in his life, busy. Days that used to creep along at a snail's pace are now sprinting past him, cackling merrily at his shocked expression over their shoulders; there's simply too much to *do*. His work on twenty-seven isn't difficult, but it is *present*, and it's becoming harder and harder to get it all done. One way or another, he keeps finding himself several floors removed from all that, ensconced instead in the increasingly familiar warmth of the *Gastronome* offices.

The footage from their late-night dinner escapade was... well, okay, it certainly wasn't *good*. For one thing, the video quality was nothing compared to what Jaelyn's fancier equipment would have rendered; when Ben sent her the first cut to make sure it was not unwatchably grainy, she sent back, *Good lord, did you film this in*

1987 somehow? Did you convert it from the original VHS? Do you have a backup copy on a floppy disk?

Still: Pete was better in it. A lot better. Ben had been amazed by the difference when he cut the edit together: how much more easily Pete moved, how many more regular human sentences he said, how much easier it was to stitch them into reasonable cooking advice. He still made plenty of errors, of course, and Ben still poked a little fun at his expense in the edit, a little, but it was gentler poking, and thus gentler fun. The overall result was something easier to consume than even the first one, for all it wasn't quite as funny. Watching it made you feel more like you were in the kitchen of your clumsiest friend, listening to his buddy affectionately razz him, than watching a trained professional beef it for views on camera. The latter of which was, for better or worse, what their first two attempts evoked.

Ben had been nervous, sending the video he'd come to think of as "Heaps for Dinner" off to Dave in S&P. The first video had done well; the second video had followed its footsteps; a tone shift in the third one was a risky choice. On the other hand, it was less risky than their other option, which was submitting nothing and giving Miranda the chance to cheerfully send Ben packing, so. He'd sent it off and tried to focus on other things.

But it had, in the end, gone even more viral than the first one, outperforming their second attempt by a wide margin. And then the video they posted after that, which Pete filmed while Ben was stuck in a multi-hour retrospective meeting for a project on twenty-seven he'd only been an ancillary part of, performed worse than any before it. It wasn't that anything Pete did in it had been so much more horrible than what happened in the others—dropping multiple sheets of painstakingly hand-rolled pasta while making butternut squash ravioli was about par for the course—but the blank misery and frustration radiating off Pete had spoiled the vibe, no matter how Ben cut it.

So Ben decided he was going to be around for filming after

that. For the good of the show, and everything. For the *numbers*. For his *career*.

God, Ben's not even convincing himself. The truth is, he's hanging around while Pete films because he *likes* being around while Pete films; he's hanging out in the *Gastronome* offices because he enjoys being there more than in his own. He's come to know the other test cooks a little—Adina, whose background is in pastry, is a particular friend of Pete's, so she'd been the first one he connected with. She's bright and funny and incredibly laid-back about everything except her work; about that, she is an absolute, unrelenting lunatic, which made Ben take an immediate liking to her. She's also very generous with scraps and samples, and though Ben's not exactly proud of it, he's not above being bought by a solid pâte à choux, or a thin slice of apple tart.

She's probably Ben's favorite, but the rest of the test cooks are nice enough, too. Ben is not, by nature, the sort of person who generally gets on well with others, so they're not all a personality match. Brogan, whose focus is primarily on fish and vegetables, is so easygoing that Ben has no idea what to say to her, and Ezra, their meat and butchery expert, seems like he might be someone else's cup of tea but isn't exactly Ben's. Ben, by nature more than intention, is the sort of gay man who's never quite grasped "camp" as either an adjective or a verb; whether you cover him in sequins and feathers or drop him in the middle of the woods, he's going to find himself wishing, in fairly short order, that he was at home in his sweatpants. Ezra, on the other hand, is the sort of gay who gets his nails done professionally, and flirts salaciously with anyone who happens by, and often feels called to express himself by bursting out in song. It's entertaining, of course, and he's got quite a good voice, but being around him sets Ben's teeth on edge a little, leaves him with the raw, uncomfortable itch of not quite fitting into your own community. It's not that Ben begrudges him expressing himself—if anything, he wishes that he, Ben, had more to express.

Still, it's nice to have someone else openly queer around. If nothing else, it's helping Ben solve a little mystery for himself—in the back of his mind, for the last few weeks, he has been compiling a mental dossier without letting himself notice he was doing it. While he worked on editing, and thinking through the production schedules, and considering the best methods to get reasonable human behavior out of Pete, he'd just stuck everything he could find in that folder, every little piece of evidence. But only now has Ben allowed himself to mentally scrawl, across the folder, the actual query he's hoping its contents will answer: *Is Pete Bailey, In Fact, Gay? Or Is He Just Excruciatingly Hot and More Friendly than Most People?*

The question is driving Ben slightly insane.

It's not that he doesn't have gaydar. Ben has gaydar, of a sort. He can tell immediately when, for example, a guy his sister is dating is gay, or a celebrity is gay, or a couple dining at his parents' restaurant is gay, as opposed to a pair of middle-aged business associates who are about to be very offended by Ben's father's well-meaning assumption. But the minute he, himself, actually likes a guy, all bets are off; somewhat relatedly, Ben has now spent several weeks convinced by turns that Pete is either straight, gay, or bisexual, which he's sure means absolutely nothing at all. And it doesn't matter, anyway, since there's one thing Pete definitely and categorically is, and that's being so far out of Ben's league as to be beyond rendering. Even if Ben could determine whether or not Pete liked guys, it wouldn't mean Pete liked *him*.

And Ben doesn't care if Pete likes him, of course. Why would he care? It's not as though *he* likes *Pete*. Or, well, no, that's not fair—Ben likes Pete, of course he does, as a friend. They're friends, now; Ben thinks that's fair to say. They've had a variety of meals together, mostly in the test kitchen but also a few quick cafeteria lunches, and that one rainy afternoon towards the middle of the month, where they each scarfed down a hot dog from a street vendor under the protection of some nearby construction scaffolding. Ben's also gone along for drinks with the test kitchen staff after work twice now and, both times, ended up wound in a long conversation with Pete about some topic or another. And they text, sometimes, about inconsequential stuff, or sharing memes and videos—so, normal friend stuff. Nothing weird there at all.

But in terms of *liking* Pete, in a less-than-professional, more-than-friendly way: Ben doesn't. He doesn't. He *does not*. Pete is a perfectly lovely and very competent person so long as the camera's not rolling; he's kind to animals and children; he never seems to forget anything Ben tells him about himself, even though he does regularly forget almost everything else. And that's all fine and good and wonderful, Ben is sure, but he's not about to go and let it make him into some sort of idiot. He knows how things go, with guys like Pete and guys like him—it's not an even match. Straight or gay, there wouldn't be any point in Ben nurturing a fixation, or crush, or whatever. He'd just be setting himself up for heartbreak.

This is a good argument, a strong argument. It holds up admirably, despite several tests of Ben's internal resolve, right up until the Halloween party.

The night of the event, Ben decides, after waffling about it through his entire dinner with Mrs. C, to take a cab to the party.

It's not the sort of choice he would typically make. Cabs are expensive; if one is going to spring for a cab, best to save one's money for the ride *home*, when one is likely to be far less sober, and thus far more incompetent at navigating the labyrinthine maze of the subway.

But tonight is not Ben's typical party experience, because Ben's typical party experience, at least here in New York, is something like a networking event, or the wedding of a family friend, or a public restaurant opening advertised online, which Ben is typically just dropping by at for the food, anyway. *This* is a real, genuine party. A food media party. A *food media Halloween party*. It's apparently an annual thing, held in some warehouse space owned by one of Rick's friends, and invite-only. That Ben has an invite, if a somewhat last-minute one, still feels like maybe it's a prank, or the result of a critical error, like mixing up his name with someone else's.

Nevertheless, Rick had pressed the invitation into Ben's actual hands himself only yesterday, breezily saying, "Kid! There you are. You don't come to our staff meetings, so I keep forgetting to give this to you. Learned my lesson about emailing it out a few years ago; if that creep from the sports desk on twenty-three shows up this year, I'm going to end up getting arrested, so try not to spread the news around the building, okay? But I promise, it'll be worth canceling your plans." Ben had laughed in what he hoped was a convincing impression of someone who might, conceivably, have plans to cancel.

He'd unfolded the invitation with slightly trembling hands; even now, as he hails and climbs into the back of a cab, it's burning a hole in his pocket. It's a crude, handwritten thing in the style of house party invitations in eighties films, photocopied onto a half sheet of neon printer paper, and he knows he's being stupid bringing it with him—it's not like someone is going to be checking them at the door. But, pathetically, Ben knows himself well enough to know he'll need the proof, the piece of physical evidence that he's wanted here, to make himself walk through the door.

He sweats through the cab ride, relieved that he has landed a stoic, silent driver. For the thousandth time, he looks down at his outfit, even knowing that it's far too late, at this point, to do anything about it—he just hadn't known which *direction* to go. For gay Halloween in Michigan, at least in his teens and much of his twenties, Ben had generally thrown on some messy eyeliner and whatever band T-shirt he felt would play best to the crowd, called it a day. It had always gone over well enough. Since then, he has transitioned into what he thinks of as New York City Introvert Halloween, which, depending on the year, either involves wearing pajamas and handing out Twix bars to kids in his building, or hiding in his apartment with the lights off, pretending that he isn't home. But this is semi-professional Halloween, the dress code on the invite offering the guidance,

Costumes required. Dress to impress but not to kill; if you wouldn't want it on your LinkedIn, don't wear it.

With very little time to decide, and even less time to shop, Ben had made the executive decision to half-ass it. Really, it was his only move, and when he climbs out of the cab, he takes a minute in front of the large brick building to assess the clothing under his gray wool peacoat. Staring down at his well-worn maroon chinos and the branded ketchup T-shirt Renata sent him for his birthday a few years ago, he hopes to God he's made the right call. He's looking to come off like a cool, understated guy who doesn't care very much about his costume one way or the other, as opposed to what he is, which is something more akin to an alien meeting human beings for the first time.

Still, he's made it here, and he's bound to know a few people—he'd asked Pete about it, and Pete grinned and said, "Oh, yeah, everyone will be there, it's a blast," but then they'd both been distracted by trying to solve for a missing element of a bolognese Ezra was working on (it needed some simmering time with a parmesan rind, in the end) and the conversation had been lost. But "everyone" both sounded promising and implied Pete would be there, which Ben is, admittedly, counting on. Rick had said he invited everyone else in the *Gastronome* staff meeting, so there will probably be one person Ben has exchanged pleasant conversation with, but he'd prefer a proper ally.

He is not going to find one by way of loitering outside the building awkwardly. He takes a breath, steels himself, and steps inside.

It's clear from the moment Ben steps through the door that the party is on the first floor, and close by. Taking off his coat and draping it over his arm, Ben follows the sound through the large, high-ceilinged, and mostly open-concept warehouse space, brick outer walls and cement floors broken only by white plaster dividers that don't reach the ceiling. Ben would truly hate to work in a space like this, with sound bouncing around every wall, but it does make it easy to find the gathering, which is centered in a large, heavily windowed back area.

It's not at all what Ben expected, which is to say he hadn't known quite what to expect. What he'd hazily pictured had featured things like a tower of shrimp, or little hand-passed canapés with intricate flavor profiles, and guests standing around with very erudite expressions, critiquing each bite. Instead, what he sees reminds him more of parties his parents would occasionally throw for morale at Trattoria Luciana, or the annual Fleur de Sel Halloween blowout, at which everyone would have a little too much fun, and after which the following day's openers would wish a variety of horrors on everyone involved. There's a *lot* of food, on every available surface that isn't covered by the staggering variety of booze, but it's a disconnected hodgepodge of different cuisines, dishes, presentations. After a few minutes of looking around the room, he's able to connect some of the faces he sees—faces famous enough, in the food and restaurant world, to make Ben's eyes bug out a little—with some of the food on the tables. He realizes, a little staggered by it, that this party is essentially a potluck: Anyone here who owns a restaurant must have come with some catering to offer.

His eyes skip dizzily along the labels affixed to the various trays, chafing dishes, bowls, and plates—some of the most iconic restaurants in the city are represented. The spread is so high-end that it's a little difficult to parse when compared to most of the guests. Ben's imagination, never brilliant with things like fashion, had fallen short here as well, but he'd envisioned complicated, impressive costumes, or ones that left him shaking his head at their wit. Mostly, instead, the other guests are dressed like him, or in costumes they clearly purchased hastily at some point in the last ten years. There are, in fairness, a few people in more elaborate getups, but all of those seem to be surrounded by a team of hangers-on aggressively filming them; Ben writes them off as influencers and does his best to avoid them.

He gets a drink. He sips his drink. He finds himself, as he

usually does, drifting over to one corner of the party, to lean against a wall and observe other people having fun.

It's not what he should do, of course—he should get out there, mingle, introduce himself, *participate*—but this, above anything else, has always been Ben's problem. It's why he's never made any friends in New York, or taken anything out of those stupid networking events: Ben is not built to network. The people who do well at those things are like those phone board operators they used to have in the forties, charting every new connection and flipping between them with ease, calmly managing dozens of conversations at once. Ben is more like an answering machine, happily receiving incoming transmissions but not designed to make even one outgoing call on his own, let alone dozens of them.

He always ends up feeling it most acutely in moments like this, entirely alone in a room full of people; it would be easier, probably, if he didn't. In this, he realizes, his expression twisting into a slightly wry smile, he's like Pete, telling himself it will be a disaster so aggressively that it becomes one. It's just that knowing that doesn't help.

Ben is seriously considering the merits of slipping back out before he can run into anyone he knows, when, from his left, he hears: "Kid! There you are!"

Ben bites down on a groan, swallows it, turns; Rick is there, of course, and dressed, horribly, as a fish. After a second, Ben realizes that it's not just a fish costume—he is dressed as one of those mechanical singing bass that swept the nation as a craze when Ben was a kid.

"If you start singing, I'm walking away," Ben warns, his tongue slightly looser from the booze. "I mean it; I don't care who you are."

Rick laughs. "You're always a riot; thanks for coming. Come on —I want to introduce you to some of my friends."

The next twenty-five minutes pass in a haze. Ben meets chefs and critics and executive producers, two celebrities whose books he's read, restaurant owners, a wholesale distributor who moves citrus across half the country. This last is Rick's juice hookup, and

Ben ends up in a conversation about the intricacies of breeding and growing oranges for flavor, which becomes a conversation about marketing and branding the resulting product, which becomes a discussion of Larry's plans to fly out to a farm in Ohio next week to source apples for a new product. The interaction goes on for so long that eventually Rick wanders off to seek entertainment elsewhere. Ben's surprised to find, when he turns around and realizes he's alone, that he misses Rick a little, had appreciated the company, the introductions.

The thought that he might be growing genuinely fond of Rick is too horrible to contemplate, so he turns back out to face the party, scanning the crowd for familiar faces. There's Adina, who looks occupied in conversation with a stranger—there's Ezra, who doesn't look occupied at all, but if Ben's honest, he's looking for—

—*there*. Pete is standing near the door, only his head visible over the crowd, laughing at something. Ben throws back the last of his drink, for all it's mostly melted ice by now, sets the cup down, and makes a beeline for him.

He's confident, for the first three-quarters of the walk. He's feeling good. He's riding on some nice liquid courage; he's met an incredible number of fascinating, influential people; he's not dressed wildly incorrectly for the circumstances. Everything is coming up Ben, and that means it's the perfect time to say hi to Pete, be calm and witty and not at all awkward or weird, and then *leave* before his atypically successful impression of human socialization can crumble. That way, he can leave the best possible impression behind, as people always want to do with their friends, acquaintances, colleagues, business associates, and other contacts about whom they have absolutely no romantic feelings at all.

But when he's nearly reached Pete—when it's already too late to turn back without being spotted in the middle of a crouching, awkward retreat—Ben stops, frozen, a deer convinced that if it blinks hard enough, it will stop seeing the headlights. But, in spite of enough attempts that his eyes go a little dry, the vision before him simply does not clear.

Ben is dressed as ketchup; Pete is dressed as a hot dog.

There is a long, cringing moment in which Ben has seen Pete, but Pete has not seen Ben, in which Ben experiences a series of emotions he most closely associates with middle school. Panic and embarrassment vie for first spot, but hot on their heels is the deranged but undeniable spike of terror that somehow everyone at this party, Pete included, will take a look at their unintentional matching outfits and decide, through some power of collective consciousness that everyone but Ben possesses, that Ben's costume choice is in fact a frightening, stalker-esque declaration of affection. He thinks, for an unsettling but very real second, that he might scream from the sheer stress, which would add to the overall Halloween vibes.

But then Pete turns his head and catches sight of Ben. He's already starting to smile even as he meets Ben's gaze, but when his eyes flick down over the ketchup outfit, they widen, then crinkle decidedly at the corners. He laughs, shaking his head, and then says, "Well, we gotta find mustard, I think. Start a band."

"If you have musical talents you haven't shared with me, now is the time," Ben's mouth says, while Ben's brain is still busy trying to veer off the expressway to Panic Town. "Given the givens of Miranda, it might genuinely save my job at some point if I can throw you in front of the camera and make you play 'Wonderwall.'"

Pete grins, rolling his eyes. "Well, it's me, so if I *did* have any musical talent, I'm sure I'd lose track of it the minute we started rolling. But no, no skills to think of; I just think it would be funny to be in a band called the Hot Dogs."

"Oh, and now you're *headlining*," Ben says, tutting in a mocking impression of annoyance. "Didn't even ask about it or anything; I see how it is. The fame's gone to your head... We're all second banana to you now, is that it?"

"You're the one who decided to be a condiment," Pete says loftily. "It's not my fault you're not reaching for your true potential —oh, Chris, hey." This last is in a slightly different tone, mellower, less amused, to someone approaching from the left, blocked from Ben's view by someone unhelpfully tall. "I thought the drink line would take longer than that to get through."

"Oh, I cut to the front," says—well, the muscular, tanned, bleached-blond vision of a man who steps out from behind a cluster of people has got to be Chris. Ben blinks, taking in his costume: a seventies-style disco outfit fully done in gold lamé, a pair of chunky platform heels, and absolutely no shirt. He's pulling it off, which is actually the worst thing about it, and Ben's trying to bite down on a queasy smile before he fully processes what's making his stomach flip.

Then Chris passes Pete his drink and throws an easy arm over his shoulder, and: Oh. Suddenly, Ben's processing.

"You know you shouldn't do that kind of thing," Pete says, frowning. "It's rude, for one thing, and—"

"Yes, yes, and it'll make you look bad, and I get you into trouble whenever you take me out, I *know*," Chris says, rolling his eyes. "Stop nagging—you're the one who's being rude. You haven't even introduced me yet. Who is... this?"

He inclines his head pointedly at Ben, the expression on his face suggesting he'd rather be looking at a pile of elephant dung, or a moldy slice of cheesecake. Pete seems to shake himself slightly, says, "Oh, right, sorry. This is Ben Blumenthal, the amazing video editor I've been working with—"

"On those viral videos, you mean?" Chris says. He raises an eyebrow at Ben, his gaze cool, assessing. "Those are... fine, I guess. And the costume that matches Pete's—did you plan that, or are you just a creepy stalker? Maybe not so great with the old appropriate boundaries?"

"Chris!" Pete snaps, flushing bright red and breaking out from under his arm to glare at him. "Of course he's not a *stalker*. We were literally, one second ago, addressing you being rude. They're just costumes! I'm wearing this because it's the only costume I own, and I'm sure Ben didn't plan to—"

"You're not such a good judge of these things, though, are

you?" Chris says, reaching out to tap very lightly on Pete's temple. "You have a blind spot for—"

"I have a blind spot for *you*," Pete growls, visibly uncomfortable now. Ben can relate. "Because if I was smart, I wouldn't take you anywhere, because then you couldn't embarrass me—"

"Keep an eye on you—"

"In front of my coworkers—"

"Oh my God, Pete, come on, just *look* at him. It's so *obvious* that he's—"

"Will you *shut up!*" Pete nearly snarls this, so emphatic and freaked out that Ben all but physically jumps.

Chris, too, seems taken aback, his eyes widening before he narrows them, crossing his arms over his chest. Whoever he is to Pete—though Ben thinks, grimly, that the answer there is looking increasingly likely to be "boyfriend"—he obviously didn't care for that at all, and his voice is very cold when he says, "Fine, then. I will. I'm going to go enjoy the party on my own, if that's the way you're going to be, but we *will* be discussing this later. I'll try not to ruin your reputation in the meantime." He rolls his eyes on this bitterly sarcastic last, and then, managing to imbue the word with a vast reserve of icy bitchiness that Ben both fears and respects, he adds, "Blumenthal," before he turns and walks off.

Ben doesn't quite know what to make of it, but he knows he doesn't like it.

But before he can ask, he and Pete are being approached by a little knot of people with a certain—energy. Ben has encountered this a few times in the last month or so, only ever when he's out with Pete; now and then, they're starting to get recognized. Or, well, Pete is starting to get recognized, anyway. But sometimes, if Ben is with him, a particularly eagle-eyed fan will realize who Ben is, either from his voice or from the wacky credit sequence featuring embarrassing photos of everyone who worked on the episode. Ben had started slapping that in at the end of every edit after the first video, and he hasn't had any cause to regret it until now.

Well, okay, last week someone *did* approach them and ask for both of their autographs while they were having lunch in the Formica cafeteria. That had been a completely wild experience, although Ben thinks he handled it better than Pete did. Ben, at least, had responded with some recognizable words in the English language; Pete had said something that sounded to Ben like, "Squirgle," and then, "Whoop!" and then hared off out of the room, leaving his lunch behind. When Ben had texted him, *????* Pete had not replied for hours, and then only said, *sorry, think i ate a weird breakfast burrito or something*, which was so obviously a lie that Ben could not think of a polite way to call him out on it.

It does suggest that whatever is about to happen is not going to go well, and Ben finds himself half reaching for Pete's arm before he corrects the impulse sharply. After all, his boyfriend, or whatever Chris is, probably wouldn't like it.

"*It's them!*" someone in the group hisses excitably; someone else gasps, "You have to *show* them!" and then, before Ben can begin to brace himself properly, the gaggle seems to spit out two young men, dressed in familiar clothes.

It takes Ben a second to place the outfits. The shorter guy, in the dark, curly wig, is wearing a black-and-gray flannel shirt that looks a lot like the one Ben himself wears three times a week and holding a fake prop computer; the taller man is dressed head to toe in the kitchen blacks Ben has been insisting Pete film in since the Heaps for Dinner video, with a comically large splatter of fake sauce laid across the top.

"They're... us," Ben says, blankly. Then, because even having one of the most surreal moments of his entire life, he doesn't want to risk looking like a total idiot, he adds, "I mean—aren't you?"

"Yeah," the taller guy says sheepishly; the shorter one, the one dressed as Ben, is blushing crimson and staring at the floor. Ben thinks vaguely that maybe he's method acting, and if so, that he deserves the Halloween Oscar—that is more or less exactly what he, himself, would like to be doing right now. He can't bear to look at Pete as his be-sauced doppelganger continues, "We love the videos, guys, and imitation is the sincerest form of flattery, right?"

"I've heard that." Pete sounds like he's containing hysteria, but whether positive or negative Ben is not at all sure. "So I guess. Thank you?"

"Anytime," says Not Pete. "Can we get a photo?"

"I," Ben says, meaning to continue with, perhaps, "don't think so," or, "would rather you didn't," or something else along those lines. But he doesn't have time; both men are crowding up against them and snapping the selfie a second later, then shouting, "Thanks!" as they retreat, their tittering crowd traipsing after them.

"Good Lord," Ben says, blinking, as the group vanishes into the crowd as if it was only a horrible mirage. "Was that—am I awake? Am I hallucinating? Is there... peyote in those short rib pierogies? Because, admittedly, okay, I ate like six of them, but if I'd known they were full of hallucinogens, I would have stopped at four, tops."

This, Ben knows, is not helpful. He is babbling; babbling, in his experience, is almost never helpful, and almost always even total silence would be better. But he's forced himself to look, wincing, at Pete's face, and it is frozen in an expression Ben's never seen: a stone wall, rigid with tension, the veins unusually visible along the side of his neck. It seems to pull the words out of Ben against his will, like salt leaching bitterness from an eggplant, or sugar relaxing strawberries into a loose, lazy sauce.

"I need a drink," Pete says, eventually. His voice is flat, empty; Ben swallows.

"You have a drink," he points out.

Pete looks from Ben to the drink in his hand, cocks his head, considers. After a moment: "So I do."

Pete lifts the drink, which is, in terms of information Ben can tell by looking at it, in a medium-sized glass and brown; Pete drinks the drink. When Ben, not an hour ago, had been miserably drowning his own despair, he'd been doing it in small, determined sips of a clearer beverage that had contained quite a lot of soda.

Pete does not drink like that. Pete downs the whole glass in one long, unbroken swallow, his throat working rather distractingly, without pausing for so much as a breath. Ben has never once been able to take a sip of anything that wasn't significantly watered down without coughing—he has shamed his father for years, being drunk under the table at restaurant parties even by Renata. But Pete throws his drink back with the slightly unsettling ease of the long-time chef who came up in an era where you had to learn to hold your liquor if you wanted to keep pace. It's impressive. Worrying, but impressive.

Pete winces when he's finished, wipes the back of his mouth as he says, "The man has awful taste in booze." Then, his face sliding back into that same stony expression, he adds, "Need, uh—another drink. Sorry."

"Me too," Ben says, his brow furrowing. "If you want, we could—"

"The bathroom," Pete says, slightly wildly, and then he's off, slipping between party guests and disappearing into the crowd.

"Crap," Ben mutters, craning his neck trying to see where Pete's gone, and then giving it up almost immediately as futile. Figuring he might as well, he does go ahead and get another drink, although this time, already one round deep, he allows himself the luxury of something tart and sweet off the night's specialty drink list. It has some ridiculous name, which Ben forgets as soon as he orders it. It is served up to him in quite a large glass, and after a single sip Ben knows it is a beautiful, delicious, perfectly balanced mistake; it doesn't taste a bit like alcohol, just like lime and elderberry and very faintly of juniper. It will punish him tomorrow—the hangover will be brutal, a thrashing—but he figures he's already in it, so he takes several more sips, and finds a certain resolve hardening within him as he swallows.

Drifting, as ever, to an open spot against the wall, Ben decides slightly drunkenly to formulate a plan. He has to think like Pete. He knows Pete, right? Sort of, anyway? He didn't know that Pete had a *boyfriend*, okay, that's not great. But, counterpoint, Pete's boyfriend probably doesn't know that Pete's left eye starts twitching when he's about to beef something up in the middle of a four-hour cooking shoot, so who's really in the dark here?

Ben takes another steadying sip of his drink—he has to focus. He's Pete; he's thinking like Pete. Where would Pete go, if he was kind of, not to put too fine a point on it, losing it a little? Probably he doesn't want to be around people, because he does seem to run off, whenever he can, at least in Ben's experience. Also, Ben himself wouldn't want to be around people if his brain was throwing up options like "Squirgle" as words, either, so he thinks the logic follows.

This is a party full of people; there is nowhere at this party without people; so Pete has left the party, at least temporarily. He could be on another floor, but Ben has to assume and hope that they're locked off, or otherwise closed to guests. He could have gone home, but Chris is still here—naturally, Ben can see *him* across the room, merrily chatting with someone dressed as a box of Cheerios—so by the rules of basic logic, Pete's still in the vicinity *somewhere*. Maybe he went out front? But there isn't anywhere to hide out there, since the facade opens right out onto West Twenty-Third Street, and costumed people are still spilling into and out of the party through the main doors.

A single word occurs to Ben, bright and clear and obvious, the refuge of unhappy city-dwellers the world over: *roof*. He makes his way, a little tipsily, out of the main party and over to the elevator bank he passed on entry, hits a button, does an embarrassing little fist pump when the doors open, which he's very glad no one is around to witness, and steps inside. He is pleased to see a button labeled Rooftop Terrace, and even more pleased when, upon pressing it, it lights up and stays lit, and the doors ding shut.

Ben is whisked up to a glass-fronted elevator bay with doors that, as advertised, open onto a large rooftop terrace. It's obvious this warehouse has been here many decades, maybe even centuries, and has lived many lives; there are brick archways leftover from a time that Ben could bother to place, if he cared more, was less drunk. As it is, he sips at his beverage and follows his hunch, wandering vaguely across the open rooftop until—

—there. Leaning against the far wall, weight balanced on legs kicked out in front of him, bent nearly double and looking, honestly, somewhat tragicomic in his floppy hot dog costume, is Pete.

For a hanging second, a little part of Ben—his sober self, maybe, or his single self-preservation instinct—claws its way to the surface. It informs him, in rather a shriller tone than is entirely necessary, that what he should do, right now, is *turn back*. Pete came here to be alone, physically ran away *specifically from Ben* in order to achieve some solitude, and Ben has no business tracking him up here like a bloodhound.

But—God, Ben had gone through this phase in middle school, or maybe early high school—oh, he doesn't remember now. He'd been young and angry, that was the important thing, an unhappy, slightly smelly little cauldron of unfamiliar hormones and haunting new insecurities and the creeping suspicion that maybe he *wasn't* going to find himself developing an interest in girls any day now. Little things would set him off and he'd blow up, say something about how it was so *stupid* and they were all *stupid* and being alive was *stupid*, because he was in that awkward period of teen rage where frustration cut off access to his inner dictionary. Then he'd storm out and go stand outside, committed as a postman, stubbornly waiting in the rain or the snow or the dark of the night until he felt less like he was going to explode.

Ben wanted to be alone in those moments; of course he did. Ben is so, so good at being alone. He wants to be alone when he locks himself in the bathroom on twenty-seven so he doesn't scream in Jessica's irritating but undeserving face, or when he stays in his apartment on a Friday night instead of trying his luck at another meetup group or speed dating event. It's better, in his experience, to be alone when you're on fire—easier to avoid burning anyone. Easier to keep anyone from knowing who you are in that kind of agony, to sidestep the sick vulnerability of being seen that raw.

But he would be lying, wouldn't he, if he said he hadn't wanted someone to come out after him, every time. If he said that he hadn't been desperate, standing out there sizzling in front of the restaurant in whatever weather, for someone to step through the swinging doors and dump a bucket of ice-cold water over his head. If he said that, when he'd eventually stopped doing it, it was for any reason other than wanting to cut away how much it hurt—to ache for that relief, to have it never, ever come.

It's this that pushes his hesitant feet one in front of the other, footfalls sure but largely silent, regretting leaving his peacoat behind downstairs as he makes his way across the rooftop. Pete doesn't seem to notice him coming, doesn't look up, but as Ben gets closer, he can see that Pete's back is heaving under the cheap fabric of the hot dog costume.

When he's a few yards away—far enough that it will be easy to slink off if Pete makes it clear he wants Ben to go—Ben takes a deep breath, and squares his shoulders, and says, "Hey."

Pete, unsurprisingly, jumps. It's an impressively small jump—Ben would have flailed like Kermit the Frog, not remotely intentionally—but his whole body seems to shudder, after, and he quickly turns his face away. His voice is low, rough, when he says, "Uh—hi. Sorry, I'm—you're not catching my—best moment."

"I'm actually weirdly familiar with a wide variety of moments you might categorize as less than your best," Ben says, before he can stop himself. "Not that I'm judging, or anything—the opposite —but like. If I was going to care about that sort of thing, probably I would've thrown in the towel about six minutes into the first video, you know?"

To Ben's surprise and considerable relief, Pete lets out a shaky laugh and runs a hand over his face. "Well, that's... probably true, yeah."

Ben, emboldened by the magic of the beautiful beverage he'll curse in the morning, decides to take this as permission to approach. He steps closer, then leans against the low brick wall next to Pete at what he hopes is an appropriate distance away as he says, "Anyway, I wanted a break. I will always take one person over a whole party full of people—easier to keep track, if nothing else. Plus, did you know, I heard someone put peyote in the pierogies? I call that shocking."

Pete laughs again, realer this time. "I did hear that somewhere, yes. Just from the one source, though, so I'm not sure how trustworthy it is."

"Really? I heard that guy's basically a genius," Ben says lightly. "Speaking of which, here's another banger of an idea—you want some of this drink? I don't remember what they called it, but it's *good*. Gin and lime and—St-Germain, I think?"

Pete takes a deep breath through his nose, as if trying to gather himself, and then releases it slowly through his mouth before he smiles lopsidedly at Ben and says, "You know what? Yeah, that sounds nice."

Ben passes the glass over, and Pete takes a considering sip, then smiles. "Mm, yeah. A gin Collins, I think, with lime instead of lemon, and maybe some juniper infused in the simple. It's good." He takes another sip before passing it back. "Thanks."

"Sure," Ben says, and takes a sip himself. Then, half-convinced it's a critical error even as he does it, he adds, "Are you okay?"

"Oh," Pete says, and blinks at him for a second. Then: "Yeah. Of course. Why wouldn't I be?"

"Well. To be honest. You don't... seem okay," Ben says, wincing slightly. "No offense."

Pete pauses for a moment, taking this in. Then he sighs, and there's a capitulation in his voice when he says, "None taken. I guess I probably don't, do I."

It's not really a question and Ben doesn't think it needs an answer; he offers Pete an apologetic little shrug instead and looks away, trying to make space for him to talk if he wants to. The silence stretches, and Ben fights the urge to fill it with chatter, sarcasm, anything that isn't the yawning void of anticipation—

—and then Pete says, low and unhappy, "Listen, the stuff in the videos, the way I... kind of... freak out?"

Ben tries not to let his voice go too dry as he says, "I'm familiar, yes."

"It's not... I'm not doing it as a bit, or a schtick, and I'm not, like, allergic to cameras." Pete punches out a breath, like it's a marathon to get the sentence out, before: "I get like that when I'm trying not to have a goddamn panic attack. I've got some weird stuff about, uh... fame, or whatever. So being in front of a camera like this is... It kinda... makes it hard to... hold it together."

"Oh," Ben says, a little surprised, but only by the bit about fame being at the root. As far as Ben's early cursory Googles turned up, Pete Bailey's fame extends to recipe bylines, but he doesn't think this is the moment to pry. "I mean—jeez, man. That sounds like it really sucks."

Pete takes another huge breath. "Yeah, I don't love it, to be honest with you. I *really* thought about quitting, but—look, it would be too hard to explain, but I can't afford to walk away from this right now, even if it means I have to be in front of a camera. I just can't. But seeing those guys—their *Halloween* costumes... I don't know. I couldn't deal."

"Yeah, that makes sense," Ben says, trying to keep his voice gentle. It's not one of his more typical registers, outside of trying to sweet-talk Roux into taking necessary, life-saving medication, so he hopes he's hitting the right note. Knowing he's going to hate the answer, he can't help but ask: "Do you have a panic attack after every shoot, then?"

Pete winces, looks away for a second. But then he looks back, and his voice is steady if sheepish as he admits, "I, uh... Yeah. Pretty much."

Ben thinks, but does not say, a variety of colorful swear words; that's *bad*, is what that is, and not at all sustainable. For himself, an incredibly anxious and neurotic person who can get stressed out over a glass of water, Ben tries to hold a hard limit at three work-related panic attacks per business quarter—anything more than that is edging into territory too damaging to his equilibrium to be manageable. But someone like Pete, who seems by and large to be a fairly affable person, not easily rattled, calm and unbothered in the face of change, should not be having *any* work-related panic attacks per business quarter, let alone five to ten, and maybe dozens. How often is he getting recognized? Does this happen every time? Ben's been harboring secret, silly thoughts about making a real career out of this show, but he's not going to be able to do that if it's eating away Pete's will to *live*.

This isn't the time for any of that, though. This is not about Ben; this is not about the show, or *Gastronome*, or stupid Chris downstairs, not bothering to pay Pete any attention at all. This is about Pete, who is here, right now, on this cold, empty rooftop, breathing faint little clouds into the air, telling Ben something he can tell without having to ask that he has not talked about with anyone. This is exactly the kind of moment that Ben traditionally mishandles, and so he tries to think slowly and carefully, to move with purpose and forethought.

What he decides, eventually, to say, is: "I'm so sorry, Pete. That sounds really hard. I know—obviously—I'm probably tangled up in the whole nightmare of the thing for you, but. Is there anything I can do? Anything that helps?"

Pete turns to look at him, his expression abruptly wide-eyed, his mouth parting slightly in surprise. He reaches up a hand to run through his hair, pushing the top half of the hot dog suit off of his head as he does, so it sits behind his neck like a hood. Pete's hair is wild and mussed from its time in this costume, and for a second Ben can feel his whole body thrum with the urge to reach out and work it back into place, rake his fingers through the curls until they're tamed into something approaching an order. He wants to do it so badly his *fingertips* itch, and he rubs then slightly frenetically against the rough edge of the brick, trying to override the sensation.

Luckily, Pete doesn't seem to notice this. He's still looking at Ben like Ben himself is a peyote-short-rib-induced hallucination, a ghostly apparition, or some other impossible phantasm. Ben... can't totally work out why. It was a simple enough question, wasn't it? Maybe he has something on his face, or in his teeth; he hopes not. But surely, if that was the case, Pete would have noticed before now?

Ben has no choice but to sweat it out, so he waits for what feels like an eternity even though it can't be more than a few seconds.

Finally, Pete says, "I don't know, actually. What helps. I'll... think about it."

"You do that." Ben offers him a small, hesitant smile. Then, thinking longingly of his peacoat, he adds, "For now, though, did you want to like—stay up here? I can leave you alone, obviously. Or I could go get Chris—"

"No," Pete says, and shudders. Then, more quietly, he adds, "Sorry, that's not—Chris is great, this just isn't really, uh... his area." Ben decides, with the help of another sip of his drink, that he hates Chris. Pete does not seem to notice this as he continues, "If you don't mind. I don't want to stay up here all night or anything, but would you just hang out with me for a few more minutes?"

"Oh," Ben says, warmed through suddenly, forgetting about his jacket. "I mean—yeah, sure. If you want."

Pete nods, and Ben settles back against the wall. Within a minute, the conversation has turned to the food downstairs; within five, they're laughing about some nonsense joke Ben doubts he'd even be able to explain to anyone else. By the time they return to the party fifteen minutes later, Pete's smile is bright and his eyes are clear, and he breaks off to check in with Chris in a great mood, his earlier despair forgotten for now.

Ben sighs, watching Pete smile at something Chris whispers in his ear, swallows down the last sip of his drink, and walks away. Through the party; through the empty halls; through the coat check, where he is reunited at last with the glorious warmth of his peacoat.

Abruptly too drunk for logic or good decisions, Ben makes his unsteady way to the nearest subway station essentially on autopilot, and rides the twenty-five minutes home in the slightly swaying fashion of the properly sauced. He doesn't talk to anyone, but he watches as he rides, taking in the uniformed woman struggling to keep her eyes open, the old man reading a Tolstoy novel, the scowling teenager glaring into space. He's struck, suddenly, with the knowledge of how separate they all are, even packed tight into the same densely layered city, the same unlikely tin car bulleting under the ground: together, undeniably—but, equally undeniably, alone.

As Ben walks the few blocks from his usual station back to his apartment, under the sort of soft, forgiving street lamplight he's grown fond of lately, he thinks again of Pete. His easy laughter; his complicated competence; the way he always seems to get Ben's jokes, no matter how stupid or off-kilter or strange. New York never sleeps, so the streets are still pockmarked with anonymous people, striding and shuffling about their singular business; surrounded by the safety of just being another soul amongst the rabble, Ben's drunken, treacherous heart twists in his chest, and opens the door beyond which he keeps things he doesn't want to know.

Ben takes a long, sobering look at the looming truth behind that door, its inarguable shape and unmissable features, the way it seems, already, to be threatening to break containment.

Then he takes a firm grip on the door's metaphorical knob, and slams it shut.

SEVEN

The first week of November dawns cold and bracing, matching Ben's mood. After spending the bulk of Sunday both hungover and viciously down on himself, he battles his way grimly to the office on Monday morning, regretting, as always, the fact that New York's eye-catching skyscrapers have the unfortunate side effect of creating, in certain weather, a series of interconnected wind tunnels. He's buffeted along Forty-Second Street, and then blown sideways onto Sixth Avenue, before managing, barely, to make his way into his own office building.

Another sign of the state he's worked himself into: He doesn't even make a cursory stop by twenty-seven on his way to the *Gastronome* offices. Instead, he guilelessly and with malice afore-thought hits thirty-four when he gets in the elevator, and makes sure to stand in the back, so if the doors do open on his more usual floor, none of his coworkers can catch a glimpse of him.

He's the first in, when he gets to the test kitchen; this doesn't surprise him, as the chefs here, like chefs in general, are typically a later crowd. Really, Ben should continue through the test kitchen to the editing bay, where someone else will inevitably already be working, and where he truly belongs. But Pete is supposed to film today, the first of three Thanksgiving videos they're set to turn in this week, and Ben doesn't see the point getting ready anywhere but here. He'll just end up drifting in while Pete films, using a variety of excuses to explain his presence, before eventually sticking around, trying to make it seem organic and natural and like that was his plan all along.

Ben's had enough of being organic and natural. He's had enough of silly little plans built around a silly little idea of some silly little life Ben's not even sure that he wants, and that isn't possible or remotely in the cards for him in any case. Pete's not suited to this job; Pete's got a boyfriend; Pete's having a panic attack after every shoot, at minimum. Ben's vague, gauzy plan, the one he had not allowed himself to so much as think about but had been drifting loosely towards even so, is not going to work. And, anyway, while all this has been going on Ben's been doing what, exactly? Ripping Pete to shreds for the entertainment of the masses, that's what, while Pete lived his long, unrelenting nightmare, more or less as a direct result of Ben's tendency towards evisceration. There's nothing he can do about it now—for better or worse, that's the job, and it would damage both of their careers if he abruptly changed the whole tone of the show.

But the other thing Ben's been doing—the dancing around what he'd normally say, what he'd like to do, here in the *Gastronome* offices, because he wants to... to... *impress* Pete, or whatever? Give a convincing impression of being someone cooler and more cavalier than he is? That's going to have to stop, and it's going to have to stop right now. *Someone* is going to have to get bossy, and insistent, and demanding. Someone is going to have to make this easier for Pete, since it's clear he can't make it easy for himself.

So Ben sets up at the station next to Pete's that he knows is always empty, hooking up his laptop to his external hard drive and prepping programs he won't need for hours yet. Then he sits and waits to execute his plan.

Pete comes in first—also not a surprise. He's almost always the first cook in, which Ben knows is because he has a complicated daily system timed out with the ferry ride from Jersey City; if he's ever more than five minutes late, it's always because he's missed his boat, and will be delayed at least half an hour. He smiles when he sees Ben; Ben tries to smile back.

"Ben, hey! I'm glad you're here—I was hoping I'd catch a moment alone with you." Pete lowers his voice in spite of the aforementioned solitude. "I just... I wanted to thank you for the other night, for being so chill, and everything. I tried to find you again at the party, but I couldn't, so, just. Thanks. I appreciate it."

"Oh," Ben says, blinking. He's spent the past thirty-six hours steeping in a simmering tea of self-loathing, born partially of hangover and partially of realizing the sheer depth of the trouble he, specifically, has brought upon this specific man; he wasn't exactly expecting thanks. "That's—don't be stupid, it was nothing. You don't have to—just—forget it."

"Oh, you're one of *those* people," Pete says musingly, as if to himself.

Bristling in spite of his better instincts, and biting even though it's obvious bait, Ben snaps, "I'm sorry, one of *which* people, exactly?"

"You know," Pete says, taking off his jacket and folding it precariously over a stool, "people who can't take gratitude, or a compliment, or whatever. Look, I'll prove it: Your editing is really good."

"God," Ben groans, running a hand over his face, "*don't* do this to me right now. I haven't even had good coffee yet; I had to throw out my bodega cup halfway through this morning, something went *wrong* when they were making it, it was like drinking a cup of straight hair dye—"

"And yet you still drank half of it," Pete comments lightly, shaking his head, but he lets the compliment thing go. Ben doesn't think he could take continued praise of his work from Pete right now—in his current mental circumstances, it might actually kill him.

Instead of this, he offers, "Hey, I'd drink hair dye too if it had caffeine in it."

"I think we can do a little better than that," Pete says, rolling his eyes. "And if we can't, we have no business calling ourselves 'America's cooking standby,' or whatever it is—"

"'North America's culinary stalwart,'" Ben says, without thinking. Then, as he realizes it probably makes him sound like a brown-nosing, obsessive weirdo, heat begins to prickle at the back of his ears.

Before he can rush to correct himself, though, Pete's saying, "Stalwart? Really? That can't be right—what does that even mean?"

"It's like a—reliable supporter," Ben says, figuring he might as well go ahead now. "It's an old-timey word, but it's been the slogan since the magazine was founded in the twenties." When Pete raises an eyebrow, Ben feels the blush spill from the tips of his ears onto his cheeks as he admits, "I may—*may*—have been, um... a bit of a big fan. Of the magazine. As a kid." When a grin begins to break out across Pete's face, Ben holds up both hands and protests, "Go easy on me! Think of the hair dye! You can't expect me to bear mockery under-caffeinated; I won't be able to take it."

Pete laughs and shakes his head, but he does, encouragingly, start pulling out various items that look as though they might, eventually, produce a cup of coffee. "Is that why you're in here, then? To throw yourself on the mercy of whatever test cook arrived first in exchange for caffeine?"

"Oh," Ben says, sitting up slightly straighter as he remembers. "No, actually. I'm in here because—I had an idea. You know how you said, the other night—" He pauses, noticing Pete's sudden wild-eyed glance around the still-empty room, and, taking pity, changes course a little. "Just... I was thinking about what you told me, and I thought—three Thanksgiving videos in a week is probably not the best for you, is it?"

Pete's brow furrows, his expression flickering as though unsure where to land. Eventually, he says, "It... No, to be honest. It's not."

"Right, so," Ben says, and shrugs. "I sort of thought—why don't we just, you know. Shoot it all today? We've got two Thanksgiving videos due this week, and one next week, so what if we just... barrel through all of it? I know it'll suck, but, plus side, then it'll be over, and it's like ripping the Band-Aid off, right? And I figure maybe we can give some of the staff the extra food, a surprise Thanksgiving feast, and—uh." Ben pauses, clears his throat, aware that he's probably been talking too long and also that Pete's face hasn't moved at all since he began. "Anyway, if you hate it, we don't have to. Obviously."

"No, I," Pete says, blinking. "It sounds *great*, but don't you have to turn in the first video tomorrow? If we're shooting all day, when will you... edit it?"

"Oh, whenever," Ben says airily, waving a hand. "Tonight, tomorrow during the day—it'll be fine." In fact, Ben rather suspects it won't be fine, that he'll end up working into the wee hours and will, by tomorrow, regret ever having had the whole idea in the first place; he's made his peace with that. There is a little Post-it note already stuck to his pillow, in case of moments of weakness, which reads, STICK TO THE PLAN. You chose this!

Pete frowns. "You're sure?"

Ben thinks of the long comment threads laughing at the antics and mishaps of Pete in what he now knows as the early stages of a panic attack, and swallows. What's a sleepless night or two, really? It's not like he's going to be getting much sleep, anyway. "Totally sure. Honestly, it'll be easier for me, too—the sooner these are in the can, the sooner I can work on them, and that gives me more time to build up a buffer. Less stress all around. Look, I even pulled together a rough run of show—I mean, technically *runs* of show, since it's multiple videos, but we're going to do it all as one big shoot, so who's counting—and a shopping list. I figured we could send someone out while we're shooting the early stuff, since everything for that should be around here already."

He turns his computer towards Pete, who bends in to look at it, leaning against the counter. He's abruptly so close that Ben could tip forward the barest inch and snatch off Pete's beanie with his *teeth*; he wouldn't, of course, because *who would*, but the proximity is upsettingly intoxicating. Hoping it doesn't show in his voice, Ben scrolls through the agenda as he says, "So the first thing here is the vegetarian/vegan-friendly options one—we talked about that last week, so I pulled the casserole you suggested and that stuffed pepper—and then there's two more we hadn't roughed out yet. One video of standard sides, and then one for entrees, which I think they probably mean for us to do a turkey for? But Miranda didn't specify, and turkey sucks, so I vote chicken. Game hens, maybe? But we can do ham if you want." Realizing, for what must be the millionth time in a long, embarrassing life, that perhaps he has become carried away, Ben finishes, awkwardly: "Anyway, I... I have some thoughts on all of it, obviously, and that's what I pulled together here, but you can switch out whatever you want. I pretty much used your recipes anyway, since I figured you're probably already familiar." Pete's recipes have also, especially for the last few months, tended to be the most highly trafficked on the site, according to Ben's new buddy in data analytics, Findley, who he met while drinking an entirely unnecessary afternoon coffee at Brew a few weeks ago. Ben is not interested in approaching anything related to fame or audience right now so he doesn't mention it.

Pete is silent for a moment, scrolling through the document. Ben considers several options, including letting out a long, uncontrolled yodel of anxiety, or jumping out of his own skin in anticipation, but none quite seem to suit the moment. When, eventually, Pete speaks, his tone is hard to parse, distant and faintly disbelieving, like someone trying to remember a dream: "When... when did you *do* all this?"

"Oh, yesterday," Ben says, shrugging. "You know how sometimes you just get an idea and run with it?"

"I mean," Pete says, shaking his head and laughing slightly, "*no*, dude. Not really. You know, sometimes I get an idea like, 'What about baklava but with the syrup from torrejas instead,' but that's, you know, a pretty straightforward next step. This is like *homework* —it would have taken me a week and it wouldn't have been half as detailed. There's an *ingredient list* for each shoot and for the whole *day*... Oh my God, wait. This link—is this an actual list of the ingredients we have in stock? In the test kitchen? Right now?"

"Oh," Ben says, and blushes slightly. This is the sort of thing he struggles to do for himself but learned young to do for others, because it was the only way to keep the restaurant running smoothly. He prefers to do tasks like this unnoticed, the way it was when he was a kid; being spotted at it always makes him feel unaccountably embarrassed. "Yeah, I put it together a couple of weeks ago? It was just easier, you know, to keep track of everything, and I used to do inventory for my folks at the restaurant and I couldn't find yours—"

"We don't *have* one," says Pete, in reverent tones, as he scrolls. "No one's been able to keep up with it since Miranda fired Josie, and that was *years* ago. We don't even do normal ordering anymore, we just run on 'who kills it, fills it' and have everyone expense it—oh my God, you have *brand names* in here! Listen, can I print this out?"

"Oh," Ben says, blinking. "Sure, if you want to, but it's updating in the document, so it won't be accurate for—"

But the printer is already whirring, and Pete bounds off towards it before Ben can finish his thought. It's at the other end of the test kitchen, near the far door, and Ben watches in bemusement and, if he's honest, a little fondness as Pete bounces on the balls of his feet, waiting for the last sheet to spit out. When it does, he clutches the little sheaf of papers in his hands, raises it over his head, and lets out a long, reverent note, an "aaaaaah" sound that carries on long enough that Ben walks over to investigate.

Before he can say anything, like, "What are you doing?" or "Have I, in attempting to balance out some of the damage I have caused here, driven you past your breaking point?" or "You know that's just paper, right?" the far door opens, and Adina walks in.

"What are you doing?" Adina says, and then, "You know that's just paper, right?" which is, at least, handy.

"It's *not* just paper," Pete says, wild-eyed, without dropping his arms. "Ben made an *inventory*. An up-to-date, accurate *inventory*. Of everything in the test kitchen. *Everything*, Adina. The *brands* of the *salts* are in here, okay, it's better than *Josie's* was, and this is just a printout! It's a document! An editable document!"

"You're joking," Adina says, with overly brash confidence that indicates a sliver of doubt.

Pete shakes his head, grinning at her. "I'm really *not*."

Adina stares at Pete for a second, then whips her head around to stare at Ben, then turns back to Pete. Then, to Ben's astonishment and slight horror, she too raises both hands in the air, as if in worship of the paper, and joins Pete in another long, reverent "aaaaaaaaah."

"Good Lord," Ben says, trying not to laugh. "If I'd realized an inventory was going to be such a hit, I would have sent it over to you weeks ago. Here, if you come over, I can show you my basic system and share it out."

Adina is so eager for access to the file that she refuses to take off her coat or put down her bag, which is half her size and looks like it weighs about seven thousand pounds, until she's watched Ben send her the link. Then, as the other test cooks start trickling in, she oohs and aahs over Ben's level of detail and organization, the way he's set it up to track intervals of time between refills, and any changes to those intervals. This tips off the rest of the staff to the fact that the inventory exists, and suddenly Ben is being showered with promises to be taken out for a drink, or a few drinks, or to be given Brogan's firstborn as a tribute, although that one is quite clearly a joke.

Ben is *also* being inundated with compliments, which is somehow both incredibly nice and deeply embarrassing. He keeps trying to explain to them that it's nothing, that it's just a slightly updated version of the system he created for the restaurant when he was thirteen, but this makes Pete stare at him with glassy astonishment and say, "You could do this when you were *thirteen*?" which doesn't help things at all.

"I just wanted my parents to stop accidentally double-ordering the imported tomatoes my mom insists on," Ben says, shrugging. He keeps to himself the reason he'd wanted that: to avoid the doubled bill arriving, and the subsequent screaming fight his parents would have in the walk-in, which had never in Ben's lifetime been as soundproof as Daniel and Lucia imagined it. Sometimes he and Renata could hear them at it even from upstairs, going back and forth about whose fault it was and then, eventually, about who was at fault for everything else either of them felt was wrong in their lives. "So it wasn't like a great act of organizational altruism or whatever."

"Still," Pete says, shaking his head in what appears, to Ben's amazement and confusion, to be admiration. "Still."

And then Ben doesn't have time to talk about it anymore; too much is happening. Jaelyn is arriving—Ben, not actually wanting to take his life into his hands, had emailed her about this plan yesterday, and had her enthusiastic sign-off in the event Pete agreed. She's a contractor, too, with a variable schedule; Pete has to be here all day regardless, but he wasn't about to spring this concept on *her* with no notice. He gives her a thumbs-up when she steps into the kitchen with her camera bag, and Jaelyn grins and groans in relief, says, "Thank God! Ripping the Band-Aid off, I love it, I'm going to get *such* a nice check for Black Friday. My wife and I have been eying this couch for like six months, and I *know* it's going to go on sale—"

"Ooh," an arriving Ezra says, as he takes off his coat. "Color, size, shape, tell me *everything*," and they, along with an enthusiastic Adina, descend into a furniture conversation while Ben helps Pete gather the ingredients for the first video. He does it almost automatically, following Pete first to the potato and onion bins, then into the walk-in, selecting their produce on muscle memory while Pete scoops up dairy and eggs.

And it's there, in the chilly depths of the walk-in fridge, when

Ben's arms are full of ingredients and he has nowhere to run, that Pete turns to him and says, "That run of show—look, Ben, can I ask you something?"

What a horrible question—he could ask *anything*—what if he asks if Ben has—no, no, it's better not to speculate. Carefully, Ben says, "Sure! Why not."

"You asked Jaelyn to stop calling 'cut,' didn't you," Pete says quietly. It's not really a question. "Way back at the beginning. You didn't say anything about it, or ask me if you should, you just did it. Because you could tell... Because you could tell. Right?"

Oh, God, couldn't you have asked any—almost *any—other question?* Ben does not say this through an amount of effort that frankly staggers him; instead, shrugging somewhat miserably, he says, "I mean, I couldn't tell—what you told me the other night, or anything. But I... did, yeah. I thought the cuts maybe were... not helping."

Pete stares at him under the flickering fluorescents, measuring, evaluative, oddly loaded. Ben thinks, *Probably there's something on my face?* and then, treacherously, *Does he look at Chris like this?* and then tries to banish both thoughts.

Eventually, his grin a sharp slash across his face, Pete says, *"Thanks."*

"Oh," Ben says, weakly. "Don't mention it. Wasn't any trouble at all."

The morning moves fairly quickly, after that. Pete makes a classic sweet potato casserole first, roasted marshmallow layer and all, with an optional miso-maple-pecan topper, and all in all, it could be worse. Sure, he says "mashmellow" instead of "marshmallow" in literally every instance, except when he's explaining that viewers could easily substitute vegan ones; in that case, the word "viewers" seems to be a bridge too far, and what comes out of his mouth instead of "marshmallow" is "mushmallop." And, okay, while peeling a sweet potato, Pete does launch it in the air in such a way that it manages both to hit the boom mic and the side of Ben's head. Ben laughs it off, though, and after a second

Pete does, too—a little nervously, maybe, but at least he's laughing.

The stuffed pepper dish afterwards goes a little better, maybe because Pete goes on a long rant about how he'd rather be doing this with poblano or Anaheim peppers, but every time he posts a recipe with the faintest whiff of heat, he gets eight million emails from readers complaining that he burned their tongues off. None of the audio is remotely useable, at least not if Ben wants to make it to December without Rick hunting him like "The Most Dangerous Game," but Pete's so distracted he chops the vegetables, assembles the spiced rice and squash filling, and stuffs the peppers without making a single mistake. Granted, when he goes to sprinkle cheese over the top, he seems to remember the camera is there, and immediately casts about three handfuls of cotija all over the floor, but Ben can deal with that in post.

Still, they're wrapped on the content for the first video by 11:30 a.m., which is the quickest they've ever managed to finish shooting. Ben doesn't point this out, of course—the goal, ideally, is for Pete to *forget* that they're shooting—but he notes it with satisfaction for himself. And when he passes her, Jaelyn offers him a subtle low five out of Pete's eyeline, which Ben gladly accepts, pleased with his success.

People start drifting in to taste the first round of dishes as Pete starts on the second. All of them are effusive with praise, and after a threatening growl from his stomach, Ben snags a slice of the sweet potato casserole himself. He takes a bite heaped with pecans and beautifully browned marshmallow, and lets out an embarrassing groan at how unbelievably good it is—he doesn't even usually *like* sweet potato—which he regrets the second it's out of his mouth. He looks up from his plate like a startled rabbit, hoping no one heard him—

—but Pete is staring right at him, his eyes crinkled at the corners, his smile brighter and more real than any Ben's ever seen from him while the camera was rolling. It's all Ben can do not to choke.

He focuses, instead, on the work, asking Pete questions he already knows the answers to, on the theory that the audience won't. And Pete answers him easily as he chops and sautés and stirs, conversational, accidentally providing a lot of soundbites that will, stripped of Ben's half, sound like genuine cooking instruction. He doesn't spill boiling water all over the stove while he's making mashed potatoes, or forget the roasting garlic in the oven and burn it. When he's prepping mirepoix for stuffing, he pulls out a food processor and explains his personal system for making huge quantities of the stuff and freezing it, which is so cogent and sensible that Ben can already mentally scrub through the short, bonus shareable video he's going to cut it into shot by shot.

And just after he's dumped a huge pile of that mirepoix into a sauté pan, the timer goes off on his toasting bread cubes, and he says, "Ben? Would you mind taking over this for a second? I want to get those out."

"Sure," Ben says, embarrassingly soft, half-afraid someone else here, in this kitchen full of *elite professionals*, is going to say something, insist on jumping in instead. But nobody moves, or even blinks, and Ben realizes as he slides off his stool and shuffles into place in front of the stove that none of them think this is even remotely odd. That everyone in this room, with the exception of Ben, has decided for themselves on whatever level that he's earned this, his strange, uncertain spot.

He takes the handle of the pan cautiously, with a hesitation that feels ridiculous the minute it's sitting in his hand. Hasn't he been doing this as long as he's been doing anything? Isn't his whole life a long series of events punctuated by rounds of sautéing some combination of these specific vegetables?

Pete asks him for his opinion on whether the bread's gone far enough, though, and Ben forgets to think about it. He's turning to look at the tray Pete's holding out; his arm is moving automatically, tossing the vegetables in the air and catching them in the pan without having to look, his body doing the work out of long practice with no thought at all. He's saying the bread looks fine, and

Pete's making a dubious face, and Ben's laughing as the mirepoix rises and falls again, the weight of it telling him everything he needs to know, alongside the satisfying sizzle as each tiny, oiled piece makes contact with the pan. He turns back to the stove and seasons the vegetables, answering some question from Adina about whether or not he has opinions on the kitchen's salt options, and then Pete is next to him, stepping into his space, taking the pan from Ben easily, their hands brushing as they make the exchange.

And for a second, Ben is overwhelmed by a still, sweet image of this same motion, this same moment, in a smaller, more intimate kitchen. With no test cooks, and no cameras—in less professional clothes, or at a more personal time of the day—this is the kind of moment that might pin together something larger. Softer. More private. Pete could slide a little further to the left, for example, and let one broad, long-fingered hand rest against the sharp jut of Ben's hipbone. It would be warm through Ben's T-shirt and the thin, barely-there denim of his ancient skinny jeans, hand-patched with a variety of pleasantly odd fabrics.

But that's not reality, of course. If Pete really did that, Ben would have to—he'd—well, he'd—

Ben realizes, with grave, hideous clarity, that he knows exactly what he would do. If Pete splayed a hand across his hip—if Pete backed him up with gentle but firm insistence against the nearest wall, counter, or other available surface—if Pete leaned too far and with too much intention into beanie-biting territory—well. Then Ben would have no choice but to give way to him entirely, the way a delicate spun caramel dome cracks under a pour of molten sauce: spectacularly, and perhaps even exactly as intended, but still somehow a bit macabre to see all that careful work collapse.

Work; Ben has to work. He steps away; he focuses again, or he tries to. But every thought he has is like one of Rick's stupid fish-hooks, catching him in a delicate place and dragging him back up into the cold, punishing air of understanding. He tries to untangle himself, to slam the door shut, to engage with whatever stupid internal metaphor will allow him a moment's peace from the unwelcome, unwieldy, and wholly unworkable truth. It doesn't happen. Pete smiles at him, or asks him a question, or holds out a wooden spoon and asks him to taste something, and what limited semblance of mental order Ben's managed to cobble together splinters into fragments again, leaving him back at square one.

No one notices—or, if they notice, they're kind enough not to say anything about it. And *Pete* doesn't notice, which is the important part. He is, in the one real mercy of the day, on a roll; Ben's not sure if it's the nature of the challenge, or how many people have come by expressing interest in eating the results, or the fact that after the third or fourth person said, "I've never had a game hen, actually," Pete started taking custom orders. Whatever it is, by the time a full sheet tray of game hens is resting on the counter in front of him, something within Pete has clearly locked properly into place. He turns to the camera, and smiles.

"So probably," he says, in an understanding voice, "you wanted this to be a turkey video." Ben realizes at this point that Pete is *addressing the audience*; his mouth drops open, and he sees Jaelyn's eyes widen behind the camera as Pete goes on. "Thanksgiving is the turkey holiday. But the thing is, turkey involves a lot of planning, so, you know, if you're watching this two weeks before the big day, go ahead and find a turkey video instead. If, however, you're engaging in the time-honored American tradition of figuring out what on earth you're going to feed everyone in the last twenty-four hours before the holiday, then, my friend: One way or another, you're having chicken."

Ben's mouth is still open, which he only realizes when Pete turns to look at him, and his smile changes to one of entertainment, and he *winks* at Ben. He *winks*! Ben can't decide whether to be thrilled or incensed about this, and settles unhappily on a rough mixture of both, although he does remember to snap his mouth shut.

Amazingly, though, after that, the whole rest of the shoot proceeds the same way. Pete makes eight different kinds of game hen, explaining each seasoning mixture, dry rub, or saucing choice as he applies it; he talks the audience through how much meat to allow per person, and why; he lays out how easily everything he's doing can be done to a regular-sized chicken, and how to adjust the cooking times and quantities. He makes *jokes*—only two or three, but *still*. He doesn't forget any words, or how to use a stove, and when, as he's finishing prep on the last bird, he knocks a jar of Calabrian chiles onto the floor, he smiles and shrugs and says, "My dad always says it's not a holiday until you break at least one thing, and better it be a dish—or, in this case, a jar of chiles—than your spirit. Good advice, right?" And then he just puts the chicken in the oven, and cleans up, and starts working on an assortment of finishing sauces. No panic, or series of Three Stooges-esque subsequent mishaps. Just the calm, regulated equanimity of a seasoned culinary professional.

And then the hens are coming out of the oven, and they're all congratulating each other on a wildly successful shoot, and people are streaming in, alerted through the interoffice network of buzz that all the food is ready. It's nearly five, so somebody grabs a couple of bottles of wine, and somebody else pulls some other leftover dishes from the fridge, and suddenly it's a party. Not just any party—it is, somehow, the best party Ben has ever been to. No part of him wants to step back against the wall and observe instead of participate; he knows these people, likes them. It's easy to joke and laugh with them, interesting to hear about their thoughts and hobbies and opinions on the various dishes, and whenever he finds himself drawing a conversational blank, Pete is somehow *right there*, picking up the thread as if Ben handed it off neatly instead of dropping it. He eats a plate of food so good he wishes he could box it up and send it home to Michigan, with a smug little note that said something like, *Sorry to say it, but: better than yours.*

It's almost enough to distract him from the weight of what he's been trying not to see. It's *almost* enough. But the truth is, nothing does distract him, not the fun, not the party, not even the ease of slipping into an unthinking double act with Pete, the way they have been, lately, every once in a while. Ben has made it this long on the strength of not seeing the truth, of closing his eyes, of looking away. But now that he's seen it, there is no erasing the knowledge, no force within him strong enough to wrestle it back, and no box in his mind large enough to contain it, even if he could.

Ben is in love with Pete. He thinks there's a real chance he has been in love with Pete more or less since the day they met, not that he would have called it that at the time. It is, he suspects, going to become something of a problem, and he doubts there's anything that *could* distract him, now that he's looked at it. Now that he *knows*.

Miranda tests him on this, though, by selecting this critical moment to stick her head in through the front door.

The room goes dead quiet.

"Hello," Miranda sings out. She doesn't do them the courtesy of stepping fully into the room, although Ben's not sure if that's out of haughtiness or fear; the vibes have shifted from cheerful camaraderie to barely contained hatred with whiplash-inducing speed. Everyone glares as Miranda continues, "I heard you were down here carrying on—just as well, because I have exciting news! Your little show has done so well that we've booked you for an appearance on *Late Night Live with Brian O'Malley*, Pete. Nice juicy timeslot, too; you'll be doing a little cooking demo, right at the top of his first hour. It's Friday night, and—"

"Sorry," Pete says; his face has drained of blood, and for a second, Ben considers lobbing a frying pan at Miranda for undoing all his hard work. "*This* Friday?" When Miranda nods, serene, Pete continues, "And you mean—like—*the Late Night Live*? The *nationally syndicated live talk show*? I don't... Miranda, I *can't*—"

"Oh, dear," Miranda says, her voice flat, her eyes dead. "Is that going to make things difficult for you, Pete? You know how I'd *hate* that."

Ben narrows his eyes at her, trying to puzzle her out. There's something weird here, something *personal*, but he can't seem to work out what. God knows Pete's no help—every time Ben's tried to tiptoe around the topic, ask a few subdued questions, Pete's said something vague and immediately changed the subject.

True to form, Pete grimaces now and, with the air of a drowning man, says, "Look, can we not—it's just a *bad idea*, okay? I won't be good at that! Let Ben do it, that's a good idea, *he* never forgets how to say the word 'pineapple'—"

"They don't want Ben," Miranda says, with a bright, false smile. "Just you. It'll be fun! I'll send you the details. Bye!"

She drifts out with all the happy indifference of a hurricane, heedless of the wreckage she's left behind her.

EIGHT

For the next three days, Ben and Pete have, essentially, the same conversation, just in a variety of different locations. They have it in the *Gastronome* offices; they have it downstairs at Brew; they have it at Fox's several times, because it's the test kitchen's favorite watering hole, so they keep getting interrupted and having to start again. They have it, once, on the walk from Formica Media to the nearest subway station and get so engrossed in the argument that they're already on the platform before Pete says, "Jesus, what am I *doing*, I have to get to the ferry." The details change a little from round to round, but in essence, it's always the same exchange.

First, Pete says, desperation thick in his voice, "Man, I *can't* do *Late Night Live*. I can't. I can't!"

Then Ben, in wheedling tones that he hopes don't communicate his own deep apprehension about the prospect, says, "Sure you can! You've done plenty of videos and—"

"I *can't*," Pete generally interrupts at this point, "you don't *understand*, have you ever even watched *Late Night Live*?" Pete, as it turns out, has watched a lot of *Late Night Live*. "Because it's not, like, a merciful show, okay, it's *live*, things go wrong all the time, they *want* things to go wrong, they're all going to be *looking* at me—"

"Maybe that'll help!" Ben does not believe this—how could anyone believe this, in the circumstances—but he certainly wants to, which he hopes counts for something. "Maybe the extra pressure will be, uh, grounding—"

"It never has been before," Pete tends to mutter, slouching down into himself, around this point in the discussion.

"Well." At this stage, Ben is always fishing wildly for something to say, and yet somehow consistently turns up the same useless advice: "Maybe the move is to try to believe things will go well, right? Envision the reality you wish to transpire, or whatever?"

At this point, Pete groans. "The reality I wish to transpire is one where *Late Night Live* is cancelled between now and Friday."

Unfortunately for them both, Ben can never think of anything better to say to this other than, "Yeah, that's fair." He, too, is hoping the show gets cancelled, or there's a freak city-wide blackout, or that Pete will get stuck in a subway car for seventeen hours and end up on the news for totally unrelated reasons where he doesn't have to talk.

Regardless, this tends to end the conversation, until something —a shift of the wind, a reminder of what day of the week it is, catching sight of the unfortunately placed *Late Night Live with Brian O'Malley* ad directly outside the Formica Media offices— cycles it back up again. It never takes very long.

It takes Ben a few days to place what the loop reminds him of, and then, two nights before the episode is set to film, he figures it out. It's like talking to his sister, Renata, about her hideous tendency, in spite of more than a decade of avowed bisexuality, to be all but exclusively inclined towards dating terrible, poorly behaved men who treat her like dirt. She'll go on and on and *on* about some fresh new jerk she's grown attached to, and his unlikeable antics, and his unfortunate traits, and all the ways that he bothers her, and Ben will say things like, "It doesn't sound like he deserves you," or, "It doesn't sound like you like him very much," or, "Just because our parents annoy the ever-loving hell out of each other all day long doesn't mean that's a great model to work off of in seeking romantic happiness."

This last tends to backfire on him, as Renata will generally reply with something along the lines of, "Oh, is that right? And you're the expert, huh? So the key to romantic happiness, then, is... hmm, let me check my notes here... ah, yes: 'Living like a cross between a hermit and an artist's rendering of the concept of depression'? Do I have that right?" Sometimes she says something a lot more cutting, of course—it depends how annoyed she is with him—but whatever she says, it's always humbling.

Still, it does occur to Ben, as he thinks about it, that she *is* probably the person he knows who will have the best advice in this situation. Renata's a stage manager; surely, she deals with this sort of thing all the time, between flighty actors and pissy directors and theater donors trying to throw their weight around. God knows she's told him enough stories about it all. Really, he should have thought of calling her sooner, but—Ben squirms, a little guiltily, to realize it—it rankles, a little, to think of asking for her advice. They're both adults and have been for a long time, and Ben's not a jerk and understands that it's not fair of him, but. Well. She's his *little* sister. The dynamic between them is one where the advice has, traditionally, flowed in the other direction, and it feels shamefully humiliating to have to ask her for something.

But it's for Pete, not for him, and Ben is starting to worry the stress might *kill* Pete; he's looking more and more haggard by the day, as though he hasn't been sleeping. Before he can think better of it, he calls Renata.

"Are you *dead*?" Renata answers on the second ring.

"What?" Ben blinks at the wall, surprised to hear this instead of the anticipated "Hello." "Uh, no, I'm not—"

"Is Mom dead, then?" Renata demands. "Dad? Who's dead?"

"No one is dead!" Ben should have trusted his instincts—he regrets putting this call through. He regrets ever considering putting this call through. "Why does someone have to be dead?"

"Because it's *one in the morning*," Renata says, in a dangerous voice, "and you *never* call me after seven, so I figured someone had to be dead!"

Ben, shocked, glances at the clock and winces. "Jesus Christ, Ren, I'm so sorry—I was editing, and I lost track of time. I thought it was ten thirty, latest."

"If only there was some sort of timekeeping tool," Renata says, in a faux-musing voice, "that was visible upon the device you used to contact me—"

"Yeah, yeah, I know, all right, I'm sorry," Ben says, rolling his eyes even as guilt shifts uneasily in his stomach. "I'll go, sorry to wake you—"

"Oh, I wasn't asleep," Renata says, sounding suddenly cheerful. "Just got in from a wrap party, actually; I just wanted to establish that if you call me at this time of night again, without texting first, I'm going to assume someone is dead. Anyway, what's up?"

Ben wrestles down a small scream of frustration. But then, this is the price of dealing with one's family—no one ever quite hits your buttons like they do. He doesn't want to say it, especially after that little opening salvo, so badly that it feels a little like it's giving him a chemical burn as he spits it out of his mouth, but: "Actually, I was hoping for... God. Some advice?"

There is a pause. Then Renata cackles; it is, Ben notes wearily, quite reminiscent of the cackle she perfected at age nine, to accompany her witch Halloween costume. At every house he took her to she let that cackle out, delighting some of the neighborhood homeowners and deeply unnerving others. As Ben remembers it, old Mrs. Hoffman down the road had been so badly frightened that she'd come round to the restaurant the next day and asked if anyone had ever considered an exorcism. She had, unfortunately for her, had the bad luck to catch Ben's father, Daniel; Lucia might have been more sympathetic. Daniel, on the other hand, had simply listened calmly, waited until she was done, and then said, "Go home before I have her curse you, then, Carol," which he had found quite funny.

"Some advice, you say?" Ren's voice is almost painfully entertained, now that she's stopped laughing; glad she can't see him, Ben grits his teeth. "How can I guide you, brother dearest? What tangle have you fallen into that only your wiser, prettier, younger sister can solve?"

"You know what, forget it," Ben starts, "I don't—"

"No, hey, come on," Renata says, sounding more serious now—or, at least, as serious as Renata ever sounds. She's always had their mother's talent of taking life fairly lightly, up until such a time as she becomes angry, annoyed, frustrated, or too hungry. "I won't be mean about it—what is it?"

"Ugh," Ben mutters, and then, figuring he might as well, says, "Well—you know how I'm doing these videos for *Gastronome*?"

He lays out the problem for her, explaining, as vaguely as he can bring himself to, about Pete and his stage fright, the performance issues, and how guilty he, Ben, feels about having accidentally created this whole situation in the first place. And, to her credit, Renata listens actively, making little "Mm-hmm" noises or asking the occasional question, sounding utterly unperturbed by all of it. It's honestly soothing, and Ben realizes, slightly embarrassed that it comes as a surprise, that she might in fact be quite good at her job, which to his understanding is, at its core, about playing the chords of various difficult personalities in such a way that they produce beautiful music, instead of unintelligible noise.

And then, even more miraculously, Renata does have some useful advice, which is: "Honestly? Your best bet is probably distracting him. You said the cayenne pepper worked, right? That other sensation to process? I've got actors who have to wear over-tight shoes, you know that, or have a tag stuck inside their clothes just the right way; something to distract them. That's what your boy needs—or, at least, that's what I'd try."

"Huh," Ben says, thoughtfully. "Yeah, that's—thanks."

"No problem," Ren says cheerfully. Then, a note of wickedness entering her tone, she adds, "Now that business is complete, did you want to talk about how you're totally in love with this dude, orrrrr—"

"Good*bye*, Renata," Ben snaps, and hangs up on her before she can say anything else.

When he sets his phone down on the table, Roux, who, Ben thinks darkly, has always liked Ren, leaps up next to it and, with one swift paw, knocks it to the floor. Ben, in getting it, nearly pitches off his chair and decides that perhaps it's time for bed before Renata's dire premonitions are proved right after all, and he dies of his own incompetence. He tells himself, very firmly, that when he wakes up in the morning, he'll come up with an idea for an adequate Pete distraction.

He does not, the following morning, come up with an idea for an adequate Pete distraction. In fact, he tries so hard and comes up with so little that by the time he has a single idea, it seems like a great one.

It is not a great idea. It is, at best, a mediocre idea; in fact, in the hours after he begins to put it into motion, Ben realizes it might be quite a *bad* idea. If it were a morning show Pete were filming, then the idea of getting him so drunk the night before that he was a little hungover would be... Actually, Ben realizes a little grimly, that would still be quite a bad idea. A hangover might be distracting enough to help Pete function, but it also might make him throw up on live television; probably not worth the risk.

But it's *not* a morning show; it's *Late Night Live with Brian O'Malley*, which begins taping at 9:00 p.m. and runs until nearly midnight. Even if Ben gets Pete absolutely sloshed tonight, his hangover will almost certainly be gone by then, so it's not a plan that will solve his problem at all.

However, by the time Ben realizes this, he's already suggested a night out to the kitchen staff, and Pete has already moved some plans around, and Ezra and Adina have already started arguing about which bar they should all go to, so. It seems a bit late to put a stop to things, and Ben doesn't figure it can do any harm. If nothing else, it will be relaxing, right? A nice night out with friends before the hammer falls?

At this point, Ben realizes he's thinking about this evening as something not dissimilar to a last cigarette before the firing squad. Feeling equal parts guilty for his faithlessness and utterly sure it's less faithlessness than an accurate grip on reality, Ben does his best to put such thoughts from his mind and heads out with the group in the genuine spirit of having a good time.

And, for the first hour or so, he has a good time. They all do. They end up at Fox's, a seedy hole-in-the-wall bar that's only a block and a half away from the office, and Pete explains as they walk that they *always* end up at Fox's, because the proximity ends up outweighing any argument. The air is cold and crisp as they make their way up Sixth Avenue, little snowflakes so small as to almost look like a trick of the light drifting lazily around them. Pete's dark hair, peeking out from under yet another beanie, seems to be catching it as they go. The bright white flakes under his striped knitted cap, against his black bomber jacket, make him look like a catalogue model. It makes Ben self-conscious in a way he's not entirely familiar with, and he finds himself trying to subtly scrub the snow from his own dark hair until he sees Pete looking at him, smiling.

The quality of that smile—the soft, knowing warmth—Ben can't parse it or place it at all. It stays with him, though, as their little group digs into a corner of the bar, wrapping around his heart the way a vine can grow around a tree: gently enough at first, and then tightening to the point of exquisite, reshaping agony.

Maybe that's why he's not prepared for what happens; maybe it's because he doesn't know enough to *be* prepared. Maybe it's because when the conversation turns to most embarrassing moments, Ben's two drinks deep, and not entirely at his sharpest.

Regardless, he doesn't see the harm in it when, after Adina confesses to some shame about a mistake she made during a class she taught last week, Ezra suggests a little contest.

"Everyone submits, for the judges, an embarrassing moment," Ezra says, with a sharp little grin. "Adina, you can go with that one or submit another, if you want. Regardless, everyone goes, and the most embarrassing moment wins. Does everyone agree to the rules?"

There's a chorus of yeses; later, Ben will kick himself for not noticing whether or not Pete was one of them. They're separated by a few people—Ben had been ordering drinks when the table had been claimed, and couldn't very well say, "Get up, Ezra, I want to sit next to Pete," when he returned. Not with any dignity, anyway. He doesn't hear Pete's voice among the rabble, but then, it's hard to pick out anyone's voice from a chorus of yeses in a crowded bar. Ben doesn't think anything of it.

This is a mistake.

Ezra goes first. He tells a very amusing story about getting caught backstage *in flagrante delicto* with Kenickie during a college performance of *Grease*; the detail of it having been at his conservative, all-male college adds to the humor, as does the fact that apparently, they were making creative use of some of the props. But Ben notices, as Ezra tells it, that he doesn't seem that embarrassed by it, and that ultimately it isn't a story that makes him look particularly bad. In fact, by the time he's done, he seems very pleased with himself and the reception the tale has received from the group, and Ben half wonders if he brought up the topic for the excuse to tell it.

Brogan goes next, and that's a good and proper embarrassing story, one involving a fishing boat, a malfunctioning bikini top, and the particularly ill-timed emergence of both a passing whale-watching cruise and a humpback whale. Ben laughs nearly to the point of tears as she tells it; the only thing that takes away from it is her brash, no-nonsense energy, how clear it is that, while she knows objectively it's embarrassing, it never bothered her. Also, she goes into such extensive detail about the fish she caught on the journey that Ben, who is starting to really feel his third drink, begins to hazily suspect her of being Rick's daughter.

Adina, whose honestly fairly milquetoast work story kicked the whole thing off to begin with, volunteers to go next, and tells a frankly equally milquetoast story about a childhood family trip, which revolves around her laughing so hard that she shot milk out of her nose in the middle of a packed deli in Cleveland. This makes Pete, usually so affable, mutter, "God, is that the standard for an embarrassing story? I'd better sit this one out."

It is, Ben realizes, the first time Pete's spoken in a while. For once, he hasn't been paying attention; the stories have been revealing and interesting, if not necessarily in the way the people telling them meant them to be, and anyway Ben's been doing his level best not to stare at Pete too obviously. He regrets it now. There's a quality to Pete's tone, to the hunch of his shoulders, to the strained, tight look in his eyes, that reminds Ben of the energy he puts off when the camera is rolling.

Naturally—and oh, Ben could kill him for it—Ezra, several drinks deep himself, seems to take this as a challenge. "Come *on*," he says, in a wheedling tone. "The *rest* of us are doing it—"

"Famously a great reason to do something," Pete says, his tone ringing with so many obvious warning sirens that Ben's amazed Ezra can't seem to hear a single one. "Not at *all* the sort of sentence that has led to some of history's worst decisions—"

"Oh my *God*, don't be a such *baby*," Ezra says, rolling his eyes. "You can just tell us a boring story like Adina's—"

"Hey!" Adina snaps, glaring at him over the rim of her glass. Ben notices, warmed by it a little in spite of his growing apprehension, that her eyes dart briefly to Pete as she says it, as though she too has picked up on the same tension Ben's noticed. "Just because my story doesn't involve the worst thing I've *ever* heard of someone doing with a pom-pom—"

"You need to get out more," Ezra says, although Ben, having also heard the pom-pom story, thinks that the reality is maybe that Ezra needs to get out less. Even so, he finds himself wishing Ezra *would* get out, would go *anywhere else*, when he turns back to Pete and says, "Seriously, man, it's your turn. We all agreed—"

"Did we?" Pete's voice is low, rumbling now. "Or did you all agree, while I sat here silently, because I would *never* agree to—"

"Listen, you should let me go; I'm going to win anyway," someone says; oh no, wait. *Ben* said it, before he could think about it, before he could remind himself that the last thing he wants to tell Pete is the story that lead-in demands. But, God help him, it's already *come out of his mouth*, and Pete is giving off a trapped-animal-lashing-out energy that, in Ben's experience, never leads to anything good. So, in for a penny, he carries on. "I can pretty much guarantee you I've got the most embarrassing story here. Might not be any point hearing Pete's, really. You'll see what I mean if you let me tell it."

Ezra looks at him like he's bitten a lemon; Ben raises an eyebrow back. Finally, sounding irritated about it, Ezra snaps, "Oh, *fine*, then. If you must."

"Well, I started messing around with video editing when I was in middle school," Ben says. He tries, as he talks, to lean into how much he's had to drink, to sound confident and over it and like it never bothered him at all. It's easier, now, than it's ever been—it always is, with each telling of it. "So by high school, I sort of knew what I was doing, and I started helping out with some audio-video stuff in my spare time." He keeps from them, though it's the more complete truth, that he'd done this mostly because it kept him out of Trattoria Luciana until as late as five or six at night, and thus generally got him out of being asked to cover a call-off.

"Thrilling so far," Ezra says, with a pointed yawn.

Ben ignores him. And since he can't bring himself to look at Pete, or anywhere that might risk making eye contact with Pete, as he tells this particular story, he focuses his eyes on the dartboard on the far wall as he continues, "And every year my school did this big boring assembly right before Christmas break, giving out like, honors to the teachers, and talking about the year to come. So they were doing one of those, and I was supposed to play a video on the big screen, a like 'Our District's Year in Review' type of thing? Only..." Ben swallows, trying to force back the resistance clawing at his throat—it was years ago. It's funny! It's not like it matters now. Still, he's proud of the way the ache doesn't show in his voice as he says, "It, uh. It wasn't that video... that I played."

For all Ezra's complaining, he sits for a beat of breathless, anticipatory silence with the rest of them, and then, very satisfyingly for Ben, snaps, "Well? What was it?"

"It was," Ben says, and closes his eyes briefly, surprised to find himself laughing on the words a little for all they're still mortifying. "Well, it was a shot-for-shot recreation of an episode of *Star Trek?* The one where Kirk and Spock seem, um, really gay for each other? More than the usual amount of gay, I mean. And I was kind of... playing all the parts." In the yawning silence, unable to totally stop the words as they tumble out of his mouth, Ben can't help but add, "And, um... once it started playing, the computer I was using froze, so it took—about ten minutes? To get it to stop? And the whole school was there? So. Ah. You know. Hard to top that one."

The silence is, for a moment, quite painful. Then someone snickers; a second later they're all laughing, some harder than others, even Ben. There are tears running down Brogan's face; Adina has gone so red from amusement she looks like a tomato; even Ezra is howling, shaking his head, chuckling, "All right, all right—you're right. Can't beat that, good *Lord*."

The only person who isn't laughing is Pete: When Ben finally turns to look at him, there's a smile on his face, to be sure, but not an amused one. He looks—glad, maybe, or grateful. The word "fond" floats by in Ben's slightly overserved mind, and he tries, as it does, not to notice it.

But Pete mouths, "Thank you," while the rest of them are looking away, so clearly sincere that Ben can hardly bear it. They hold eye contact for a long moment, and then Brogan asks who wants another round, and the conversation turns, and before long the bar is spitting them back out again, all a bit unsteadier and somewhat worse for the wear, but in good enough spirits.

In a happy coincidence, Pete and Ben are both walking the same way for a few blocks; they break off from the others and set out again, the air colder now than it was a few hours ago. The snow is still falling, the flakes thicker and more aggressive, and Pete sounds almost wistful when he says, "Okay. Don't tell the others or anything, but: You want to know my most embarrassing story?"

"Oh," Ben says; it's an exhalation more than a word, and for a hanging, confused second Ben entertains the thought that it's shock freezing his breath in the air. Then, recovering himself enough to speak, he stammers, "Oh, but you didn't want... You don't have to—"

"It's okay." Pete shrugs, and then, slanting a wry, slightly self-effacing glance at him, adds, "It's not like you haven't seen me at my lowest, right? Anyway, you told me yours; it's only fair."

"But," Ben argues, not sure why he's doing so even as the words come out of his mouth—after all, he *is* desperate to know. "So did the others, and you didn't want to tell—"

"Eh," Pete says, waving a hand. "They didn't really. Ezra *wanted* to tell that story, you know? I think he brought the whole thing up just to tell it. Brogan, okay, that *was* a good one, but she wasn't *embarrassed*, I don't think. She knows it would be embarrassing, for someone who embarrassed more easily than she does, but I'm not sure anything embarrasses Brogan. And Adina..." Pete sighs, and shakes his head, a little smile slipping onto his face that makes a brief and irrational jealous rage flare within Ben, for all he likes Adina, and knows her to have been happily married to Tom for more than a decade. "Both those stories were genuinely embarrassing *for Adina*, but I'm not sure she's ever been bad at anything in her whole life. She's great, don't get me wrong, I love her like a sister, but she doesn't know, I don't think. Not what it's *really* like, to be properly, publicly humiliated, and then have to carry it around with you, how that felt. None of them know." He slants another glance at Ben, assessing this time, before he sighs and says, "But *you* do. Don't you?"

"Yeah," Ben says, after a second, with an uncomfortable shrug. "I guess I do."

Pete nods sharply, just the once. "Right. So it's different, okay? Telling you is—it's not the same. It's just not."

"Okay," Ben says quietly, afraid to put too much volume behind the word. A little part of him, less than logical but quite upsettingly strong, is sure that Pete will take it back, say he didn't mean it, if Ben draws too much attention to the fact that he's said it at all.

He's distracted anyway, as they reach the edge of Bryant Park; to his surprise and pleasure, Ben realizes the Winter Village has opened for the season at some point in the last few weeks. It's always up this time of year, transforming the park's open courtyard into a series of little pop-up shops and restaurants, but he hasn't been by, too wrapped up in everything at work. There's a large, if temporary, outdoor ice rink set up in the center of everything, multicolored string lights and a steady backdrop of Christmas music making even the sloppy, stumbling skaters currently on the ice look picturesque.

The holiday season has never meant much to Ben; every year back home in Michigan had been pretty much the same, with his parents constantly trying to balance things out between Hanukkah, Christmas, and the restaurant, and inevitably ending up giving the bulk of their attention to the restaurant. But he likes the Bryant Park Winter Village, and has ever since he stumbled upon it his first year here; it was his first taste of New York's tendency to deliver unto you, on an otherwise unremarkable day, a small wonder.

"Want to go in for a minute?" Pete asks, following Ben's gaze. "I haven't been yet this year, and I could really go for a beverage that *doesn't* have alcohol in it. And, uh. It might be easier to talk about this not, you know." He ducks his head and looks away for a second. "Surrounded by a bunch of people?"

"Oh," Ben says, surprised and pleased both to have been asked to go in, and that Pete had noticed he wanted to go in at all. "Sure, yeah. If, um... if you don't mind. That sounds nice."

They end up getting hot chocolates, which is to say Pete gets them each a hot chocolate, and Ben manfully resists the urge to shout, "DOES IT COUNT AS A DATE IF HE BOUGHT ME A HOT CHOCOLATE??? ISSUE A RULING AT ONCE," at random passersby. But it's good, rich and nicely spiced and warming, and Ben follows Pete over to a tiny wrought-iron table tucked up against one of the hedges marking the park boundaries. It's in an odd place and looks like maybe it was forgotten or left behind when they reset the area for the Village, but it gives a good view of the ice rink and is fairly well isolated from everyone else.

They sit in silence for a moment, sipping their hot chocolates. Then Ben says, "Did you want to tell me the story, or...?"

Pete grimaces briefly, then shakes his head, then sighs, then nods. "Okay. Yeah. God. So—do you remember, back in like the eighties and nineties, a show called *America's Best Home Videos*?"

"Oh, sure," Ben says, his brow furrowing as he tries both to bring up the show and imagine why on earth it would be relevant. "The host was—that guy from that show, right?"

Pete gives him a sideways little smile, and says, "Okay, well, technically, that could be anyone, but I'll grant you that I know who you mean, so. Yeah, that was him." He sighs and takes another sip of his hot chocolate with the same energy that someone might sip at a stiff whiskey for strength. "Anyway, my parents recorded this, well... home video, right? Of me. And I was maybe seven or eight, and learning to skateboard, and so I was kicking around in front of the restaurant, and I hit a rock." He shrugs, his mouth twisting. "Sometimes that's all it takes, you know? You hit a rock and then, ten years later—hell, sorry, I'm getting ahead of myself."

"It's really fine," Ben says, a little at sea but hoping to be encouraging. "I'm not, like, grading you here. There will be no scorecards at the end of this process."

Pete nods, and takes a breath, and says, "Well, I hit the stupid rock, right, and I went flying through the air, and I happened to be holding a water bottle, which I squeezed in surprise, and so I also managed to squirt myself in the face. But I landed on the grass, which was lucky, and didn't get hurt, and when my dad watched the footage back later, he realized he'd inadvertently zoomed in while it was all happening, and that the video was pretty entertaining. He and my mother showed it to a few people who all found it really funny, and then one of them—they're *still* arguing about which one, even ten years after splitting up—decided to send it into the show, which aired it."

Ben grimaces. He knows how bad it was to be humiliated as a kid in front of his own school; on a national television show sounds horrifying. "Dude, I'm *sorry*. That must have been hard."

Pete laughs, though not as though he finds it funny; it's a bleak laugh, a sad one. "Honestly, it wasn't; I wish it had just been that. I didn't even see it air, and the kids I was at school with mostly didn't watch it, either—it was on pretty late. If the parents and teachers knew, they kept it to themselves. But." And here Pete's shoulders square, and his jaw works, and his voice is tight when he finally says, "Someone videotaped it, back then. When it aired. Someone videotaped it, and they liked that particular clip so much that a few years later, they uploaded it to one of the very first streaming video sites, where it was one of the very first videos to ever go viral. And then someone else—no way to know who—but *someone* else enjoyed that viral video so much that they made it into a meme. You might remember it; imagine this face I'm making, except on like a seven-year-old version of me, and over the words Womp Womp." Pete contorts his face into a pantomime of shocked distress before, wincing, he adds, "Ringing any bells?"

As he stares at Pete, Ben feels the blood drain from his face, because—yeah. *Yes*. Ben has never been particularly online; Renata had been the one, of the two of them, willing to fight to the death for use of the desktop computer the whole family had shared when Ben was growing up, and it had set the tone for the rest of his adult life. He has social media, an online presence, but he doesn't use it very much, and he's certainly not up on whatever memes are circulating at any given moment.

But... the early 2000s Womp Womp Water Bottle Kid meme? Of course Ben had seen that; *everyone* had seen that. It was like that stupid interrogative owl, or the cats and their insatiable desire for cheezburger, or that one movie still full of information vis-à-vis whether or not one can simply walk into Mordor: a foundational piece of the early internet, something built into the weird, unconstrained bones. It would have been seen and saved and shared by people all over the world, been written into the code of websites as a gag, and then on sheer longevity become part of internet history, to be preserved *forever*. It's probably, Ben realizes with a wash of horror, in *textbooks*.

"Oh my *God*," Ben says, putting his hot chocolate down a little too abruptly. Still full, it splashes a little out of the top of the lid, sliding down the side of the cup; Ben doesn't care. He feels, honestly, a little nauseous. "Dude, that's—that's *horrible*, Pete. It must have been—" Ben blinks, trying to cast the net of his own creative empathy as far as it will go, and pulls in nothing but air. "I can't even imagine how it must have been. I'm so sorry."

Pete stares at him for a second, his head cocked to the side, and then huffs out a soft laugh. "Oh, thanks. I wouldn't say it was a great experience, no." He grimaces, and then waves a hand, like he's trying to wipe some of the grime of the memory away. "But, you know. It all happened out in front of my father's restaurant, so. Castillo's ended up getting famous off it, which I guess is kind of nice."

When Ben's face creases in puzzlement, Pete explains: His father's restaurant, Castillo's, sits under a big eighties neon sign bearing its name near the Newark waterfront. The logo on Pete's shirt that day had been a printed version of the sign. When he went on *America's Best Home Movies*, traffic from locals saw a little bump, but when the meme went viral a few years later, the restaurant took off with it. Apparently, there are all kinds of people on the internet who enjoy doing things like taking photos in front of the sign, or recreating the meme themselves, to the best of their ability. "It is," Pete admits, when he shares this part, "pretty funny to look out the window and see people squirting water in their own faces, but I wouldn't call it worth it."

"Honestly, I'd think it was worse," Ben says, as lightly as he can. "Not the water part—that does sound funny—but, like, it making the restaurant famous or whatever. That just sounds... complicated." Ben winces, and adds, "Then again, the whole thing sounds complicated, and like a total nightmare, so what do I know?"

"No," Pete says, and sighs. "You're right. It is complicated. It's hard, and weird, and I don't know how to talk about it, even now. When I was a teenager, it was *so* awful—I still hadn't grown into my face, so I looked a lot like I did as a kid, so people recognized me all the time. *And,* because my name was Pete Castillo back then, even if they didn't know it was me at *first,* the second I introduced myself, I'd see it wash over them." He shakes his head, an unusual sour note entering his tone. "I didn't want it to follow me all my life, so I changed my name, and now I'm a Bailey, like my mom's family. Even though it was my dad's family who raised me, and all my sisters kept Castillo even after they got married, and made sure their kids were Castillos, and I haven't even seen my mom in years—but what does that matter, really? Oh, and she remarried, and she took *his* name even though she never took my father's, because of course, right? So now there are a bunch of new little baby Castillos running around, which is great, and she's Laurie Cholmondeley, which is great, and I'm the last Bailey standing. Which is great."

It does not sound like Pete thinks this is great. It sounds like Pete thinks this is so far from great that he'd like to scream for one thousand years, or take a baseball bat to a series of china shops, or drive an ATV through a garden party about it. Ben does not, however, think it would be helpful to point this out.

Unfortunately, before he has time to process what he's just learned, let alone consider what *would* be helpful, Ben's stupid, reckless mouth decides to soldier on ahead. "I have to say, I have some questions about your mother's logic, in terms of last name decisions. Keeping Bailey—fine, respectable. My own mother told my father that if he insisted she change her name to Blumenthal, he'd live to regret it, and I think my sister, Renata, intends to tell whoever she eventually deigns to marry the same thing, so I get that. But... Cholmondeley? She wouldn't take Castillo, but she'll take Cholmondeley? No offense to anyone named Cholmondeley, of course, but she's going to spend *so* much time telling people how to *spell* it—"

It's a silly line of conversation, an asinine one. But Pete is laughing anyway, his slightly shaking shoulders seeming to dislodge the dark blanket of despair that's been draped over them since they left the bar. "You know, I never even thought about that? But you're right, I bet it's a nightmare."

He seems relieved to find them swimming in lighter conversational waters, so Ben lets them paddle in the shallow end for a few minutes. The conversation drifts, from name spellings to whether or not either of them had any childhood nicknames to a riotously funny story about Pete and two of his three sisters attempting to sneak out in the middle of the night, in hopes of conning their way into an R-rated movie at the cinema down the street. They had all been under the age of twelve, and also the man working the cinema counter that day had happened to be their uncle, from whom they had heard about the movie in question in the first place. He had ended up chasing them all the way back home, yelling at them about how much trouble he'd be in with their father, which had woken their father, who had, indeed, been annoyed.

It's a nice story, one that feeds, though does not satiate, Ben's vast appetite for details about Pete's early life. But mostly, he's grateful for the way it makes Pete sit easier, sound easier, than he did when they arrived. It's getting harder and harder, as the weeks pass, for Ben to bear the anguish of Pete's unhappiness, to hold himself together while Pete's obviously struggling. He cares too much, he thinks, shifting uncomfortably to realize it. No one had ever warned him it would be such a liability.

He's still curious, though, feels in some ways like he has *more* questions than he did before Pete told him this story. He's opening his mouth to ask his most pressing one—that is, why on *earth* Pete is still *doing the show*, if this hideous story is, very understandably, the source of his hatred of cameras—when the tree branch next to them, which has been slowly gathering snow, reaches a breaking point. It snaps, dropping snow across the table, and all over Ben and Pete; they both jump up, shocked first and then laughing, and brush themselves off.

And from there, as Ben finds it often goes with Pete, things just... happen. They're falling into step in mutual, tacit agreement that it's time to go; they're walking to the closest subway stop, even though Pete doesn't need to go to the subway, and surely, Ben realizes as they reach the entrance, needed to turn off the other way a block or two back. When he says as much, Pete shrugs easily and says, "I wanted to walk you. Thanks for listening. Have a good night, okay?" Then he's walking off, black bomber jacket disappearing into the haze of the snow.

Who walks you to the subway, Pete? Ben thinks at his retreating back. It's pointless, nonsensical; surely, the answer is Chris, if nothing else. But knowing that it doesn't matter, doesn't stop the rest of it from lining up inside his mind: *Who makes sure you get home all right? Who checks in to make sure you're not doing too much? If you're the last Bailey standing, and you're always looking after everyone, then who's looking after you?*

Pete's back, barely visible now, doesn't reply. Ben sighs, and shakes his head, and descends into the station, certain the thought will dog his heels all the way home.

NINE

The next morning dawns painfully—some might even say *agonizingly*—bright. At least, Ben thinks so, although it might be his hangover talking. He pours himself out of bed like so much blackstrap molasses, feeling equally bitter and ill-suited to most basic cooking tasks, and elects not to bother making himself breakfast. He stops at the nearest bodega, waits in an interminably long line, and orders a bacon, egg, and cheese instead, grimly housing it on the sidewalk directly outside. He barely tastes it, but dutifully chews and swallows anyway, willing the grease to revive him.

It doesn't really, and so Ben makes his way through his Friday morning meeting block on twenty-seven with bad grace, snappish and jumpy and sharper than he usually allows himself to be at the office. People notice; Jessica, standing ten feet away and holding a can of disinfectant spray in front of her as though it's some kind of weapon, asks if he's feeling all right. He is not feeling all right—he is feeling as though someone has taken a jackhammer to the back of his head, and also as though he'd like to be roundly sick into whatever trash can's nearest. When she eagerly shoos him out before the next conference call can start, he happily goes.

He stops up at the *Gastronome* offices intending just to say hello—his edits on the Thanksgiving videos are all done and submitted to S&P, and he's already thrown together a run of show for each Christmas video, and he does like the thought of being a lot less conscious for a good long while. But he wants to make sure that Pete's... well, that Pete's not laid up with a worse hangover than Ben's, or wigging out too much about being only hours away from tonight's dreaded *Late Night Live* appearance. That Pete's *okay*. That's not such a horrible thing for Ben to want, is it? Friends want their friends to be okay, after all, don't they? Ben could mean it in an entirely platonic way, this concern he feels for Pete. He *doesn't*, of course, but the fact that he could seems important.

But Pete isn't okay, as it turns out. He isn't okay at all.

Ben can tell, from the minute he walks in, that Pete's starting to really panic, but he's not sure the rest of the kitchen can. They seem to dismiss Pete's pacing and muttering to himself, the way his hair is all but standing on end from the times he's run his fingers through it, as "Pete being Pete," and nothing worth worrying about. Ben, however, is worrying about it, both the rest of the staff's comfort with it—how often has he been *like* this?—and how this sort of energy is going to play on *Late Night Live with Brian O'Malley*. Ben thinks the answer to that second question is probably "very badly," but he can't think of a tactful way to point this out.

But when Pete turns to him, a pleading look in his eyes, and says, "Look, Ben, I'm sure you have plans already, right, and I'm sorry to even ask, but I'm freaked out about this, honestly. About how it's going to go tonight. And with the videos, it's always—you always make it—ugh." He stops, makes a frustrated little noise, and then, sounding like it's costing him to do it, says, "Would you, um... Is there any chance you might come with me? I'm supposed to be there at eight thirty tonight and I don't even know what I'm *wearing* and the lady on the phone said I could bring a guest if I wanted and I *know* it's last minute but—"

"Sure," Ben says, quiet and steady, mostly to stem the tide of increasingly anxious words flowing out of Pete's mouth. "Sure, I can come. Where should I meet you? When?"

"Really?" Pete's staring at him with round, shocked eyes, like Ben's water in the middle of a desert, or an unexpected six-figure check. "But... you don't have plans?"

Ben's plans had in fact been to call in three orders of soup dumplings from Nom Wah, eat about half of them, and then fall asleep on the couch in front of whatever movie appealed to him most in the moment. Smiling winsomely, his hangover utterly forgotten, he says, "I think I can move some things around."

By the time he's standing on the corner of Sixth Avenue and West Fiftieth Street waiting to meet Pete that night, Ben is feeling less confident that he's made the right choice. He's beginning to think his original plan for tonight was really the way to go. It's not that he minds being Pete's moral support—it's that 30 Rockefeller Plaza, where the show films, is only a few blocks away from the Formica Media building, so Ben had suggested they get dinner before they go. This was a mistake, since then he'd had to try very hard not to take it personally when Pete begged off, apologizing, saying something about having to head back to Jersey early, and that the turn-around was going to be tight to get to the studio. It's not that Ben didn't believe him when he said it—Pete had certainly seemed sincere enough, and he's not the type to lie—but his belief has waned somewhat since then. In its place is the dark, snarling, persistent thought that Ben had *made it weird* by suggesting dinner, and that when Pete does arrive, he'll wish Ben had stayed at home.

The street corner is cold, and the building Ben is leaning against to stay out of the crush of people is cold, and the world itself is cold, the air biting and sharp. Perhaps that's why Ben feels almost frozen, as though a thin sheet of ice has descended over him like a cloak, a transparent, frigid barrier between him and the rest of the city. Pete's late, almost ten minutes past the time they were set to meet—maybe he already went in. Maybe he got here early in order to avoid Ben entirely, so that later he can send Ben a text that says, *Hey, I know you were coming onto me earlier, but fyi I've got a boyfriend, and am way hotter than you, and think you're gross, and have filed a sexual harassment claim, and also you're fired.* Maybe he and the other test cooks have *all* decided they *hate* Ben, and never want to *see* him again, and this is *exactly* why it's easier not to put himself out there in the *first* place, and—

"Oh, thank God, I thought maybe you'd have left," Pete gasps, all in one breath, bursting through the flow of people to collapse against the wall next to him. The icy sheet of despair around Ben shatters spectacularly, and he smiles as his world warms up. "I'm sorry, I'm sorry, my sister promised me she'd be back at six and she didn't show up until six fifteen and then the *ferry* was slow and I couldn't get service—"

"Pete, hey, take a breath," Ben says; he looks down and realizes his hand is on Pete's arm without having ever received clearance to land, but Pete doesn't shake him off, so he decides, for now, to press on. "It's fine. You're still ten minutes early for your call time; I didn't leave. It's all okay."

Pete stares at him for a second, and then nods, sucking in a huge breath. And then another. And then a third. After the fourth one, Ben says, "Pete? Are you... um... good?"

"I don't want to do this, man," Pete says, his voice low. "It's going to be so bad, everyone's going to *see* it, it's going to be that whole mess when I was a kid all over again—"

"Hey," Ben says, with a confidence he doesn't feel, and squeezes Pete's arm lightly. "It's not going to be like that again. For one thing, it's not the early 2000s anymore; when's the last time you've seen someone rolling around in a pair of Heelies?" Pete laughs, so Ben, encouraged, continues. "Also, you're an adult, and also, sorry, but: You're a disaster on camera like multiple times per week anyway?"

"Thanks," Pete says dryly, but he sounds grimly amused now, as opposed to panicked. "That means a lot, really."

"Hey," Ben says, letting go of Pete's arm because he *definitely* should have already, "I'm not knocking you being a disaster on camera! As it turns out, that works for people. It's practically a superpower, so there's no point in worrying about it. This? One measly little five-minute segment on a show people regularly forget is even on? It's all going to be fine, man, even if you screw something up. You'll see—there's only so off the rails this can go."

Ben means this very sincerely. He's also very sincerely wrong.

The first impression Ben has of Studio 8B, where *Late Night Live with Brian O'Malley* has apparently been filming for the last fourteen years, is not dissimilar to stepping into some incredibly loud mass event, like a rock concert, or maybe gladiatorial combat. There are so many *people*, all of them running and shouting urgently to one another—someone is frantically doing makeup on an actor who appears to be asleep across a desk—there's a large sign plastered up against one wall which reads: LATE NIGHT LIVE: IF YOU CAN READ THIS, GOOD LUCK!

He glances over at Pete, and is unsurprised to find him looking terrified.

Ben doesn't get a chance to say anything to him, though. Frankly, Ben doesn't even get a chance to take in their surroundings, beyond observing that they seem to be in a long, wide hallway containing several chairless desks, off which there are a number of doors leading to God knows what. Regardless, they aren't there long; they're approached immediately by a harried-looking, dark-haired woman holding a pen and a clipboard, who snaps, "Pete Bailey? Jesus Christ, finally, it took you long enough! You were supposed to be here an hour ago."

"I was?" Pete looks baffled. "Miranda told me—"

"Who on earth is—actually, you know what, I don't care and it doesn't matter," the woman says. "I'm Priyali; I'm the associate director. Is this what you're wearing? Who are you?"

It takes Ben a second to realize she's speaking to him; she's still looking at Pete, seeming to be attempting to measure him with her eyes. Feeling enormously stupid about it, Ben says, "Oh, I'm, uh... Ben? Ben Blumenthal? I'm the video editor, um, on the—"

"We didn't ask for you, Ben Blumenthal," Priyali says, glancing briefly at her clipboard, before sighing and shaking her head at Pete. "Well, it's too late now, it'll have to do. Why are you here?"

Again, it takes Ben a second to parse that he's the one being spoken to. "Oh. I'm..." God. Why *is* Ben here? What could he possibly say? *I'm the reason this all happened, so I am performing ritualistic penance by observing what dread horrors my hubris has wrought?* Or, perhaps, would it be more accurate to offer, *Since you ask, I am desperately in love with this man who I have trapped in his own personal version of hell; he asked me to be here, and I'd do basically anything he asked me to do, simply because I'd be so pleased to be the one he asked to do it!* Maybe he should just go for broke and say, *Sorry, lady, you'll have to ask Pete, because if I were him, I think I'd be about the last person I'd ask to come with me for—*

"Moral support," Pete says, bringing Ben's entire train of thought to a grinding, shuddering halt. "Is why he's here. Is that allowed? I'm not saying he has to come onstage with me or anything, just—"

"Fine, whatever, I don't care," Priyali says, and points her pen at Ben. "Don't burn the studio down or anything, got it? If you being here becomes a me problem, that's going to become a you problem, are we clear?"

"Crystal," Ben mutters, sinking into the heels of his shoes. "It'll be like I'm not even here."

Ben means this as a promise, not a prediction, but in the end it *is* a little bit like he isn't even there. Pete is whisked into a room full of mirrors and makeup chairs and seen to briefly by a makeup artist who is not currently occupied with a passed-out actor in the hallway, while Ben stands awkwardly behind him. Then Pete is, after all, pushed into wardrobe, where he is made to exchange his button-down shirt and bomber jacket for a clinging black T-shirt, while Ben stands awkwardly behind him. Then Pete is dragged into a greenroom, where he is briefed extensively and pointedly by Priyali on what's going to happen, while Ben stands awkwardly behind him.

They don't get a chance to talk, or even exchange more than one or two speaking looks, before Priyali is saying, "Well, that's it, you're up, if you wanted more prep time, you should've been *on* time, let's go, up and at 'em," and dragging Pete off towards the stage doors. Ben tries his level best to follow awkwardly behind, but Priyali shoos him off, telling him to go lurk on the side of the soundstage if he must, but to leave her alone. Pete casts a desperate look over her shoulder, but when Ben tries again to follow them, Priyali snaps, "One more step and I'm calling security, Blumenthal; I don't have the time *or* the energy tonight." Ben, at this point, has no choice but to hold up his hands, a gesture both of surrender to her and, rather more emphatically, apology to Pete.

They're out of sight a moment after Ben stops walking, ducking through a door and vanishing to parts unknown, so Ben follows the signs in the large hallway for the soundstage.

The second he walks through the double doors into that enormous, open area, Ben realizes his mistake. Or, rather, Ben realizes his mistakes, plural; there are several. He's been on soundstages before, hasn't he? In college, on various trips and studio visits he got the chance to attend through his classes, and once or twice as an interested visitor in adulthood, justifying it as an education experience to pay for a guided studio tour. Plus, of course, there's the fact that he's made a *career* in the video and film industry, and so has spent a fair amount of time thinking and talking about the mechanics of how any given show or movie is shot.

So it hadn't occurred to him, the way it *should* have occurred to him, the way it is occurring to him *now*, that he should have *prepared* Pete. He should have warned Pete that shows like this are shot on a large, constructed soundstage with, and this is the important part, anywhere from *three to five huge cameras* pointed directly at it. This particular soundstage, Ben notes with a slightly hysterical alarm, has four huge cameras; great. Only three more than Pete already can't bear to be in front of.

But, of course, the cameras are not the only problem. It's not that Ben isn't familiar with the phrase "Filmed before a live studio audience." It's not even as though he's never *seen* a live studio audience before—he's seen several studio audiences, and been in a few himself, and they've all been, to the best of his knowledge, one hundred percent populated by fully alive people only. But Ben has never seen a live studio audience for an actual *live production* before; every time he's been in or around one, it's been for something that was being taped, and would pass, before being broadcast, beneath the merciful eyes of an editor.

No such eyes will pass over *Late Night Live with Brian O'Malley*, unless you count Ben's helpless ones; the audience knows this. Ben's not even totally sure how he can tell—if it's something about the body language, the looks on their faces, what. But somehow, to look at the crowd in front of that stage is to know that everyone in it is thinking something along the lines of, *God, I hope something crazy happens tonight.*

Ben swallows as the theme music begins to play; when Brian O'Malley walks onstage, he takes a breath. Pete's the first guest, and according to Priyali, he just has to chat a little bit about himself, like a normal person, for two minutes. Then there will be a commercial break, and then he'll have a brief five-minute cooking segment. Barely a cooking segment, really! Pete's just making a cocktail and searing off a steak that's already been cooked sous vide —even Renata could do that, and she's always been hopeless in the kitchen.

"It's going to be fine," Ben whispers to himself, more a prayer than anything else. "It's going to be fine."

Thirty minutes later, when he and Pete are shivering together in front of the studio, bathed in the striating red-and-white glow of the fire truck lights, Ben says, "Do you know, I think I jinxed it?"

Pete's voice is hollow, like his eyes, like his laugh, which is less a laugh and more a flat and toneless, "Ha. It was you, huh? *You* turned the burner up as high as it would go, and then *you* glugged enough oil into the stupid pan to *country fry* the damn steak, and then *you* were the one who dumped *water* on a *grease* fire? That was you?"

"Ah," Ben says carefully, because, no. That had all been Pete. "Well. That's not *exactly* what I'm saying—"

"Water on a grease fire." Pete shakes his head, looking haunted. "I've known better since I was ten—younger, probably. If my father sees this, I'm *never* going to hear the end of it. Why did I *do* that? And why did I *say* any of that stuff, in the interview part, that was... I mean, *why?*" He folds his arms over his chest, still wearing nothing but the tight black T-shirt Priyali put him in, and moans, "I couldn't stop thinking about all the *cameras*, and all the *people*, and it was like my body was just... moving on its own! Making terrible decisions! He asked me if there were any signs in my early life that I'd be into cooking and I said *Virgo*, Ben! I'm not even a Virgo! I'm a Taurus! And it doesn't matter! I only know because one of my exes told me it's why I was so stubborn, and I think he just wanted me to pet-sit for his turtle!"

Ben, who *is* a Virgo, and who knows this because Renata is constantly sending him weird memes that say things like "Big Virgo Energy" invariably followed by the words *it u*, decides now is not the moment to say so. Instead, carefully, he offers, "Anyone could have been confused—"

"Could anyone have burned down the studio?" Pete says this with a wildness that makes Ben grimace.

Still. "You didn't burn down the studio," Ben says, in the most soothing voice he can muster. "You, okay, you lightly singed a small section of the soundstage; I'm sure that's happened hundreds— well, dozens—*well*, I'm sure you're not the first person to set something on fire in Studio 8B, anyway. But it's all still there—"

"They had to evacuate the *building*—"

"Only the floor we were on!" Ben protests. Then, at Pete's

narrow-eyed glare, he admits, a little more honestly, "Well, okay, and the two floors above us and the three floors below that, so a total of six floors, but! It's a big building! There are—uh—well, the elevator had buttons up to seventy, so that's, what? Six over seventy, uh... like, eight percent? They had to evacuate eight percent of the building; that's practically no evacuation at all. That's *closer* to no evacuation than it is to evacuating everyone."

For the first time since they walked—well, ran, pursued by an employee in an orange FLOOR FIRE SAFETY OFFICER vest screaming, "This is real, people! This is not a drill!"—out of the building, Pete looks something other than dead inside. One eyebrow quirking up, he asks, "Did you just do that calculation in your head?"

"Oh," Ben says, surprised, but before he can answer, Brian O'Malley is walking up to them. He's still wearing the tailored blue suit he was sporting behind the desk during taping, and there's a dark jacket in his hand, swung up over his left shoulder. His carefully structured coif of thin, wheat-blond hair is being utterly destroyed by the wind, but if he notices, he doesn't seem to care. He walks up to Pete and Ben with the confidence of a man who has been famous long enough to burn away any concerns of what anyone thinks of him, and claps Pete, hard, on the shoulder.

"I tell you what," Brian says, shaking his head, "I'm still not sure if your little schtick is on purpose or not—it *has* to be, right? But if it is, having met you—then you're *too* good at it, man. It's unsettling. The ratings for tonight are *crazy*, and Priyali got our social team to upload the clip right away, and it's already everywhere." Hand still on Pete's shoulder, Brian peers at him, his expression tightening. "But if you're not doing it on purpose, right, then ratings or not, I think maybe I did a bad thing, asking the team to book you. The sort of thing that wouldn't sit right with me. If that's the case—" And here he swings the jacket off his shoulder, pulls out a business card, and tucks it into the inner pocket. Ben realizes it's Pete's bomber jacket at the same moment, handing it back to Pete, Brian finishes, "Then you give me a call, all right?"

Pete stares, blankly, from Brian to the jacket he, Pete, is now clutching tightly in one hand. "But... I burned your studio down!"

Brian grins. "Nah," he says, waving a hand. "It's seen worse. Anyway, anything's better than the week we had the horses." He nods to Pete, and then, to Ben's surprise, to Ben, before saying, "Gentlemen." Then he's walking away, whistling something under his breath which Ben realizes, in the seconds after Brian vanishes from earshot, is in fact the *Late Night Live* theme song.

For a moment, they just stand there, the jacket dangling from Pete's hand, staring after him. Then, because he thinks someone really *should*, he asks, "Um, Pete? Are you... all right?"

Pete blinks for a second. Then, slowly, he says, "I think... that I'm great. Because—stay with me now—I must be asleep. This is all some kind of insane anxiety dream! And any second now I'm going to wake up, and I'm going to say to myself, 'Pete, you idiot, I can't believe you really thought any of that was real, you never have to worry about making a fool of yourself in front of Brian O'Malley, because that kind of thing doesn't *happen* to people!'"

"I regret to inform you that this is reality," Ben says, hating himself for it a little.

Pete groans. "In that case? I need a drink."

Ben thinks that's fair, in the circumstances. He thinks that if he were Pete, he, too, would want a drink. Perhaps several drinks. There is the chance that he might want to move past drinking and progress to attempting to sustain an amnesia-inducing head injury, but decides it's best not to suggest that just now.

Instead, they attempt to get a drink. They try first at the bar nearest to 30 Rockefeller Plaza, which, Ben realizes as they walk in, is an obvious mistake. Because the whole place banks on its proximity to the building, and the various shows filmed inside, it is often playing those shows for its patrons. Tonight every screen within is lit up with images of the burning *Late Night Live* set, Pete's hapless, trapped expression immortalized next to the dancing flames; when they step inside, Pete blanches, turns on his heel, and walks right back out, which Ben can't blame him for.

But the next two places they try aren't much better. At the first one, they only make it ten feet past the door before someone calls, "Oh my God, wait, that's him! That's the guy from my phone! Dude, we were *watching* you, you straight up burned that *set* down —" Ben never finds out the end of this sentence, because he's too busy following Pete, who had turned tail the minute he heard the words "that's him." And at the third place, they manage to get all the way to the bar without incident, but as they're halfway through placing their order, the bartender's face lights up with amusement, and she says, "Holy crap, wait, aren't you that guy from the—"

"NO!" Pete yells this so loud several bar patrons turn to stare; Ben wishes he could flip some switch that made Pete invisible, or unrecognizable, until he was back to a more even keel. "I'm not *anybody*, from *anything*, you don't *know* me, you've never *seen* me, good*bye!*"

When Ben catches up to Pete this time, he looks frustrated nearly to the point of anguish. That's why, before he can think better of it, Ben hears himself saying, "Why don't we just go back to my place?"

It's not the sort of sentence Ben usually says. In fact, if he's going to be entirely honest about it, Ben is more the type to come up with excuses why someone *cannot* come back to his apartment. If the place had actually been fumigated as many times as Ben has claimed, it would be an unlivable toxic hazard, killing anyone who stepped foot inside. But it's just easier, isn't it, to claim fumigation, or that a fictional roommate is hosting a party, than it is to tell the truth. Ben has never found a situation where it was socially acceptable to say, *I don't want you to come back to my apartment because it's the place where no one bothers me and you're bothering me.* And, indeed, *I don't want you to come back to my apartment because over the last month and a half every cup and bowl I own has slowly migrated into the general region of my editing desk,* is also not, in his experience, a winner.

However, he *has in fact asked Pete to come back to his apartment,* and when Pete immediately accepts, he looks so relieved that

Ben can't bear to take it back. Instead, he spends the short walk to the subway trying to behave like a normal person while mentally cataloguing things like the last time he did dishes, or laundry. He is relieved to remember, feeling like it was a long time ago, that he spent the time between getting home from work and leaving to meet Pete tonight stress-cleaning the place, so it should be in fairly decent shape.

This leaves Ben, on their fifteen-minute ride to his usual subway stop, to instead try to behave like a normal person while thinking histrionic thoughts like, *Pete's going to be in my apartment!* and *My apartment is where my bed is!* and *You know what kinds of things people get up to in beds, Ben, don't you? Or has it been so long that you've forgotten?* It is, in a word, distracting. Ben's fairly certain he isn't pulling off "normal person," and honestly, he'd be pleased to discover he was even managing "only slightly off-putting."

Luckily, Pete does not seem in a state to notice. He spends the subway ride hunched forward, head down to keep his face hidden, all but curled in on himself. It makes Ben want to hiss and spit at everyone who so much as glances at him, but also, in a horrible, contradictory way, to go soft and soothing, cocoon Pete in a brief but beautiful world a little less punishing than this one. At very least, it would be nice to give in to the urge to put a hand on Pete's back, to rub in long, comforting strokes until some of the tension bled away from his shoulders.

Ben doesn't do that, of course. It would be weird; it would be inappropriate. But he thinks about it, so hard he half expects Pete to see it written on his face, the whole way to the Upper West Side.

When they escape the bowels of the MTA and surface, Pete's still grayed-out and mostly silent, so Ben simply leads him to the building, welcomes him inside, gestures for him to take a seat on the couch. Pete does, murmuring thanks and then dropping his head into his hands, groaning softly. As he has several times in the last half hour, he murmurs, clearly to himself, "Why did I *do* that? What was I *thinking?*"

After a moment, Roux, who is usually wary of strangers and sometimes wary of even Ben, comes creeping out from Ben's bedroom. She looks assessingly at Pete for a long moment, and then at Ben, as if to say, "You know about the sad guy on the couch, man?" Ben, feeling silly about it, nods subtly to her; then, to his amazement, she leaps onto the couch, steps gracefully under Pete's arm, and settles comfortably in his lap. After a second, she starts purring.

"Oh!" Pete moves, but carefully, clearly not wanting to startle or unseat her. "Hi, uh—?"

"Roux," Ben says, staring at her in shock. Then, seeing Pete lift a hand to pet her, he hastily adds, "Listen, I wouldn't, she doesn't usually like... Oh." Transfixed in spite of himself, Ben watches as Pete scratches Roux on the back of the head, and then under the chin, and then along the ruff of her neck, all actions that would get Ben mauled six days out of ten. "Wow. I guess—never mind."

"She's a nice cat," Pete says, stroking her absently. She gives Ben a smug look.

"She's not," Ben says, still staring at her. "But she does seem to like you, so. What do I know? Look, you wanted a drink, right? I have—uh," Ben, abruptly remembering that he does not drink very much and these last few weeks have been an unfortunate, booze-soaked exception, winces. "Well, um. Actually. As I think about it. We might be looking at, like, a really old bottle of vermouth, or a couple of beers from the back of the fridge?"

Pete laughs. It's not what Ben would call a hearty laugh—it's thin, and wan, and sounds like he's forcing it slightly—but it's better than nothing. "I'll take a fridge beer, man. Even after that, I don't think I'm desperate enough to drink your vermouth. Why do you just have vermouth?"

"I'm not usually a big drinker," Ben admits, unearthing two beers that have surely been in there at least a year. "But I *do* make a chicken dish with vermouth that I really like, so I try to keep it on hand. Usually, I'd have red wine, too, because my mother would kill me if I tried to make half her dishes without it, but I'm out right now. My folks'll probably send me back with some when I go home for Thanksgiving in a couple of weeks." He sits down next to Pete on the couch, passing him one of the cans, and adds, "If that tastes disgusting, don't say I didn't warn you; I think I purchased it during a previous presidential administration."

"I didn't know you were going home for Thanksgiving," Pete says, cracking his beer and taking what looks like an evaluative sip. He shrugs, offers, "Tastes fine to me," and then adds, "Michigan, right? That's home for you? Do you go back for Christmas, too?"

"Nah," Ben says, trying to sound cool and casual, and not at all like his heart is beating faster because Pete remembered where he's from. Love, Ben has realized, is above all else so *embarrassing*, but knowing that doesn't seem to help. "Christmas is traditionally a disaster back home? So I prefer to swing by in November, say hello, eat some turkey, and dip back out of town before things start getting tense." Feeling like he might as well offer a little more context, since Pete is clearly still teetering on the edge of the canyon of despair, he adds, "My dad's Jewish, and my mom's Catholic, and they always tried to do all of it, you know? But in the end, what they really cared about was the restaurant, and each always blamed the other's holiday for getting in the way, and it— never brought out the best in anyone. It's easier, like this."

"Ahh," Pete says, and sips his beer. "My family is pretty chill about Christmas, but Easter—that's a bloodbath," and Ben laughs, encouraged to hear him telling a joke, until he realizes that it isn't one.

The conversation of holiday family grudges carries them for a few minutes, but Pete's burst of distracted semi-decent cheer seems to fade away as they go. Eventually, Ben realizes why, but it's not until Pete barks out a humorless laugh and says, "God, they're all going to have seen it. My dad, my sisters, my sisters' husbands; when I turn my phone back on, it's going to be calls and messages and 'How could you throw water on a grease fire,' and 'Don't you know how this makes us look,' and—" He cuts himself off, clearly frustrated, and then admits, "You know what? Just once, just one time, I'd like to not be the *embarrassing* one. The one who makes everyone *else* say things like, 'Wouldn't want to be you, Petey.' Just *once* I'd love to be able to say that to someone else!"

Ben drums his fingers on his knee for a moment, considering this. Then, without saying a word, he stands up, walks to his office, picks up his laptop from his desk, types and scrolls for a moment, and then takes a deep breath.

When he returns to the living room and sets the laptop down in front of Pete, Ben says, "I want you to know, okay, that I would not show you this if the circumstances were not so extreme, and that, upon having shown it to you, we will *never speak of it again.* Do you understand me?"

Pete's brow furrows in confusion. "What?"

"Do you understand me or not?"

"I mean," Pete starts, "I do, but what are we—"

Despairingly, Ben says, "I don't think it'll take that long for you to figure it out," and hits play. The screen fills with his teenaged self in a blue Starfleet uniform, a lot of blue eyeshadow, and thick, Vulcan-style eyebrows he'd drawn on with his mother's eyeliner pencil.

"Oh my *God*," Pete breathes, sitting up in sudden, rapt attention, "is this—"

"Yes," Ben snaps, mortified but willing to do anything that pulls the miasma of anguish from Pete's expression. "It is my teenage directorial debut, and if you tell *anyone* we work with that you've seen it, or that a copy still exists—"

"I won't, I won't," Pete says, flapping a hand at him. "Shhh, I'm watching." And Ben, with effort, goes silent. Then, with somewhat more effort, he, too, turns his head and forces himself to watch his life's most embarrassing work.

He's surprised and somewhat pleased to find, as the minutes tick on, that it's not as mortifying as he thought. The *content* is awful, of course, but it's fun, watching it with Pete. Ben can see the humor in it, from this vantage point, in a way he couldn't when he was fifteen, or even twenty-five. But here, as he approaches thirty, the spotty, wildly overeager teenager yelling out sound effects is somewhat hilarious, and Ben finds himself more amused than he would have expected by his antics.

Pete, for his part, tries manfully not to laugh for the first five or six minutes of viewing. He loses the battle during a particularly overacted moment, letting out a single shout of laughter that becomes a peal when the next take is a brief, extreme, and obviously unintentional closeup of one of Ben's ears.

By minute fifteen, they are both absolutely howling with mirth, clutching at each other for support, having scared Roux off in a huff some time ago.

"What," Pete gasps, barely able to get the words out, "what are you doing to that pillow?"

"I'm... Oh, God. Well, I'm supposed to be, uh? Wrestling it? I see now that that's not what it looks like." This sets Pete off laughing so hard Ben's a little afraid he's going to choke on it, and, chuckling through it himself, he offers the best defense he can, which is: "I mean, listen, okay, *you* try to wrestle a pillow—"

"Oh, I don't have to," Pete says, gesturing at the screen. "Because you've helpfully showed me exactly what it would look like—oh my *God*, are you using a banana as a *gun*?"

"It's a phaser," Ben says as loftily as possible, "and it's set to stun," and then dissolves into hysteria again the second Pete catches his eye.

And it's fun, Ben realizes, as they progress through the video. It's fun, to watch this with Pete. It's fun to laugh, gently and without malice, at the person he was when he made it; it's fun to see Pete laugh, too, entertained by this younger version of Ben in a way that, somehow, doesn't feel sharp or judgmental or mean.

Ben has spent the bulk of his adult life trying to avoid being known, sliding away from intimacy and closeness the way oil slips through water. It was easier, he told himself, not to be known. It was easier to avoid the sting of being found wanting; easier to sidestep having his darkest fears about himself confirmed. It was easier for him to exist, for him to *be Ben,* without having to look at the proof that the condition of being Ben was somehow, inherently, a mortifying one.

Letting Pete know him doesn't feel like that. Letting Pete know him feels like... like... like the way sometimes, when Ben was a teenager, he'd take his camera out in the woods and stand very still, and after a while, the forest would forgive him his humanity and forget he was there. They'd come out, the birds and squirrels and chipmunks, and go about their business, as though having assessed him as worthy of knowing their secrets, not dangerous enough to hide from. The benediction of a chickadee landing on top of his head—that's what it feels like, showing Pete this video. Like being chosen as worthy of something rare and singular through some mechanism Ben doesn't understand, but is desperately grateful for.

It is, all in all, an upsettingly good time. It's such a good time that Ben would probably stay up half the night worrying about it, except that by the time the video ends he and Pete, exhausted by the day's events, have both fallen asleep on the sofa.

TEN

Ben learned young the folly of falling asleep on the couch. Renata, like their mother, could cheerfully bed down anywhere, waking up fresh as a daisy whether "anywhere" was an air mattress or the backseat of a car; Ben had inherited their father's tendencies instead. Sleeping anywhere but in a proper bed, ideally his *own* bed, and most ideally his own bed with the assistance of an assortment of sleep hygiene rituals he habitually doesn't practice, is almost always a mistake. If he is foolish enough to let himself fall asleep, say, half-slumped against the arm of the couch while agreeing sleepily with Pete's mumbled comment that they should really get up in a minute, there are always consequences.

Tonight, Ben pays for his folly by having an exceptional, exquisitely detailed dream, which doesn't, at first, seem like a punishment. Within it, he wakes in the exact same position in which he fell asleep, and Pete's waking up, too, and Ben's hand accidentally lands on Pete's thigh as he tries to stand up, and Pete's eyes meet his with a charged, hungry desperation, and then—well. Then Ben's subconscious gets quite granular on the detail indeed, which he appreciates, in the moment.

He appreciates it less when, just as things in the dream have reached a crescendo, a tinny, unpleasant sound rips him towards wakefulness. He fights it, thrashing internally to stay in the dream, but after what feels like a few fractured seconds, it slips away from him, lost.

Ben *does* blink awake in the exact same position in which he fell asleep, which seems promising, for a second. Then it mostly seems like he, Ben, is the punch line in one of the universe's cruel little jokes.

Pete is not sitting on the couch next to him. Pete is standing, tense, on the other side of the room, whispering into his phone. A *ringtone*, Ben thinks, feeling abruptly hollowed out inside, is what had pulled him from the dream. He can tell from Pete's body language alone that he would have been happier staying asleep—as always, reality is clearly planning to underwhelm him.

"I know what I *said*, Chris," Pete is hissing, trying fumblingly to put on one of the shoes he kicked off earlier, around ten minutes into the screening of Ben's teenage theatrical efforts. "And I meant it, it was an accident, I didn't intend to be out this—oh, like you haven't ever—well I wasn't *expecting* to set the stupid set on fire, was I? *No*, Jesus, I'm not in jail—no, I am not out *getting some strange*, Chris, what's wrong with you?" He turns, at this point, to grab his other shoe, and sees Ben staring at him in the dark. Quickly, he snaps, "Look, I'm heading back right now. I'll get a cab, okay, it'll be fast—you know what? I can't do this with you right now. Bye."

Pete hangs up the phone and, sliding it into his jacket pocket, gives Ben a pleading expression. "Sorry to, like, run out in the middle of the night," he says, his tone changing to one Ben can't quite place—guilt? Regret? Ben's not sure it matters. "I didn't mean to fall asleep, *and* I didn't mean to sleep so long, and now it's all... ugh." He runs a hand over his face, sighing, and says, "It would be too hard to explain it all right now but I've kind of... messed some stuff up at home, and it's going to be a whole thing, and I really need to go deal with it before it gets worse."

"No worries," Ben says, ashamed when it comes out thin,

reedy. Forlorn, he thinks, is the word, although he wishes he'd never thought of it. "Worse seems—bad."

Pete laughs, not that there's much humor behind it. "Worse is bad," he agrees, "and the story of my life, in some ways, but—just, thanks, man. Seriously. I don't know what I would have done, and if you want to—"

"Oh, don't," Ben says, waving a hand, like it's nothing to him. Like it's easy. "It was no problem at all. Your basic act of Good Samaritanity. Samaritanism? Never mind, it doesn't matter—whichever it is, that's all that it was, so. No big thing. Would've done it for anyone. Safe trip home, okay? I'll see you at work on Monday."

"Oh," Pete says, blinking at him. "Yeah, okay. See you... at work, then?"

"Yep," Ben says, nodding with the firm good cheer of someone who definitely doesn't care at all about Chris, or Pete leaving, or, in fact, Pete, at least in anything other than a strictly friendly, platonic, collegial way. "Good night."

"Good... night," Pete says slowly, before he sighs, and lets his shoulders drop, and sees himself out Ben's front door.

Ben waits. He waits until he hears the door click shut; he waits until Pete's footsteps have faded down the long hallway; he waits until he hears the faint ding of the elevator, and the distant, barely audible metallic hum of the doors sliding shut. Only then, well and truly sure that he's at no risk of Pete bursting back in, does Ben let himself curl up in a hard, tight little ball on the couch and sink into a misery that prevents him from sleeping at all.

By the following Monday, Ben's managed to patch himself up a little.

Okay, so, Pete has a boyfriend; Ben already knew that. Or, he'd already suspected it—Friday night was confirmation, for all intents and purposes, and *that* sucks, but it's not like it's such a shock. And, yes, of course, it *had* obviously stung to have such a vivid dream of how things could have gone, followed by the immediate nightmare scenario which had played out for him instead. How could it not have stung? Anyone in Ben's shoes might have, just for example, spent Saturday morning watching terrible romantic comedies and unwisely eating most of a family-sized bag of salt and vinegar chips for breakfast, feeling equal parts self-punishing and indulgent. Granted, Ben's specific shoes also come along with Ben's specific stomach, which can no longer handle that much acid, hence the self-punishing aspect of this particular coping mechanism. It's what Ben used to do as a teenager, whenever he found out the guy he'd been harboring a crush on was either incredibly straight or absolutely gay enough to be getting on with, just not with Ben. He got a lot of experience, over the years, on both sides of that particular line.

But by Saturday afternoon, Ben had resolved to pull himself together, and on Monday, when he walks into the *Gastronome* offices, he feels—well. Not *good*, per se. Good would be a significant stretch. But he feels ready, at least. Equipped. Prepared.

This is for one reason only: Ben has a plan.

It isn't, Ben is aware, a good plan. He wishes it were a good plan, the sort of plan that might make someone say, "Nice plan, Ben!" or "Wow, you've really thought this through!" However, he suspects it is more the type of plan that, were he to express it to anyone with more than a few brain cells to rub together, would be met with the response, "Yeesh. Good luck with that."

Ben doesn't feel great about that, no doubt. But a plan is a plan, and above anything else, a plan is something that makes Ben feel less like he's going to lose his entire mind, so. A plan is what he's got. It runs as follows: Pete has a boyfriend, sure, but he doesn't seem to have a *happy* relationship with that boyfriend. Ben's not a homewrecker or anything, but it's not wrecking a home to hang around, is it? To see what happens? To demonstrate to Pete that he, Ben, is a fine enough person, and a decent friend, and, yeah, *not* exactly a certified beefcake like Chris is, or like Pete himself is, but maybe that doesn't have to matter! Maybe it's about timing and compatibility and anything ever going right, even once, in Ben's whole stupid life.

Or maybe Ben's convincing himself of absurdities to get through the day—it wouldn't be the first time. Either way, though, it allows him the grace and composure to walk through the *Gastronome* doors on Monday morning, to talk to Pete like everything's normal between them, to get to work. After the success of last week's triple-Thanksgiving shoot, Ben's decided to do the same thing for the three Christmas videos they're slated to produce next. Pete will have an easier time if they shoot them all at once, and when they've delivered those videos, they'll have completed the nine videos they were contracted for, and can hopefully relax for a few weeks.

Here, too, Ben's dreams are dashed—in this later case via a courier, who arrives at the office with several large packages around 9:30 a.m. on Monday.

The courier's arrival interrupts what was, in Ben's opinion, shaping up to be a very nice morning. He and Pete, as usual, were the first ones in and, as has become Ben's new normal over the last week or two, quickly threw together a breakfast to share. It's nothing exciting today, just leftover Greek yogurt from the easy galette recipe Adina was testing last week, a selection of random fruit that was nearing the end of the line, and the very last of the dried coconut flakes, but still, Ben was enjoying it. Between that and his nearly successful impression of a normal man with no recently bruised romantic feelings at all, things were looking up.

But the courier is followed by Jaelyn, who bears a camera on her shoulder and an apologetic expression. Pete freezes, the spoon halfway to his mouth, which is when Ben realizes the red light is on, indicating the camera is rolling.

"Uh," Jaelyn says, looking uncomfortably between Pete's frozen rictus of horror and Ben's abrupt, ferocious glare. "So... someone from Formica social media? Emailed me? And said that it might be good to, um... get your organic reaction? To this delivery? For the social channels?"

Ben opens his mouth to tell her in no uncertain terms what he thinks of that idea, but before he can, a sentence comes out of Pete's mouth. It is an *utterly* unrepeatable sentence, a sentence featuring so many swear words that, if anyone did try to use the footage, they'd have to replace the entire thing with one long, unbroken bleep. As Pete says it, Jaelyn sucks in a breath, and Ben's eyebrows climb up into his hairline, and the courier, after what seems to be a long, careful moment of thought, crosses himself, hands Pete an envelope, and walks back out of the office.

The envelope, Ben notes with trepidation, is branded with the official Formica Media logo, under which Pete's name is printed in a bold hand. It's a *card* envelope, of the size and type one might see on a gift—who bothers to have those printed up with the official company logo?

"Well," Jaelyn says brightly, dropping the camera off her shoulder and hitting the switch that cuts the red light blessedly off, "great news, I'll just tell them my memory card melted." Glancing at the envelope in Pete's hand, she adds, "Are you going to open that, though? Because, listen, I don't know what this is about, either, and I'm dying of curiosity."

Pete glances at Ben, who shrugs, eying the envelope as though it might explode, but saying, "I'd rather we didn't find out what's in there, honestly, but the sooner we do, the sooner we can deal with it, so. I say go for it."

"Rip the Band-Aid off," Pete mutters to himself, which makes Ben smile slightly in spite of his dread anticipation. "Yeah, all right."

Pete rips the envelope open, pulls out the card, and stares at it.

And stares at it.

And stares at it.

"Ben?" he says eventually.

Ben swallows. "Yes?"

"I would like you to look at this, please," Pete says. He passes the card over to Ben with one hand and pinches the bridge of his nose with the other, closing his eyes. "Because maybe, you know, maybe this is some kind of—of—*stress break*, right—and it doesn't say what I think it says?"

Noticing the card is trembling slightly in Pete's fingers, Ben hastily plucks it from his hand, opens it, and reads:

Dear Pete,

Congratulations! Viewership on your little show has been high enough to attract a few sponsors. Christmas is a big season for all of them, so for your upcoming Christmas videos, please only use the cookware that's been delivered today. I'll be emailing you a list of sponsor names, and of the specific sentences they'd like you to make sure to work in, later today. You'll need to include sponsor shout-outs in each video, but make it feel natural. That should be no problem for you, right? I hope not; there are other paths we could use to drive traffic, but I'd hate to have to resort to those.

This is an exciting opportunity for you and Gastronome! If these videos move the sales needle far enough in the right direction, there is interest in ordering a longer run of your show. Don't mess it up!

Best,
Miranda Culter
Executive Director of Creative Strategy
Formica Media

"Good Lord, who takes the time to handwrite their email signature onto the bottom of a card?" Ben mutters, too overwhelmed by the content of the letter to focus on anything but granular, irrelevant detail. Attempting to move past this, he instead finds himself in the somewhat worse territory of telling frantic, ill-conceived jokes, as though they will somehow bleed the tension building within him. "I think that's the sort of thing where if you do it, a therapist should appear before you? Like a fairy godmother? And start casting spells for the betterment of your human experience.

Bibbidi-bobbidi-basic-perspective.   Abracadabra-work-life-balance—"

"Oh my God, would you give me that," Jaelyn snaps, apparently at the end of her patience, and snatches the card out of Ben's hand. "Useless, the both of you—" She falls silent, reading, and then, when she's finished, glances at Pete and whistles softly. "Woof. Sorry, man. I know that's probably going to be rough." When Pete doesn't say anything, just stares off into the middle distance, she jerks her thumb awkwardly over her shoulder and adds, "Do you know, I remembered that I promised to meet, uh, Emma, from—marketing, we need to, uh... market? I'll be—back." Pete doesn't even seem to hear her, but when Ben quirks his eyebrows at the obvious lie, she mouths, "Good luck," and flees without another word to either of them.

"Ben?" Pete's voice is small.

Ben bites back a scream of wordless hatred at a pile of still-sealed boxes full of free, brand-new cooking equipment, which is not a situation he ever expected to find himself in. Instead of mentioning this, he says, "Yeah?"

"You know I can't do this." It's not a question; there's brittleness to the statement, but Pete doesn't sound uncertain. "You *know* I can't. I mean, I can barely hold it together with my own equipment, that I'm *used* to. They want me to say specific *sentences*? I can barely say specific *words*, man! How the f—"

"Hey," Ben says, holding up a hand to pause the flow. "Look—it's all going to be okay, you'll see. We can still do the Christmas videos all in one shoot, like we did for Thanksgiving, and if you need a couple of extra takes, or a couple dozen, then whatever! That's fine. Worst-case scenario, there *is* a reason so many people live and die by the phrase, 'We can fix it in post,' although I will say, as a video editor, that phrase is responsible for a lot of sins, and people should have to be issued a license before they're allowed to say it, but that's a topic for another time."

Pete doesn't look at all reassured by this, which is fair enough, so Ben lets go of caution for a moment and reaches out, allows himself two light pats on Pete's arm before pulling away. This, at least, makes Pete meet his eyes, and Ben holds his panicked hazel gaze as he says, "Pete, listen. It's just three more videos, and then we're at the end of the contract; whatever happens next, the whole company is always shut down between Christmas and New Year's, so it'll be next year before we have to worry about this again. This is the home stretch, and you're better than you were at the beginning, and I'll help you, I promise. How badly could it go?"

As it turns out, the answer to this question is "quite badly indeed." To say the next two weeks are grueling would be putting it mildly; they are some of the most difficult professional weeks of Ben's life.

It would be a gross understatement to say that Pete's progress in terms of on-camera work regresses. Ben *wishes* it was just a regression, that he was dealing with Pete as he was in the first handful of videos they worked on together. Christ, he would even take the Pete in the *pilot* footage over the Pete of mid-November, who has progressed past comical panic and into something more classically tragic. If, for example, a fifteen-pound ham had slipped out of Pete's hands and gone careening towards the floor few weeks ago, there would have been a slapstick attempt to catch it, and then a series of creative swear words, and then probably Pete would have tried to cut the part of the ham that had not touched the floor off of the larger chunk of meat for a minute before saying, "Wait, what am I doing?" Ben could have made good content out of that.

Instead, when a fifteen-pound ham does slip out of Pete's hand and go careening towards the floor, he doesn't even bother reaching for it, just watches it fall with a defeated, resigned energy. When, with a resounding *splat*, it lands on the tile, he stares at it for a second, saying nothing at all.

Then, despairingly, he looks into the camera and says, "Floor ham! Brought to you by our sponsors!" Finally, he sits down next to the unfortunate entree, puts his head in his hands, and won't speak to anyone for fifteen minutes, except to say, "I'm done for today; that's it. I'm done."

They do not, as Ben had hoped, get through all the Christmas videos in one day. They do not even get through all the Christmas videos in one *week*; it takes them two and a half days to get enough workable footage for Ben to scrape together the first video, which he's editing frantically on set as they film the second one, which takes them *four* days to shoot. That puts them at Tuesday morning of the third week of November, and the final video, a Christmas dessert spectacular, Ben honestly thinks might kill Pete. He's supposed to be making a Yule log, and he spends the back half of Tuesday and all of Wednesday being tormented by the cake, Thursday swearing up and down that he'll never make buttercream frosting again, and Friday cursing all meringues, of all shapes and sizes and flavors and purposes.

Still, it's not all bad. Work's a depressing nightmare, but it's still better than things used to be on twenty-seven, where Ben hardly spends any time at all these days. For one thing, everyone's pissed at Miranda on Pete's behalf, so Ben gets a lot of good gossip. Apparently, she'd been the Formica executive who oversaw the *Gastronome* buyout a few years ago, and they'd all been stuck working with her for a while. Ben notes with grim satisfaction that she is roundly hated, even by Brogan, usually too even-tempered to bother with hating anyone, and Ezra, who seems to find almost everyone he meets at least a little annoying but rarely expends the energy to work himself up to a proper loathing. And Ben gets the sense, too, that something was going on between Miranda and Rick at one point, although no one will give him more detail, and all of them clam up guiltily when he presses. Ben, knowing all too well Rick's tendency to chat, has to wonder if he didn't confide in all of them individually at one point or another, unthinkingly asking each of them not to tell anyone.

But within a few days of the courier's delivery, the conversation turns to the upcoming *Gastronome* centennial party. The celebration of the magazine's hundredth year is taking place the

Saturday before Thanksgiving, something Ben really wishes he had been told before he booked an early-bird flight out on Sunday morning. Granted, he booked that flight before he even worked for *Gastronome*, and, sure, okay, he *could* have afforded to pay the nominal additional sum to switch to one that left at a less punishing time than four in the morning, but he hadn't seen the point. It's not as though he ever slept the night before going home to Michigan anyway; the way he figured it, if he was going to be awake no matter what, it might as well save him a little money.

In spite of the fact that it dooms him to a long, complicated night of navigating travel logistics, Ben is looking forward to the party. It will be nice to relax a little, to cut loose, to spend some time with Pete that's just *fun*. It's not that Ben hasn't had fun with Pete since the *Late Night Live* fiasco—Ben *always* seems to have fun with Pete, no matter what kind of mood he's in or what they're doing. This fact, while inarguable, makes Ben feel warm, soft, gooey, and slightly nauseated, like a toasted marshmallow dropped at the last moment in a patch of yellowing snow.

Pete, however, does not seem to be having very much fun. Pete seems to be swimming through a waking nightmare every day, and there's only so much Ben can do for him. The videos are one thing —Pete, as predicted, cannot say a scripted sponsor-submitted line to save his life, but Ben's able to do it in voice-over in a way that plays, so it's fine. But Ben cannot, alas, reach in and cut out the long stretches of miserable silence from Pete's day, splicing in some more pleasant experiences instead. All he can do is be around, and encouraging, and tell Pete that it's not as bad as he thinks, and he's doing fine.

It's a rough two weeks, no doubt. But it is, Ben has to admit, almost worth it for the moment after their very last shot, when, with Jaelyn's nod to indicate they're clear, he smiles at Pete and says, "That's it. We're done. No more filming." The light that flares in Pete's eyes for the first time in days—the way he whoops with delight, and steps close, and scoops Ben into a huge, back-slapping hug as he yells, "YES! DONE!"—well. Ben would do it all again a hundred times, for that reward.

He is, if he's honest, still riding the high of that moment as he walks back into the Formica Media building the following evening, feeling strange to be entering on a Saturday night. He knows that he's not in the wrong place; the entryway is brightly lit and set up with a comprehensive fleet of valet drivers who certainly aren't usually on duty. A line of expensive cars is blocking a whole lane of Sixth Avenue, various fancily dressed people climbing out of them and making their way laughingly inside. Ben, who rode the subway here like he does every other day and is wearing a suit he originally bought for his grandfather's funeral, slips quickly past them, walks round the building to a more subtle entrance. The sustenance of Pete's firm, warm hug seems to be draining rapidly away from him in the face of so much glamour, and he'd rather slide unobtrusively into the back of the party than face walking boldly in the front door.

But, as it turns out, Ben needn't have worried about it. He barely makes it through the *back* door without being pulled into something by someone he knows—Adina, looking stunning in an emerald-green cocktail dress, spies him from across the room and makes "rescue me" eyes at him. Ben walks over and pulls her away from conversation with a man who, as she explains once they're out of earshot, had been eagerly trying to convince her to visit his lake house upstate, despite having met her only minutes before. They chat for a moment, and then Brogan joins them, and introduces her partner, Charlie, and then suddenly, Ben is being dragged away by Jaelyn and ends up in a twenty-minute discussion of cinematographic techniques with someone who turns out to be a very famous food photographer whose work Ben has admired for years.

It's around this time he sees Pete arrive, looking windswept and a bit rumpled from his ferry ride, but with a spirit and energy about him Ben has sorely missed. They grin at each other from across the party—Ben's all the brighter because Pete has not brought Chris with him tonight—and start progressing towards one another.

But progress is slow; Ben sees Pete get flagged down into conversation at the same moment that he feels a hand land on his shoulder.

"Kid!" Ben turns, torn between fondness and despair, knowing before he manages it that he'll see Rick. "Good to see you. You remember my buddy Larry Kobald, right?"

Ben experiences half a moment of blinding panic, having absolutely no idea who Larry is, before he gets a look at the man standing next to Rick. Then he relaxes; Ben remembers him, all right, he just isn't sure he ever got a name. This is Rick's juice guy, with whom Ben had a nice chat at the Halloween party, and they greet one another enthusiastically.

As happened the previous time they met, the conversation flows naturally between them, Rick drifting off to find something more interesting to do after a few minutes. It surprises Ben a little that the two men are such good friends—Rick's grown on Ben these last few months, but his personality is still a bit grating and tends to leave Ben walking away slightly raw with annoyance. Larry, on the other hand, he finds easy and relaxing to talk to, like an old friend instead of someone he's only meeting for the second time.

Larry must feel similarly, because, as their conversation wraps up, he says, "Look—it's Ben, right? I've got to run, I can see my wife is locked in mental battle with an emissary of the devil, but I'm going to give you my card. I know you have a good gig going here, but I can't imagine they're paying you what you're worth, and I need someone at my facility on the west coast. A video editor," he clarifies, chuckling, correctly interpreting Ben's creased brow. "Not just some guy to hang around keeping the oranges company or whatever. I'm launching a juice line into the retail market next year. I'll need commercials and pitch videos, someone to film a guided tour of our production facilities, stuff for social media, the works."

Ben stares at him, agape. "What, *me*? Seriously? Just because we get along at *parties*?"

Grimacing, Larry says, "Depressing though it is, that's how the world works a lot of the time. Didn't Rick tell me he met you in a coffee shop?" Ben opens his mouth to argue and, realizing he has no rejoinder, snaps it shut again. Larry laughs and claps him on the shoulder. "Look, the truth is, hiring for these creative jobs is always pretty much a crapshoot. I like your work; we seem to get along; Rick likes you, and he's got a good eye for this sort of thing. What I see there is an easy solution to my problem, if you're into it, and one thing about me: I'll work pretty damn hard to make things easy." He smiles at Ben, passing the card over, and adds, "I'd make it worth your while, and one California winter will make you forget why you ever liked New York in the first place. Think about it."

"I... will," Ben says, staring from the card to Larry's cheerful, slightly ruddy face. "Thanks."

Larry nods and hurries off; Ben stares after him, gobsmacked at first, although this does turn to amusement when he sees Larry approach a redheaded woman who seems to be deep in conversation with none other than Miranda Culter. An emissary of the devil, indeed.

Chuckling slightly to himself, Ben decides to put Larry and the job offer out of his mind for the moment. After all, had it really been a *job offer*, or had Larry just been a little overly friendly after one drink too many? And, anyway, it's not like Ben can make any employment decisions right now—he doesn't even know if the show is going to be renewed, or if he *wants* it to be renewed, given the agony filming every episode seems to trigger for Pete.

Probably getting to be time to figure that out! The part of Ben that points this out sounds both urgent and, if he's honest, more than a little annoyed. *Because you've filmed the last video, and you don't know what's going to happen with your contract at all, and you don't want to go back to spending all your time on twenty-seven, and pretty soon, it's all going to come up!*

Ben, very firmly, tells himself to let it go for now. After all, this is a party.

He turns, intent again on finding Pete, and pauses, breaking into a grin: Pete has found him first, is standing with his arm frozen in the air, like he was midway through reaching up to tap on Ben's shoulder.

Ben is surprised to find himself feeling shy, suddenly. It's nonsensical; he's known Pete for weeks now, and saw him *yesterday*, and only a few hours ago, they were exchanging ridiculous texts betting on what appetizers would be passed around tonight. But still, Ben can't help but scuff a shoe against the floor, grinning up at Pete like some soppy, lovestruck teenager, totally blanking on anything to say which is just embarrassing, isn't it? But there's nothing for it. He would stop smiling if he could, but when he tries, he finds it entirely impossible.

As if having taken this thought as a challenge, an image of Chris floats across Ben's mind, still perfectly chiseled and unfairly symmetrical in Ben's imagining of him, which is just cruel. His own mind can't throw him this one bone? Give the guy an unfortunately placed facial infection? Poison ivy? *Something?* But no: He's smooth and shiny even in Ben's head, and looking down his nose at Ben in irritation and disgust. This does, Ben has to admit, dim the wattage of his smile somewhat, though he finds he *still* can't crush it entirely.

At least, Ben thinks distantly, Pete is smiling back at him. That's something. A pleasure to witness, if nothing else.

"Hi," Pete says, eventually. His eyes flick down the length of Ben's body, quick and barely noticeable; Ben notices anyway. "You look great."

"I don't," Ben says, automatic. "I'm not a suit guy, but the invite said formal, and I didn't have anything more formal than this so— uh. *You* look great, though. Like, actually great."

Pete flushes slightly but rolls his eyes. "Oh, thanks, but if that's true, it's only because I made one of my sisters dress me. Or, at least, I asked for her help in choosing an outfit, which somehow ended up with both of us in a department store and her wielding my credit card like a sword, but." He shrugs, glancing down at his cream knit sweater, which he's wearing under a camel-colored coat, and over a pair of woolen dress trousers in a complementary light brown. "I have to give it to her, I *do* feel more professional in this than my canned beans T-shirt." He winces, and adds, "Not that I've been at my most, um, professional, these last couple of shoots. I hope the edit hasn't been too brutal?"

Ben, who did in fact spend much of the night awake, and who did only get the last video sent off to Dave in S&P an hour before leaving the house tonight, says, "Oh, it was nothing, really."

Pete, ducking his head slightly, says, "It isn't nothing to me. Thanks for—just, thanks."

Warmed, Ben smiles at him, and then feels that smile grow brittle as he runs abruptly against the wall of realizing he's not sure what to *say* to Pete. All they've talked about for days now is work—the videos, and the content of the videos, and how to make it easier to film the videos, and how much they both wish they didn't have to *do* the videos, at least not in this specific way.

It's not that it's been unpleasant conversation. If anything, the opposite; Ben's cracked up laughing a dozen times over jokes about Miranda, or the sponsored products, or the abysmal quality of the scripted lines meant to sell those products. But he doesn't want to bring any of that up now, not when Pete's clearly so happy to be on the other side, and the last thing that happened between them that wasn't work-related was that cut-short evening after *Late Night Live*. They have not talked about it at all since then, and the only evidence that it even happened is Pete's beanie, which he'd left behind on the back of the sofa, and which Ben, to his great shame, has not been able to bring himself to return.

Thinking about that night once again brings up the mocking mental image of Chris; feeling a little like he's generously salting an open wound, Ben forces himself to ask: "No Chris, huh? Where's he tonight?"

Pete's brow furrows briefly, as if in deep thought. "Hmm. Weehawken, probably? I'm not sure what he's up to this weekend —why?"

Because a normal person would bring their boyfriend to an

event like this, Ben does not say. It is, if nothing else, a sentence that would disqualify him from being a judge of normalcy the moment he uttered it, and he does his best to avoid letting those escape. Instead, in what he hopes is a tone of casual inquiry and not desperate interest, he says, "Oh, because, um... he came with you to that Halloween thing? So I thought—"

"Ah, yeah, no, different vibe," Pete says, on a slight laugh. "This isn't his kind of party—it would need to be either three degrees fancier or four degrees less fancy to meet his very exacting standards for attendance." In slightly self-deprecating tones, like he thinks it's an entertaining joke, he adds, "In a real sense, I am merely a vessel through which Chris attains access to parties. If he doesn't want to go, what would be the point?"

Chris sounds like a terrible boyfriend, and I'd like to throw him into the Hudson River. Ben, again, keeps this to himself on the argument that saying it would be both mortifying and utterly incompatible with his general mission of projecting "It's me, your colleague Ben, a regular guy who has never even thought about putting my tongue in your mouth." He thinks it quite hard, as instead he says, "Okay, talk to me about this fanciness points system. Is there actually a scale? Or does it run on vibes?"

The question has a very simple answer—it does, indeed, run on vibes—but somehow, the conversation that springs out of it covers them across the room, through both the drink line and the wait for their ordered beverages, and halfway through drinking said beverages. By the time they've established that they are, honestly, pretty bad drinks for a food industry party, they've also come up with a comprehensive set of metrics and qualities on which to measure and rate the fanciness of events, complete with a little chart Pete draws on the back of a cocktail napkin.

Ben doesn't know, suddenly, why he was worried about this. It's easy, talking to Pete. It's delightful. It *always* is.

It's interrupted, of course, by a wide-eyed, round-faced man, who is wearing what appears to be his most formal sweater vest, hurrying over them. "Pete? Ben? Is that you?"

Ben stares at the man, confused, as under his breath, Pete mutters, "Do you know this guy?"

"No," Ben hisses back out of the corner of his mouth. "Gathering you don't, either?"

"Not a clue," Pete whispers, and then the stranger is upon them, sticking out a hand for first Pete, and then Ben, to shake.

"Hi, hi, so good to meet you both in person, finally," the man says, as he pumps each of their hands up and down exactly three times before releasing. "Sorry to be rude—I know you, of course, from the videos, but you wouldn't know me. I'm Dave! From Standards and Practices! Ben, we've exchanged a lot of emails—"

"Ah," Ben says, finding it's suddenly a struggle to keep his voice neutral and friendly. "*Dave*. Yes. Good to—put a face to the name."

"Likewise!" Dave grins at Ben, broad and guileless. "Although I've seen you before, of course—you pop up in the show here and there—and *you*, naturally, I've seen a lot." Dave doesn't notice Pete's brief, hastily concealed grimace, but Ben does and wants to echo the expression himself. "But it's different in person, isn't it?"

"It sure is, Dave," Ben says, to spare Pete from having to think of anything. Then, because he can't quite help himself, he adds, "You know, speaking of being in person—I've got a question I've been wanting to ask you for weeks, Dave, and since we're here—"

"Oh, shoot," Dave says, patting his own stomach lightly twice, as if in invitation. In invitation for what, Ben is unsure and hopes not to find out, but it's what the gesture communicates just the same. "I'm an open book."

"Why," Ben says, keeping his tone casual and trying to conceal the enormous irritation he's felt about this since he first saw the schedule, "the varying deadlines, Dave? Some weeks S&P needs the video one day in advance—others three—others four! My last delivery time for you was barely two hours ago, and I know you can neither be applying whatever standards nor doing whatever practices you typically get up to, Dave, because you're *here*, Dave—"

Pete's voice is low, and amused, and close in his ear; Ben is abruptly very aware of the rush of Pete's breath, warm air tickling over the sensitive skin. "Just a heads-up: You're saying Dave's name a lot."

Ben, not trusting himself to answer with any degree of composure at this moment, just nods, taking the note. But Dave doesn't seem to notice. His brow is creased in what appears to be very deep thought.

"Let me give that one a little ponder," he says. He reaches up a hand and for a few moments just stands there, tapping his chin in contemplation. Eventually, dropping his hand and shaking his head, he says, "I'm sorry, fellas—I can't say I know what you're talking about. There must've been some confusion."

Even without knowing what the man is about to say, Ben feels his blood pressure ratcheting up. Immediately forgetting Pete's note, and ignoring the soft snort of laughter from behind him as he says it, Ben snaps, "*What* sort of confusion, Dave?"

"Well," Dave says, slow and thoughtful, "I'm not sure. I can tell you I only need about an hour for most videos that come through; yours take me even less time. They're fun to watch, you know? So forty minutes or so usually does it!" When Ben's jaw drops open in a mixture of shock and fury, Dave grins at him and pats him on the shoulder. "Aw, you're nice, but it's not that impressive; I could always go faster if it was crunch time. Anyway, nice to meet you!" And he walks off, smiling sunnily, clearly one of those people for whom the toast always lands buttered side up.

Ben, who has never dropped a piece of toast without buttering the floor in the process, stares after him in wordless, boiling rage. "Do you know," he says eventually, "how many hours of sleep I have lost since I started this job? Because of Dave? Because of needing to send our videos? To Dave? Because it was *so* urgent that Dave get them *exactly* by the set deadlines, it said so in that email *so* many times, and he was—it—he—forty minutes, Pete! He only needs forty minutes!" In tones of genuine hysteria, he adds, "He could go faster! If it was crunch time!!!"

"I think," Pete says, in grave and, very kindly, only slightly entertained tones, "you may have been Miranda'd here. Nobody likes it when Miranda is a verb—believe me, I know."

"*Why* is she even *doing* this?" Ben complains, because it's been bothering him. "It's good for her if the show does well! Does she just hate me? Does my face inspire in her a fountain of rage? Will she not rest until she and Dave have driven me to the very brink of despair?"

For a second Pete's face changes. It looks almost scared, or worried, or nervous, or *something*. But then Pete laughs and takes him by the elbow, murmuring, "Ooookay, I think maybe we need to get you a drink better than the swill they're serving down here. You seem like maybe you're about to snap and kill someone."

"No jury would convict!" Ben says wildly, even as he lets Pete steer him towards the doors out to the main lobby area. "Crime of passion!"

"I'm reasonably certain juries do convict for those, you know," Pete says dryly. "Come on, come up to the offices with me? I can make us something worth drinking up there."

A little part of Ben wants to stay and track Miranda down in the crowd, pick a fight just for something to *do* with all this annoyance, but Pete's hand is warm at his elbow, and his suitcase is up in the offices anyway, and: "Oh, all *right*," Ben says, and lets himself be led out of the party.

Ben can almost feel his blood pressure dropping as the elevator rises towards the thirty-fourth floor, a weird, inverse reaction. Pete's telling him some story about one of Miranda's previous crimes—something about a cancelled shipment of very particular cheese—and while Ben's not paying a huge amount of attention, the sound of his voice is calming. Slowly, he feels his shoulders lower from where they've been bunched up around his ears and allows his breathing to settle into something that less resembles a rage-induced pant.

It occurs to Ben, too late, that this perhaps was not the most alluring side of himself to show to Pete. Renata's always told him that he's like a cartoon character when he gets into that particular mood, stomping and stamping and looking like he should have steam coming out of his ears; it's not one of his more attractive qualities.

But when Pete quirks an eyebrow and says, "Feeling better?" he doesn't sound annoyed, or resigned, or like he thinks Ben's made an ass of himself. He looks entertained. "I *am* sorry, you know, about the lost sleep. I know some of that's my fault—"

"Oh, shut up," Ben says, no rancor behind it at all. "I didn't mind *doing* it, it's just that it *didn't have to be done*. He *only* needed *forty*—"

"Okay, okay, let's not start that again," Pete says, laughing, as the elevator doors ding open. He steps behind Ben, puts a hand on each of his shoulders, and begins frog-marching him out of the elevator. "Come on, that's it, onward. No more talk of Dave."

"*Dave*," Ben mutters darkly, though his heart's not in it. He's too busy enjoying the warmth of Pete's hands against his shoulders, the way he could close his eyes and tell himself this moment was happening in another context, in another place. Somewhere private, where they could be completely alone, and Chris was guaranteed not to be around. Somewhere they would be unlikely to inconveniently fall asleep, or get distracted, or otherwise be pulled away from what sometimes, to Ben, feels like a personal altered gravity between them, like they're asteroids falling into the sun.

The motion-triggered overhead lights flicker on one by one as Pete pushes Ben down the hall towards the test kitchen, leaving his hands on Ben's shoulders long after he could have pulled them away. It occurs to Ben, in a moment of brilliant, sparkling clarity, that he doesn't have to close his eyes to imagine the ideal conditions to find himself in with Pete right now: He's *in* them, accidentally but entirely. All he has to do is play his cards right.

And, well, okay, live with a little bit of guilt, probably, about attempting to seduce Pete away from his hot, mean boyfriend in hopes of being his... well, somewhat less hot and still fairly mean boyfriend, but! Ben wouldn't be mean *to Pete*, that's the important thing. The critical crux of the issue.

When they reach the kitchen, Pete stops pushing. He does, however, squeeze Ben's shoulders lightly as he says, "Drink?" before letting him go.

"God, anything," Ben says, feeling drunk just on the proximity to him, the sheer privacy of the moment. Obviously, anyone *could* come up to the test kitchen tonight, but Ben can't imagine why they would. It's all closed down for the weekend: everything in its proper home, all the dishes put away, all the surfaces sanitized, various floor mats hung over the sinks to dry. It would be a pain to come in here and cook now; you'd have to get everything set up and then broken back down again, at least for whatever station you wanted to use.

Easy enough to make a drink, though. Pete grabs a few highball glasses out of the dishroom, liberates a jar of something labeled only with PETE's from the Keeps fridge, and then pulls a few bottles off the liquor cart in the back corner. He pours and mixes for a minute, tasting off a tiny spoon, then nods and dumps the mix into a cocktail shaker with a large cube of ice he snatches from the freezer.

He lifts it to shake and—pauses, glancing down at his outfit. Sheepishly, he says, "Okay, can I be honest here?"

"Oh, definitely," Ben says, as much out of curiosity as kindness.

"My sister really *does* have expensive taste," Pete admits. "But I'm not exactly rolling in it, so I may or may not have left the tags on this coat? And... the sweater? So I can return them? And I feel like—" He glances grimly from the cocktail shaker to his station and shakes his head. "I know there's not any cameras here *now*, but it feels like tempting fate, doesn't it? After so many mishaps?"

"Oh, *definitely*," Ben says again, because it's that or say, "You know, just to be safe, maybe you should get totally naked. And I, too, should get totally naked. And then we, once totally naked, could determine our next steps from there. What do you say?" It doesn't seem like his best move.

He doesn't have to make it, anyway. To Ben's absolute delight, Pete nods, and takes off his jacket, which he drapes carefully over Brogan's station, out of harm's way. Then, with a little shrug, he pulls the sweater up over his head, too, revealing that he is wearing nothing but a ratty black tank top underneath, one that looks like it has seen better days.

Oh, hell, Ben thinks, dry-mouthed and distant, *I've miscalculated here. He's too hot and I'm going to die*, but then Pete picks up the cocktail shaker. Ben watches, transfixed, as Pete shakes the drink, lost in the ripple and flex of the muscles in his shoulders, his arms.

Pete, does your boyfriend know you're here sexily shaking drinks at me as though I have some sort of bartending fetish and you're determined to show me a good time? Ben neither says this nor wants to say this; it's a thought that pops up unbidden, determined to sully his happiness, and Ben wrestles it quickly aside.

"What, ah." Ben pauses, noticing his voice is coming out as more of a dried-out croak than anything, and clears his throat. "What are you making?"

"Oh, remember that drink you let me try at the Halloween party?" Pete grins when Ben nods, and, tragically, sets the cocktail shaker down, breaking the seal, putting ice in their glasses, and pulling a tiny strainer from a drawer as he talks. "Well, it was *good*, but I kept thinking about it, because I thought it could be, you know, better. So for the last few weeks, I've been letting these finger limes infuse in this mezcal, and I strained that out as the base and shook it with ice and simple syrup and a little bit of the lime pulp. Oh, except juniper wasn't quite right with the mezcal, so it's a brown sugar grapefruit simple now, and as I lay it all out, basically it's a totally different drink, but." He sets a glass in front of Ben and strains the cocktail into it as he finishes, his smile going small and sheepish. "I'm still going to call it the Hot Dog Panic Attack."

"How could you not?" Ben says, after a beat in which he wrestles back the urge to attempt a vault over the counter for reasons of sheer attraction, which would both be embarrassing and, likely as not, end in the emergency room. Ben is a lot of things, but athletic? Not so much. He contents himself, instead, with saying, "Didn't seem like a great experience, but a great name for a cocktail."

"I don't know," Pete says, still smiling. "It could have been worse. If you have to have a panic attack, and that panic attack has to be while you are, for all intents and purposes, a hot dog, I think doing it in such good company is probably the best-case scenario." He takes a sip of the drink while Ben, sure he's flushed bright red, searches for a response to this, and adds, sounding satisfied, "Mmm, yeah, that's how I wanted this to taste. Go on, try it. I think you'll like it."

Ben doesn't doubt at all that he'll like it; he's concerned that one single additional sip of alcohol is all that stands between him and letting go of the paltry remains of his self-control. But he picks up the glass anyway, holding eye contact with Pete as he swallows for far longer than he should and releasing an embarrassing little moan of satisfaction when the beverage—nothing like the one from the Halloween party and somehow akin to it anyway, managing to be both brighter and smokier while hitting in the same refreshing, citrusy spot—has finished sliding down his throat. "*God*, that's *sublime.*"

Pete doesn't reply; as Ben greedily takes another sip, he notices Pete's eyes are fixed on his throat and nearly chokes as he swallows.

At this point, a little voice begins to sound in the back of Ben's mind. He can barely hear it through the haze of desire and, admittedly, growing tipsiness, but it's saying something along the lines of, "Hello, Benjamin, it's me! Your conscience! Things are going a little far here, my good man, wouldn't you say? A bit beyond the old pale? So this seems like the perfect moment to point out to Pete that he does have a boyfriend, and that you, Ben, have never been involved with any sort of cheating, and that even if he is, okay, the hottest human being who has ever shown even a glimmer of interest in you, that doesn't mean—hey! No! Oh, God, wait, don't make me go back there, there are *so* many neuroses running around—"

Having shoved this voice firmly back into the recesses of his mind, Ben turns his attention, once again, to the man before him. Pete's taking a pull from his own drink, then grinning down at it, smiling in satisfaction.

"You know how sometimes," he says, turning his gaze on Ben and letting his smile go smaller, "there's just the best possible version of something? Or maybe not the *best*, but the version that's most yours. That works the best for *you*." He swirls his still-full glass in his hand without looking away from Ben; Ben, at something of a remove, thinks it really shouldn't be so hot, the way he doesn't spill a single drop. "I love figuring out stuff like that, don't you? The right way to approach a given dish, or a given drink, or." He pauses, tilting his head slightly, almost a question, but not quite. "A given person."

"Pete?" Ben's heart is hammering in his chest, but he tries to tell himself his voice comes out smooth and cool. This lie becomes less convincing the longer he talks. "To be painfully, excruciatingly honest here, I feel like we've entered the territory where, like, how it's supposed to go is you say something smooth, and then *I* say something smooth, except I'm not going to say something smooth, okay? I'm *never* going to say something smooth. You have to assume I'm like someone who was raised by wolves or in a cave or on the *moon*, I'm not *suave*, I'm going to say something weird! Or off-putting! Or become completely convinced that I'm reading the signals all wrong and you really *are* trying to have a conversation about the joy of recipe development or whatever—"

And then Pete is rounding the counter, chuckling slightly as he closes the distance between them with all the easy confidence Ben's never seen him summon on camera, seemingly not nervous at all. He steps into Ben's space with grace and ease, crowding him back against the counter just enough to force Ben to look up at him, breath caught in his throat, as Pete says, "I'm not trying to have a conversation about the joys of recipe development, Ben, no."

Ben should wait for Pete to kiss him, give himself some scrap of plausible deniability, not to mention dignity; he does not. His self-control gives way all in one go—in spite of weeks of telling himself he had it all under control, it snaps like a twig the very instant Ben's certain this whole thing hasn't been in his head. He grabs Pete by the worn straps of his tank top and pulls him down into the kiss, letting go of one strap to slide a hand up Pete's neck, into his hair, when Pete snakes an arm around his back and pulls him close.

"My good man!" Ben's conscience screams, as though briefly surfacing from the ever-churning sea of anxiety that is Ben's internal landscape. "Wait a moment, please! We can talk about this! A nice breath of fresh air, that's what you... Oh. Oh, well, I must say, this *is* quite a good kiss, isn't it? Of course my objections stand, but he does seem to know what he's—wait, is that his *hand* against your thigh or—do you know what? You seem to be handling this without me anyway, so. No hard feelings! See you for our guilt trip later, already got it scheduled, looking forward, bye!"

Ben forgets very quickly about his conscience, and then about ever having even had one. He forgets about Chris, and about the party downstairs, and his dreaded early bird flight to Michigan in a few short hours. He forgets about the videos, and *Late Night with Brian O'Malley*, and Pete's horrible, unlucky history with the internet. Who, he thinks, when he can think at all, could remember anything right now? This is a time for recording the present, not sifting around in the past, and for the moment Ben lets everything go but the here and now.

He kisses Pete like he's wanted to kiss Pete for weeks: hungrily, and intensely, and possessively, with an amount of himself in it that would usually scare him. It doesn't scare him. Pete's kissing him back too thoroughly and too well for Ben to access that brand of terror right now.

Ben had assumed, based on Pete's personality, his daily struggles to find items like his keys, wallet, or phone, and essentially everything else about him, that he might be a bit unfocused in this arena, easily distracted or hard to follow. After all, anyone that hot wouldn't have to try very hard, not if they didn't want to. God knows Ben, in his various imaginings of things, had not minded the thought of having to direct Pete a little. It wasn't exactly his usual vibe, but for Pete, and Pete's body and hands and face, and the way Pete wears a pair of jeans—well. Ben would have been more than happy to cover any gaps.

But to his surprise and pleasure, Pete focuses on Ben the way he's able to focus on a complicated culinary process, at least if no camera is rolling. He's not scattered and in need of direction; he kisses Ben meticulously, with an attention to detail that steals Ben's breath from his chest. His hands are everywhere—stroking Ben's neck, sliding up the back of his shirt—and then both dropping low, fingertips sinking into the soft flesh of Ben's thighs through the thin fabric of his suit trousers. He lifts Ben as though he weighs nothing, as though he's a side of beef or a Christmas ham, and deposits him gently on top of the counter, *all while kissing him.*

"God," Ben gasps, half laughing, when Pete pulls away to press a kiss against his jawbone, "we're going to have to re-sanitize all the surfaces—"

"To be honest," Pete breathes, low and hot in Ben's ear, "I wouldn't say I'm concerned about that right now." And then they don't talk anymore.

TWELVE

A few hours later, as though it was all some kind of wild fever dream, Ben finds himself wandering dopily around JFK, smiling at every Hudson News as though it's a wonder of the world. He feels... different, inside his skin. Like his glorious hour and a half with Pete pulled his soul out of his body, gave it a good shake, laundered it, darned up the holes, and slipped it back into place, just in time for the afterglow to be cut short by the insistent ringing of Ben's "LEAVE FOR THE AIRPORT NOW, YOU IDIOT" alarm.

Pete had been good about that, though. Pete had been good about everything.

Pete had been... *good*. Ben can't quite stop thinking about just *how* good he'd been, how skillful and attentive, how playful, how *responsive*. Some of the sounds he'd made—

—no, Ben cannot *think* about this here, in the migraine-inducing fluorescent lighting of JFK's underwhelming halls. This is a place for waiting for an airplane, boarding an airplane, or partaking in one of a variety of miserable side-quests that can occur between one and the other. It is not a place for remembering what Pete's body had felt like against his, or under his hands, or the way he'd kissed Ben goodbye and whispered, "Fly out of LaGuardia next time, yeah? It's closer to the office; you wouldn't have to go just yet."

Ben can see, now, that this would have been a great opportunity to say something like, "I think you'd better take me to dinner before you go dictating my airport choices," or, indeed, "Will next time be before or after you break up with the hot guy who considers you a party ticket, your commitment to whom we have never otherwise discussed?" Instead, he had squeaked, "Next time?"

Pete had just grinned, and shaken his head, and kissed him again before sending him off, saying he'd take care of the various surfaces which needed re-sanitizing. It was a good kiss, one Ben is reliving in spite of his internal admonishments not to, when he hears, once again, from his conscience.

"It's not that I don't understand why you did it," it begins, hesitant in the back of his mind. "But I wonder, I do, if you have considered the consequences. Considered them thoroughly, and all the way through to the end. If, for example, you were walking through the airport, and you happened to *see* Chris, *walking directly towards you—*"

"Oh my God," Ben breathes, stopping dead in his tracks and then, in a moment of true insanity, ducking behind a vending machine so as to remain unseen. He tries to tell himself it's a waking nightmare, a hallucination born of guilt, but no: *Chris himself* is indeed walking towards him. That's bad enough on its own, but he appears to be with—

—walking hand in hand, with, actually—

—*stopping to kiss another man*, a man who is *not* Pete, right here in the middle of John F. Kennedy Airport. For anyone to see!

In this particular moment of Ben's life, a variety of seemingly unrelated things are true. True: He has had several drinks over the course of the night, and is still, if he's honest, a little less than sober. True: He has, for some weeks, been harboring a private well of rage for Chris for many reasons of his own, and to see him stepping out on Pete like this is simply a bridge too far. True: Ben *does* happen to know Pete is *also* stepping out on Chris, extensively and with great enthusiasm, because Ben was there and ecstatic for the entire event, and it was only about an hour ago. And, true: Because of all of the above, the smart thing for Ben to do is put his head down, let them pass, and keep his big mouth shut.

But when someone blows your mind in the bedroom—or, as the facts run in this case, the *Gastronome* test kitchen—it apparently takes out a few of your *critical brain cells*. Surely, it's this, or perhaps a combination of this and his unwise second, post-coital Hot Dog Panic Attack that has Ben striding ferociously out of his hiding spot, stalking across the floor, and, when Chris has broken apart from his damningly not-Pete paramour, snapping, "Well, well, well. Aren't you supposed to be in Weehawken?"

Chris stares at him, visibly confused. "No? *What?*"

"As if you don't know what I'm talking about," Ben says, crossing his arms over his chest. "What would your *boyfriend* think of you being here, huh? What about that?"

"Who even *are* you?" Chris demands, his brow creasing. "What would my boyfriend think? I'm with him! Right now! Behold!" He holds up their joined hands, as if in evidence, and adds, to him, "What do you think, babe? About me being here?"

"I think you better not be cheating on me with some guy in Weehawken," the man says, but mildly enough. "But as far as I can tell, all your dad's neighbors are ugly, so. I'm not that worried about it."

"Thanks, baby," Chris says, sounding touched. "Your trust means a lot."

"So," Ben splutters, a growing and embarrassing awareness that he's maybe been projecting here starting to surface, "so—so if *this* is your boyfriend, then, you're, what, *using* Pete? For free *tickets* to things?"

Chris's eyes bug for a second, and then his hand flies to his mouth and he says, "Oh my God, you're the *ketchup* guy. From the Halloween—Luke, remember I told you about the—"

At this point, Chris's Boyfriend—Ben's going to go ahead and assume his name is Luke—cuts in. "Oh, you mean from the food—"

"Right, and Pete was all—"

"And this is *him*," Luke says, giving Ben a brief once-over, "and he thinks that you and *Pete...*" He, too, puts a hand over his mouth, but Ben realizes with a sinking feeling that he is concealing laughter. "God, I'm sorry, I'm going to go stand over there until I can get myself under control."

He walks off as Chris puts his hands on his hips and stares at Ben.

Ben wilts under the 5,000-watt intensity of Chris's stare; he thinks *glass* would probably wilt. "Okay, I can see I've read this wrong somewhere, but I was—"

Chris, looking irritated, holds up a finger. "Stop; I'm trying to work out the fastest way to explain the enormity of your mistake, because I have things to do, shockingly enough, with my time. So, you know Pete pretty well?" Ben nods. "You know about him changing his name, back in the day?" Ben nods, wincing slightly. "You know what his name used to be?"

At Ben's final nod, Chris nods back, then makes a thumbs-up, points it at himself, and says, sounding very annoyed, "Chris Castillo. His *cousin*."

"His... cousin." Ben stands for a long, silent moment, horror seeming to have turned all his blood to an icy sludge. Then, hideously, before he can stop it, what comes out of his mouth is, "Are you sure?"

Though Ben can't see him, he hears an enormous whoop of laughter from somewhere nearby that sounds suspiciously as though it came from Luke.

Chris does not look amused. "Am I *sure* that he's my *cousin*? Well, let's see. His father's my uncle, check. *My* father's *his* uncle, check. But, wait, are our fathers brothers—why, who could believe it, they are! Like, what do you *mean* am I sure? He's my cousin! He's been my cousin since the day I was born. Are you asking if I think he's been bodyswapped? Because my answer is no!" There is another peal of laughter at this point, which confirms for Ben that it's coming from Luke, wherever he's gone to, since Chris snaps, "You shut up, Luke, this isn't that funny!"

"I don't know," Luke calls back, "I think it's at least medium funny."

"I personally would like to die about it," Ben says, in the brightly brittle tones of someone who has moved past simply being mortified and into a plane of existence where mortified is the only thing they've ever been, or shall ever be again. "If that's helpful at all. I'm going to go and, um, stop having this interaction as fast as possible, if it's all the same to you. Thanks so much, and sorry for the, um, interruption to your morning, and is there any chance that maybe you won't tell—"

"Pete? About this conversation? No," Chris says, flat, one eyebrow up. "There is no chance of that. None whatsoever. I'm already anticipating retelling this story at every family holiday for, and this is an estimate, the rest of my natural life, so. Nice seeing you—what was your name? If you give me a fake one, I'll just tell him that, too, you know."

"Ben," Ben says, on a sigh, "I'm Ben, and I'm sorry, and I'm leaving," and then he's hurrying away to one last peal of laughter from Luke, before he can screw up anything else.

The flight that follows is punishing, in that Ben tries to close his eyes and get some rest but can't quite manage it. Either he's treated to a Technicolor replay of everything that happened with Chris, *or* he experiences two or three moments of exquisite memory of his evening with Pete, before the thought of how Pete will *react* to what happened with Chris crashes in to spoil his fun. All in all, by the time he lands in Michigan, weathers an uncomfortable Uber ride, and lets himself into his parents' building around 5:45 a.m., Ben is vibrating with tension, semi-hungover, and sure to his bones that he's ruined everything. He crashes onto the twin bed in what was once his childhood bedroom and is now ostensibly the guest room, expecting to lie awake in anguish until he hears his family start getting up. Since this room's actual purpose has become housing his father's model plane building hobby somewhere his mother doesn't have to look at it, there is, if nothing else, plenty for his exhausted eyes to behold. It's reminded him for years of a page from an *I Spy* book.

But to his surprise, Ben finds himself blinking awake three hours later to the sound of his phone ringing instead. Rolling over as though he's in his full-size bed at home, and nearly pitching off the mattress as a result, he scrambles around looking for it. It could be his cat sitter saying something happened to Roux, or Mrs. C calling to say she's fallen and she can't get up, or—

—Ben swallows hard, having found the phone. *Pete.*

He almost doesn't answer, but the thought of letting it go to voicemail makes him feel like such a coward he forces himself to pick up the call. Still, he's hoping as he lifts the phone to his ear that maybe Chris had a change of heart and this is a work emergency—a follow-up from last night—*anything* but Pete calling to say that he heard Ben's a total freak show and so he'd like to strike everything that happened between them from the official record and, also, file a restraining order.

But when he's finally got the little speaker in range, Ben realizes that Pete is laughing. Not a mocking laugh, or a mean one—a breathless, wildly entertained laugh, a laugh that sounds like it has survived several attempts to get it under control. He gasps, "Do you have *any* idea how many *weird* conversations this explains," and then, "I'm sorry, it's not that I don't see why you thought—Ben, I can't tell you how many times I watched him eat rubber *cement* as a kid! You couldn't have known but—I mean, even the *idea* that we'd be—" and then he's howling again, clearly too amused to speak.

After a second Ben finds, to his surprise, that he's chuckling, too. Pete's not laughing *at* him, not exactly—Ben knows what it is to be laughed at, a sad corner of his soul trapped for eternity in that auditorium when he was a teenager, trying everything he could think of to shut the feed off. This isn't like that. Pete's laughter is warm and delighted, so obviously tickled by the whole stupid, embarrassing thing that Ben, in spite of himself, can't help but feel a bit better about it.

Still, he groans, as good-naturedly as he can manage. "I'm glad this is how you're taking it. I thought maybe, instead, you might be calling to lie to me out of misguided kindness? Tell me you're, just to give you a random example that's definitely never been used on me before, unexpectedly moving to Nebraska in three hours, and not to worry if I never hear from you again, or if I see someone around the city who looks *just* like you but seems not to know me at all—" This make Pete's laughter, which had been quieting down, kick off again, which is weirdly gratifying. "So, like, I'll take this. But I am *sorry*, for the record. I'd like to use this opportunity to officially lay the blame at the feet of the Hot Dog Panic Attack. A wonderful, delicious, and above all *dangerous* drink."

"I'll be sure to issue a warning when I publish the recipe," Pete says, on a final chuckle. He takes a few breaths—there's a sound like maybe he's wiping tears of mirth from his eyes—and then he says, still a little amused, "I think it's sweet, for what it's worth. You trying to defend my honor like that. Misdirected, sure. And I guess you *could* say a *little* hypocritical, given that about an hour before-hand I had you—"

"I *know*," Ben groans again, though he shivers a little at the memory of the position he suspects Pete's talking about. "Even as I was *doing* it, I knew I was being a hypocrite. I don't normally *do* things like that, for the record. I'm normally, like, chill! Low-key!"

"Are you?" Pete sounds, if possible, even more entertained. "Are you really?"

"Okay, no, of course I'm not," Ben snaps, no real heat behind it. "But I keep it to myself! Inside! Where inside thoughts belong! I have a very good grasp, okay, usually, on that line, and I don't want you to think this is like—my *vibe*—oh, God." Ben stares, despairingly, up at the ceiling. "Can we talk about something else?"

"Sure," says Pete, "one sec," and, muffled as though he's

covered the speaker with one hand, Ben hears him order a cup of black coffee from what must be a newsstand. After barely a minute, he's back, and now that Ben's had a second to wake up, he can tell from the background noise that Pete must be walking, on his way to whatever his Sunday morning entails. "Sorry; I have to undo my sister's purchasing spree this morning, and I can't face that without caffeine."

"God knows I get that," says Ben, who, now that he is fully conscious, is already considering the fastest route to coffee. "I'm reasonably sure that at this point what's running through my veins is more dark roast than blood." As always when he comes back to Michigan, he remembers too late that he should have packed some of those awful canned lattes, or even some chocolate-covered espresso beans—anything to ensure that his path to caffeination doesn't have to run through either parent. Lucia's coffee is punishingly strong, even for Ben, and Daniel's might as well be tar. Ben will drink either if he has to, but he won't be happy about it.

He's distracted from this utterly when Pete says, "Okay, you wanted something else to talk about, right? How about this: Is it too early to ask what you're wearing?"

Ben both flushes with pleasure and, grimacing down at himself, wonders if this is the sort of situation in which a man is supposed to lie. Honesty has worked out inexplicably well with Pete so far, so he sighs and says, "Uh. The same undershirt I had on last night and... a pair of my sister's Hello Kitty pajama bottoms from like 2004?" Ben glares accusingly down at the pants, which had been sitting on the top of a basket of Renata's laundry when he'd stumbled inside, and which he'd unhesitatingly swiped on the theory that he was too tired to dig his own out of his suitcase. "Uh. In a hot way?"

Pete laughs again, warm, almost musical against the sounds of the city behind him, like a lifeline back to the world Ben chose. In spite of himself, and his pajama bottoms, and the room full of tiny bottles of paint and weird miniscule airplane parts and so many sticks of balsa wood that Ben half wants to call the fire department on his own father, he starts to feel like maybe his toast is finally going to start landing buttered side up.

It's not what Ben would call a *good* week, the next week of his life. He's not sure he and his family have ever spent an *entirely* good week together, at least not since he and Renata hit adulthood. It's never an entirely bad time, either, what time they manage to spend as a family these days; it's not as though they're cruel or hateful to one another, driving each other to tears or screaming. It's just that each one of them seems, in whatever undefinable way, to be designed to subtly irritate the others, like a small-scale pearl farm.

On Mondays, for example, the restaurant is closed, so they agree on Sunday morning they'll all go out to dinner the following evening, as a family. Then they spend all day Sunday and most of Monday morning going back and forth about the place—Renata wants to go to the Chinese place downtown, but Daniel has some long-standing personal beef with the owner there (one which is, in Ben's opinion, Daniel's own fault), and couldn't it be a steakhouse? He gets one night out a year, basically, it couldn't be a steakhouse? But then Lucia's offended—one night out a year? How could Daniel say that? Does their monthly bridge night mean *nothing* to him? The salsa lessons they took last winter? And, also, she doesn't want steak *or* Chinese, she wants a good sandwich, doesn't anyone make a good sandwich anymore? And Renata says a sandwich isn't dinner food, and Lucia says she didn't raise her children to be too good to eat sandwiches for dinner, and then Daniel says *he* didn't raise *his* children not to offer an opinion, and everyone turns, expectant, to stare at Ben.

But when Ben shrugs uncomfortably and mutters, "I honestly don't care what we eat? I just don't want to argue about it," Daniel huffs out an annoyed breath, and Lucia rolls her eyes, and Renata gives him a look that clearly communicates, "Ooof, a swing and a miss, you hate to see it," which is... great. It's juuuuust great. It makes Ben feel totally awesome.

The truth is, in a perfect world, things would have worked out differently in Ben's family. In a perfect world, after they made their little deal—Lucia would name any daughters, and Daniel any sons —and then, by luck of the draw, had one of each, his parents' favoritism would have broken out more evenly. Perhaps Lucia would have preferred Renata, having named her, but Daniel would have focused his attentions on Ben, committed to building a strong bond between father and son. Or, equally acceptable, it could have gone the other way, with Lucia preferring Ben, and Daniel preferring Renata, each enjoying the reflection of the other they saw therein. In a *truly* perfect world, of course, they would have simply loved both of their children equally. Even in his fantasies, though, Ben can never quite imagine that.

In any case, Ben doesn't live in a perfect world, and in this one, it broke out that *both* his parents prefer Renata. Ben doesn't entirely blame them; between himself and his sister, he, too, prefers Renata. People tend to. Renata is loud and charming and vivacious and funny, like their mother, but also grounded and rational and never misses a trick, like their father. Ben loves her, of course—she's his sister, and he has to—but he genuinely does *like* her, enjoys her company and the person she is, especially when it's only the two of them. It's only that after a couple of days of watching her communicate with their parents in a language he has never been able to learn, the obviousness of the difference between those relationships and his... rankles.

But Pete helps. He helps so much that Ben is honestly embarrassed about it; he keeps pulling out his phone to look at his messages in quiet moments when no one else is around, looking over both shoulders as though afraid of being caught in a crime. It's ridiculous—it's not as though blushing, or smiling soppily down at the screen, is illegal. It's not as though his father is going to snatch his phone away, start scrolling through his texts, get to the dirty ones (this, in fairness, wouldn't take him long), and then scream, "My eyes! My eyes!" while instantaneously dying of sheer horror. Ben could say, "I have to jump on the phone with this guy I'm talking to, back in a bit," instead of making up some weird lie about going on a walk for his mental robustness and fortitude on the recommendation of a podcast. If, as he knows they would, his family pushed and pressed him for details, he could say no, and refuse to give them, and weather the evening of sulking awkwardness that would result.

He doesn't want to, though. It's so *new*, of course, that's part of it, still undefined even between them because it isn't a conversation Ben wants to approach over the phone or in text, but it's not just that. He spends the week puzzling over it, turning it over and over in his mind as he covers several shifts at the restaurant, and cooks two-thirds of Thanksgiving dinner, and peels potatoes with his mother for an hour while she complains about Ben's father, and watches the parade for an hour with his father while he complains about Ben's mother.

But it's not until Thursday night that Ben figures it out. It's after everyone's partaken of The Thanksgiving Meal, and moaned, and claimed they couldn't eat another bite, and made room for dessert, and groaned, and said they couldn't possibly bear to eat a single thing more, and made room for one more dessert, and collapsed in a heap on whatever piece of furniture was nearest. This is all normal enough for Thanksgiving, but Ben finds within him a very nontraditional burst of energy after about an hour in the heap stage, when he receives a text from Pete that says, *free from dinner. u around?* And then, a second later, another text, that's just a phone emoji.

"I'm going out for, uh, air," Ben says, standing up. Normally, someone would offer him a "What, so the air in here isn't good enough for you?" It's a sign of how stuffed everyone is that all he receives in response to this is a series of semi-agreeable groans, and a wave—more of a hand-flop—from Renata.

But Pete is bright and cheerful when Ben gets outside and calls him, bubbling over with energy; it was a good Thanksgiving at his father's restaurant, better than he expected, and he's so pleased to have the nice memory, and for nothing to have gone horribly wrong. He laughingly relates several humorous anecdotes about his nieces and nephews, tells a story that leaves Ben in stitches about his sister Michelle, a cabbie, and her neighbor's illegal pet lemur, and in return Ben tells him the story of the Thanksgiving of his fourteenth year, when his cousin Billy, all of five years old, had screamed out, "I'M A MAGIC MAN," and attempted to pull the tablecloth out from under the spread. He had not achieved this—he had dumped the entire Thanksgiving feast to the floor—and the collective meltdown which had followed ultimately resulted in each branch of the Blumenthals having their own separate Thanksgiving celebration, which was safer for everyone.

Pete clearly enjoys this story, but then he says, voice going wry with a different brand of amusement, "Speaking of annoying little cousins with a reputation for ruining family parties: Chris says hi."

Ben groans, sure he's blushing so deeply that it would be visible to random passersby; he's glad it's Thanksgiving night, and basically everyone in town is either passed out or might as well be. "I was really hoping he was kidding when he said he was going to tell your entire family that story. But he wasn't, was he?"

"He was not," Pete confirms; Ben thinks he must be grinning. "But if it's any comfort, I think it made my family like you? They all agreed that your heart was in the right place, and I didn't exactly mention to them what we'd been getting up to right beforehand, for reasons I hope are obvious, so you're in the clear there. My dad says he wants to meet you; he says you should come by the restaurant sometime."

"Really?" Ben asks, embarrassed that it comes out slightly squeaking. "That wouldn't be weird for you?"

"Nah," Pete says, his tone easy, open, unafraid. "You're welcome anytime."

It's cold on the street, under the forever-glowing red neon Trattoria Luciana sign; it's always cold here this time of year, the wind biting under the tightest-pulled scarf. But when Ben shivers, it's from warmth: not just in Pete's voice, not just in the nature of the invitation, but at the slow, sinking-in-all-over realization of how easy it is to talk to Pete. How easy it is to just *be* with him. How it's never a long, intricate argument; how Pete never makes him feel disappointing, or like he's singing a slightly different song than everyone else, and in the wrong key, to boot. How Pete, outside of the miasma of his own traumas and anxieties, looks for the good things, and not the bad ones, even though those traumas and anxieties *should* have made him as misanthropic as Ben is.

I want to go home, Ben thinks, on the street where he grew up, close enough to his parents' restaurant to be within the sphere of the neon sign's light. For all these years he's lived in New York, he's thought of coming back *here*—at Thanksgiving and sometimes Passover, and for an always-grueling week over the summer—as coming home, but something has shifted within him since his last visit.

When he was in his early twenties, Ben ended up dropping by his old elementary school, visiting a friend who had gone into teaching. He'd been amazed by the way the reality didn't match up against his memory, doors he remembered as toweringly tall turning out to be simply regular-sized, rooms he recalled as enormous being small-to-average at best. It had taken him several disorienting moments to work it out: *He'd* been smaller, when he formed those memories. The building had stayed the same—it was Ben who had changed.

Being here, now, Pete's easy, familiar voice pouring into his ear like honey, is like that. It's the same street, the same collection of brick buildings, the same neon sign it always was; it's Ben who has changed. He feels, all at once, like laughing out loud at all these years he's spent living a small, quiet life, braced for the worst. He wonders why he never considered before the glaringly obvious answer: that home isn't a place, or a building, or a sign. Home is being with people who make you feel like yourself.

"I'll be back in town Saturday night," Ben says, allowing himself the risk of wild abandon, of imagining a future where a home with Pete isn't metaphorical. "You guys do Sunday brunch? I love a good brunch, unless that's creepy and too soon, in which case I hate brunch and all who are associated with it; down with brunch."

"We should let brunch live to fight another day," Pete says, laughing, and Ben settles back against the brick wall of the restaurant, against the sound of Pete's voice. Soon enough, he'll be back where he belongs.

THIRTEEN

The rest of Ben's time in Michigan passes quickly, probably because it isn't very long. He has to weather all day Friday helping his parents prep for the weekend—they'd kindly given the staff both Thursday and Friday off for the holiday, though no such allowances were extended to Ben—but texting with Pete makes the time move faster. Rick has asked Pete out for a Saturday evening drink, and so they spend a lot of the day speculating about what he could want, the concepts getting increasingly more absurd. By the time Ben goes to bed Friday night, Pete has fully steeled himself to be sworn into the Fish Crusades, though he's planning to turncoat Rick and fight on the side of the sea if it really comes down to it. The whole thing is insane, but Ben falls asleep laughing anyway.

On Saturday, Ben's flying out in the early evening, so he's able to bail out of family bonding time after lunch. Everyone seems a bit relieved to see him go; it doesn't bother Ben as much as it once did. After all, he's a little relieved to see the last of *them* for a few months, although he'll also, in a strange way, miss them. He's often wondered if that's the universal nature of family: being with them feeling both good and bad at once, like scratching a mosquito bite, or poking a bruise. Maybe it's just the nature of *his* family; he supposes it wouldn't matter either way.

Regardless, he and Pete text back and forth all day, right up until the point Ben's boarding the airplane. His flight, landing at around nine thirty, will run right over Rick's proposed time for drinks with Pete, and Ben spends it looking forward to turning his phone back on, and finding out what exactly it was Rick wanted. Pete's actual best guess was that this was some kind of bonding ritual, and holiday related—apparently it wouldn't be the first time.

But Ben's not so sure: He's been watching the numbers climb on the first of their Christmas videos, the ones with the sponsored content worked in, which had posted the day before Thanksgiving. The numbers are *high*—not only for sponsored content, but for *their* content. It's probably the seasonal draw, and while Ben, if he's honest, hates to give Christmas credit for anything, he has to admit it's worked nicely for them here. *He* thinks, though he's kept this thought to himself, that Rick probably has some news about the future of the show, or what Formica's planning to do with them next.

All in all, by the time his plane lands at JFK and the captain releases him from cell-signal jail, Ben's a little excited, and a little nervous, and jiggling slightly with both anticipation and how much coffee he consumed during his long airport wait.

But when he turns his phone on, there are no messages from Pete. Not one.

A tiny sinkhole, barely bigger than a pea, opens in the pit of Ben's stomach.

Still, he tells himself it's fine. Of course it's fine—Pete's probably still out at drinks with Rick, that's all. Ben has no right to be worried about the frequency of Pete's texts anyway; they've hooked up once, they haven't even technically had the dating conversation, and if anything, up until now they've been messaging *too* much. This is fine. Normal. Nothing to get worked up about.

The last text Pete did send him, before Ben turned on Airplane Mode, had said Ben should let Pete know when he lands. So he does, typing and deleting several drafts before eventually going with, *Made it back to NYC, still in one piece! Hope you can say the same. Just send a hook emoji if you need extraction from the Fish Wars.*

But Pete doesn't answer; not while Ben's in the airport, and not in the cab ride back, and not while Ben listens to an incomprehensible earful from Roux, who is clearly deeply offended to have been left at the mercies of a highly paid cat sitter for a week. When Pete finally does reply, it's nearly midnight, and the text is short, and clipped, and weird: *sorry for radio silence. too much to drink. catch u tomorrow.*

The sinkhole in Ben's stomach, which has been growing for the last few hours, yawns out now to be the size of a small car. But... Pete said he'd catch Ben tomorrow, right? So they're still on for their brunch plans; not all is lost. Ben doesn't have to panic, or lie awake gripped with dread, or castigate himself for a week of thinking it was all going to work out. He doesn't. He *doesn't.*

He does it anyway, of course, but he tells himself he's choosing to, and could opt out if he wanted.

On Sunday morning, it takes such an unbelievable amount of effort to keep himself from texting Pete something like, *DO YOU HATE ME SUDDENLY?* that he, instead, texts roughly everyone else he knows. He also spends a frankly unnecessary amount of time reading and rereading the Castillo's menu, looking for throughlines to Pete's cooking, pieces of him on the page. He finds a lot: Pete clearly *wrote* this menu, the descriptions matching the voice he uses in his work for *Gastronome.*

By the time 10 a.m. rolls around with no reply to the text Ben sent Pete late last night—*No worries at all, feel better!*—the sinkhole in the pit of his stomach has grown teeth, and become more of a gaping maw. He seriously and passionately considers texting, *Are our plans still on? Let me know if I should still come to brunch???*

But looking at it written out, the cursor blinking accusingly at him after the last question mark, makes Ben feel so weak-willed and pathetic that he deletes it furiously, shoving his phone deep into the pocket of his charcoal-gray jeans.

"Do you know what?" Ben says to Roux, who is watching him

inquisitively from her current perch on top of a basket of what was, until she climbed into it directly out of the litterbox, clean laundry. "I'm going. I'm going! The man invited me to brunch—come *anytime*, he said, and I asked if Sunday worked, and he said that it *did*. And then, at the end of the call, he said he'd see me Sunday! That's a *plan*, my feline friend. It would be weirder if I *didn't* go."

Slowly, and somehow managing to communicate an enormous amount of doubt, Roux flicks her tail back and forth.

"Okay, *yes*," Ben admits, trying not to think about the fact that he is being successfully cross-examined by an animal who can't figure out how cupboards work. "Yes, he's been a little strange! And silent! And yes, I *have* considered the possibility that he's decided I'm not worth the trouble, or that Chris sat him down and impressed upon him how *nuts* I am, or that Rick told him—told him—oh, I don't know!" Truthfully, Ben can't work out *what* Rick might have told Pete to make him reconsider the way things have been going between them, though he's put a lot of effort into trying. "But regardless, if he *does* want to tell me he's decided I'm annoying, or intolerable, or *whatever it is*, after all this, he's not going to ghost me! He can tell me to my face if that's how he feels."

Roux seems to consider this. After a moment, she lowers her head so it's resting atop Ben's second-favorite knit sweater. Making direct eye contact with him, seeming to be trying to communicate very intently, she sticks out her rough tongue and begins licking the sweater, creating pulled threads and pills immediately.

"Oh, what do you know," Ben mutters. "You'd eat twist ties if I let you." Ignoring her irritated mew, he grabs his coat and heads out the door.

On the journey, which somehow manages both to take a long time and to move too quickly for Ben's liking, his anxiety swells within him, seeming to crowd out room for even his breath. He tries to wrestle it back down, to crush it away into something manageable, but it's a bit like trying to close an overfilled suitcase, or shut the door on a burning fire. By the time he finds himself standing on the pavement in front of Castillo's—in the same spot, he realizes with an abrupt pang, where Pete's infamous childhood home video was filmed—he is half-ready to turn around again, so sure his bad vibes will poison the entire encounter.

Then he steps foot inside the restaurant and realizes immediately that *his* vibes won't make any difference one way or the other.

The average diner—or, the average diner who has never spent any time in the food service industry—is not generally aware of what Ben privately thinks of as "restaurant vibe rancidity." This is not because they have never encountered it before. In fact, nearly everyone who has dined in restaurants has, at some point or another, eaten in one on a high-rancidity night. To those guests without specialized knowledge, it would likely have manifested very subtly, only at the edges of things: the sound of breaking china and swearing in the kitchen, a curt edge to the waiter's tone as she asks if there's anything else she can get you, the sense that certain members of staff are bristling as they pass one another between tables. Perhaps a few plates of food slightly below the place's usual standards might be laid before the diners, or a round of drinks that isn't what was ordered. They might leave murmuring, amongst themselves, "Off their game tonight a little, huh? Maybe the regular chef's on vacation."

But to Ben, and to anyone who has spent time working in restaurants, a high-rancidity night is obvious from the moment you step through the door. The causes are infinitely varied—interpersonal drama, financial drama, staffing issues, management issues, all of the above—but the results are always the same. Left to fester, low rancidity can become high rancidity with disquieting speed in the back of house, one person's bad mood dispersing like noxious gas to infect everyone else. Having grown up in a restaurant and thus been the Patient Zero responsible for more than a few high-rancidity nights there, Ben's senses for these things are finely tuned. Even Renata, hopeless though she is with a knife or a pan, can tell a good vibe from a bad one; more than once she and Ben have met somewhere for dinner, walked inside, looked at each other, and walked right back out, not needing to exchange a word. It wasn't *worth it*—high-rancidity nights, in addition to being unpleasant, were the nights with the highest chances of cut corners and mistakes. If you had, as Ben did, the ability to sense when it was happening, you were always better off just coming back another time.

The vibes in Castillo's this morning are so rancid that Ben almost *does* turn on his heel and walk out, on sheer instinct alone. There are so many signs it's hard to count them all—the diners look gray-faced and uncomfortable, first of all, many of them staring down at their plates in awkward silence. The waitstaff, also, look unhappy, though there's an air of desperation to them that the diners don't possess, which Ben knows implicitly is because the diners can *go home* without risking their jobs. The hostess, white-knuckling a lovely, art deco-style stand which Ben would admire if circumstances were different, gives Ben a wide-eyed look, one which clearly reads, "Your brunching spirit will die a slow death here today; run! Flee! Save yourself!"

All of this pales in comparison to the screaming coming from the kitchen. Ben thinks, honestly, that it probably would have tipped *anyone* off as to how things are going at Castillo's today, whether they had Ben's food service background or not.

"When I want your damn help, I'll ask for it!" This voice is deep and unfamiliar, lightly accented, and, above all else, furious. "I'm not a *child*, and this is *my* place. If I say I can do it—"

"But you *can't* do it!" This voice Ben knows; it's Pete's, and it's *very* upset. Ben winces. "This keeps happening over and over again! What was it last week—*oh*, the pot of stuffing for the chile rellenos—"

"I wouldn't've dropped it if one of you hadn't spilled oil on the—"

"Dad, c'mon." Pete sounds pained, now, though still perfectly audible out here in the dining room. "There wasn't any oil. It was the same thing as *this*, the same thing it *always* is: You say you can do it, and I say, 'Are you sure? I'd be happy to help you,' and you tell me to shove it and stop talking down to you. So I back off, and then you *can't* do it, because it's *too heavy*, and then it's a big mess that sets back the whole—"

"Too heavy? Too *heavy*? Ridiculous! I'm strong as an ox, you know that. It was the damn slippery handles. Look, stop being such a worrier and get out of the—"

"Aw, Jesus, Dad, don't—"

There is a loud, resounding crash, which is followed by a long beat of dead silence.

When Pete's voice sounds from the back again, it's much quieter, but still perfectly audible, since absolutely nobody else in the building is currently making so much as a peep. "Well. Okay. There it is. So much for the atol de elote! But for the record, this is *exactly* what I said would happen."

There's a sound from the kitchen like someone scoffing, but it's Pete's voice that carries on, dropping into a despondent register Ben recognizes from filming. "Hell. Somebody needs to clean this up, and we'll have to eighty-six it off a bunch of tickets; there isn't time to make a fresh batch before those tables are turned. But I'm sorry, I... I need to take a fifteen. I'll come back after and deal with—"

Pete's father's voice is a roar now; Ben's whole body tenses up on Pete's behalf even as he wonders if it's embarrassment driving the older man's rage. "I didn't *say* you could take a—"

"You're not *paying* me," Pete snarls, as he pushes the double doors to the front of the house open. "I'm here to *help* you, as I keep *trying to do*, so I can do whatever I want..."

He trails off, his mouth parting slightly in surprise, as he spots Ben waiting next to the hostess stand.

Ben realizes, in a hideous moment of perfect clarity, that he has absolutely *no idea* what to do. Not one. His mind is a vast and yawing abyss, into which any request for something to say falls like a stone, bouncing back to Ben with an echo that sounds a lot like, "Gooood luuuuuuck wiiiiith thaaaaaat, brooooo."

With no other options before him, Ben finds himself raising one hand in the air and pasting on a queasy smile as Pete visibly shakes himself, then hurries forward. He wishes, very much, that he'd listened to his cat and stayed at home.

"Christ, it's Sunday, isn't it," Pete says when he reaches Ben, instead of "Hello." His voice is the opposite of the agonized bellow of moments ago; now it's quiet, hushed, like he doesn't want to be overheard. Ben doubts that'll be much of a problem—now that the dramatics seem to be over, the diners have cautiously returned to their conversations and meals. "I'm sorry, I'm not—I woke up this morning thinking it was still *Saturday*, and it's been one of those days where—"

Another huge crash sounds from the back, followed by a female voice crying, "God *damn* it, Adrián, do you not want there to be anything *left* for us to serve this morning?"

"How *dare* you," booms Pete's father—whose name Ben can only presume is Adrián—even louder than before. "To speak to me that way in my own restaurant—"

"God, okay, I need to get *out* of here," Pete mutters. "Just... just come on."

Ben follows him, mute and panicking, out of the restaurant, around the nearest corner into an alley, and then into a small alcove out of the wind. There is, in this alcove, a single metal folding chair, and in spite of the circumstances, Ben relaxes a little to see it, and to see Pete sink down onto it. Clearly, this is the Castillo's unofficial smoke break spot, and somehow, for Ben, that makes this all feel ever so slightly less... personal. Obviously, this is Pete, for whom he has some devastatingly intense feelings, and to whom he is so attracted that half of his thoughts feel as though they might burn through his brain and body to drop to the floor, like a hot coal in a vat of butter. And, of course, Pete's personal, emotional, and family life are heavily tied up in what Ben just witnessed, and that means the stakes here are high.

But out here, right now, Pete's also just a guy in kitchen blacks, sitting on a crappy metal folding chair with his head in his hands, having had his ass handed to him quite unreasonably by management. That, at least, is familiar to Ben, even if the specifics here very decidedly are not.

"So that seems like it sucked," Ben offers. "For, well... everyone, maybe? But for sure it seemed like it sucked for you. Are you good?"

"God," Pete says, on a little laugh. It's not a happy one. "Am I good. *Am* I good? I'm sorry, but I'm not sure I know the answer to that right now."

After a beat, Ben says, "Fair enough," although, in his heart of hearts, he feels it's not. In his heart of hearts, what he'd *like* to say is, "For the love of *God*, man, you're obviously *not* good, it was a *rhetorical question*! Why are you being so *weird* with me all of a sudden? Did something happen with Rick? Did I do something *wrong*? Is it that this stuff with your dad is so messed up right now that you've shut everything else off? Because I'd get that, okay, I'd be so understanding, if you'd just *tell* me!"

But Ben doesn't want to seem desperate, or clingy, or pathetic. So instead he says, "Do you, like, want to talk about it?"

Pete looks up at this question and meets Ben's eyes with an expression that genuinely startles him. For a second, there's such raw, naked openness there, such obvious gratitude for being asked, that Ben's muscles are tensing to move towards him before Pete's face changes, abruptly, to an anguished one. Then it goes carefully blank, all traces of either emotion wiped away before Ben can so much as lean forward.

"There's not much to talk about," Pete says on a sigh. "And I'm sure you gathered a lot of it from the dining room, unless—you wouldn't happen to have come in only seconds before I walked out of the kitchen, would you?"

"I could say I did?" Ben offers, wincing slightly. "If it would make you feel any better."

"Ah," Pete says, in a tone flatter and grimmer than Ben's ever heard him use. "So you heard all of it, then."

Silence falls between them for a beat or two, Ben not sure what to do. Surely, he *didn't* hear all of it—enough to get the gist, of course, but it was obviously in progress when he arrived. But he can't imagine Pete wants to hear, "Actually, I turned up just in time for 'When I want your damn help, I'll ask for it,' and then lingered like a fool instead of leaving, if that gives you an accurate time-stamp in your mental file scrub!" He's equally certain he wouldn't be convincing if he tried to lie, since Ben's never been that good a liar.

It doesn't end up mattering, anyway; it's Pete who breaks the silence: "He has multiple sclerosis. My dad, I mean. Diagnosed about ten years ago. For a while it was the kind that comes and goes, and that was—it's not like it was a blast or anything, but it was okay. Manageable. But last year something changed, and now it's the kind that just... comes." He drops his gaze, looking down at his hands as he says, quietly, "That wasn't him, not really. I don't want you to think—he's not like that, not when he's himself. He's fun, usually. Still loud, to be honest, big personality, but chill, more or less. But now he gets confused, and combative, and that thing where he's so stubborn *is* him, which is hard to work around. And I shouldn't *talk* to him like that, I *know* it's the damn disease, but it's so *frustrating*. I've put so much time and work into helping him, and I'm so *tired* all the time, and I've tried so hard to keep it sepa-rate, you know? To not let it eat into my life, or turn me into a different person, or become all I think or talk about, or make me think of *him* differently. But he just—"

Pete stops talking abruptly, the words cutting off as though they've dried up in his throat, which is when Ben realizes he's stepped forward and put a hand on Pete's shoulder.

"God, sorry," they say together, Ben jumping backward even as Pete springs up and out of the chair. Ben's confused—he's not sure why Pete's apologizing, or jumping away, or even why he, Ben, is doing those things, beyond that the way Pete is acting makes him feel as though he *should* be doing them.

But Pete looks like he knows why he's doing what he's doing. He's looking at Ben with an expression of total panic with which

Ben is intimately familiar, having seen it in person and on film enough times now to commit it to memory. To be the person who put it there is... non-optimal, Ben decides, as if from very far away. To not know how or why, though, is a particularly corrosive brand of torture, pouring acid on the already flimsy lock holding back Ben's self-doubt.

"Sorry," Pete says again, too quickly, walking backwards down the alley away from Ben now. "Sorry, I didn't mean to dump all that on you, or to forget about our plans, or for you to see—it doesn't matter, okay? Just, I'm sorry, it's only that it's such a bad day, and it's going to take ages to clean up that damn elote, and we'll reschedule, and I'll see you—"

And here Pete's face goes utterly stricken, the expression genuinely making Ben think for a second that they're about to be mugged, before he smooths it away and finishes, "Uh. Soon."

"Okay...?" Ben says, when Pete stops at a door in the alley a few feet away, puts one hand on the knob. Stepping closer, he realizes it must be the back entrance to Castillo's; their logo is painted on the surface, faded and peeling away. Aware that he has maybe seconds left before Pete vanishes down a path upon which Ben has neither the permission nor the non-slip shoes to follow, he says, "Pete, listen, I'm *really* sorry if I did something to—"

"*God*," Pete says, sounding so upset all of a sudden that Ben's mouth snaps shut in shock. "Please don't apologize to me. *Please*. It isn't you, just... I can't talk right now, okay? I have to go."

And before Ben can reply, Pete's disappearing back into his father's restaurant, the door slamming shut behind him.

FOURTEEN

Ben doesn't bother attempting to sleep that night; he knows better. He's simply not built for this, to bounce from feeling so good to feeling so bad in such a short amount of time. Ben, in general, doesn't bounce. If people who can roll with the punches are made of rubber, then Ben is terracotta: Drop him from a height and get the dubious thrill of watching him shatter.

So Ben can't get into bed, because if he gets into bed, he thinks there's a real chance he won't get out again. He stays awake at his desk instead, poking at old projects and updating his reel, too miserable to notice whether or not he's tired. Around 5:30 a.m., on a whim, he gets dressed, buys a coffee and a bagel with lox and cream cheese from his favorite spot, goes down to the subway, and rides it all the way across the island to the Financial District. Then he walks the few minutes from the station to Battery Park, to eat breakfast while he watches the sun rise over the water.

It's a cold day to be doing this; Ben doesn't care. He used to do it when he first moved to New York, when he felt alone and stupid and certain that whatever happened, no matter how unhappy he was, he could *not* crawl back to Michigan and prove his parents right about his inability to hack it in the big city. He'd been adrift within the seas of himself at that point, the only soul sailing upon a strange and lonely ocean, and so the temperature hadn't mattered to him then, either. It had just mattered to *be there*, watching the sun peek up from over the horizon line and illuminate the Statue of Liberty from behind, and feel like he was part of this complicated, storied city. Like he was really *experiencing* living here, even if he was doing it somewhat pathetically, and utterly by himself.

Today he's not looking at the Statue of Liberty. He's staring in shivering, wistful silence across the river at New Jersey, which looks to be just waking up.

It's not that he *knows* what's going to happen; Ben doesn't know *anything*, not anything at all. Two days ago, he *thought* he knew some stuff, but he was—kidding himself, probably, about all of that. If this weekend was anything to go by, he couldn't possibly have had any of it right. He spent a good chunk of the previous day trying to work it all out, solve for what could have happened to make things take such a dramatic wrong turn, but around two in the morning, he realized it was pointless and gave it up. Ben knows *nothing*, and the uncertainty is dreadful, but the *most* dreadful part about it is in fact the single thread of information running through it, the one thing about which he is, right now, absolutely sure.

Ben might not know what's going to happen, but he knows it's going to be something *bad*. He can feel that inevitability tingling and buzzing within him the way he used to be able to predict what kind of night the restaurant would have, the very edge of the catastrophe curve starting to give way under his feet. It's so unfair it makes his *chest* hurt, his *teeth*—Ben got, what, a week? Of something good? A single week of feeling like he might have a shot at a real *relationship*, of caring about someone who cared about him in return, and now it's all going to go *wrong*? Nearly a decade of being alone and he gets a *week*? What kind of a deal is that?

There isn't anything to be done about it, though, so Ben watches night become day, trying to think about nothing at all. When the sun is up, he throws away his trash, gets back on the subway, and lurks in a coffee shop a few blocks away from Formica headquarters until just before nine. He people-watches to avoid looking at his phone, which he knows is not going to show any new texts from Pete, as none have come in since yesterday, not even after Ben reached out to say he hoped everything was all right. As he sits hunched in the table closest to the coffee shop's large picture window, he tries not to scowl to see the whole block shift into Christmas mode before his very eyes: people changing out their window displays, wrapping street poles with garlands and twinkly lights. He, himself, has never felt less festive in his life.

It's in this Scrooge-like spirit that Ben makes his way into Formica headquarters, having moved past anxiety and into a state of mind he would characterize more as a desire to be put out of his misery. He keeps his head down as he walks through the building doors, fishing his contractor ID badge out of his bag as he has every weekday morning for years now. Wearily, as he reaches the small bay of electronic security gates that grants access to the employee-only elevator bank, Ben waves the badge over the reader without bothering to slow his pace and—

"Ow!" Ben snaps, surprised, as he walks directly into the plastic security divider. It should have moved—it always moves—and he waves his ID over the reader again, puzzled. The divider stays stubbornly closed.

Taking a step back so he can fully take in the gate before him, Ben narrows his eyes. Then, with an air of a man reaching into a tiger enclosure, he waves his ID badge over the reader for the third time.

In this attempt, which also does not work, Ben can see the light below the reader flash a judgmental, punishing red. Terror begins to churn in his gut, freezing anything it touches as though he's swallowed liquid nitrogen. Face flushing, he realizes a few of the other employees milling around are looking at him now, watching as though they're trying to work out what's happening, and whether or not he's going to make a scene.

Hastily, Ben retreats a few steps, out of the flow of traffic to the elevators. Leaning against the nearest wall, he pulls out his phone with shaking fingers and checks his email.

And there it is, right at the topic of his inbox, sent only a few minutes ago: Just what he was afraid he was going to see, and hoping so much that he wouldn't.

To: Benjamin Blumenthal <ben@blumenthalediting.com>
From: Erik Aaronson <erik.aaronson@formica.com>
CC: Miranda Culter <miranda.culter@formica.com>

Subject: Termination

Dear Ben,

We regret to inform you that your contract position with Formica Media has been terminated effective immediately. As you know, all of our contract workers are hired at will, and subject to termination due to fluctuations in budget, work availability, project planning, etcetera. Though we cannot discuss specifics, your services will no longer be required.
Thank you for your time here at Formica. Wishing you all the best.

Regards,
Erik Aaronson
Associate Co-Director of Human Resources
Formica Media

For the space of Ben's next few breaths, time slows down.

He drags his eyes up from his phone screen as if pulling them away from the abyss, an agonizing, grueling effort, to look at the people milling around him. They, too, seem to Ben to be frozen in place, caught in the amber his memory is pouring frantically onto this moment, determined to capture every punishing angle whether Ben likes it or not. He knows none of them—there are too many people working here to know everyone—Ben has never *liked* working here, at least up until the last few months. But somehow this collection of people hurrying in for their Monday morning meetings, this hideous fluorescent lighting, this overdone eyesore of a first floor that Ben has prowled a thousand times looking for someone to talk to, have all become part of the fabric of Ben's reality. He has constructed his life around being here, telling himself it was just for now and it didn't matter to him anyway, that he was *fine* with the inherently tenuous nature of contract work, that it was only a paycheck. That it wasn't like it was *important*, in the long term, what happened, so long as he could cover his rent one way or another. That he wasn't going to become one of those people who let some crappy, exploitative job define him.

Ben realizes, too late, that he was wrong, but it's not as though it will change anything. After all, he's just a guy who doesn't work here anymore.

The sound of his own breath is what, eventually, pulls him back into the flow of time; it's ragged, as though he ran here from the subway instead of walking with the slow, steady pace of a man to the gallows. He tries, desperately, to gather himself. Hadn't he known, after all, that something bad was going to happen? Okay, granted, this exact scenario had not played out in even his most anxiety-riddled imaginings, but maybe there's an upside. Maybe Ben's sense of impending doom was strictly professional. Maybe it *wasn't* because he's blown his shot with—

Pete.

Ben's gaze, which had been pinging around like a trapped animal's, fixes on the other man, who has clearly just arrived. He looks cold, red-cheeked and shaking snow from his hair, but he freezes when he sees Ben, his expression changing in an instant.

It is not, Ben notes with some trepidation, an expression that suggests Pete is pleased to see him. It's more an expression you'd see on someone who has opened their refrigerator, expecting perhaps to be mildly disappointed by its contents, and found, to their surprise, a very angry raccoon who wasn't in there before.

Still, the part of him that is fizzing and hissing with shock can't help but take a few steps towards the lifeline of a familiar face, however uncertain he currently is of that face's *entire deal*. And

Pete, as though being reeled in by one of Rick's long lines, is walking towards him, too, stopping when they're only a few steps apart.

"Ben, what are you—" Pete starts to say, in the same moment Ben, unable to contain it, snaps, "I just got *fired*."

"You—what, just *now*?" Pete stares at him with wide eyes.

"At eight fifty-nine!" Ben says a little wildly, shoving his phone at Pete. "That's the timestamp on this email! Where they fire me! Not just from *Gastronome*, by the way, but from *Formica at large*—"

"What the *hell*," Pete mutters, staring down at the phone. "Rick told me—I mean, Christ, he said it was a *rumor*! Just whispers! I thought we had *time*, that I'd be able to figure out how to—"

"Sorry," Ben says, a ringing starting up somewhere in the back of his mind. "Rick told you—what?"

Pete doesn't say anything, but his abruptly caught expression tells Ben more than enough.

"*Sorry*," Ben says again, feeling as though the wind has been stolen from his lungs, "are you saying you *knew*? You *knew* this was going to happen? This is what you and Rick *talked* about on Saturday night?" A thought occurs to him, one that applies a hesitant break to his growing anger. "Wait... did they fire you, *too*? Did they cancel the show? I thought the numbers were—"

"They didn't fire me," Pete says. He's staring at the floor now. "Or cancel the show. They want another twenty-four episodes, but they just want... me. They think their in-house editors are the more... practical choice."

For a second, there is dead silence between them. Finally, hollowly, Ben says, "Oh."

"I..." Pete says, and grimaces. "God, I'm sorry, I was trying to figure out how to tell you, and then everything was happening with my dad, and—"

"But Miranda said." Ben's voice is small, which is horrible, but he presses on anyway: "She said that if the videos did well—the voice argument—and they *did* do well."

Now staring at the ceiling, in tones that suggest Pete's opinion of the statement is not a favorable one, he says, "She says that because the spon-con one did the best, and that one had an internal editor inserting the content from those sponsors after you submitted the first cut, that it's proof that's the best way forward."

This enrages Ben so much that for a moment he can hardly speak. "But they didn't have to do *anything*! They were *flat images*, I left them the file with a PLACEHOLDER frame for each one, even! And I would have done it myself except the stupid sponsors didn't send the files over until *after* I had to send it to *Dave*, who apparently *only needed forty minutes anyway*, and now I'm *fired*, and—" His cycling thoughts, having looped back to where he was a few minutes ago, return to a salient point: "And you *knew*, and you didn't *say* anything! You don't even *want* to do the stupid show—"

"No," Pete says; now his gaze is fixed on a point over Ben's shoulder, and he's grimacing. Louder, he says, "I *don't* want to do the show, but—"

"Pete, how many times do I have to tell you? It's not always about what you want." The female voice behind Ben is familiar, but not welcome, and he wheels around to glare at Miranda Culter.

"For God's sake, can't we just," Pete starts, low, but then Miranda lifts a single finger to her lips. If she had done this to Ben, he would probably have stared at her in incredulity and then asked if she thought he was a toddler. But Pete, to Ben's mystification, falls and remains resentfully silent.

"Ben!" She smiles brightly at him; what Ben does in response is more a baring of teeth than a smile. "Sorry you had to make the trip all the way down here for nothing today, but no hard feelings, right?"

"I think," Ben says, through gritted teeth, "I might have one or two hard feelings, actually."

"Because it would be a shame," Miranda continues, as if he hadn't spoken, "for you to burn a bridge with *Gastronome* like that. After all, the team on twenty-seven isn't too pleased with you;

doubt you'll get a good reference *there*. They were *so* upset to hear how cavalier you've been with the option to work elsewhere in the building. 'Shocking,' is the word Jessica used, when I pulled up the door camera footage and showed her how often you're simply leaving the premises without letting anyone know."

Even as he feels himself flush bright red, Ben sees the expression echoed on Pete's face. He remembers, too late to do anything about it, that it had been *Pete* who suggested Ben interpret that section of his new contract a little more loosely than he otherwise would have.

Still, he splutters, "But I got all my *work* done—"

"But you abused our generosity," Miranda says, with an expression of such wide-eyed, innocent surprise at his behavior that it loops around to being somewhat mocking. "You're lucky that Rick's willing to overlook it. *He* said he'd give you a reference, and we won't remove your name from any of the existing videos, of course. Between the numbers on those and, though I hate to give it to him, the strength of Rick's word, you should be able to find another job easily. So long, of course, as you don't make a scene." The smile she levels at him this time might as well be a glare, it's so pointed. "But after all, why would you? Formica Media has *helped* you, Ben. You're in a much better position than you were when we hired you. Really, you should be saying thank you."

Ben stares at her, his mouth hanging half-open, for a long moment, trying to formulate a reply to this string of bad-faith nonsense. When he fails, his gaze swings towards Pete, who is standing there like a statue, silent and drawn.

"Are you seriously not going to say *anything?*" Ben demands of him, hating himself for it, feeling pathetic and worthless and small. "You're just going to *stand* there? After everything? After we—" He cuts himself off before he can say, "slept together," but Pete reacts as though he had anyway, a vicious, full-body cringe. Ruthlessly, ignoring Miranda's smirk and the way his own voice sounds near tears, Ben carries on. "You couldn't even have *made* the videos without me, you were—no. You know what? It doesn't matter. I don't *care* about the videos, or my *job*, even, not really. It's just a job! But I thought..." Ben sucks in a harsh breath, trying to get a handle on the thread of real despair he can feel seeping into the words. "God. But you *knew* this was coming on *Saturday*, and you just stopped *talking* to me and let me walk into it like a—"

"Sorry—you think Pete found out about this on Saturday?" Miranda lets out a tittering little chuckle. "Honestly, you're adorable. So naive! I warned him this would happen right at the beginning, didn't I, Pete? Go ahead: Tell Ben what I told you after we first hired him. The very same day we did, if I remember correctly." When Pete hesitates, her tone goes sharper, more pointed. "Go on. Unless you'd like *me* to tell him? I'm sure some of what we discussed that day would prove very interesting to him. All things considered, it might be a public service."

Ben doesn't understand this comment at all, although an expression crosses Pete's face as if she struck him. Sounding like it's costing him his life savings to do so, Pete grinds out, "You said... that I shouldn't bother to get attached. That these things always go internal in the end." Then, perhaps because he can see the flickering pilot light to Ben's heart precipitously blowing out, he starts, "But I—"

"Ah, ah, ah," Miranda says, silencing him this time simply by lifting her index finger. "That's enough, Pete, thank you; wouldn't want to get you all worked up before our next big meeting! Lots of important sponsors to impress. Ben, if you don't mind—time for you to leave. After all, it would be *so* embarrassing to have security walk you out."

"My things," Ben snaps, remembering them suddenly. "At my desk upstairs, I—"

"We'll have them couriered," Miranda says. She reaches up to place two fingertips lightly against the ball of Pete's shoulder and, as though he is a marionette, turns and steers him towards the elevator banks. Without looking around, she raises her free hand in a lazy wave and calls, "Ciao!"

Pete looks around, though. He stares over his shoulder at Ben like a drowning man, an expression of anguish on his face that, mere hours ago, would have driven Ben to distraction trying to figure out how to help him.

Now he meets Pete's agonized gaze in furious, stony silence, before turning his back on it and walking out.

FIFTEEN

Ben *had* been planning to spend the first week of December more or less resting on his laurels, hanging out in the *Gastronome* offices and maybe trying to feel Pete out vis-à-vis whether there might be a workable version of making the show going forward. Traditionally, the time between Thanksgiving and New Year's is fairly dead at Formica, setting aside the various commerce-related teams, for whom it's the equivalent of tax season for accountants. But Ben had thought, like an *idiot*, that because the videos were doing so well across the board, and because the *sponsored* videos had been such a smashing success, that maybe he and Pete would have some leverage to work with. That maybe, between them, they could figure something out that would make filming less horrible for Pete, and then find a way to sell their plan to Formica. Ben had been planning to suggest that they go in front of the camera *together*, which is so embarrassing now that he wants to *die* about it, in spite of never having mustered the courage to say it out loud.

Anyway, instead of resting on his laurels, Ben spends the rest of the week in a frantic haze of activity. It is his only choice.

Over the years, Ben's heard depression described in a lot of ways, some more resonant than others. A deep, dark hole in the ground, sure, is apt enough; a yawning emptiness, too, bears a resemblance to the truth. But for Ben, depression has always brought to mind an untethered shadow, like some twisted nightmare born of too many viewings of *Peter Pan*. It stalks him through the week, lurking at the edge of his vision, never more than a step or two behind. He tries to tell himself, with the increasingly frantic desperation of a sick antelope being pursued across the savannah by a completely healthy lion, that if he stays busy enough, it won't be able to catch him.

This works, at first. Ben tells himself it works, anyway. He tells himself it works while he catches up on the household tasks he's been putting off for weeks, and then months, and then years. When being in his apartment becomes too oppressive with memories of Pete, in spite of Pete's only having been inside it *one single time*, Ben leaves and tells himself keeping busy is absolutely holding his depression at bay in various locations across New York. He pointedly does not think about his job, or Pete, or his losing his job, or losing Pete, or how he's going to need to figure out a new source of income, or Pete's sweat-soaked body in the soft light of the half-illuminated test kitchen, or *anything else at all* while he goes about his business.

He visits bookstores and favorite restaurants; he reads three great novels he's been meaning to get around to for years, and one that's only fine; he applies for twenty-six jobs from the comfort of at least five different coffee shops. He goes to museums and interesting little stores and unfamiliar markets. He goes down to St. Mark's, and gets dumplings, and sits on someone's front stoop, and burns his mouth eating them, and considers getting an ill-advised tattoo.

None of it shakes the shadowy figure on his tail, no longer bothering trying to hide itself, smiling patient and sinister whenever Ben glances over his shoulder.

Hoping that clinging to structure and routine will keep the worst from happening, he cooks for Mrs. C every night that week—

complex, intricate meals that stretch and challenge him. For the first time in many years, he can only bear to drop these meals off at her door, apologize for not staying, and disappear back down into his own rapidly dirtying apartment. He can tell she's worried about him, like he can tell Adina and Brogan and even Ezra are. All three of them have messaged him a few times, expressing their condolences and offering to hook him up with job leads, saying Miranda sucks. Ben can't bring himself to answer them.

And Pete has messaged him, too, of course. Dozens of times by now. Ben hasn't read any of them, had muted the chat in squirming self-disgust when he couldn't bring himself to block Pete's number entirely, but every time he glances at the steadily climbing number, the lurking specter of depression lurches a little closer.

It's just... what could Pete say, really? What could he say, that would make it okay with Ben that he knew, the *whole time* he knew, that this was the likeliest outcome? It's not that Ben doesn't *want* there to be a good answer, a plausible answer. It's not that he doesn't want Pete to come to him and explain that Miranda has been *blackmailing* him, or *brainwashing* him, or has his whole family at *gunpoint*, somehow! *Anything* other than the Occam's Razor answer, the one Ben can't quite bear to hear: that, for Pete, it had been a *showmance*, the attraction tied up entirely in the situation, and it had drained away immediately when Rick explained that Ben was getting fired. Without the thought of the show binding them together, Pete had simply—come to his senses, that was all. Realized that he was *him*, and Ben was Ben, and there were not just leagues but galaxies between them.

But that he hadn't even had the courtesy to *warn* Ben, had sat there in the alley acting weird, and then *run off*. God, but Ben can't let himself think about it. The shadow's so close now that Ben can sense it borrowing his movements, learning his exact size and shape.

On Friday night, while Ben is eating the remains of the dinner he made for Mrs. C directly out of the pan instead of putting together a plate for himself, there is a knock on the door. He walks over to it wearily, peering out through the peephole expecting to see the super, and freezes when it's Pete instead. After a second, his hand reaches for the knob, lands on it, and... doesn't turn. He can't bring himself to open it.

The knob must jiggle enough to alert Pete to his presence, though, because he calls, "Ben? Ben, I can tell you're in there—can we just talk? For a minute? I want to *apologize*. I can't exactly explain, not without—ugh. Look, I didn't mean for it to go this way, all right? Sometimes Miranda is just talk, and I thought—"

"Go away, Pete." Ben says it hollowly, though loud enough to carry through the door, which he leans back against, sliding down to the floor. "Just... go away."

There is a long silence. Then, very quietly, Pete says, "All right, Ben. If that's what you want."

As his footsteps fade off down the hall, Ben lets his head thunk back, hard, against the door. And depression settles over him like his own shadow, fitting against him like a second skin, so achingly familiar it's suddenly impossible to remember having ever lived without it.

It's *not* a good Saturday. Ben oozes slowly into wakefulness, regretting it immediately, and then just never *stops* oozing, dripping like so much slime through his day. Trying to shake off his foul mood, he goes to the Union Square Greenmarket, wandering aimlessly through the shrunken, winterized selection of stalls and stands. When nothing there strikes his fancy, he attempts to go to the Union Square Holiday Market next door; it reminds him too much of the one in Bryant Park and thus Pete, and so he hastily backs out again before he starts doing something embarrassing, like wailing in anguish, or screaming in rage. Instead, he eats lunch at a little cafe nearby, one of his favorite spots in the city, finishing the entire plate even though, to him, the food is tasteless. Then he walks the few blocks to the Strand, his favorite bookstore, and wanders aimlessly again, flipping through novels and books on film craft that would normally be interesting to him without even processing what he's reading. When it feels like an appropriate time to give that up, he gets on the subway and goes to the Museum of Modern Art, to stare blankly at paintings and statues in the hopes of feeling something.

He *tries* to go to the MoMA, anyway. To his displeasure and misfortune, he forgets until he is walking past that the nearest subway exit is right next to 30 Rockefeller Plaza, where, only a few weeks ago, Pete had lightly singed the set of *Late Night Live with Brian O'Malley*.

Ben's feet stop moving without his telling them to, without any input from his brain at all. He stands there, stock-still, as the wash of humanity that is constantly ebbing and flowing over New York City's sidewalks parts around him like so much water. He stares at the iconic golden sculpture in front of Rockefeller Center, the enormous, towering Christmas tree, alight and glittering over the huge ice rink that won't be here come spring. He can almost feel Pete huddled next to him, goose-bumped and shuddering in his black T-shirt, groaning about having made a fool of himself.

It hits him brutally and out of nowhere, like a pen that slipped out of a skydiver's pocket: What has Ben *done*? Three months ago, he was—okay, well, no, he wasn't *happy*, Ben is not so deluded as to imagine he was *happy*, but he was fine, wasn't he? He was *fine*. He had a good apartment and a solid enough job and, sure, all right, no social life to speak of, but two out of three wasn't bad! Practically killing it, is what he was doing, compared to where he is now, which is apartment and *nothing else*. Probably not even the apartment for long, if he can't work some method of paying rent. *Why* hadn't he kept a *handle* on himself, instead of crossing the streams between professional and personal? Hell, why hadn't he just told Rick to *piss off* that very first *day*, the instant he realized there was more to this whole thing than met the eye—

Because it was fun, the shadow of depression whispers in his ear, in a voice so much like his own it's hard to tell the difference. *Because it was fun and you felt comfortable and you let your guard down, didn't you? And now it's all ruined. It's like I've always told you: Better not to risk it in the first place. If you don't try, you can't fail.*

Ben sighs, and gets back on the subway, and rides it to his home stop. He walks the few blocks to his apartment and pauses on his building's slightly pitted stones stairs, about halfway up. It's just a few more steps—it's cold out here—he should cook something, or do some of his dishes. He doesn't *have* to get sucked into a spiral of despair if he goes up there. It's not as though it's the apartment creating that. He should go in, and he's going to. Any second now.

After three minutes, he puts his bag down.

After five minutes, he sits down next to it and pulls out his phone.

It takes about twenty minutes for him to really start feeling the cold; it's nice, in a strange way. Grounding. Hard to think about anything else, which, right now, is welcome. He puts his phone away and hunches over himself, past the point of thinking he should go inside. At some point, surely, he will, the miasma of his mood failing against his basic survival instincts... but he's not there yet. He has time left to sit here and shiver, in the blissful, blank void of being too cold to sustain any of his more heated emotions.

After thirty-six minutes, a sharp, familiar voice behind him demands, "Well, Benjamin? Are you going to be a gentleman and help an old woman down the stairs, or do you plan to sit there as an obstacle for me to clamber over? Perhaps I could give breaking my other hip a try; might be nice to have the full titanium set."

"*Mrs. C?*" Ben is already scrambling to his feet as he gasps this, staring at her in shock. "But... why... You haven't left your apartment in—"

"Seventeen years, darling, give or take," she says, and stares up at him severely. "Well? Are you going to help me down or not?"

Automatically, as if she's puppeting him, Ben offers her his arm, which she takes as he stammers, "But... you're an *agoraphobe*—"

"I am no such thing." Mrs. C says this mildly, as though she's not offended, just correcting him. "I'll grant you, I'm nearly one—functionally, I might as well be—but it's not that I'm afraid of the outside world. Let a bus hit me, as far as I'm concerned; it's been an interesting life, and I don't have any regrets." She sighs, letting go of him as they reach the sidewalk. "I just can't bear to go to all the fuss anymore. It's been years since I've seen the point."

"I know how that is," Ben says, his mood enveloping him again as he stares glumly down at the sidewalk.

"No you don't!" Mrs. C raps her cane—cherry wood with a carved lion's head at the top and, Ben's always thought, an oddly masculine choice for her general aesthetic—hard against the ground. "You're, what—twenty-three? Twenty-four?"

"I'm twenty-eight, actually," Ben says, dry.

"Oh, psh, same thing," Mrs. C says, waving a hand. Ben notices she's wearing rather a lot more glittering jewelry than usual, as well as her best mink coat and its matching hat. "You're too *young* to go giving up on life; it's unseemly. Wasteful. Look at you, with all your healthy organs and working joints! Sitting out here freezing to death like you don't even *appreciate* still being able to bend both your knees. I won't have it, you know. You're coming with me."

"I'll come up in a minute, Mrs. C, I promise," Ben says, not meaning it.

"Not *upstairs*, Ben," says Mrs. C, as though the suggestion that she might want to return to the apartment she has refused to leave for nearly two decades is asinine. "I am out. Therefore: We are going *out*."

Then, to Ben's absolute amazement, she steps up to the curb, lifts two fingers in the air, and hollers, "TAX-AAAAAAAAAAY," with the lung strength and commitment of a much younger New Yorker, if one was dropped here via time machine from a different era. It works immediately, a yellow cab pulling up next to them before Ben can so much as pull out his phone to suggest a ridesharing app, and she turns to him, arching a brow.

"Well?" she demands. "Are you going to help me in or not?"

Ben, seeing no way around it, does so. When she is safely

tucked inside the cab, she makes and holds direct eye contact with him, pointing at the seat next to her with a firm, unyielding, gnarled finger. Helplessly, he shuts her door, walks around to the other side, and climbs in, rolling his eyes when she pats him on the leg like he's a little dog.

Before he can say it, the cabbie asks the question on his mind: "Where are we headed tonight?"

"Lillian's," Mrs. C says, grinning. "And step on it."

"*Lillian's?*" Ben demands, as the cabbie nods and lurches back into the flow of traffic. "Like, the steakhouse? Mrs. C, listen, it's not that I fault your taste, but—it's *Lillian's*! It's one of the most famous restaurants in the city! It's Saturday night! And the *holidays*! There's no *way* there's going to be a table free; they'll *never* seat us—"

"He's right, you know," the cabbie says, in congenial tones. "Not for nothing, but if you don't have a reservation, you've got a better shot of eating on the moon than at that place tonight."

"I think," Mrs. C says, patting Ben's leg again, "you should stop trying to tell an old woman her business, hmm? And *you*"—she fixes the cabbie with a fierce glare—"have been hired to *drive*, not to opine. We would like to listen to some light music, and keep the conversation to a minimum. I haven't had the chance to observe this city in some time, and I would like to do it in peace, *if* you don't mind."

The cabbie, a man in his mid-fifties, makes amused eye contact with Ben in the rearview mirror. It could not be clearer that he thinks Mrs. C is Ben's grandmother, and not seeing the point in breaking the illusion, Ben makes wincing, apologetic, grandsonly eye contact in reply. She might as well be his grandmother, honestly; she's more involved in his life than either of his own ever were. Daniel's mother had died in a car accident a few months before Ben was born, and while Lucia's mother, Alessia, was alive until Ben's late teens, she never left Italy once from birth to death. Consequently, Ben met her three times, and all three of those times she had looked him up and down and said what seemed to Ben to be a paragraph in Italian, which his mother had always then summed up as, "She says she's glad to see you," before hastily changing the subject.

He's probably due, is the point, to be lightly humiliated at one of New York City's oldest and most revered restaurants by forcibly following the whims of a stubborn old lady. It's something to do, anyway; it's keeping him occupied.

But to his amazement, when they arrive at the steakhouse, Mrs. C stalks right up to the host stand and demands a table for two. And when, unsurprisingly, the host sneers down at her and suggests she try making a reservation next time, she smiles at him like he's given her a birthday gift, one she's been secretly hoping for.

"Young man," she says, leaning close and letting a note of crackling, grandmotherly kindness slip into her voice, "I think, if you were smart, you might pause for a moment here. You might say to yourself, this little old lady seems awfully confident, doesn't she? And then you might consider calling up the owner—or getting tonight's manager, perhaps, if you don't know how to reach the owner yourself—and letting him know that DiDi Collins is here? Just a suggestion, dear. We'll be happy to wait."

Ben stares at her. The host also stares at her. Then, slowly, he holds up one finger, places a little card on the desk that says, WE WILL BE BACK TO ASSIST YOU SHORTLY, in ornate script, and steps away, muttering darkly to himself.

Three minutes later, he returns, muttering now firmly silenced, flanking someone who Ben would guess is the floor manager, based on her clothing, headset, and general vibe. Walking with her is another woman who looks to be waitstaff. He braces himself to be told that the reason multiple people have come to speak to them is so they can be escorted out promptly if necessary, in order to avoid disturbing the other guests.

His mouth drops open slightly when, instead, the floor manager zeroes in on Mrs. C like a homing pigeon and bursts into a huge, fake smile. "Mrs. *Collins*, it is an honor. I'm Jackie, and I could hardly *believe* it when—"

"Let's not make a fuss, dear," Mrs. C says, smirking at Ben. "It's not that I don't appreciate it, you see, it's that if anyone finds out I'm here tonight, I'm going to have to talk to them, and I can't be bothered. You can keep a secret, can't you, Jackie? And find us a nice table, out of the way?"

"Oh, *yes*, Mrs. Collins," Jackie says, and, to Ben's absolute astonishment, begins leading them back through the restaurant. "It's all ready for you now, if you'd like to walk this way?"

As they follow Jackie back, Ben should be looking at the art crammed onto every inch of the dark wood-paneled walls, or craning his neck to take in the who's who of New York ringing the various tables. But he can't stop staring at Mrs. C in absolute astonishment, to the point that she rolls her eyes at him and says, in a pointed tone, "Jackie, can you tell me, is there any tongue on the menu tonight?" When Jackie apologizes that there is not, Mrs. C leans over and whispers in Ben's ear, "There you go: no tongue served tonight. So maybe you'd better roll yours back up into your head and close your mouth, hmm? You'd think you were raised in a barn!"

Ben, realizing at this point that he has been looking at her semi-agape this whole time, snaps his mouth firmly shut. Then he waits patiently as they are seated, poured water, and given menus, and as he orders himself a gin and tonic and a strip streak, and Mrs. C, with absolute relish, orders herself a Cosmopolitan and the prime rib. When their waiter departs and they're truly alone, he turns to her, eyebrows up, meaning to ask a dozen questions.

He only gets as far as, "Mrs. C, *what*—" before she interrupts him.

"It was my Harry, you know," she says, her eyes going distant. "That's why I can do that, even now. That was Harry: People remembered him. He was a financier"—she gives Ben a bit of a hairy eyeball at this, as though daring him to make a comment—"but most of what he did was finance restaurants. He had a real eye for which places would hit and which would bust. Lillian's wouldn't be here without him, and plenty of others wouldn't be either."

"Is *that* why," Ben says, his eyes widening, "you've met so many famous chefs? Julia Child, and—and James *Beard*, and—"

"Oh, James was a dear friend," Mrs. C says, putting one hand on her chest at the memory even while waving the other dismissively at Ben. "*My* friend first, in fact, *I'm* the one who introduced him to Harry, not that I ever got any credit for it. But the rest, yes, generally. Harry and I met late, you know, married late—he was in his early sixties, and I'd just turned forty-five—but for twenty years we had a *ball*." She sighs and then occupies both hands with cutting and buttering a roll as she adds, "And then, you know, for three years we had more of a nightmare than a ball, and then I lost him. But that's how it goes, at the end. Wouldn't trade it, and until then, oh, it was parties and dancing and theater and music and the most delightful, delicious food—I wish I could take you back in time and show you around. Harry had this way of making everyone around him have fun, like his good mood was contagious. Everywhere he stood, the light shone a little brighter."

This is the most Mrs. C has ever told Ben about her lost love; he should be touched, honored that she trusted him. Instead, he's suddenly neck-deep in the mire of thinking of Pete—of the way he, Ben, would have described Pete much like this only a *week* ago—of how Pete had always seemed to make more space unfold for everyone in any room he entered—

"All right," Mrs. C says, rapping her knuckles sharply against the table. "That's enough of my nattering, and enough lollygagging from you! Tell me your troubles. I insist."

"Oh," Ben says, badly wrongfooted. "Look, you don't want to hear my troubles, Mrs. C. They're stupid, for one thing, and not that interesting, and I'm such a disaster that hearing about it would probably be like watching a car crashing into a train—"

"Benjamin, my dear boy," Mrs. C says, fixing him with such an affronted look that Ben can't help but fall silent, "if you say another word like that about yourself, I'll have to scream. You are, if nothing else, quite an excellent cook, and atypically kind to the elderly. As for boring, I'll have you know that you are at *least* as interesting to follow as half my soap operas." She glances at him and then adds, "The other half, I must tell you, are more compelling, but you could up the stakes for me if your current issues happen to be about that hot young thing you brought up with you a few weeks ago—"

"Mrs. C," Ben gasps, scandalized. "That was the middle of the night! Are you up there watching from the window twenty-four seven like a Hitchcock character?"

Mrs. C cackles but then abruptly drops into a serious manner and fixes him with an intense look. "You should be glad I do! If I didn't, you'd still be out on those steps, wouldn't you? Flirting with freezing to death? Come on." She fixes him with a crooked smile. "Indulge an old woman. It's been so long since anyone told me a really *juicy* story."

Ben takes a long sip of his drink and a deep breath. Then, figuring it can't hurt, he gives the woman what she wants.

It takes Ben long enough that they're about halfway through their entrees by the time he finishes talking. Or, Ben is halfway through his entree; Mrs. C has eaten exactly six bites of prime rib, seeming to relish every one. He'd been planning to ask her why she'd ordered the prime rib, a slab of cow nearly the size of her head, but given the intensity with which she savors each forkful she eats, he's decided to leave it alone. He's a little afraid she might turn the steak knife on him if he asks her too many questions about it.

Also, he's been busy laying out the excruciating details of his personal life for her like so many slices of carpaccio, so. It's not as though he's had the time.

"Well, that certainly *was* more compelling than my soap operas," is her conclusion, when Ben realizes, to his mild surprise, that he has run out of story to tell. "I have a few things to say, but to start with: Don't worry about rent, dear. I'll take care of it until you're back on your feet."

Ben feels his eyes bulge out of his head as he stammers, "Mrs. C, I—that's—it's so generous, but I couldn't possibly—the *expense*—"

"Wouldn't matter to me either way, and we *could* call it a Christmas present, but it's moot," she says, and pats him lightly on the hand. "It was Harry's building, you know; that's why we chose it as a hideaway, back when we were sneaking around. It's been mine since he passed." She pauses and, scowling at him, adds, "Oh, don't look so shocked. Why do you think *you* got your apartment, and at such an oddly reasonable rate, too?"

"I... thought it was a testament to my talent for stalking real estate listings?" Ben says, feeling stupider about it with each word.

Mrs. C shakes her head, chuckling now. "No, no, though I *am* sorry to burst your bubble. I never set out to *be* a landlord, but I'll die before I sell Harry's building off to anyone, so. To balance things out, I try to choose tenants who wouldn't get a shot otherwise." Smiling, she adds, "I believe what I liked best about you was a note you wrote on your rental application; it was something like, 'I know that on paper I may not look like your best candidate, but I promise if you let me move in, I will never bother anyone, and cook you whatever you'd like to eat.' Harry would've liked that, I thought. Gumption."

This is flattering, in a way, but Ben is still processing the realities of the situation, and he's drawn back to pointing out: "But you never said!"

Settling back in her chair and sniffing haughtily, Mrs. C says, "You never asked."

For a moment Ben is engulfed in a wash of guilt—the elderly really *aren't* appreciated enough, are they? So many precious memories, such deep wells of important wisdom to share, all lost to the seas of time because selfish young people never think to—

Abruptly, Ben's brain catches up to his emotions, and he crosses his arms over his chest. "Oh my God, yes I *did* ask! I can't believe you almost *got* me like that—I asked you *so* many times, Mrs. C! To tell me about your life and your past and your husbands and everything, and you *always* told me that it's gauche to ask a lady for her *secrets!*"

There's a beat, and then Mrs. C lets out another cackle. Eyes twinkling, she says, "All right, all right—that usually works on people, you know. I never told you because I never wanted you to know before. It's fun, being mysterious. I have to take my thrills where I can get them."

"Well," Ben starts, and then, suddenly realizing that he *hasn't* yet: "God, *thank you*, if you really don't mind waiving the rent—"

"No, no, none of that," Mrs. C says, waving a hand. "It's done, I'll handle it, no need to discuss it further. We have more important topics to get into, like your man problems."

Ben groans. "I don't have man *problems*. I have a problem, one, that, yes, okay, does happen to be a man—"

"In fact, Benjamin, darling, you're half-right," Mrs. C interrupts. "You do have one problem. But that problem is *you*."

"*Me?*" Ben can't help the outrage in his voice as he demands, "What did *I* do? I mean, sure, I ruined Pete's life a little by posting the first video, but other than that all I've tried to do is *help* him and *support* him and—"

"Yes, you're like that, aren't you?" Mrs. C cocks her head and peers at him, curious. "You'll help and support anyone but yourself."

Ben can't think of a single thing to say in response to that. She's right, of course, but he hadn't known it about himself until it slipped out of her mouth.

"Do you know," Mrs. C says, as she slices a seventh sliver-thin piece from her prime rib, "how I knew Harry was the one for me? The only man who would ever make my heart beat that fast?"

"I don't," Ben says, his tone jokingly grouchy, "because you've never *told* me even when I've *asked* you."

"Well," Mrs. C says, "he was with someone else, when we met. The connection was there right away between us, that spark, but the spark can lie. After all, I felt a strong pull to my first two husbands, too, not to mention a number of partners in between, and they were brutes and liars, the lot of them. So even though Harry started taking us seriously right away—hell, even after Harry left Suzanne and moved me into his place in Westchester—I was jealous, insecure. Waiting for the moment he'd decide to trade me in for a younger model."

Ben nods, understanding but not wanting to interrupt her flow. Then he ends up having to wait a minute anyway while she pauses to eat the piece of prime rib that's been absently waving around on her fork as she talks. He's used to this from years of dining with her, though, and knows better than to interpret it as an invitation to offer a reply.

Sure enough, when she finishes, she continues as though she hadn't paused: "So one night, we're out at this benefit, all these hoity-toity rich people milling around, gathering gossip like their lives depended on it. And Harry and I were fighting—I was upset some woman had been flirting with him, I think? Oh, who can remember now. In any case, we went back and forth a while, and then he said he was going to get a drink. And suddenly I heard someone tapping the microphone, and I looked up to the podium the evening's speakers were supposed to use, and there was Harry!" Her eyes go a little misty, her face softer than Ben's even seen it before. "And do you know, he pointed right at me, and he said, 'Hello, good evening! Eligible bachelors and bachelorettes, I want to let you know: that woman there? She's my lady, and I'm with her. So if you're hankering for a slice of this balding, middle-aged pie, you'd better keep your filthy mitts to yourself, you hear?' And then he sang the first two verses of 'The Way You Look Tonight,' before he was escorted off the stage."

"Wow," Ben says, after a moment's pause. "And he pulled that off?" When she glares at him, he holds up his hands and says, "No, no, listen, it's very romantic! I'm not knocking it, it's just that if I tried to do that, it... wouldn't go well. But I guess maybe he was a good singer?"

"*Dreadful*," Mrs. C says cheerfully. "One of the worst voices I ever heard; like if Donald Duck drank acid. But that's part of what it was for me. His voice was awful; it was an enormously tacky thing to do in a roomful of his peers, especially since many of them had known Suzanne a long time. Everyone, in the end, found it quite funny—Harry had that way about him—but it was the *risk*, you understand? It was him caring about my opinion more than any of theirs. He was willing to stand up and make a fool of himself for me, and so I was willing to trust him, and risk him making a fool *of* me. Which, I'm happy to say, he never did. Not once."

"I'm glad," Ben says. Then, looking for a way to say it that won't offend her and not finding many good options, he goes for broke and asks, "Uh. Why are you telling me, though? Not that it's not interesting, just—"

"This Pete of yours sounds, in many ways, like a lovely man," Mrs. C says. "And I'd wager there's more to this story than meets the eye. But whatever it is: His backbone's weak, I'd say. It sounds like he's not willing to make a fool of himself for you, or for whatever is between you." She reaches over and places a chilly, wrinkled hand over his. "You deserve someone who will. If this Pete won't, well, then, he's not your Harry, and you should go out and try to find the man who is." Winking at him, she adds, "Maybe he's in California. With that job in—wine, was it?"

"Juice."

"Same thing," Mrs. C says, patting him twice and moving her hand away. "Just don't *stay still*, that's my real advice. Whatever you do, move forward. You've got so much left to do—you owe it to yourself not to shrivel up." Perhaps catching Ben's thoughts reflected on his face, she adds, "And I do know I, of all people, have a lot of nerve saying that. But: I, of all people, know what I'm talking about."

Ben has to give her that; the conversation turns to lighter fare, and they have a pleasant rest of the evening, and journey home. When Ben walks her up to her door, she kisses him on the cheek, and swats at him when he tries to thank her again for waiving his

rent, and tells him maybe she'll let him take her out again sometime, if she can muster the energy for it.

Then he goes downstairs and sits on his living room couch,
holding the card Larry the juice guy gave him. He sits there for
nearly an hour turning it over and over between his fingers,
thinking about California sunshine and what he might find
under it.

SIXTEEN

Things move quickly after that.

Speed is not what Ben was expecting—it's the holiday season, after all, and surely, Larry has better things to do with his time than woo a freelance video editor. Ben figured he'd send Larry an email and maybe get a leisurely reply somewhere in the back half of the week, and then they'd exchange a few more emails and maybe a couple of calls, before eventually Larry suggested Ben come out and see the property. He'd anticipated *that* as a brief, mid-week visit, maybe sometime in early January, with accommodations at a Best Western or Embassy Suites near the airport. That, in his view, is what would have been normal.

Instead, Larry replies to Ben's email, which he sends at 10:31 a.m. on Sunday morning, at 12:30 p.m. Sunday afternoon, asking him to jump on a call the following morning. On that call, Larry makes it clear that what he's looking for is not a contract video editor, or a freelance video editor, but a full time, in-house video editor, and one with an unusual amount of creative oversight. The benefits are excellent, the salary enormous, and could Ben come for a week? Next week, maybe? Of course Larry would cover flights, and put Ben up in their guest house, and have him back in time for his Christmas plans—oh, he doesn't have Christmas plans? Well, he's welcome to stay through if he likes, so long as he accepts the job! Larry and his wife and their children and what sounds to be roughly forty of their closest friends would love to have Ben's company.

Ben hangs up dizzily, and spends the next week feeling dazed, and excited, and sad, though that last feeling plagues him without being identifiable for the bulk of the time. He has to spend several days turning it over in the back of his mind like a Rubik's Cube, puzzling at it absently while he handles the huge pile of logistical challenges he's unwittingly dropped in his own lap. As he hires a cat sitter for Roux, and asks his super to keep an eye out for any packages that might arrive from Michigan while he's gone, and coordinates with Larry's team on travel info, and updates Mrs. C on his plans, and re-cuts and updates his reel, and cleans out his fridge, and does all his laundry, and packs, and unpacks, and repacks, he pokes and prods at the emotion, trying desperately to identify it.

It only hits him properly the following Sunday morning; he's set to fly out that night, landing in LAX early and then picking up a car that's been rented in his name. He's packed and organized and ready, so he goes down to his preferred local bodega and orders a bacon, egg, and cheese on a hard roll with ketchup, knowing without asking that they only use his preferred brand. And when he takes his first bite, it hits him—not just the tang of cheese against crisp, salty bacon and rich scrambled egg, but the fact that he is considering—really, genuinely considering—*leaving New York*.

He wants to cry suddenly, here on the scuffed and yellowed linoleum floor of the bodega, next to the aggressively humming glass-fronted refrigerator holding a variety of energy drinks. Is this really where he is? What things have come to? After all these years of living here, letting himself become part of the city, letting the city become part of *him*—he's just going to flee? Run away? What will he *do* in California, when he's not working for Larry? Where will he eat breakfast, get coffee? Where will he go when he's upset, or anxious, or excited, or bored? Is he even a California *person*, the sort who blooms in the sun? If he's honest, Ben would expect himself to be more like a raisin: shriveling up under all that direct heat until he can barely even remember the grape he was before.

But: *Move forward*, that's what Mrs. C had said. With no job, and no relationship, and no desire to watch the little friend group he's finally managed to gather fall away because they're still close with Pete, California is Ben's path forward. West of what he'd hoped for, maybe, but still forward.

That's what he tells himself for the rest of the day: *West but forward, Ben. West but forward.* It's running in the back of his mind as he kisses Mrs. C on the cheek that night after dinner, thanking her again for everything. It's playing on a loop as he apologizes to Roux, and tells her he'll be back soon, and promises her groveling in the form of tuna when he returns. It's what he's thinking while he loads his large suitcase into the trunk of a cab, and as he slides with his laptop bag into the backseat, shuts the door, and asks to be taken to Newark Airport.

He's annoyed, honestly, to be flying out of Newark—anything that has to do with New Jersey makes his thoughts slide treacherously towards Pete—but beggars can't be choosers, especially when the person buying the tickets is a potential future employer. Still, he indulges in staring out the window as the cab creeps through traffic, watching light snow fall in little flakes over the slowly passing city. In spite of his general Grinch-like inclinations, he finds himself wondering if he'll be back in time for Christmas, and then if he'll *ever* spend another Christmas in New York. If last year's holiday celebrations, which amounted to eating dim sum alone in his apartment, were, without his even knowing it, his last shot.

He's only distracted from this maudlin line of thought when he receives a text message from Adina, one so distractingly cryptic it immediately consumes him with curiosity.

ADINA:

Hey again, Ben. It seems like you're not in a place
to talk right now, and I understand. I might not be
in your shoes, either. But I thought you'd still want
to see this. You should click through. i think it'll be
worth it. Hope you're okay. <3

He stares at it, mystified, the city streaking by unnoticed out
the window of the cab, until a message containing a link appears
below it. Then, too intrigued to let it go, he fishes his headphones
out of his pocket, pops one earbud in, and clicks through.

Ben's heart clenches in his chest when he realizes the page
that's loading is hosted on the website for *Late Night Live with
Brian O'Malley*. It's a clench of anger, admittedly, at first—for a
second, until it finishes booting up, Ben thinks it's going to be a
Pete blooper reel, or some other mention of his original appearance
on the show. He's so annoyed that Adina would send him something like that right now, would imagine he'd want to think about
Pete at *all*, that it takes him longer than it normally would to realize
that what's loading is not a clip from a former episode. It's a live
feed of the episode that's happening *right now*, the camera
zooming in on the stage as the next guest is introduced.

When it's Pete's name that falls out of Brian O'Malley's
mouth, the clench in Ben's chest shifts from one of anger to one too
complicated to identify. Anger's still in the mix, to be sure. But
there's also trepidation on Pete's behalf, and on his own behalf, and
sympathy for the hash Pete's inevitably going to make of this, and,
in spite of everything, the desire to send Miranda two hundred self-
dispersing boxes of glitter for making Pete do another live show.

But Pete, Ben notes with growing shock, does not look
panicked, or semi-hysterical, or like he is about to throw up. He
looks... resolute, maybe, is the word. Stalwart. *Ready*.

"Pete!" Brian O'Malley is saying; Ben's barely looking at him,
his eyes riveted to Pete's tiny, pixelated face. "Good to see you
again, in a way. We've neglected to give you a cooking segment
today at the advice of the fire marshal. Hope that's cool."

"Probably smart," Pete says, with good enough humor. But his face is serious, and his tone tilts that way, too, as he adds, "And it's for the best, anyway. I'm not in much of a cooking mood."

Brian turns to the camera. In confiding tones, he tells the audience, "Pete's here to tell us a juicy story full of industry gossip, apparently. That sounded fun to me—does it sound fun to you?" His audience roars, and Brian smirks at them, and then at Pete. "Well? Go on, then. The anticipation is killing me."

Ben knows that this can't be true, at least not for Brian O'Malley. Brian O'Malley was surely briefed on what Pete is planning to say, because surely Pete had to explain it to the terrifyingly competent Priyali before he was booked in for a slot. The anticipation cannot be killing Brian O'Malley; he's acting, playing a role, for the benefit of the audience.

On the other hand, Ben really *might* die from anticipation. There's every chance that, if Pete doesn't start talking soon, his unfortunate cab driver will find herself in the Newark drop-off zone with a corpse.

Luckily, the camera swings back to Pete, who takes a deep breath and says, "Okay. Well. If you know me, you know me from the web show I do for *Gastronome*." There is a round of raucous cheers; in response, Pete smiles queasily. "Ha, thanks. You guys are fans, then?" Another round of cheers; this time, Pete nods. "So you know, then, that I'm only really half the show? And that the person who makes it watchable is my video editor, Ben Blumenthal?"

Tears prick at the corners of Ben's eyes as Pete says his name and then threaten to overflow when the audience cheers a third time, every bit as loud as before. Distantly, he registers that it was foolish to think the anticipation would be his cause of death. Clearly what's going to give him a heart attack is what Pete's actually *saying*.

"I'm glad you guys know Ben." Pete's smile looks more genuine, this time. "There wouldn't *be* a show without Ben. And I think there *shouldn't* be a show without Ben; it wouldn't work, and more importantly, it wouldn't be right. But two weeks ago, our bosses at Formica Media fired him anyway."

The audience gasps, this time. Then, after a shocked pause, there is a round of boos, to which Pete nods, grimly satisfied.

"Yeah," he says. "That's about how I feel about it, too."

"So what's the plan here, Pete? Did you just want to come on and tell us about it? Are you hoping to appeal to fans of your show, asking that they contact Formica Media and tell them what's what?" Brian O'Malley is doing his best to appear innocent, as though he doesn't know what's coming, but through his swimming vision, Ben can tell the mask is starting to slip. There's a glimmer of devilish excitement in the man's eyes: A true professional, a veteran of the industry, O'Malley is a man who knows good television when he's about to make it. With the hand that isn't clutching his phone, Ben grips at the leather seat of the cab and digs his fingers into it as the camera swings back to Pete. *What* is he going to *say?*

"No, I hadn't thought of that," Pete admits, and then adds, "Yeah, honestly, if anyone watching *does* want to do that, don't let me stop you. It couldn't hurt." He pauses, taking another deep breath and seeming to steel himself. "But really, if someone is going to right this wrong, the person with the best shot at it is me. I could refuse to do the show without Ben—they could fire me, too, sure, but it would be wasting all that momentum I built up for them. All I'd have to do is tell them we're a package deal, and they'd probably reconsider."

Ben, no longer remotely aware of where the cab is in the city or even whether or not it's moving, nods furiously at the screen. He's had that same thought a hundred times in the past two weeks, and it's gratifying, in a strange way, to hear Pete say it, too. *So why didn't you?* he wants to scream at his phone, holding it in only out of respect for his cab driver, who so far has been mercifully non-chatty.

But Brian O'Malley, thank God, seems to be on the same page that Ben is: "So why didn't you do that, then?" He's hamming up the innocence so much now that he might as well be dripping with it; his eyes are gleaming with excitement. "Why *not* tell them no, if you think the show needs Ben?"

"Well, Brian, the truth is, I have a secret," Pete says. "And a few years ago, I trusted someone at Formica with that secret. That person and I were friends, when I made the choice to tell them—soon after, we stopped being friends, and I realized it was a huge mistake. Too late, though. It was made clear to me that unless I did anything and everything this person asked of me, my secret would... stop being a secret. And I have to tell you, man, I really did not want that to happen. I put a lot of work into burying that particular truth—I even changed my name—and so for a long time, I just went along. Did what was asked. It seemed better than letting all that work go to waste, or dragging all that old stuff back into the light."

"But, Pete," Brian says, with dramatically widened eyes, "that sounds like *blackmail!*"

Pete shrugs, obviously uncomfortable. "I'm not here to name names, or to throw accusations around. That's not what I want; that's never what I wanted." He looks directly into the camera, and Ben nearly bites his tongue off with surprise, with the sense that Pete is looking right at *him* even though he knows, he *knows*, it's impossible. "I thought what I wanted was to live a quiet life, under the radar, anonymous and unknown. But it turns out that's a lonely way to exist. What I really wanted—what I think we all really want—was the opposite: to be *known*, truly and deeply, by someone *worth knowing*. Someone who makes me want to get out of bed in the morning just to talk to him." He swallows, still making direct eye contact with the camera. "I had that, or I think I did, and then I screwed it up, and you know what? Living without it sucks more than living with the secret out in the open ever did. If it's a choice between one of the other, as it turns out? Easy call."

Ben lifts a hand to his mouth as Pete squares his shoulders, takes one final deep breath, and says, "My name's Pete Bailey these days, but I used to be Pete Castillo, and even before the

Gastronome show blew up, you might have seen my face. Brian, do you want to roll the—ah, yep. There it is."

And Ben watches in overwhelmed silence, his heart so full he thinks it might burst in his chest like a tomato left too long in a hot pan, as the video and then the associated famous meme of Pete as a child plays for the entire audience of *Late Night Live*.

"Wow, yeah, I remember this," Brian says, his tone light, after the clip ends. "It was everywhere for a while, wasn't it? What was that like?"

"It was hell," Pete says grimly. "I was a teenager when it went viral overnight, and I still hadn't grown into my features yet, so I looked a lot like I had as a child, which is what I was in the original film. So, suddenly, it felt like *everyone* recognized me, and uh, not in a good way. The bullying got so intense at one point that I had to change schools—and eventually, like I said, I changed my name, so it wouldn't follow me." He sighs and shakes his head. "But it followed me anyway, in the end, and I don't want to spend my life hiding from it. It's too... I don't know. Absurd, maybe? Wasteful? Stupid?"

"Maybe the best conclusion here is," Brian says, clearly as much to the audience as Pete, "'Don't put embarrassing videos of your kids on the internet'?"

"Yeah," Pete says. His tone is still heavy, but then he seems to get a handle on himself, and half-smiles. "I think that's a good takeaway."

"Always bizarre to revisit the ghosts of internet past," Brian says conversationally. "I feel like maybe I should ask you if I can haz cheezburger, just for the sake of continuity. Can't quite bear to, though, so instead: Anything else you'd like to say to your viewing public? Before I have someone escort you out with a fire extinguisher at the ready?"

"Two quick things," Pete says, looking back to the camera. "Ben, if you're watching—I'm sorry, okay? I'm so, so sorry. I just panicked, and I know I handled it all wrong, but if you'll give me another chance, I promise you, I'll never make you regret it again."

He pauses, seeming to rein back emotion, which makes Ben's own heart twist in his chest.

Then, now sounding less pleading than angry, he adds, "And, of course, to my pals at Formica Media—you know who you are—this is my official notice that I'm not doing your show without Ben Blumenthal. I straight-up won't. You can try to mess me around however you want, but even if you do manage to force me in front of the camera, I'll make sure every take is unusable. You know I'm good at that, right? It's practically my job description." He grins, looking abruptly and entirely wolfish. "Anyway. Your move."

And then the camera's panning back to Brian O'Malley, who's saying, "Pete Bailey, everyone! After the break, we'll be joined by our next guest—"

Ben doesn't care about the next guest. He shuts his phone screen off and sits there, staggered, for a long moment. Then:

"Stop the cab." The words are scraped out and hoarse, so quiet Ben almost doesn't hear them; it takes him a second to realize they came from his own mouth.

The driver seems confused, too. She glances at him in the rearview mirror and says, "Hmm?"

"STOP the CAB!" Whoops; it's too loud this time by such a wide margin that Ben and the cabbie both wince.

"Jesus H., dude, you don't need to blow my eardrums out," she complains. "I heard you the first time—you having some kind of freakout back there or what?"

"I'm not having a freakout," Ben says, in the reedy tones of someone who is only a breath away from doing exactly that. "I just want you to stop the cab! So I can get out!"

Patiently—like she's talking to a child, or an animal—the cab driver says, "The cab is stopped, man. We've been sitting in traffic for ten minutes. Are you *good*?"

"No," Ben says, automatically, and then, as a smile that he's sure looks totally unhinged breaks over his face, "Or, uh. Yes, actually, I *am* good—I'm *so* good. I just, uh... I have to—change of plans—oh, hell, my *suitcase*." He pulls out his wallet, and, as he riffles through and glances at the meter, says, "Look, you know what? I'm not normally a trusting person, or somebody who's rolling in dough, or someone who asks service workers to go outside their job description, okay? But I will give you the entire fare I owe you, and another—uh—forty-three dollars? If you will just take my suitcase back to the building where you picked me up and leave it with the super. Tell him it's for—you know what? Tell him it's for Mrs. Collins, and she's sending Ben to bring it up for her. Okay? Will you do that?"

"There a bomb in it?" The question is calm, measured. More inquisitive than concerned.

"Of course there's not a bomb in it," Ben snaps, annoyed, eager to be done with this conversation. "Why would there be a bomb in it?"

The cabbie shrugs. "You never know. Drugs, then? Contraband?"

"Underpants!" Ben cries, at the end of his rope. "Shirts! More shoes than one person probably needs for a week in California! God, you know what, screw this, everything valuable is in my bag anyway. Here!" He shoves the handful of money at her and says, "I hope you don't steal my suitcase, but if you do then—then—whatever! Who cares! I have to go." And he throws himself out of her cab, laptop bag firmly slung over his shoulder, before she can reply.

It takes him a second to orient himself in the chilly evening air, half-blinded by the haze of headlights, streetlights, and brightly lit signage that is New York at night. He spins around in the light snow that's currently dusting over the road, briefly lost a few blocks from home, before he recognizes DeWitt Clinton Park just behind him. That means it's nearly a straight shot to Rockefeller Center, and Ben knows he can't be more than six or seven blocks away. Granted, they're avenue blocks, and that means it's probably a twenty-minute walk—does Ben have twenty minutes? *Damn*: If only they hadn't been hustled out so fast last time due to the blaring fire alarms, he'd have a better sense of how long it will be before Pete steps out of the building.

Of course, Ben could just *call* Pete. He could get back in the cab, even, and sit in traffic for as long as it took for the driver to take him, along with his suitcase, back home. He could send Pete a text, or an email, setting up a time and place to meet; Ben could even go down to Castillo's one day this week, if the most important thing was seeing Pete in person.

But the most important thing to Ben, in this moment, is not seeing Pete in person. It's seeing Pete *right now*, this *instant*. It's not wasting another second they could be spending together on stupid misunderstandings, or problems born of corporate vampires, or having mistaken his cousin for his boyfriend.

All his life Ben's believed in waiting and seeing, in not getting too invested, in adapting to whatever situation arose. He's done his best to crush down his impulses to say harsh, judgmental things, or to insist that any given situation be handled his way, even if he knew to his bones that his way was right. It's not that those impulses haven't *been* there all his life, but he's had the decency—or, what he thought until now was the decency—to manage them, keep them under control. Life has, as a whole, taught him roundly that it's better that way. Safer. Not worth the danger inherent in sticking your neck out. Not worth the cost of the argument.

But tonight, after watching Pete lay it all on the line on live TV for a chance, just a *chance*, that Ben would forgive him—tonight, Ben looks deep within himself and finds there is a man of action after all. And so, with Mrs. C's words about risk and Pete's whole impossible speech fighting for the opportunity to ring loudest in his ears, he runs.

Man of action or not, Ben is not much of a runner. He never has been, for the very good reason that he was, until this moment, totally unable to understand why anyone would ever want to be good at it. Survival situations, sure, but Ben is more or less doomed in one of those anyway, having been crafted since birth for very exacting indoor specifications. He hadn't ever seen the point.

He sees it now, though, as he huffs and puffs his way across the island as fast as he can, dodging and weaving around pedestrian traffic. The thud of his feet on the ground matches the drum of his heart in his ears, and as he hurries past cheerful holiday window displays, and under lampposts wound in spruce garlands and thick red ribbon, he finds himself wishing he had ever in his life cared about cardio.

The wish becomes more of a fervent prayer to a higher power when Ben sees, approaching at speed, two women carrying a Christmas tree. Their vibe suggests they're a couple, which would normally make Ben vaguely happy in the oblique way seeing a queer couple always does. In other circumstances, perhaps he would smile, and nod, and they'd all walk away with that indefinable sense of having been seen by one another.

However, the women are carrying the tree slung low between them, about two feet off the ground—at, Ben thinks grimly, precisely kneecapping height.

Also, Ben has seen them too late to slow down without eating the pavement hard, and so is definitely, absolutely not going to be able to stop in time to avoid a collision with them.

With no other option, Ben shrieks, "I'M SO SORRY," and leaps into the air, barely clearing the tree and sending a scattering of needles across the ground. "SORRY!" he cries again, though he can hear the women cracking up behind him, without looking around.

As if in response to this—as if in response to every uncharitable thought Ben has ever had about the holiday season—the rest of his journey is essentially a Christmas-themed obstacle course. He nearly collides with a very foul-mouthed Santa at the intersection of Fifty-Third and Eighth Street, and then heartily offends a red-and-green-swathed, Broadway-bound couple only minutes later, by shrieking a swear word of his own when they step out of a cab right in his path. Barely dodging them, he makes it through the crowd of people always massing in the theatre district and then spots a stand of rentable bicycles. Heartened by the thought of wheels, he pays for and attempts to extract one, only to discover to his absolute rage that some incompetent bastard has, in stringing the bike stand with twinkly lights, *run those lights* through the spokes of *every bicycle.*

At this point Ben, pushed past any semblance of composure, tips his head back towards the sky and lets out a brief, wordless yelp of frustration.

Someone nearby says, "Hey, man, chill out—try to get with the spirit a little, you know?" When Ben turns to look, he spots the speaker on a nearby stoop: a fellow New Yorker drinking something concealed by a brown paper bag and wearing an upsettingly well-rendered Grinch costume.

This could, Ben knows, be a stress-born hallucination, but probably not. It *is* New York City, after all. A drunk stoop Grinch is hardly the weirdest thing he's ever seen; just last week a guy outside the local laundromat *barked* at Ben, a full, unsettlingly accurate dog bark, and Ben hadn't even stopped walking.

Still, he doesn't have *time* for indulging the Grinch, or for untangling twinkly lights from bicycle spokes, or anything else. Grimly, without saying a word, he leaves both the bikes and the Grinch behind and once again takes off running.

"This... is... Stupid," he pants to himself after a few minutes, when he's only a block away from Rockefeller Center. It *is* stupid, and the closer he gets, the more difficult that is for Ben to ignore. What, exactly, is his plan? Is he going to go inside the building and say, "Hello, Ben Blumenthal here, I don't have a visitor's pass or any permission to be on the premises, and I look like I'm seconds away from expiring, which, in fairness, I am! But a guy on one of your shows just said my name like fifteen minutes ago, and that guy has only set this building on fire the one time, and it was only a little, *and* it wasn't *my* fault at all—"

No. Even in the safety of his own head, Ben can't imagine a version of himself *he'd* let inside of *any* building, let alone one currently recording a live television show. But—when else, then? Is he going to wait *outside* like a *creep* until Pete leaves? What if Pete's already left? What if Ben chooses the wrong entrance to stake out and misses him entirely? Would he have been better off heading to the *ferry*, maybe, and hanging out there on the theory that at some point Pete will have to return to New Jersey?

None of these thoughts slow his footfalls, though, so he's approaching the building, dashing along the sidewalk that runs above the famous Rockefeller Center ice rink, when—

"AHHH!" This distracting exclamation is emitted by a small child of utterly indeterminable age and gender, holding a large stuffed Rudolph the Reindeer, and so bundled up that all that's visible is their eyes. Those eyes look very frightened. This, perhaps, is because a strange, gasping man running at full speed is seconds away from crashing into them; Ben would probably scream in the circumstances, too.

In fact: "AHHH!" Ben screams in reply, and leaps wildly to his left, towards what he realizes too late is a line of shrubs which serve as the barrier between the sidewalk and the sunken ice rink, which sits about a story below him. The moment slows a little as Ben realizes he's hitting it at a terrible, overbalanced angle, too high and with too much momentum—he's teetering on the edge of the shrubs, scrabbling for purchase or, at very least, to direct his weight back towards the sidewalk instead of towards the ice below—crap, *hell*, it's not enough, he's tipping forward, he's going to meet the ice skull-first and crack his damn head open and then Pete will *never know* that—

"Ben!" And suddenly he is being gripped by one large, strong hand, and then another, as he is hauled back to the safety of the earth. "Hey—I got you. You're all right."

Gasping for breath, his life flashing before his eyes, it takes Ben a second to realize his rescuer is Pete.

"It's... you." Ben wheezes this more than he says it, out of breath from the run and the adrenaline and, a little, the abrupt proximity of Pete, which is asinine. Surely, he wanted to see Pete; surely, he nearly killed himself *getting* here, more literally than he'd have preferred, in order *to* see Pete, immediately and at once. And yet somehow being in front of him, with one of Pete's hands firmly gripping his shoulder and his other arm loosely looped around Ben's waist to steady him, is a breath-stealing, brain-emptying shock.

"Are you *okay*?" Pete's looking at him with such unmasked concern, like these last two weeks never even happened—like Ben never stopped talking to him, or told him to go away without even hearing him out. "Jesus Christ, for a second there, I thought—"

"I'm okay," Ben says. Letting the words out of his mouth seems to loosen his tongue—or maybe it's the way Pete hasn't stepped back yet, hasn't let go even a little—but whatever the reason, Ben suddenly finds whole sentences he hasn't thought through pouring out of him. "I was running, because I saw the show. Your show? That you did just now? And I wasn't far away—I mean, it was far to *run*, that's why I probably seem, like, mostly dead? But it was pretty close, and I was supposed to be going to California, which, oh, Christ, I have to call Larry, but that's a later problem. Sorry! Anyway! I was trying to say that I was running, because I thought if I ran, I could get here, to talk to you, to tell you that you didn't have to *do* that and I'm so sorry Miranda's been *screwing* you, and I should have let you *explain*, and I didn't mean to make you—"

"You didn't make me do anything." Pete's smiling down at him now; his arm tightens around Ben's waist, pulling him in close. "Or, if you did, it wasn't in the way you mean." The hand that was on Ben's shoulder is sliding now, long fingers spreading out over Ben's coat to lie flat along his back. "I did it because of something you made me realize."

"And what was that?" Ben feels giddy, dizzy with proximity and happiness and relief, but the curiosity underneath is real.

Pete's eyes are warm and fond under his snow-flecked beanie. "Well, as it turns out, nothing scares me as much as the thought of you never talking to me again. In the face of that, what's a little camera time? A little internet fame?"

"Oh," Ben says, semi-hysterically. "Is that all? Just the single most romantic thing anyone has ever said to me in my whole life, no biggie? How am I supposed to respond to that, Pete? I'm not going to say *thank you*, that seems *insanely* awkward, but my reference points for things like are *old movies* and I can't imagine that my most dignified move here is to *swoon*—"

"You can if you want to," Pete says, sounding amused. "But, honestly, I'd settle for hearing that you forgive me for getting you fired? Because, if it's all the same to you, I'd like to get around to kissing you at some point."

"Forgiven, forgotten, let's skip ahead," Ben says hastily. "Don't let me delay you." And then Pete's leaning in and Ben's tipping his face up and the world's falling away, leaving nothing but a distant echo behind.

SEVENTEEN

For a long, blissful series of seconds, Ben is aware of nothing but Pete. Pete's lips, warm and soft and opening under his own; Pete's hands sliding possessively over him, pulling him close. The long and only half-familiar line of Pete's body, flush against his, and the warm, stubbly skin of his neck under Ben's palm. This is a good series of seconds. Excellent, even. It's an experience Ben would be happy to have for much longer than a few seconds. An amount of time measured in minutes would be acceptable, but Ben would prefer hours or, ideally, days.

Unfortunately, after those seconds have passed, Ben's ears interrupt his happiness with several urgent reports.

The sound is distant to Ben, at first. Maybe it's more accurate to say that it's drowned out by the roaring in his own ears, internal and external fading deceptively together; he tries to ignore it, to write it off as his brain playing tricks on him. But... *would* his own brain be shouting, "Yeah, boy! Get some!" He doesn't think so, although, admittedly, he doesn't disagree with the sentiment at all.

Pete, too, must notice that something is amiss; he pulls back from Ben, resting their foreheads together for a moment, and then they both open their eyes and—

"Oh, *Christ*," Pete mutters. He doesn't pull away from Ben, but he does lift one hand to slide over his rapidly reddening face. Ben can't blame him; he's sure his own face is the color of a summer tomato, or maybe a strawberry.

Loosely surrounding them, pressing in from every side, is a small but dedicated crowd of people who have been distracted from the enormous Rockefeller Center Christmas Tree. Wearily, and a little amused in spite of himself, Ben can't help but recognize them as quintessentially New Yorkers: immediately abandoning the famous icon they came here to see in favor of watching a private moment of human drama play out before them. Ben can't say he blames them, or that he wouldn't have done the same in their shoes, but it's more unnerving than he would have guessed to be on this side of things. He feels a bit like a butterfly pinned to a board, desperate to squirm and equally sure it would be a huge mistake to do so.

This last is mostly because a few members of their audience have clearly realized who they are, or at least who Pete is. These onlookers are holding up their phones, obviously filming, with the hungry, slightly manic expressions of people who expect to make a lot of money very shortly.

"Crap," Ben mutters, under his breath. He looks up at Pete, bracing to be met with wild-eyed panic, or the blank, dead-eyed expression that means he has descended into the pits of despair. Ben's even prepared for Pete to be looking around desperately for escape routes, and to dash off into the crowd before Ben can so much as try to talk him down.

But instead, Pete is looking down at him with cheerful, sparkling eyes, not seeming remotely perturbed by the crowd. Smiling small and secretive, just for Ben, he leans in and whispers, "Oops. Probably should've thought that one through a little more, huh? You want to get out of here?"

"God, yes," Ben breathes, and then Pete's breaking away from him, taking his hand, and pulling him towards the street.

"Pete!" The onlooker who yells this out is small and reedy but obviously tenacious; he's clearly fought his way through to the front of the crowd, and keeps elbowing people to get past them as he follows Pete and Ben across the sidewalk, a camera phone trained on them. "Listen, man, can I get a quote? I saw you on *Late Night Live*, and this is Ben, right? Who you were talking about?" To Ben's surprise, Pete nods at the man as he reaches the street, raising a hand for a cab. "Okay, great, so: Anything you want to say? That you'd like people to know? Updates? Anything?"

"Why?" Pete says, cocking his head curiously, as though he doesn't already know the answer. "Do you think the footage will be worth more if I tell you something juicy?"

To his questionable credit, the man doesn't look at all caught or called out by this question. He just says, very fervently, *"Yes."*

A cab pulls up, and Pete opens the door for Ben, smiling warmly at him and gesturing for him to slide in first. Ben does, but, intrigued, lingers near the door instead of scooting over, not wanting to miss Pete's response.

He's glad he waited: For his trouble, he is rewarded by seeing Pete, his hand on the open cab door, turn an enormous grin on the man with the camera. "I do have quote, actually. Something I really want everyone seeing this to hear, and know that I mean very deeply, with all of my heart. Are you ready?"

"Yes," the man says again, leaning closer. Ben, his own breath catching slightly—Pete has surprised him more than once tonight, after all—leans a little closer, too, and sees the rest of the crowd doing the same.

Pleasantly, as though he hasn't noticed this, Pete says, "You sure? You don't need a pen or anything?"

"No," the man snaps, a whining note entering his tone now. "I'm *recording* you, man, go ahead! Say what you want to say!"

"You got it, buddy." Pete touches his lips and gestures outwards as though spreading the good word unto them all as, cheerfully, he says, "Mind. Your. Own. Business." Then he waves jauntily, climbs into the cab as Ben scrambles back to make room, and shuts the door.

"Where to?" The cabbie, thank God, does not seem at all interested in what just happened, or who they are. "*Please* don't say Greenpoint—I've been back and forth three times already tonight and I'm over it."

Ben looks over at Pete, and nearly chokes when he finds Pete already staring at him, his eyes soft, wondering. It's only barely that Ben manages to say, "Um. My place? Unless—if you need to go back to Jersey for your dad, that's—"

"No, Chris is with him," Pete says. He reaches out and pushes a piece of Ben's hair out of his eyes, which reminds Ben that he still probably looks like he fought his way here through a series of wind tunnels. "And my sister is taking over later. Your place sounds *good*." He growls this last word low and right in Ben's ear, which sends a shot of adrenaline through Ben.

Or, at least, it sends a shot of *something* through Ben. Adrenaline might not be the right word, especially since it seems to be focused in a region rather below Ben's heart, but it does make him briefly forget his own address, or even the nearest cross street.

He recovers himself after a second, though, and once he's given their destination to the driver, he and Pete spend the next fifteen minutes trying not to commit lewd acts in the back of a taxicab. It's harder than it should be by such a wide margin that after those fifteen minutes, when they realize they've only made it about five blocks, they elect to pay the fare and get out, walk the rest of the way. It should take them about twenty minutes, but, in the end, it's nearly an hour before they stumble through the front door of Ben's building, snow-dusted and freezing and attached at the lips, laughing into one another's mouths. The whole journey was a series of interruptions, one of them pulling the other into every alley or alcove they passed, each too impatient to touch again to make it one more step.

When they do make it to the lobby, Ben notices, out of the corner of his eye, that his suitcase is sitting up against one wall, out of the way of foot traffic. He considers stopping to grab it, but then Pete is crowding him back into the otherwise empty elevator; Ben decides he can live with it, honestly, if one of his neighbors steals a third of his wardrobe. Who needs clothes? Ben certainly doesn't, not for what he and Pete are about to do, and in this frame of mind, he's got one hand halfway down Pete's pants, still kissing him like it's his last hour on earth and he intends to make it count, when the elevator doors open with a ding on his floor.

The ding doesn't do much to distract Ben, honestly. But the sharp voice snapping, "Oh, God, I didn't need to see that!" manages it, and he whips his head around to make horrified eye contact with his across-the-hall neighbor, Deena. Deena is in her late fifties, the proud owner of more cats than Ben thinks her lease strictly allows, and possessed of a surplus of personality, but a deficit of tact. True to form, she clutches slightly at her bathrobe, the bag of garbage she was obviously en route to depositing dangling judgmentally from her hands, as she says, "Now every sound I hear tonight, I'm going to think it's you two... well, doing it! Boinking! Thanks a lot!" And she wheels around and storms off, trash still in hand, throwing over her shoulder as a parting shot: "This is totally going to throw off Roast Beef's vibe with our animal communicator tomorrow, if you even *care*. He's very sensitive to... ugh, *lustful vibrations*."

Ben and Pete both manage to keep straight faces as they proceed down the hall, somehow. Maybe it's by dint of not looking at each other at all; certainly Ben, at least, is not looking at Pete, and furiously biting his own lip to keep a shout of laughter inside. He unlocks the door as fast as he can, and the second they're inside, both Ben and Pete crack up, gasping and wheezing for breath.

Ben tries, for a moment, to gather himself, but all he manages to get out is, "Did she say the cat is sensitive to—*lustful vibrations*—"

"*Doing* it," Pete howls in reply, shaking his head. "*Boinking*—"

"Thanks a lot!" Ben says, and then loses himself to hysteria, listing forward into Pete's body as he shakes with laughter. Pete, still cackling himself, throws an easy arm around Ben's shoulders, and for a moment they stand there together, letting the mirth flow through them.

But as their chuckling dies down, they both seem to realize, in the same moment, that they have made it: They are safely inside Ben's apartment, where no one can arrest them for committing lewd acts in public, or accuse them of disturbing Roast Beef with their wanton ways.

Grinning down at Ben, Pete tightens his grip as he says, "Well? What do you say? Should we give her the show she's expecting, do you think? She *did* already thank us."

"Practically rude not to," Ben agrees, smiling wide and embarrassingly happy up into Pete's face.

The communication between them becomes more physical than verbal at this point—it's all pressure and suggestion, stumbling steps towards the bedroom, clothes being peeled off and tossed away without so much as a glance as to where they'll land. Ben hears something fall, at one point, as he chucks Pete's T-shirt somewhere to the left; it doesn't matter. He'll figure it out tomorrow, or a week from now, or whenever Pete decides to be done with him: Ben can't be the one left to make that call. It'd be years, probably—they'd starve to death—but Ben's increasingly sure with every passing minute that it'd be worth it.

Sometime later, after thoroughly exhausting one another, briefly napping, and then waking up ravenous around 4:00 a.m., Pete and Ben order a pizza. It's New York, so this pizza shows up quickly in spite of the hour, although it does arrive in the hands of maybe the most stoned person Ben has ever encountered. Pete hides a smile behind his hand when the guy asks if they mind if he takes a slice of pie for the road, and then doesn't bother to hide his fondness when Ben says, "I mean—yeah, why not," and offers him one.

It's a good pizza, even minus a slice, and as they sit on Ben's bed eating it, Pete explains about Miranda.

"She actually kind of... got me this job? In the sense that she straight-up *did* get me my original job at Formica." Pete shakes his head, and then laughs and thumps Ben on the back when he chokes on a mouthful of pepperoni in surprise. "Sorry, probably that was a between-bite disclosure, but. I was. Uh. Well—are you sure you want to hear this? It's a pretty long story."

Ben raises a single eyebrow at him and then makes an expansive hand gesture, one meant to encompass all that's happened between them as, apparently, a consequence of this woman's involvement in Pete's life. "I'm very, very sure, Pete."

"Okay," Pete says, and sighs. "So this is going to seem like a tangent, but it's not one: The summer after high school, I started dating this guy, Neil. And Neil was..." Pete's face falls into complicated expression, one Ben can't quite read, before he says, "Neil was... a lot. There were ways in which the two of us were compatible, I guess, but mostly he was, uh." Running a hand through his hair, obviously uncomfortable with every option he considers, Pete finally says, "I think maybe. Inconsistent? Is the best word for it?"

"Is it the best word?" Ben can't help but ask, his ears pricking at the shift in Pete's tone, the uncharacteristic hesitation. "Or is it the most generous one?"

Pete makes a face like he's bitten a lemon and doesn't answer the question, which is answer enough. Ben contains a wince as Pete continues, "He was hard to describe, let's just put it like that. But we were together, on and off, for... God, I don't even totally remember, now. It's all a little blurred, those years—it was always so volatile, you know? Hard to keep track of the particulars. It was more than half of my twenties, though, for sure." He sighs again, more heavily this time, and looks down at his hands. "We met at the restaurant I worked at back then—he was waiting tables to cover expenses his last few years of school—and it was fine, sort of, for a while. We fought a lot, broke up a few times, but usually we got along well enough. And he liked my family, and my friends, and I liked his, and when it was good, it really *did* feel like it was all working. We got a place together, even. But then he got this Wall Street job, and he started wanting to, uh. To party a lot harder than I was interested in partying."

"I... see," Ben says, and winces. He's had his own run-ins with the sort of hard-partying finance guys he thinks Pete's describing, mostly as the direct result of checking Grindr in certain parts of the city, and it's never gone particularly well. "Coke, then? Or...?"

"Oh, it started there," Pete says, with an uncomfortable shrug. "And if it had stopped there, I mean—well, I still wouldn't have loved it, to be honest, but. It's not like the restaurant industry is so clean and sober, right? So in the beginning, when it was just him doing a bump or two at a party, I figured: Whatever. He's an adult. It's not my job to look after him, and I know plenty of people who indulge like that every once in a while, and..." In a smaller voice, one that sounds ashamed, Pete admits, "I just really didn't want to have to fight about it? I know that sounds horrible, but I was already so tired of fighting with him."

Ben briefly resists the urge to put a soothing hand on Pete's back, and then has the glorious, crowing realization that he doesn't *have* to resist that impulse, and does it with perhaps slightly more gusto than is strictly necessary. "I don't think it sounds horrible, Pete. I think it sounds... really understandable, honestly."

Pete smiles at him, but it's a queasy smile. "I'm not sure you'll still think that when you find out what happened."

"Oh, I'll take that bet happily," Ben says, not even having to pause to think. With even this much information, he's fairly sure he can see the shape of this story in the marks it left behind on Pete and the people around him, and he doubts very much Pete did anything truly wrong. "You're on. What do you want to say—ten bucks? Or maybe it's easier if loser buys the coffee tomorrow morning."

"Assuming you still want to have coffee with me in the morning," Pete mutters. But then, louder, he says, "God, I have to just tell you right now or I never will, so: He started going out more and more, and partying more and more, and we kept breaking up, and making up, and breaking up. That was... hard, because we were on a lease together and neither one of us could afford a place alone, and Neil was out more and more, using more and more. It was just coke at first, but pretty soon it was meth and GHB and God knows what else. He got... erratic." Pete gives Ben a desperate look, a look that breaks Ben's heart; it's like he thinks Ben is going to call him a bastard and kick him out if he's not generous enough to this man who, reading between the lines, clearly treated Pete quite poorly for the bulk of their relationship. "You have to believe me: I did try to get him to go to rehab, visit a clinic, talk to someone, anything. I drove him to a fancy rehab center upstate, even—I had to wait until the day after my twenty-fifth birthday so I'd be old enough to rent a car. But when we got there, he wouldn't go in, and he never wanted to go in, and for a year or two, I really tried, I promise I did—"

"Hey," Ben says quietly, rubbing his back and then figuring he might as well go for broke and pulling him into a hug. "I can hear you freaking out, you know. I was specially trained like a Navy SEAL by watching you do it over and over for—and this is an esti-mate—eight million hours of footage." When Pete doesn't laugh, Ben lowers his voice and, more seriously, says, "Pete—come on. Of course I believe you. Take a breath."

Miserably, Pete says, "But I *broke up* with him! Not just in a fight, or for a month or whatever; for real. I told him to lose my number, I moved out, I couldn't take it anymore. It was all so—so *messed* up, all the time. I mean, God, he came to my niece's quinceañera and called my sister a *bitch*. To her *face*! In front of my aunts and uncles and everyone! She just asked him if he wanted a bottle of water! And at the apartment..." Pete shudders at the memory, and Ben shifts them both, they're lying back together on the pillows. "It was just... awful. It was always, always awful. So I left, and I moved back in with my dad, which ended up being a good thing because it turned out he shouldn't have been living alone anyway, except that after that Neil—I guess Neil kind of. Bottomed out." So quietly Ben can barely hear him even inches away, he whispers, "Nobody's heard from him in years, Ben. He... he disappeared into his habit. Fell off the face of the earth. For all I know he's—" He shakes his head, unable to finish the sentence, holding himself taut as a wire in Ben's arms. "You can tell me to leave now, if you want. I'd understand."

Ben glares, briefly, up at the ceiling; his rage at the world has to go somewhere. Then, as kindly as he can, he says, "That's okay, Pete. You can hit the ATM for my ten dollars in the morning, or we can just go with the 'loser buys the coffee' plan. I've got plenty of flaws, but I'm not a sore winner."

There's a beat, and then Pete pushes himself up on one elbow to stare down at Ben in shock. "*Really?*" he demands, sounding breathless. "You're not—you don't think I'm—like an extremely horrible person? I mean, I *left* him and he—"

"It sounds like he wasn't very nice to you, Pete," Ben says, reaching up to push Pete's hair, flopped forward and messy, out of his eyes. "Even before he started going down that heavy road. And obviously it's awful, and I'm so sorry it happened to you, and to him, and I hope he's all right, wherever he is. But. It sounds to me like he was going to do what he was going to do? I don't think you staying with him, miserable, would have changed much, in the end."

"But maybe I could have... Oh, I don't know." Pete shrugs, helplessly, down at Ben. "Helped him. Fixed him. Something."

Ben frowns up at him for a moment, considering. Finally, carefully, he says, "I don't... really think it works like that? You can't fix other people—they have to do that for themselves. All you can do is support them, if they'll let you, and try to patch up your own gaps in the meantime." He shrugs, both heartened and saddened by the hope in Pete's eyes, because it reveals how badly he's felt about this, and for how long. "And you're not responsible for his choices, Pete. They were *his* choices."

Pete bites his lip, looking as though he wants to believe this but can't quite work out how. "You're sure? You're not upset? You don't think I'm a monster?"

"I'm so, so sure," Ben says, smiling up at him, and then Pete's leaning down, and kissing him like he'll die if he breaks away for more than a second, like Ben is oxygen and Pete's spent decades gasping for breath. Since they're conveniently already mostly naked and sprawled, legs lazily entwined, across the bed, this proves to be a *bit* of a distraction, and they lose rather a lot of time—no. "Lose" is not a word Ben would apply in this circumstance. They make a glorious and far better use of the time than they otherwise would have, and between a delightful interlude that Ben *really* hopes Mrs. C can't hear from upstairs and several hours of sleep, they don't pick up the thread again until the following morning over coffee at Ben's favorite local shop.

"Okay, you can tell me to back off if you don't want to talk about this anymore," Ben says, sipping the pistachio latte Pete obligingly bought for him. "But, last night—I'm so glad you told me about what happened with Neil, and I'm really sorry if I missed this in all the, um, everything, but—how? Exactly? Does that relate to... Miranda getting you your Formica job?"

"Oh, God, right," Pete says, and shakes his head with a self-deprecating little laugh. "Naturally, I told you every detail except the most relevant one—Neil? Is Neil Culter. He's Miranda's little brother."

"Ahhhhhh," Ben says, with a wince, because: Yep. That would do it.

"We were friends, at one point," Pete says, morose. "She used to be fun, you know—she was the partier of the two of them, when we met, and he was the serious, focused one. That's how she found out about the meme thing from when I was a kid: I told her at a bar one night. We were getting hammered while Neil studied for his CPA exam." He rolls his eyes, and adds, "I think that was the same night she told me her job title should be Bullshit Artist, actually, because everything she did all day was bullshit. I'm not sure she'd even recognize herself now."

"What changed?" Ben asks, even though he imagines he knows the answer.

"Oh, Neil did, mostly," Pete says, with a shrug. "I think, now, that he must have told her I was the one giving him drugs, that started him down that path—I know for sure she blames me." He takes a long pull from his coffee, and admits, "She told me she did, a couple years ago. I hadn't seen her since Neil and I split—that job she helped me get was at Clean Eats, a smaller health food magazine, but that wasn't ever really her area, she'd just pulled a few strings. It's a big company, and we swam in totally different waters, right? So by the time Formica bought Gastronome—and I applied for, and got, the test kitchen manager job—I wasn't really thinking about her as a factor anymore."

"But then she turned up," Ben prompts, when Pete goes briefly and painfully silent. "Right? I mean, I know she did; everyone in the kitchen hates her."

"Oh, she was dating Rick," Pete says, with a sigh. "As it turned out. The worst thing is, none of it really even had to happen; I think they were pretty happy together. But she came by to see him for lunch one day about six months after I started there, and realized he'd hired me, and..." Pete winces. "I guess she... tried pretty hard to get him to fire me? And he wouldn't, and she told him about Neil, and he, I guess, said that he was sorry, but he didn't think it sounded like it was my fault, and it all. Uh. Went... wrong, from there. Rick didn't exactly give me all the details, but he wanted to—warn me, afterwards. That she was gunning for me, I mean. He's good about that kind of thing, usually. And it's good he did, because about a week later a meeting with her turned up on my work calendar, and she took me out to lunch, and she..."

Pete has to pause here, and take another sip of his coffee, and stare out the window. Ben waits for a minute and then puts a hand over Pete's, gives it an encouraging squeeze.

It must help, because: "She told me I'd ruined her brother's life," Pete says quietly, obviously half believing it himself. "She told me that he'd been fine and normal and wonderful until he met me, and I had destroyed him, and she'd never forgive me. She said if Neil wasn't going to get to be happy, I didn't deserve to be either.

And ever since..." He waves a hand, miserable. "She went after the other staff, first, and Rick could only do so much, especially if she found anything even remotely actionable. She has something on him, too, I think, but he won't tell me what."

"Maybe she has a sex tape of him," Ben suggests, just to pull Pete up out of his dark headspace a little. "Maybe all his dirty talk is about lures and, like... bite rate, and the walls of his boudoir are lined with professionally mounted fish carcasses, and he can't bear the shame of the world knowing his truth."

In reward for this absurdity, Pete cracks a smile. "He'd probably be proud of that, horribly. I've always assumed it's something to do with the Formica-*Gastronome* deal, because I know she was involved in that, but I've never gotten it out of him. It doesn't matter, anyway; his hands were tied, and Miranda made it clear if I pushed back at all, or said anything to anyone about what she was doing, she'd put that meme back out there for the world to see. So I just *watched* as she tortured my friends at work, and made our jobs tense and stressful, and I swear she arranged for extra health inspectors to come by the restaurant and harass my father, although I can't prove that. And anyone it even seemed like I was dating—*God*." Shaking his head, Pete mutters, "I just had to stop dating, eventually. I didn't really go anywhere but home and work, so everyone I met worked at Formica, and within a few weeks of seeing me they'd get demoted, or fired. She got *Josie* fired, for God's sake, and I only kissed her on the cheek! Because she brought me a baklava tray and a book about multiple sclerosis when she heard about my dad! I don't even like *women*!"

"I know you don't," Ben says, with the sympathetic tones of someone who has completely forgotten he ever wondered about this for even an instant. It just seems so obvious, now. "Also: I'm no lawyer, but I'm pretty sure that kind of vindictive retribution in the workplace is wildly illegal, just for the record. If it isn't, it should be. That's awful; I'm sorry."

"Well, it was... I mean... awful, honestly, yeah," Pete admits. The words are pouring out of him now, so fast Ben gets the sense he couldn't stop them if he wanted to. "And then she said I had to do the videos, and I didn't want to do that, but it seemed less bad than having the *meme* go everywhere, except then the video went viral, *too*! And then *you* turned up, and you were—you, and you looked like that, and treated me like—and I tried so hard to keep things professional, Ben, okay, I really did! But I couldn't hack it, and then the *minute* I let myself believe that maybe it was going to be all right, that she hadn't gone for you yet even though I obviously liked you, and so maybe it was really *over* and I was going to get to *have* this, Rick takes me out and tells me she's going to *fire* you, and I—Christ, Ben. I knew, Rick and I both knew, that if we warned you, she'd tell you what happened with Neil. That's why Rick took me to drinks: He wanted me to have the choice. He said that based on the conversation he'd had with her, she was determined to do something to hurt me, and he thought the least he could do was let me choose. The lesser of two evils, he said. And the meme, really, that was whatever, in comparison to the other option."

"Why didn't you want her to tell me about Neil?" Ben feels like an idiot the moment the question escapes his lips, and before Pete can reply, he's blurting, "God, Pete—did you think I'd believe her? That I'd think you were responsible for what happened to him?"

Pete shrugs, his shoulders an unhappy hunch, and looks away. "I mean. Aren't I?"

"*No*," Ben says, as emphatically as he can. "You're not." Pete doesn't look up, or look like he believes Ben, and Ben thinks regretfully that it will probably be some time before Pete *can* believe him. He also thinks, more ruefully than regretfully, that this whole story is fairly illuminating vis-à-vis his own initial encounter with Chris.

Setting emotion to the side, he decides to try a different tack. "Pete?"

"Yeah?"

"I'm sorry that happened," Ben says quietly. "Thank you for

telling me. It makes—well, a lot of things—make a lot more sense. I wish you'd explained it sooner, but I really, really understand why you didn't. It's okay." He takes a breath, watching the relief of this settle over Pete's shoulders. Then he says, "Will you tell me, next time something intense comes up?" and takes a relieved breath of his own when Pete nods.

They smile at each other for a moment in the warm glow of the coffee shop's eclectic collection of lamps, not needing to say anything at all. Distant, cheerful acoustic guitar is twangling over some unseen speaker, and Pete's fingers are warm over Ben's, and suddenly, Ben is grateful. He's grateful for Miranda, and Rick, and Jessica the germophobe, and his coworkers on twenty-seven; he's grateful for his years alone, every late night wondering if he'd live out his life like one of those solitary bees, toiling away by his lonesome until the day he dropped. He's grateful for his family, for his failed relationships and career turns, for every grating, grinding moment of aching indecision that felt, at the time, all but lethal.

It was worth it, whatever happens from this moment. Whichever way life decides to go, whatever winding road it chooses to chase them down: It was *worth it*, all the anxiety and anguish and agita. For another day like this with Pete—a *single day* more—Ben would do it all again tomorrow.

Still, there are the details to consider: "I do think that maybe we should discuss. Uh. What we do next?" Ben says cautiously, a little afraid to spoil the moment by bringing it up. "Do you have like... a plan? For the show? I know you said, 'Your move,' to a large corporation on live television, and to be clear, like, kudos. Ballsy as hell, insanely sexy, *not* complaining. Just: Once they do move, what's *your* move? Or I guess—" Ben swallows hard, tries not to sound shy, and fails: "I guess. Um. Our move? If you... if you meant what you said about—not doing it without me."

"I did and I do," Pete says cheerfully, "and I'm glad you brought that up. I don't know if you caught this, but that conversation Brian and I had on the show wasn't *actually* the first time I told him the story—"

"Wow," Ben says, very dry. "What a shock. Who would have imagined it? His acting was so subtle."

Pete rolls his eyes, but he's grinning. "Regardless, okay, he had some advice…"

Three days later, flanked by Pete on one side and an entertainment lawyer on the other, Ben returns to Formica Media headquarters. For the first time in all the years he spent working in this building, he is met by an unfamiliar, very nervous young professional, led to the elevators, and taken to a floor that is neither twenty-seven nor thirty-four. Instead, he, Pete, and their lawyer are whisked up to swanky, private-access-only forty-eight, where they are situated in a large conference room with floor-to-ceiling windows. Water, and coffee, and a selection of pastries have all been laid out on a side table, and they're encouraged to eat while they wait before the person who brought them up waves and, looking quite anxious about it, leaves them alone.

The entertainment lawyer—a woman called Veronica, who is apparently a long-time friend of Brian O'Malley—shakes her head slightly when she sees Pete eyeing the food. "What did we discuss?"

Pete sighs. "Sit still, shut up, don't take anything they offer me until you say I can."

Veronica smiles brightly at him, leaving an overall impression of dark hair, dark lipstick, and the vaguely implied threat that you'll regret not giving her your complete and total attention. "*Good*, Pete. And Ben? What about you?"

Ben also sighs, before, in a slightly droning monotone, he says, "I have the same rules as Pete, except you said, 'Shut up,' about six more times, and especially not to mention my firing."

"I also told you not to scowl like that," Veronica says, scowling briefly herself, "but close enough. Are you ready, boys? This is going to be fun."

And, to Ben's surprise, it *is* fun. Miranda isn't there, first of all, which is a huge bonus. Rick's in the meeting, though; the man is absolutely beaming, his face radiating delight. When Ben asks where Miranda is, Veronica glares at him, mouthing, "What did I say? Shut! Up!" But Rick lets out a brief, cut-off guffaw and then sits smugly across from them, looking like a cat who has infiltrated canary headquarters.

"Miranda's talents are urgently needed elsewhere in the company," says one of the three black-suited men who had joined Rick across the table. They all introduced themselves at the top of the meeting—one of them is a Formica executive, and one is a Formica lawyer, and one is a Formica human resources representative. Unfortunately, Ben has utterly lost track of who is who, and has to settle for thinking of them in relation to their ties: Purple, Blue, and Egregiously Ugly.

"*Gastronome* has been assigned a new mid-level executive to partner with on growth initiatives, and to spearhead other internally driven changes," says Purple. "You'll meet her next week— Bethany. We hope you'll find her... easier to work with than you seem to have found Miranda."

"We're not here to discuss Miranda, though, are we?" Veronica says, cutting one more sharp look at Ben. "Or, not at this juncture."

The suits exchange nervous looks with one another. Then Egregiously Ugly, who Ben suspects of being the lawyer, adjusts his hideous tie and says, "No, I suppose not."

Veronica smiles; Egregiously Ugly winces. Negotiations begin.

It takes, in the end, quite a long time. Ben largely doesn't follow it, drifting in and out as a mixture of legalese and jargon flows over him like so much wet cement, so boring as to be totally immobilizing. His mind wanders aimlessly, picking up occasional phrases like "revenue per mille" and "points on the gross" and "sustained harassment campaign" and "corporate malfeasance." Pete, too, seems to be far away when Ben looks over, gazing out the window with a totally slack expression on his face.

But when Ben takes his hand under the table, concerned that perhaps the slackness is in fact a sign that Pete's gone somewhere dark and spiky within the confines of his mind, Pete turns to him, his eyes focusing at once. He smiles, and squeezes Ben's hand, and mouths, "I've never been this bored in my life," which makes Ben choke back a laugh.

He doesn't let go of Pete's hand, and Pete doesn't let go of his, either. He rubs his thumb slowly over the back of Ben's wrist instead, the steady, patient intimacy of the motion working Ben up even as it calms him down. When his mind drifts this time, it's to the hours he and Pete have spent together over the last few days in much less public—and clothed—circumstances. These are good thoughts. Distracting ones.

He's so caught up in them that he doesn't realize the meeting is ending until it's already over, Purple and Blue packing up their briefcases, Egregiously Ugly straightening his awful tie one last time, Rick offering them a final beaming smile and saying, "Well played," as he walks by. Pete must be in a similar headspace to his; Ben directs an urgent, questioning glance at him, meaning "What happened? Where did things end up? Did you understand anything they said?" But all he gets in reply from Pete is a somewhat desperate shrug.

"Um," Ben says, when the room has emptied out, and it's just the two of them and Veronica. "Am I allowed to talk again now?"

Veronica rolls her eyes, packing up her own bag. "Not that you listened to me *before* or anything, but yes, Ben. You can talk."

"Did we..." Ben looks helplessly at Pete, who shrugs again. "Did we win? What happened? I don't speak Corporate *or* Lawyer."

Looking exasperated, Veronica says, "Well, let's see here. You wanted to be the show's primary video editor, working for *Gastronome* in a full-time position, with benefits; you got it. You wanted Pete to have right of refusal on video concepts, sponsors, and scripted lines; you got that, too." Glancing down at her nails, she adds, "You also got a creator credit, as did Pete, and both of you will be receiving drafts of your renegotiated contracts later this afternoon, once they've passed through my office. They are, I will say, *quite* a bit more lucrative than your old ones, and more correctly structured for the kind of work you're doing. *And* you'll both be seeing a percentage of the profits on traffic and sponsorships now, so. Assuming the videos do as well as they have been, reach out if you need me to recommend a money guy." She snaps her briefcase shut, and, sighing at Ben's still only half-comprehending face, and says, "Yes, Ben. You won."

"Oh," Ben says, realizing abruptly that he's not sure how to react to this information at all. "Well. Um. Hooray!"

Veronica gives him a flat look, and Pete hides a smile behind his hand, and Ben decides it's for the best if he goes back to shutting up until he's back out in the sunshine.

But he doesn't make it back out to the sunshine. Instead, when they get into the elevator, Pete hits thirty-four and says, "Veronica, you don't mind if we say goodbye here, do you? I figure Ben and I should probably check in at work."

It hits Ben as the elevator descends the fourteen floors, as Veronica says easily that she has a meeting anyway: They *won*. He has a *job* again. Not only a job—a permanent, full-time video editing gig at *Gastronome*. He's not going to have to become a California guy, learn how to love sunshine and sand and cutting together orange juice commercials: Ben's going to get to stay here, and work with his friends, and with Pete, and *be* with Pete. Nothing, after all, had turned out to be the disaster it appeared at first, which, Ben thinks with a sigh, does seem about right.

When he gets off the elevator and follows Pete down the hall, only his own shadow follows him; he leaves the last dregs of depression behind the closing doors, not even noticing it fall away. It'll be back for him someday, probably—it does have that nasty habit—but for now, at least, he walks again without it.

Ben had been braced for a kitchen full of eager test cooks, brimming with questions, but it's early still—their meeting on forty-eight had started at 8:00 a.m., so it's only 9:15, too early for most of the staff to have dragged themselves inside. Instead, it's just the two of them, the way Ben can't help but feel it *should* be. They drift by habit over to Pete's station and take up their usual positions on either side of the enormous butcher block that serves as a counter, Pete next to the range and Ben across from him.

He looks as dazed and amazed and overwhelmed as Ben feels. For a second, Ben wants to shout with laughter, less because it's funny and more for something to *do* with all this vibrating energy gathered up under his skin. He feels a brief moment of fellow feeling for the Laundromat Barker: Suddenly, he really understands the desire to let out some kind of *sound*, if only as a release valve.

Deciding that he should probably *not* base his choices on the assumed reasoning of a barking stranger, Ben gives Pete a half-sheepish, half-pleading look and says, "So, uh. What do we do now, do you think?"

"What do we do now," Pete says, thoughtful. Then he grins, and leans across the counter, and grabs Ben by the lapels of his jacket to pull him in for a long, luxurious kiss. Ben feels himself relax to the point of near bonelessness, and when Pete finally breaks away, it's all he can do not to slither to the floor.

"Great suggestion," Ben manages, still gathering himself and his breath, "extremely compelling, will take it under *very* serious advisement, but we can't *just* do that, right? Not that I wouldn't like to, but." He glances around the kitchen slightly guiltily. "I'm not sure we can get away with defiling this place twice."

"Probably better not to risk it," Pete agrees, sounding regretful but laughing on it a little, and pulls a knife out of his block. He taps the dull side of the blade very lightly against the counter a few times, clearly considering something, before he says: "Listen—I know you were too stressed on the way in, and that's fair, but what if I throw breakfast together now? Could you eat? What're you hungry for?"

Ben smiles up at Pete, this complex tangle of a person who has become both more simple and more complicated every day since Ben met him. Pete's dark brown hair, which Ben knows now is soft and smooth to the touch and often smells faintly of woodsmoke, is falling into his eyes again, and from the expression on his face, the bounce in his step, you'd never know he had the capacity for dread and panic and despair. Ben is so desperately in love with him that he thinks there's the chance he might perish from it.

"I'm hungry for whatever you're cooking," Ben says, and smiles. "Surprise me."

EIGHTEEN
ONE YEAR LATER

Ben and Pete stumble out of Castillo's about fifteen minutes later than they mean to on Christmas Eve. They're both laughing, more than a little tipsy, and laden with bags of gifts and food. Pete throws apologies over his shoulder as the door is closing behind them, calling, "I'm sorry, but it's the last ferry of the night! We're not sleeping here! I love you!" as it slams shut.

He turns and grins at Ben, his huffed-out breath of laughter clearly visible in the cold night air, as they start walking towards the harbor. "Well? What's the verdict? Better or worse than last year?"

"Oh, better," Ben says, shaking his head and grinning himself, although his is a little rueful. "Not that last year was *bad*, exactly, just..."

"A bit much to meet my entire family and every friend my father's ever had when we'd been dating, for, oh, four days? Here, give me those." He reaches over and takes Ben's bags, adds them to the brace of gifts he's already holding, and then threads his free hand through Ben's, squeezing lightly. "I probably shouldn't have asked you to come, honestly. I just hated the thought of you being alone on Christmas."

"Hey, it *was* better than being alone on Christmas," Ben

protests. Snow is starting to fall as they walk, the sort of thick, heavy flakes that suggest the city will be blanketed soon, and they both pick up the pace without having to say anything about it at all. "I had a good time! It was a bit of a... marathon, that's all. Much easier this year, now that I know everyone."

Pete rolls his eyes good-naturedly, which is fair; Ben's more aware than anyone that he's underplaying it. The truth is, last year's Castillo Christmas Eve had been a bit of an ordeal, but it's not like it was the *Castillos'* fault. It's only that Pete has so many aunts and uncles and cousins and second cousins and people who are so close to the family they might as well be cousins that meeting all of them, in a single evening, had been intense. It's not that Ben doesn't have cousins, since *both* of his parents came from families like Pete's: big, loud, close families that saw each other regularly, were involved in one another's lives. It was just that the entire run of Ben's childhood, and every development that happened since, suggested that Lucia and Daniel had done everything in their power to *escape* living like that. They'd wanted something smaller, more insular, more manageable. Fewer moving parts.

Maybe it skips a generation. To his own surprise, Ben has found in the last year that he quite enjoys Pete's family, far more than he's ever enjoyed any of the occasionally seen, far-flung Blumenthals or Margiottas. There's something oddly comforting about it, the rush of conversation and noise and laughter, the way everyone always seems to have something to say to each other, some thread they'd left last time and meant to pick back up. The more he gets to know them—developing inside jokes with Pete's sisters, and playing video games with his nieces and nephews, and having a few genuinely wrenching conversations with Adrián, Pete's father—the easier he finds it to relax around them. Be himself.

But: "How about for you?" he asks, giving Pete's hand a light squeeze of his own. "Better now that we've changed things around?"

Pete takes a deep breath, then sighs, which isn't exactly surprising. Ben knows he still feels some guilt about hiring nursing staff to help manage Adrián's illness, even though these days, between the show and his independent sponsorship deals, he can more than afford it. Still, Ben's quite sure it was the right thing, and Pete must agree with him, because he nods. "Yeah, it—is. I don't think I quite realized how much it was weighing on me, the pressure of keeping it all managed. And you were right: It is easier, for someone who isn't related. I watch these nurses do things that *killed* me to do, and for them it's totally chill, business as usual. Another day on the job." He pauses, craning his neck as they approach the harbor to make sure the ferry hasn't gone without them, and then, satisfied, finishes, "And he seems happier, too, right? My dad? He was sharp tonight, I thought."

"I think all the flirting with his nurses is doing more for him than anything," Ben says wryly, which makes Pete laugh. Then, in fairness, he's forced to add: "Although not with Kyle, of course. Poor Kyle—he must think the man *hates* him, he's so disappointed to see him arrive."

Pete laughs again, and then, sounding abruptly serious, says, "Aw, hell, I think we might miss it—come on!" They dash madly for the boat, which is bedecked with garlands and string lights and a few large wreaths hanging from either side of the bow, and manage to run onboard before the walkway is pulled up, the horn blasted from above.

In mutual tacit agreement, Pete and Ben make their way out of the (poorly) heated interior cabin and onto the ferry's open upper deck. The snow is coming down heavily now, but in spite of that, or perhaps because of it, the deck is dotted with other people, mostly in couples or small groups, looking out over the water at one glittering city or the other. In honor of the holiday, most of them are wearing red or green, although Ben gives a cheerful, knowing nod to a man in a fluffy blue sweater with a menorah on the front. It's picturesque, and as Ben and Pete step up to an empty spot on the railing, Ben is abruptly awash with the strange certainty that he'll think of this again, later. That when he is old and frail like Mrs. C, and reliving the glory of his youth in the stunning Technicolor of his imagination, this particular moment will be one of those that pops up.

They're interrupted, briefly, before they can get comfortable: A pair of what appear to be Midwestern tourists recognize them, gasping, and beg for autographs and photos. They grant them, Pete a little more comfortably than Ben—Ben's only been *in* their videos regularly for a few months, and he's still getting used to the increase in fame. But Pete's practically an old pro by now, rattling off a few easy, noncommittal answers to their questions and then politely sending them on their way. You'd never know that this very same type of attention had once driven him to a panic attack in a hot dog costume.

When they've gone, Ben turns his face towards the water and Pete steps up behind him, putting an arm around Ben on either side, their hands next to one another's on the long railing between them and the punishingly cold Hudson River. Pete tucks his chin over Ben's shoulder, and Ben sighs deeply and relaxes into him, wrapping himself in the warmth and comfort that Pete always seems to radiate as though he's more furnace than man.

For a few moments, they look out over the water together, appreciating the view. They're facing Manhattan, and it's putting on a show for Christmas Eve: Lights twinkle everywhere, and several of the larger skyscrapers are lit in red and green in honor of the holiday. As they get closer to shore, Ben can pick out a few Christmas-themed children's drawings posted in the window of a building next to the water; in spite of himself and his traditional anti-Christmas inclinations, he can't help but find it a little heart-warming.

As if having overhead this thought, Pete, laughing on it slightly, says, "Hey—having the weirdest sense of déjà vu. You wouldn't happen to remember standing here with me on Christmas Eve last year, would you? Almost exactly here? While we had a wildly entertaining discussion of the merits of the holiday season?"

Ben groans, the memory coming back to him all at once. "Oh,

God. Yes, I remember—who could forget? You said I was a Grinch."

"Well," Pete says, leaning in to press a kiss to the side of his neck to soften the blow, "you were *being* a Grinch. You can't blame a guy for calling a thing like he sees it—"

"You can when that thing is *you* and what he's calling it is *a Grinch*—"

"My point is," Pete interrupts, chuckling, "is that *I* said that it had been a pretty good holiday season for us both, and that maybe it was unfair to declare yourself a sworn enemy of Christmas when it was obviously fond of you. And then *you* said that Christmas was probably just trying to lure you into a false sense of security, so that it could attack you when your defenses were lowered, and that you couldn't possibly reconsider your thoughts on the subject for at least a year."

"You're not supposed to remember it when I say things like that!" Ben protests, not meaning it at all. "You're supposed to be like a normal boyfriend, and not listen to anything I say!"

"Joke's on you," Pete says, light, "if you're expecting me to be normal *or* stop listening to what you say. A lot of it's very interesting, and—with so much love—really, amazingly insane." Then, his tone slipping down to a teasing one: "Anyway, it's been a year and I've been very patient, but the curiosity is eating me alive. What's the verdict? Scrooge or Santa?"

"That sounds like the name of some deeply cursed holiday game show," Ben says, hoping to distract him. Pete doesn't take the bait, just hums in amused acknowledgment and continues to wait for an answer. In a last-ditch effort to avoid giving him one, Ben tries, "Technically, it's still Christmas, you know! This could all be part of its wretched plot to destroy me! Some guy in an elf costume could be going to whisk you out from under my nose with his sensual, seasonal charms on the way back home, and then where would I be?"

"I'm not sure," Pete admits, dry. "Because I can't imagine any location on earth where that could happen, mostly. If I were you, I'd just answer the question instead of worrying about it."

Ben stares out at the water, feeling caught, but not in an unpleasant way. More like—sometimes, Pete will come home to their apartment and Ben will be at his editing desk with headphones in, and Pete will walk up behind him, unheard and unseen, and put his hands on Ben's shoulders. And for a fraction of a second, there's this moment of terror—who's here? Who's got me? Why?—before Ben's body recognizes the touch as Pete's and relaxes before it can even begin to tense. It's always such a *good* sensation, almost better for that bare moment of uncertainty, the possibility of some worse fate than the delightful one that has in fact arrived. Maybe it's that the comparison makes him appreciate it more.

Whatever the reason, that's the emotion that surges within him as Pete adds, his tone slipping into one that Ben considers quite promising, "Of course, I could always spend the last few hours of *this* Christmas making a case for it. Show you the joys of the season in the spirit of the famous song."

Ben snorts before he can help himself. "Pretty sure that one *isn't* called, 'O Noisy Night, O Unholy Night,' Pete—"

Pete makes a noise against the shell of Ben's ear like a game show buzzer indicating a wrong answer. In his best imitation of an announcer, he says, "IIIII'm sorry, but I'm afraid the answer the judges were looking for was 'All I Want For Christmas Is You.'" When Ben flushes, pleased, Pete kisses the side of his jaw and adds, "That is, assuming you'll issue your verdict on the season as a whole immediately afterwards, of course. While your memory is still fresh, and Christmas has the best shot at winning you over."

"Did Big Tinsel pay you off?" Ben demands, but he's grinning. "Is the pine tree lobby lining your pockets with hundreds or what?"

"Nah," Pete says. "Those guys are real cheapskates—they'll only pay in needles."

Ben rolls his eyes, but with his face safely turned out towards the river, he allows himself a little smirk as he considers the year he's passed. It hasn't been perfect—nothing ever is—but he'd be lying if he said it wasn't the closest he's ever come to perfect. And he'd be lying, too, if he said he hadn't felt his heart swell near to bursting the first time he walked past this year's tree at Rockefeller Center, or stepped foot into the Bryant Park Holiday Market. He'd be lying if he said he'd ever be able to look at this season again without being grateful for what it gave him.

"You know," Ben says, trying to sound casual, "maybe I'm coming around. It isn't so bad, really. I could get used to it. But more data is always better—I think you'd better check back in five years to make sure." He lets his voice go a little wicked as he adds, "Having said that, of course, I *could* change my mind at any moment. It's not *really* official until Christmas is over. So... I think it might not hurt to make sure I'm really convinced, don't you?"

Pete's lips are warm and chapped and familiar as they press against the side of Ben's neck again, the kiss longer and more promising this time. He murmurs a soft agreement and wraps an arm around Ben's waist as, although they can't be more than a few minutes from shore, a group of carolers assembles in the center of the deck. It's a slapdash, impromptu bunch and slightly drunk besides, but they burst out into a fairly well-executed rendition of "The Twelve Days of Christmas," to which Pete starts humming along.

Ben doubts he'll ever go all in for partridges and pear trees, but when it comes to gifts his true love gave him, he'd never be able to cut off the list at twelve. He lets the music wash over him, warm and spirit-lifting, as he turns his gaze towards home.

A LETTER FROM THE AUTHOR

Dear reader,

Huge thanks for reading *Recipe for Trouble*! I hope you were hooked on Ben and Pete's journey, and that reading about them entertained you as much as writing about them entertained me. If you want to join other readers in hearing all about my new releases and bonus content, you can sign up here:

www.stormpublishing.co/dylan-morrison

If you enjoyed this book and could spare a few moments to leave a review that would be hugely appreciated. Even a short review can make all the difference in encouraging a reader to discover my books for the first time. Thank you so much!

I have spent a truly unsettling portion of my one wild and precious life thinking about what I was going to have for dinner, and wanting it to be amazing. In pursuit of this goal, I have learned an amount about cooking, and about food in general, that is significantly beyond what's necessary for sustaining basic human existence. So I wrote this book for other people like me, who love to cook, or love to eat, or who connect and show love through food. I'd make you all a pot of beans if I could.

Thanks again for being part of this amazing journey with me and I hope you'll stay in touch—I have so many more stories and ideas to entertain you with!

Dylan

KEEP IN TOUCH WITH THE AUTHOR

instagram.com/dylanthyme

facebook.com/dylanjstrand

x.com/dylan_thyme

linkedin.com/in/dylan-strand-92aa43219

ACKNOWLEDGEMENTS

I did not grow up in a restaurant the way Ben and Pete grew up in restaurants. When I was doing prep work as a kid, it was usually for my grandmother. Her kitchen, with its warm red tile floor and every shelf set with some decorative plate or bowl, is where I picked up many of the cooking skills that my characters learned as children at Trattoria Luciana or Castillo's. (Admittedly, a lot of the rest of my cooking skills are from consuming an excessive amount of food content on the internet, as you may perhaps have guessed from... everything else about this book.)

But I did grow up *around* restaurants. Roy, a friend of my father's dating back so long that my brothers and I called him Uncle Roy, runs a tiny local spot serving up the best damn sausages you'll ever eat. My grandfather ate breakfast every day for the bulk of his life at the same Jewish deli in one of Cleveland's eastern suburbs, with the same group of friends and sometimes enemies; we would join him there every Saturday morning and were always greeted like family by staff. My father's work wasn't in the restaurant industry, but it was close enough to it that sometimes I found myself with the opportunity to explore a professional kitchen, or peek behind the scenes at a candy store. I was always fascinated by food and cooking, the mechanics underneath the meal.

In my twenties I had a lot of friends in food service, and then worked in the industry for a while myself. It was an education: in how wonderful humanity can be; in how terrible humanity can be; in the laws of food safety; in what it means to work as part of a team. It also taught me the difference between people (individuals, infinitely variable, can often be reasoned with, sometimes awful but sometimes deeply lovely) and The Public (a frightening, multi-headed beast with no logic or reason at all, capable of committing almost any violation of basic human decency with essentially no warning). I absolutely, categorically could not have written this book without the things I learned doing that work, or the people who taught me those things. And I promised myself then that if opportunities ever arose to do so, I would put the following sentiment out in the world:

The people who prepare and cook and serve your food are all complicated, layered, intricate individuals, with lives and loves and problems that extend beyond the bounds of plate and bowl. Restaurants run on slim margins, and most of them are closer to catastrophe or collapse than you realize, and things can generally get quite stressful and intense even at a place that's doing well. The work is rewarding, certainly, if you're the kind of person who enjoys doing it, but it's also often difficult, exhausting, hard on the human body and soul, and underpaid. So, if you enjoyed this book at all, then I'd ask you to do me this favor: Please be kind to your friendly neighborhood restaurant staff and service workers, who I can more or less guarantee are doing their best, and who deserve much more thanks than they get.

Speaking of deserving thanks, briefly but fervidly to spare you a long slog through a list of names: Huge thanks always to Kathryn for her guidance and my publishers at Storm for their help (and so much else); to Hannah for her bottomless, remarkable kindness (and so much else); to my parents Pam and Adam for their unwavering support (and so much else); to my brothers Scott and Ike for their constant encouragement (and so much else); to my friends Sophie, Lena, Shea and Kaye for their willingness to be patient with me when I fall into an ADHD black hole for weeks at a time (and so much else); to my readers, new and old, for the gift of their attention (and so much else); to so many others, for so much else. All the words I can think of to capture my gratitude seem trite, which suggests either a failing of the English language or—and this seems likelier—that I am too grateful to pin it down in words, so I'll just say: Thank you, thank you, thank you.

9 781837 001576